As a child **Sarah Morgan** dreamed of being a writer and, although she took a few interesting detours on the way, she is now living that dream. With her writing career she has successfully combined business with pleasure, and she firmly believes that reading romance is one of the most satisfying and fat-free escapist pleasures available. Her stories are unashamedly optimistic, and she is always pleased when she receives letters from readers saying that her books have helped them through hard times.

Sarah lives near London with her husband and two children, who innocently provide an endless supply of authentic dialogue. When she isn't writing or reading Sarah enjoys music, movies and any activity that takes her outdoors.

Readers can find out more about Sarah and her books on her author page at www.millsandboon.com/sarahmorgan. She can also be found on Facebook and Twitter.

Love Sarah Morgan?

Join the conversation on Twitter with #SummerReads

Sarah Morgan

Summer With Love

MILLS & BOON

Mills & Boon, an imprint of Harlequin (UK) Limited,
Eton House, 18-24 Paradise Road, Richmond, Surrey TW9 1SR

SUMMER WITH LOVE © Harlequin Enterprises II B.V./S.à.r.l. 2013

Originally published as *The Spanish Consultant* © Sarah Morgan 2004, *The Greek Children's Doctor* © Sarah Morgan 2004 and *The English Doctor's Baby* © Sarah Morgan 2004

ISBN: 978 0 263 90675 2

097-0613

Printed and bound by
CPI Group (UK) Ltd, Croydon, CR0 4YY

CHAPTER ONE

SHE'D forgotten how much she hated coming home.

Katy's breathing quickened as she looked round the elegantly landscaped garden filled with groups of people sipping champagne and laughing together. The air smelt of summer, the heady fragrance of blooms mingling with the scent of grass mown to uniform perfection.

Suddenly she felt completely stifled and longed for the familiarity of the riverside apartment in London.

If it weren't for her mother she wouldn't be here.

'Happy birthday, Dr Westerling.'

Hearing the familiar voice behind her, Katy turned with a smile of relief, her mouth dropping open as she caught sight of her sister.

'What happened to your *hair?*'

Libby tossed her long, shaggy mane and grinned wickedly. 'I did it especially for Dad. It's called strawberry blonde. Don't you love it?'

'It's pink,' Katy said faintly, and Libby's smile widened.

'I know. It's perfect, isn't it?' Her eyes moved defiantly over the throng of conservatively dressed people and Katy bit her lip, looking at Libby's normally gorgeous blonde hair in dismay.

'Will it wash out?'

'Yep.' Libby reached out and scooped a glass of champagne from a waiter who was passing. 'But hopefully not before I've caused a spectacular firework display from our esteemed parent.'

Katy tensed, anticipating her father's anger. 'You always try and provoke him. Couldn't you have worn a slightly longer dress?'

'Definitely not.' Libby wiggled her bottom provocatively. 'Think he's going to like it?'

Katy slid her eyes over the skin-tight dress that exposed almost all of Libby's perfect legs. For a nightclub it would have been barely decent and for a summer garden party it was—

'He's going to have a heart attack.' Katy's eyes darted warily over to where their father stood, broad-shouldered and unsmiling, deep in conversation with several cabinet ministers. There was going to be trouble. She bit her lip and shook her head. 'Why do you always do this, Lib? Can't you conform just once?'

'Why would I want to?' Libby reached out a hand and touched the pearls that lay around Katy's neck. 'I've never been a pearls sort of person. And neither are you underneath.'

Katy looked away.

She didn't know who she was any more.

As usual, Libby's directness had unsettled her. 'Just because I dress appropriately for our parent's summer party, there's no need to—'

'Our *birthday* party,' Libby reminded her pointedly. 'This is supposed to be our birthday party, remember? You, me and Alex.' She glanced round the manicured garden at the hordes of elegant guests and rolled her eyes. 'We're the only triplets in the world whose parents throw them a garden party and then invite all their own guests and offset it against tax as business entertaining. Well, I, for one, refuse to play the game. And you only do it because you're so sweet and gentle and hate confrontation.'

There was a light in her eye that made Katy feel extraordinarily jumpy. 'We can all go home in a few hours,' she reminded her sister wearily. 'Just play along, Libby. For Mum's sake. Please.'

'Like you do, you mean?' Libby's eyes slid over her. 'Don't you ever want to shock them all, Katy? Rip your clothes off, get drunk, take drugs, swear?'

'All at once?' Katy gave a wan smile and glanced towards a group of men who were downing champagne at a remarkable rate.

'Ah—yes. I forgot. You can't do things like that. Lord Frederick Hamilton wouldn't approve.' Libby was silent for a moment and then she gave a sigh, her pretty face suddenly serious. 'I can't believe you're going to marry that man, Katy.'

Katy swallowed.

Sometimes she couldn't believe it either.

But it was the right thing to do.

'I mean, look at him now! Why isn't he trying to drag you into the bushes for a grope?' Libby studied him curiously, her head on one side. 'He's too busy networking to even notice that you're here. You could be naked and covered in whipped cream and he'd still be mingling with the movers and shakers.'

Everything her sister said was true and Katy wondered why she didn't mind more. She chewed her lip. The truth was that she didn't mind because she didn't *want* Freddie to take her into the bushes for a grope. She was quite happy for him to be talking to his business colleagues, leaving her alone to make her own amusement.

Freddie was safe.

At that moment their mother glanced towards them and a horrified expression crossed her face. Visibly agitated, she cast a terrified look towards her husband who was still deep in conversation and hadn't yet noticed his daughters.

Libby sucked in a breath and grinned. 'We have lift-off. Ten, nine, eight...'

The girls waited as their mother hurried towards them, Katy tense and on edge, Libby amused and defiant.

Katy glanced at her sister with a mixture of exasperation and envy. How could she be so completely unafraid of their father? Instead of avoiding confrontation, she relished it.

As if to prove a point, Libby tugged her dress down to expose a little more of her already exposed cleavage.

'Elizabeth.' Lady Caroline Westerling stopped in front of her daughters and her eyes darted nervously towards her husband. Fortunately he still had his back to them. 'Your hair is a disgrace, and what *do* you think you're wearing?'

'A party dress.' Libby smiled happily at her mother. 'For *my birthday party.*'

Katy winced at her less than subtle reminder that this annual event had originated as a celebration of their birthday. Her mother seemed oblivious to the dig.

'It's indecent and common.' She ran her eyes over Libby's long bare legs and winced. 'Your father will… He'll throw a fit.'

Libby's eyes gleamed. 'Oh, I do hope so,' she said softly, and their mother gave her a helpless look.

'Why, Elizabeth? Why do you have to do this?' Her eyes flickered around the lawn. 'There are any number of suitable men that you might have been introduced to this evening, but not dressed like that.'

Libby's smile widened. 'I'm only interested in unsuitable men.'

Her mother's eyes closed and sweat broke out on her brow. 'You look like a prostitute. Go upstairs and ask Sally to find you something more conservative before he sees you.'

'I like this dress and I don't care what he thinks. And neither should you.' Libby's eyes gleamed. 'You shouldn't let him bully you, Mum.'

Katy let out a breath. 'Not here, Lib, *please.*'

Libby was staring at their mother. 'You should stand up to him.'

Caroline Westerling ignored her comment and looked away,

her breathing suddenly rapid. 'Your father has some very important guests here today.' She turned to Katy and gave a bright smile that fooled no one. 'Freddie is doing *so* well. He has something to say to everyone. Your father thinks he's heading straight for the top.'

'Hopefully he'll bang his head when he gets there,' Libby drawled, and Katy hid a smile.

What would she do without her sister? She loved her irrepressible nature and the fact that no one scared her.

No one made Libby do anything she didn't want to do.

Not even their father.

Katy watched Freddie weave his way through the crowd, exchanging smiles and handshakes.

Her mother gave a sigh. '*Such* a suitable man. You've made a wonderful match, Katherine. All we need to do now is to sort your job out. I hope that once you're married you'll give up all this doctor nonsense.'

Katy stiffened. 'I won't be giving it up.'

What did it take to convince her parents that this was the career she wanted?

'What about me?' Libby's tone was airy. 'I'm a nurse—does that count? And Alex is a doctor. Doesn't Dad want us to give up, too?'

Their mother bit her lip. 'You and Alex are different.'

'He can't bully us, you mean,' Libby said softly, and Caroline's eyes darted nervously around the lawn.

'Keep your voice down, Elizabeth.' Her mother looked pained and turned back to Katy. 'You've qualified now. You've shown everyone that you can do it. You don't need to carry on working any more. Freddie is extraordinarily wealthy in his own right and with your trust fund there's absolutely no need for you to work. When you're married Freddie will need you at home for entertaining clients. You won't have time for a job.'

Katy felt stifled again. 'I love being a doctor, it's what I do. There's no way I'm giving it up.'

Sometimes she felt that her job was the only thing that kept her sane.

Her mother rubbed her hands together nervously. 'You can't carry on doing nights and all those horrible hours once you're married.'

Katy liked the horrible hours. Horrible hours gave her a perfect excuse not to have a social life.

'I've got a new job starting in two weeks,' Katy reminded her. 'I'm a casualty officer in the accident and emergency department.'

And she couldn't wait.

'Oh, Katherine, what is the matter with you?' Her mother screwed up her face in horror. 'All those drunks and rough people—Saturday nights after the rugby. Why would you want to do that when you don't have to?'

Because she loved medicine. And it was a million miles away from the ruthless world of banking that had been her entire life.

The garden was closing in on her.

'It's just such a waste,' her mother was saying. 'I still tell everyone that you were a successful model when you were seventeen. You were on so many magazine covers and if you hadn't thrown it all in to become a doctor you'd be one of those supermodels now.'

'No, she wouldn't,' Libby interrupted cheerfully. 'Katy's grown hips and boobs since then and you're not allowed to have those if you're a supermodel. Just bones.'

Their mother's mouth tightened. 'Just promise me you'll give up this emergency department rubbish. I know Freddie's parents are worried about it, too. It's just not suitable, Katherine.'

Suitable. There was that word again.

Katy felt as though her head was exploding.

What was happening to her?

Normally she'd do anything to keep the peace for her mother's sake, but today she just wanted to run screaming into the distance.

'Start the job if you must,' her mother carried on, 'but you'll be marrying Freddie in three months and you'll have to give it up then. Oh, look, there's Freddie's mother. I must talk to her about the arrangements.' She glared at Libby. 'Elizabeth, go and change into something that hides your underwear before your father sees you. *Please.*'

She turned and walked with studied elegance across the lawn, beaming at her guests and reaching for another glass of champagne.

Libby gave an exaggerated sigh. 'It's a good job we're triplets. At least they managed to get the physical contact over in one go.'

'Libby!' Katy turned to her, her blue eyes wide with reproach, and Libby shrugged.

'Well, it's true. Look at them.' She tilted her head to one side. 'They don't show each other any affection. Their marriage is a business arrangement. It's no wonder you, Alex and I are so dysfunctional. Look at our role models.'

Katy licked dry lips. 'We're not dysfunctional.'

'Yes, we are. You've spent so much of your life trying to please Dad and avoid his wrath that you don't even know who you are any more. I'm so determined to be the opposite of everything they want me to be that I've forgotten who I am, too. And as for Alex...' Libby turned and scanned the garden, looking for their brother. 'Alex is so disillusioned about marriage that he sets a three-month rule. After three months with a woman he ends the relationship just to be sure that they don't start hearing the word "serious". He's the original commitment-phobe.'

Katy looked at her. 'So are you.'

'And can you blame me?' Libby looked at her parents and shuddered dramatically. 'If that's marriage, then I hope I die single.'

'Libby, that's an awful thing to say.'

A bee hovered close to them and Libby took a step backwards.

'Oops. Killer insects.'

Katy frowned, knowing that her sister was very allergic to bee stings. 'Are you carrying adrenaline?'

Libby grinned and tapped her tiny bag. 'Lipstick and adrenaline. A girl's best friends.'

Katy knew that, despite the smile, Libby took her allergy seriously. They all did. Libby had had a frighteningly severe reaction to a sting in the past and none of them had ever forgotten it. Particularly Alex, who had been the one who'd kept his sister alive until the ambulance had arrived. Ever since then Katy had always carried adrenaline and she knew that Alex did, too. Just in case.

The bee moved away and Katy's gaze was caught by Freddie, who was taking a call on his mobile phone.

Libby's soft mouth tightened. 'Don't marry him, Katy.' Her voice was soft. 'As Mum says, there are three months to go. Plenty of time to change your mind.'

'I don't want to change my mind.'

Libby shook her head in disbelief. 'Katy, life with Lord Frederick is going to be one long round of business entertaining. He's marrying you because of Daddy.'

'I know.' Her sister's bluntness should have upset her but it didn't. It was the truth, after all. Freddie *was* marrying her because of her father's immense wealth and influence. And she didn't even care.

Libby looked at her with exasperation. 'So why are *you* marrying *him*, Katy?'

'Because I want to.'

Because their relationship was safe and predictable.

Libby shook her head. 'It isn't right, Katy. Don't you want to be in love with the man you marry?'

Katy felt her breathing quicken. *No.* No, she didn't. Love was terrifying.

Love had almost destroyed her.

'Well, maybe you can do without love, but what about passion?' Libby was studying Freddie with narrowed eyes. 'I mean, that man would never do it for me. I want someone who's so overwhelmed by lust for me that he thrusts me against the wall, lifts up my dress and takes me there and then.'

'There's nothing to lift,' came a dry male voice from behind them. 'Your dress barely covers your bottom.'

'Alex!' Libby gave a delighted squeal and threw her arms around her brother.

He glanced over her shoulder and down her back. 'Nice knickers, Lib.'

Libby grinned and tugged her dress down. 'You're late. We thought you weren't coming.'

His handsome face was inscrutable. 'I was busy.' He released her and turned to Katy, his customary indifference momentarily suspended as he looked at his other sister. 'Hi, there, kid. You all right?'

No.

Katy hugged her brother, avoiding his penetrating gaze. 'Happy birthday, Alex.'

He tucked a finger under her chin and forced her to look at him. 'All right. What's going on? Tell your big brother.'

Katy gave a wan smile. Alex had been born first by all of three minutes.

'She's being bullied into marrying Freddie,' Libby muttered darkly, 'that's what's going on. She's doing it to please Dad. It's time for the triplets to unite.'

Alex's blue eyes narrowed sharply. 'Katy?'

Katy pulled away from her brother. 'She's talking nonsense. I'm fine. Really. Just a bit tired. And nervous about the new job, I suppose.'

'A and E is great,' Alex said immediately. 'You'll love it. I just wish you'd chosen to do it further from home. You could have come and worked in my department. We need good doctors.'

Katy smiled. 'You never stay in one place for five minutes,

Alex, so there's no point in joining you. I wanted to be in the same hospital as Libby and, with Freddie in the City, I need to be in London.'

'Well, of course you do,' Libby drawled. 'Which brings us back to the point I was making when you arrived, Alex. I just can't imagine Lord Frederick indulging in spontaneous sex. He probably gets his secretary to book slots in his diary. Is that really what you want, Katy?'

Suddenly Katy felt sick and she closed her eyes to blot out the images.

She didn't want sex with Freddie at all.

Alex frowned and was about to say something when their mother called him over.

'Back in a minute.' He touched Katy gently on the cheek, exchanged a meaningful glance with Libby and strolled across the lawn, lithe and athletic and totally confident.

'He's bloody good-looking. How come we're both blonde and he managed to have such dark hair? It's really spectacular with those blue eyes.' Libby watched him charm a group of her father's clients. 'He's everything a man should be. Sexy, strong, clever. The funny thing is, if he weren't his son I'm sure Dad wouldn't approve of him. He's just a little bit bad and dangerous, isn't he? And we all know what Dad thinks of dangerous men.'

Katy sucked in a breath.

She'd only ever met one dangerous man.

There was a tense silence. 'You still think about him, don't you?' Libby looked at her, her blue gaze penetrating. 'It's been eleven years since he broke your heart but you still think about him.'

Katy didn't even have to ask whom she meant. 'I—I don't...'

The sick feeling grew worse and her heart started to beat faster.

'Don't lie to me, Katy.' Libby's voice was soft. 'It all seems such a long time ago now, doesn't it? Our eighteenth birthday party. Do you remember that summer?'

Katy stood still, her features frozen. Of course she remembered it. She remembered every single minute.

Libby's voice was soft and dreamy. 'I envied you so much. I would have done anything to have been you.'

'Stop it, Lib.' Katy closed her eyes and then opened them again quickly. Closing them just made the images worse.

'How was it that Dad used to describe him?' Libby tipped her head on one side. 'Brilliant, but dangerous. I'll never forget the first time he came to our house for one of Dad's social evenings. We were sixteen, remember? Everyone else was in a black tie and Jago Rodriguez turned up on a motorbike dressed in black leather with absolutely no respect for English social customs.'

'That's because he's Spanish,' Katy muttered, wondering why Libby was choosing this particular moment to tackle a subject that she'd studiously avoided for years.

'That probably was half the problem,' Libby agreed. 'He wasn't British and he didn't have the right pedigree. I thought Mum was going to have a heart attack. I loved the fact that he didn't give a damn what anyone thought of him. You would have thought that being the son of our housekeeper might have made him feel awkward but he had absolutely no hang-ups about who he was or where he came from.'

'That's because Mrs Rodriguez was such a great mother,' Katy said, not wanting to remember those times. 'Spaniards are renowned for having close families and she gave him pride and a belief in himself. And then Dad gave him his big break in the City—'

Libby gave a cynical laugh. 'Don't be naïve, Katy. Dad doesn't have even the thinnest streak of altruism in his make-up. Every single move he makes is calculated and he does absolutely nothing that won't benefit him.' Her tone was bitter as she surveyed her father across the lawn. He still hadn't noticed her. 'He didn't employ Jago Rodriguez out of any sense of kindness. He employed him because he spotted raw talent and the same character traits that he possesses himself. Both of them are ruthless, ambitious and completely lacking in emotional conscience.'

Katy flinched slightly at her sister's harsh analysis. It didn't match her memory of those few glorious weeks. 'Jago was kind to me, Libby, gentle.'

'He walked away without a word,' Libby pointed out grimly, and Katy sighed, unable to argue with the truth, knowing that Libby was just being protective. And she would have felt the same if positions had been reversed. Libby and Alex were her best friends and the three of them were as close as brothers and sisters could be.

And it was hardly surprising that Libby blamed Jago. The months after he'd walked away had been the worst of her life and Libby had been the one who'd seen her through it.

She bit her lip.

But hadn't he always warned her that he wasn't looking for commitment?

Had it been his fault that she'd committed the cardinal sin of falling in love with him?

'Well, he may have been a rat, but I can see why you fell for him.' Libby broke off and looked at her with a touch of awe. 'Jago was the most stunningly gorgeous male I've ever met. And to think you actually—'

'That's enough, Lib!' Katy's nails dug into her palms as memories exploded in her head.

Rapid breathing, the rough scrape of male stubble against sensitive flesh, and heat, pounding erotic heat, heat that burned inside and out...

'You—the quiet, shy one and Mr Rough, Bad and Dangerous. Where did you ever find the courage?' Libby looked at her in admiration. 'I wonder what would have happened if Dad hadn't found out? Would it have carried on?'

Sleek, hard muscle against soft skin, flesh scorching flesh, mouths locked, bodies joined in untamed, wild passion...

'Of course not.' Katy lifted a hand to her head, trying to clear the memories. 'We were totally different.'

His strength mixed with her gentleness. Raw male power controlling her every movement...

Libby pulled a face. 'That's our father talking. To him Jago was a banned substance, right up there with drugs and smoking. He was *the* unsuitable man. Fine for fighting dirty in the money markets but not good enough for his daughter. He didn't have the benefit of Lord Frederick's bloodline.'

'Maybe Dad was right. It would never have worked,' Katy said frantically. 'Now can we change the subject, Libby, *please*?'

Dark eyes holding hers, possessing her, taking her with him as their bodies exploded.

Her sister appeared not to have heard her plea. 'Why wouldn't it have worked? Because you were the rich heiress and he was a bit of rough? Dad's protégé who clawed his way up through hard work and naked ambition?' Libby gave a wicked grin. 'I confess that I would have signed away my share of the family fortune for the chance of one roll in the hay with Jago. He might have been dangerous but he was so-o-o sexy. I've always wanted to ask you something.' She lowered her voice and glanced around to check that no one could hear them. 'What was it like with him? Was he good, Katy?'

Katy couldn't breathe.

Good?

Oh, yes, he was good. Better than good. Jago was so skilled that he might have invented sex.

And she'd trained herself never to think about it. Never to remember those few weeks. The agony was too acute.

And now, for some unfathomable reason, her sister was making her talk about it.

She never talked about it.

'That's enough, Lib.' Her voice was hoarse and she lifted a hand to loosen her collar, only to remember that her dress had a scoop neckline.

The constriction came from within.

Her memories were suffocating her.

'You loved him, Katy. He was the one,' Libby said softly. *'The one.'*

Her father in one of his terrifying rages. *It ends now, Katy. He's gone. You won't be seeing him again.*

Her childlike belief that her father was wrong.

'I kept thinking that he'd come for me,' she murmured, talking as much to herself as to Libby. 'I thought our love was strong enough to survive anything. How could I have been so wrong?'

'You were crazy about him, Katy.' Libby's tone was gentle. 'It was true love. How can you marry Freddie after what you had with Jago?'

'It's because of what I had with Jago that I'm marrying Freddie,' Katy said hoarsely. 'And Jago never loved me. How could he have loved me and walked away?'

She could see now that he'd been way out of her league. A sophisticated, ruthless man so practised in the art of seduction that someone as emotionally and physically innocent as her had never stood a chance. He'd been with her for the novelty value, whereas she'd fallen for him like a skydiver without a parachute and had been left emotionally devastated when he'd ended the relationship.

And she knew that she never wanted to experience that depth of emotional intensity again.

Which was why she was marrying Freddie.

Freddie was safe and predictable and she always knew how her body would behave around him, whereas being with Jago had been a journey into the unknown. A breathless, exciting, terrifying journey. Every look, every touch had caused an explosion inside her that had left scars.

Scars that had never healed.

'Jago wouldn't be standing around talking to your father's friends,' Libby murmured, not meeting her eyes. 'He'd be sending you hot looks and dragging you into the bushes, and he wouldn't give a damn what anyone thought.'

His voice, rough with masculine triumph. 'You're mine now, Katy.'

Desperation swamped her and she dropped her champagne glass and ran across the lawn and up the steps, ignoring Libby's attempt to stop her.

She had to get away.

Her car was parked in the front.

She'd drive.

She'd just drive, and then she'd be all right.

She could leave the memories behind.

Alex stepped up to his sister, his blue eyes narrowed. 'Did it work?'

Libby bit her lip and stared after Katy, guilt and anxiety clouding her eyes. 'Judging from her reaction, I think it might have worked a little too well. Oh, hell, Alex, are you sure we're doing the right thing? You know she hates talking about it and usually we go along with that.'

Alex rubbed a hand across the back of his neck, displaying a rare departure from his customary cool. 'She's marrying a man she doesn't love, Lib, for all the wrong reasons. Anything is worth a try.'

Libby's eyes shone a little too brightly. 'But I *hurt* her.'

'And you think she won't hurt when she finally wakes up and realises that she's made a mistake marrying Freddie? And anyway…' Alex paused and took a long slug from his glass of champagne. 'You only made her talk about stuff she thinks about all the time.'

'I felt like a total rat, not telling her about Jago,' Libby mumbled. 'What's she going to do when she finds out that he's now a doctor and working in her hospital?'

'She'll be shocked, but she needs to confront her past and

get on with her life instead of bottling it up,' Alex said firmly. 'It's the right thing to do. Stop worrying.'

Libby glared at her brother. 'How come you're always so damned confident about everything? Aren't you even remotely worried he'll hurt her again?'

Alex's jaw hardened. 'We both know that Dad was somehow responsible for the first time, which was why I didn't go after Jago eleven years ago, but if he hurts her again…' There was a brief pause and the warmth of his tone dropped several degrees. 'Then I'll kill him. Now change the subject. Dad's spotted you at last and he's on his way over. Better hitch that skirt up another inch, Lib. I can't quite see your knickers.'

CHAPTER TWO

'RTA COMING in, Jago.' Charlotte, one of the A and E sisters, replaced the phone and turned to the consultant. 'Young female had to be cut out of a car. Apparently it's taken them a while to free her.'

Jago lifted night-black eyes from the X-ray he was studying, his handsome face sharply alert. 'Details?'

'Not many. Head and chest but I don't know how bad.' Charlotte tilted her head, studying his face, marvelling at how unbelievably gorgeous he was. It didn't matter how long she'd worked with him, she still stared. All the female staff stared. As one of the cheekier nurses had quipped, 'Some staffrooms have posters of heartthrobs—we have the real live thing.' Charlotte pulled herself together. 'I can hear the siren.'

Jago nodded briefly. 'Get someone to check Resus while we meet the ambulance.' With that he yanked the X-ray out of the light-box and strode through the department, broad-shouldered and confident, pausing briefly to hand the X-ray to one of the casualty officers. 'If you take a close look at this, you can see a lunar dislocation on the lateral view, Alison. You missed it.'

Aware of his reputation for zero tolerance when it came to clinical mistakes, the young doctor regarded him warily.

'I—I didn't request a lateral view.'

The consultant's voice was silky smooth. 'But fortunately I did.'

'The AP view looked normal, Mr Rodriguez—'

'Which is why you should also have requested a lateral view X-ray.' His tone was icy cold and unsympathetic and the casualty officer shifted in her seat.

'I—I thought that was a pretty rare injury. I read in a book that it's quite common to miss that particular injury on X-ray.'

'Not in my department,' Jago said softly, visibly unimpressed by her error. 'Next time request the right views and check them carefully. Expect the unexpected. Rare injuries still happen. Refer the patient to the orthopaedic team for a manipulation under anaesthetic and then join me in Resus. We've got an RTA coming in.'

'Yes, Mr Rodriguez.' The young female SHO was pink with mortification and Jago gritted his teeth impatiently. The girl was sloppy and over-confident and he'd be relieved when she finished her six-month stint in two weeks' time. Some people weren't cut out for emergency medicine and she was one of them. And on top of that, her longing looks were beginning to irritate him. She'd made it obvious that she'd be happy to extend their relationship beyond the confines of the hospital but he had more sense than to break hearts in his own department and these days he was becoming more and more picky about who he shared his bed with.

By his side Charlotte winced. 'Ouch—you were hard on her.'

Jago lifted a dark eyebrow, his expression cool. 'You'd prefer that she discharged a patient with a dislocation?'

'No, but—'

'Patients have the right to expect the very best care when they come into this department. She has a great deal to learn.'

Ending the conversation abruptly, Jago pushed his way through the swing doors just as the ambulance roared into the ambulance bay.

The paramedics opened the back and lifted out the stretcher. 'Young female with head and chest injuries. She was shunted from behind so we've had her on a backboard. GCS of 7 at the scene but she regained consciousness fairly quickly and it's 12 now, but she's not saying much.' The paramedic frowned. 'She hasn't been able to tell us her name or anything, but we've got her bag so we need to try and find out who she is.'

Jago turned to look at the still form of the girl lying on the trolley and his powerful body froze in shock. He stared in stunned disbelief, his muscular shoulders tense as his eyes raked over the blonde hair and the endless limbs.

I love you, Jago.

'I know who she is.'

Only years of exercising rigid control over his intrinsically volatile emotions prevented him from displaying his reaction to her in a very public way.

The paramedic was looking at him. 'You do? Oh—right. Well, in that case...'

'Take her through to Resus,' Jago ordered, his eyes still on the long, primrose blonde hair, now matted with blood.

Do you think I'm pretty, Jago?

'Her air bag didn't open properly and she hit the windscreen,' the paramedic explained as they manoeuvred the stretcher into the A and E department. 'Her head bled a lot and she's going to need stitches, but we've put a pad on it for now. She might have chest injuries, too, from the way she was thrown against the steering-wheel. Weird really. There didn't seem to be anyone else involved. You should have seen the car. Frankly, she was bloody lucky to escape alive.'

Jago's expression didn't flicker, his eyes as black as night and his manner controlled and totally professional. 'OK, guys, let's get to work. Get me some gloves, please—she's covered in glass. Be careful!'

Someone handed him some gloves and he pulled them on quickly as Charlotte moved closer to the trolley.

'Hello, can you hear me, er…?' She glanced up question-ingly. 'Do we have a name?'

'Her name is Katherine.' Jago checked her airway and reached for an oxygen mask. 'Katherine Westerling.'

Huge blue eyes staring into his, innocence mingling with excitement and anticipation as his hard body moved against her softness…

'Right.' Charlotte exchanged puzzled glances with one of her colleagues. 'Why is that name familiar?'

'She's the daughter of Sir Charles Westerling, the banker,' Jago informed her tautly, and Charlotte's eyes widened.

'Wow! I've seen pictures of her in the glossies, looking glam-orous. She's seriously rich and really, really beautiful.'

And totally lacking in morals.

His relationship with Katy had been the one and only time in his life that he'd lowered his guard with a woman. And he hadn't made the same mistake since.

Her father, telling him the truth, showing him the evidence…

'That's her.' His emotions held rigidly in check, Jago didn't look up, his hands moving swiftly as he worked to stabilise Katy. *She was just a patient.* 'Now, can we stop gossiping and just get on with the job?'

Charlotte stiffened warily, cast him a curious look and then turned her attention back to the patient. 'Katherine? Kather-ine, can you hear me?'

Katy lay with her eyes closed.

She could hear voices but she didn't respond. It felt nice to hide in the darkness. There was a sharp prick in her arm and hands moving over her.

'Katherine.'

A kind female voice was calling her name but it felt like too much effort to respond.

Then she heard a harsh, male voice and her body tensed.

It sounded so familiar.

'Her X-rays are fine but she's got a laceration by her hair-line that's going to need suturing and she was knocked out so she's going to have to stay in overnight for observation.' Fingers touched her and then she heard the voice again. 'She's shivering. Get some blankets.'

Something soft and cosy covered her immediately but the shivering wouldn't stop.

'Any relatives?'

'She was on her own in the car.'

'Open your eyes, Katherine.'

Hands touching her, the prick of another needle.

'OK, she's stable.' The familiar male voice again. 'I'll leave you to get on with it. Get her a bed on the ward and call me if anything changes.'

'How's that head?'

Katy lay in the bed, watching the nurse who was checking her blood pressure. 'Aching, but I'll live.' She moved her head to look around her and then winced as pain lanced through her skull. 'Which hospital am I in?'

'St Andrew's. We put seven stitches in your head but your hair will cover it so don't worry about having a scar.'

St Andrew's?

Katy closed her eyes and suppressed a groan. Having a scar was the least of her problems. She was due to start work in this very department in two weeks' time. How embarrassing!

Should she say something?

Deciding to remain silent on the subject for the time being, she shrank lower in the bed.

'They reckon you're lucky to be alive.' The nurse pulled a pen out of her pocket and scribbled on the chart. 'What happened?'

'I don't know.' Katy frowned as she tried to remember. 'I was at a party at my parents' house and then I left to drive home.' *Running from her past.* 'I saw a rabbit in the road so I slammed on my brakes and that's the last thing I remember.'

The nurse made a clucking sound. 'Anyway, your X-rays are clear so you should be able to go home in the morning. We found some details in your handbag and called your fiancé. He's on his way over.'

Katy suppressed a groan. She didn't want to see Freddie. Why couldn't they have called Libby or Alex?

The nurse was looking at her in concern. 'You look terrible. Is there anything I can get you? Do you need anything?'

Yes. She needed to know that the voice that she'd heard in A and E hadn't been Jago's.

Of course it wasn't Jago's, she told herself.

Jago was a super-rich banker. How could he possibly be working in A and E?

She had just been imagining things and it was no wonder after the conversation she'd had with Libby.

'I don't need anything else, thanks.'

She smiled at the nurse just as the door opened and Jago Rodriguez walked in.

The colour drained out of Katy's cheeks and her breathing did an emergency stop. Her entire body was frozen to the bed, paralysed by the shocking reality of being confronted by Jago.

'Mr Rodriguez.' The nurse straightened nervously, went a deep shade of pink and dropped the chart she was holding.

Stunning dark eyes flickered to the nurse. 'You can go.'

He held the door open in the manner of someone totally accustomed to having his every instruction obeyed instantly, and the flustered nurse retrieved the chart and hurried across the room, casting a final hungry look at Jago's profile before slipping outside.

Suddenly the room seemed too small.

Jago closed the door and stood with his back to it, his long, powerful legs spread apart, his expression unsmiling. Dominant, confident and unapologetically male, not by the slightest flicker of those sinfully dark lashes did he acknowledge that they'd ever been more than casual acquaintances.

'Hello, princess.' He spoke in a deep, masculine drawl that made Katy's pulse race. 'Running again?'

Katy's soft lips parted and she struggled to sit up. She was in total shock. The subject of all her dreams and nightmares was suddenly confronting her. Jago, whom she'd thought about every waking minute for the last eleven years.

Jago, whom she'd never expected to see again.

Somehow he was standing in her hospital room, frighteningly imposing and super-handsome, displaying not the slightest discomfort at seeing her. Nothing in his body language suggested that he felt the smallest hint of guilt or remorse for the way he'd walked away from her without a word of explanation, leaving her so badly hurt that for a while she'd thought she'd never recover.

She could see that he was waiting for her to speak but she was totally unable to think coherently.

Over time she'd managed to convince herself that her starry-eyed view of him had been coloured by a hormonally driven teenage imagination. She'd decided that he couldn't have been as gorgeous as she remembered.

She'd been wrong.

Jago Rodriguez was strikingly good-looking. He wore his glossy dark hair so short that in any other man it would have accentuated the faults in his facial features. But Jago didn't have any faults. He possessed a bone structure that made artists drool and a physique that would have driven athletes to a state of mindless envy. He was impossibly, staggeringly handsome.

And to set him apart from the average man still further, he wore an exquisitely tailored suit that skimmed his wide shoulders and just shrieked of designer label.

In a strange moment of distraction Katy found herself wondering what happened if a patient was sick on it.

Growing hotter and hotter under his steady scrutiny, she lifted a hand to her aching head.

'Wh-what are you—?' She broke off, totally unable to believe his presence by her hospital bed. 'I-I didn't know you were a doctor,' she croaked, and a dark eyebrow swept upwards.

'Why should you?'

Why indeed?

After all, he'd chosen to walk out of her life without a backward glance or giving a forwarding address. To him the relationship had been over and he'd moved on. Unfortunately it hadn't been so easy for her.

She dug her nails in her palms. 'I assumed you were still in banking.'

'I lost my taste for banking,' he said smoothly, his dark eyes fixed on her pale face. 'I changed career.'

So that was why her feeble, childish attempts to track him down had failed. She'd used all her contacts at the various banks but with no success. It had never occurred to her that he might have changed profession.

Katy blinked as she did the calculation in her head. If he was a consultant now then he must have started training immediately after he'd left her father's company and he must have progressed fast. But, then, that didn't surprise her. Jago had always been frighteningly clever.

'Why medicine?'

And why this hospital, where she was going to see him every day?

She fought the rush of panic that threatened to swamp her and focused on his tie. Silk. Designer. Sufficiently muted not to induce a headache in a patient with a head injury.

'I like the adrenaline rush. When you're dealing with lives, the stakes are higher than in the money markets.'

He gave a careless shrug and she found her gaze drifting upwards to his powerful shoulders. If anything, he was even more spectacular than he'd been eleven years before. Jago Rodriguez was sex in the raw, so overwhelmingly masculine that just looking at him was enough to punch the breath from her body.

Appalled by her own thoughts and the traitorous stab of

awareness that she felt low in her stomach, she looked away from him.

What was the matter with her? He'd been in the room for less than five minutes and already her insides were turning somersaults. Did she have absolutely no sense of self-preservation?

It depressed her that she could still react to him, knowing just how badly he'd hurt her. Weren't doctors supposed to be warm and caring?

For a short, blissful interlude she'd thought that Jago possessed those qualities, but experience had shown that he was capable of being every bit as ruthless, ambitious and macho as her father.

Jago didn't have a compassionate bone in his body and she certainly couldn't imagine him as a doctor.

As far as she was concerned, he wasn't doctor material.

She started to shiver.

Why now? Why did she have to bump into Jago now, when she'd finally managed to rebuild an emotionally comfortable life for herself?

She was marrying Freddie and she was never again going to feel that breathless, stomach-churning excitement that she'd experienced with Jago.

Those slumberous eyes, as dark as obsidian, reflected not a hint of warmth or tenderness. Nothing that reflected the intense emotions which had characterised their relationship. The tension in the room sucked the breath from her body but he surveyed her with an almost indifferent coolness that made it blatantly clear he had no positive feelings for her whatsoever.

It was almost as if the very sight of her offended him, which was utterly ridiculous. After all, *he'd* been the one who'd walked away from *her* without the smallest explanation.

And maybe that shouldn't have come as such a surprise. She'd been well aware of his reputation when she'd become involved with him. In fact, his reputation had been part of the

fascination, at least to begin with, and he'd always warned her
that he didn't do commitment.

So why had she been so devastated when he'd ended it? And
did she really expect him to be harbouring romantic memories
about her? Just remembering all her innocent fantasies about
him filled her with mortification.

She'd been so naïve.

She suddenly felt horribly vulnerable in her NHS nightie
that was open all the way down the back.

If she had to face Jago she would have chosen to be wearing armour.

'I heard your voice when the paramedics brought me in.' Her
voice was a croak. 'Was it you who—?'

'Who sorted you out? Yes, it was. I seem to make a habit of
it, don't I? And it's always on the same date.' He strolled forward and sat on the edge of the bed. 'Tell me, Katy. What were
you running from this time?'

'Nothing.'

Her memories.

'You could have been killed. It took them an hour to cut you
out of the car.' His tone was matter-of-fact. 'Do you think I've
forgotten the significance of today, Katy? It's the tenth of July.
Your birthday. So the question is, what are those unspeakable
parents of yours trying to force you to do this time?'

Their eyes clashed and she knew that he was remembering
her eighteenth birthday eleven years previously. Another occasion when she'd been running and he'd rescued her...

'I'm going to be a doctor.'

Katy faced her father, her heart beating so fast that she felt
faint. There wasn't going to be a row. There couldn't be. They
were surrounded by influential people. She'd chosen to confront him in the middle of their birthday party, knowing that
he wouldn't be able to do much.

Her father looked at her impatiently. 'Don't be ridiculous,

Katherine. You're going to do this cordon bleu cookery course in Switzerland. I've paid the fees.'

Katy took several gulps of air and realised that her father was so dismissive of her that he didn't even listen to her any more.

'But I don't want to cook, and I don't want to model,' she said hesitantly, refusing to let the subject drop, digging her fingers into her damp palms as she faced her father. 'I'm going to be a doctor.'

She'd applied for a place and had been accepted subject to her exam results. Telling her father was the last step to achieving her dream.

Her father's expression became ugly, his stance suddenly menacing. 'You're not. It's bad enough that Alex has chosen to be a doctor when he's got the brains to join me and make a fortune in the City, without you doing the same thing.'

Katy refrained from telling him that it had been glancing through Alex's prospectuses from medical school that had helped her finally make up her mind. She'd already wasted enough time modelling.

Now she was going to study medicine.

'You have the looks to be a highly successful model,' her mother added nervously, lifting a hand to wave at one of the guests and pinning a false smile on her face. 'Thanks to your father, you're wealthy enough not to have to work. Have some fun until you meet someone suitable and then get married.'

'But I want to work,' Katy blurted out, forgetting that they were surrounded by people. 'I want to earn a living. *I want a career.*'

'Lower your voice, Katherine!' Her mother's tone was a soft mutter and she glanced round self-consciously. 'Your father has important guests here. We don't want everyone gossiping.'

Katy gritted her teeth. She didn't care about gossip. She just wanted him to listen to her for once. For once she wanted him to respect her opinion on something.

'Please Dad, I—'

'The subject is closed, Katherine.' Her father's face was cold and unsmiling. 'On the first of October you're going off to your cookery course and that's the end of it. Don't mention it again or you'll make me angry.'

And Katy knew exactly what that meant.

Her heart started to beat faster and she dug her nails deeper into her palms. It was the threat of her father's fury that had prevented her from saying something before now. She'd sneaked off to interviews, accepted Alex's help in finding accommodation and the only thing left to do now was to tell her parents.

And she was going to tell them.

'Dad—'

'I don't want the subject mentioned again.' With that her father strode off across the lawn to talk to the guests, leaving Katy with a desire to scream with frustration.

How was she ever going to get her father to accept her plans?

Suddenly it was all too much.

Tears springing into her eyes, she spun round and ran across the lawn, ignoring the astonished looks she received from the guests, ignoring her mother's frosty glare.

She didn't slow her pace until she reached the stables. There was only one thing that would ease her tension and that was a ride. She needed to get away from her own party.

Brushing the tears from her cheeks, she grabbed a bridle from the tack room, relieved that the grooms were obviously busy elsewhere. Then she hurried back across the yard and slid into one of the stables.

'Hi, sweetheart.' She stroked her favourite mare on the neck and slipped the reins over the horse's head and the bit into her mouth, fastening the bridle quickly. 'We're getting out of here.'

She led the mare out into the yard, slipped off her high heels and vaulted easily onto the horse's back, clattering out of the yard before anyone spotted her.

The moment she reached the fields she kicked the horse into a gallop and sped along the track at a breakneck pace.

Part of her knew it wasn't safe. She was wearing a loose summer dress and no riding hat and she was crying so hard she couldn't see where she was going, but she just *had* to get away.

She headed for the barn at the far end of her father's estate. The place she always escaped to when she didn't want anyone to find her.

As she approached the barn the horse suddenly veered to the left to avoid a ditch. Katy lost her balance and slid off the animal's back, landing awkwardly in the long grass.

She lay still for a moment, staring at the sky, wondering which part of her she'd hurt most.

'Well, that was dramatic.' The low masculine drawl came from beside her and she struggled to sit up, her eyes widening as she recognised the man staring down at her.

Jago Rodriguez.

He worked for her father in the bank and everyone knew who he was. *Especially the women.* He'd clawed his way up from what could only be described as an underprivileged back-ground. But if nature had deprived him of material wealth, it had more than compensated by giving Jago sensational good looks, a ruthless ambition to succeed and a brain as sharp as the business end of a razor. It was those qualities that had brought him to the attention of her father and had made him a million-aire several times over by the time he was in his early twenties.

He was a frequent visitor to the manor and Libby often sat on the stairs, hoping for a glimpse of him. Katy wasn't so bold. She hid in the shadows and watched in mute admiration as Jago coolly ignored her father's moodiness and childish displays of temper. He was one of the few people who remained completely undisturbed by Charles Westerling's thoroughly abrasive busi-ness manner and bully-boy tactics.

'The boy's brilliant,' her father would grunt as they ate din-ner in the formal dining room after Jago had left. Of course, he was never invited to join them. 'Has an instinctive feel for what will work and goes with it. He's making a fortune for himself and the bank at the moment.'

Their mother looked pained. 'I just wish you didn't have to invite him to events here. He has absolutely no respect for English social convention.'

'Hallelujah,' Libby muttered, and Katy stared at her plate, wishing that she had just one small portion of Jago Rodriguez's courage.

What must it be like to have such self-confidence that you didn't care what people thought?

'I think he's gorgeous,' Libby piped up, and then subsided as she met her father's glare.

'I know he's got a dreadful reputation with women, but I bet he's a brilliant kisser,' Libby said later as they got ready for bed, both of them lost in their own fantasies about Jago. 'I wonder if he'd kiss me just once so that I could find out what it feels like to do it properly.'

Lying in a tumbled heap and staring into his wicked, masculine face, Katy remembered her sister's comment and felt her heart miss a beat.

'What are you doing here?'

'Escaping,' he said dryly, glancing in the direction of the manor house where the party was still in full swing. 'Just as you are, presumably.'

He was expecting an answer but suddenly she found herself horribly tongue-tied and totally unable to speak.

He hunkered down next to her, lifting a dark eyebrow as she shrank away from him. 'Ah—the shy sister who always avoids me. You know, you shouldn't believe everything you hear.' He sounded mildly amused. 'I don't seduce children.'

She blushed hotly, mortified that he'd read her mind and self-conscious about her appearance. 'I'm not a child.' She brushed her tangled blonde hair away from her face and looked at him shyly. 'It's my eighteenth birthday today.'

She was supposed to be a woman.

'I know that. I was invited to the party. If party is the right word.' His voice was soft and his gaze assessing as it slid over her body with a thoroughness that left her gasping for air. 'So why are you galloping across the fields wearing a party dress and not much else? Why aren't you mingling with your guests?'

'They're mostly my parents' friends and colleagues. Contacts.' She stared into those lazy dark eyes and fought the temptation to blurt out all her problems. What was the point? A man like Jago wouldn't begin to understand what it was like to have someone dictating your life. He never let anyone dictate to him. 'I needed to get away.'

'Hardly surprising. If someone gave me an eighteenth birthday party like that I'd want to get away, too.' His gaze moved down her bare legs and rested on her feet. 'What happened to your shoes, Cinderella?'

'I left them at the stable.' She tried to scramble to her feet and then gave a yelp of pain as her ankle gave way. 'Ouch!'

Tears pricked her eyes and she blinked them away, determined not to cry in front of him.

He frowned sharply. 'Let me look at that.'

Without waiting for her permission he slid a strong hand down her leg and examined her ankle. She held her breath and stared in fascination at his long, strong fingers as they moved over the bone, pressing and testing her reaction. Finally he straightened. 'It's not broken. You must have sprained it when you fell. You're lucky you didn't fracture your skull.'

Strands of her blonde hair trailed onto his forearm and she marvelled at the contrast between them. He was so dark and strong and everything about him was so different to her. Hypnotised by his masculinity, her eyes fixed on the dark hairs on his forearms, travelled slowly upwards over the swell of muscle and then lifted to the stubble shadowing his hard jaw. He was breathtakingly gorgeous and so sexy that her imagination took flight.

She felt a flutter in the pit of her stomach and her eyes dropped to his firm mouth, wondering, *wishing...*

He met her rapt expression with a lazy amusement that was totally male. 'Stop looking at me like that, princess, or I just might do what you want me to do.'

She blushed and sank her teeth into her lower lip. Miles from anywhere, frustrated beyond belief with her life, she felt suddenly bold. 'I want you to kiss me.'

She stood totally still, shocked by her own impulsive declaration, but his expression didn't flicker.

'I know you do.'

His wicked dark eyes slid down to her mouth and suddenly her breathing was choppy.

'So will you?'

His gaze lifted. 'No.'

Her fragile bubble of confidence exploded and she stumbled to her feet, wincing at the pain in her ankle. 'Because you're scared of my father?'

He threw back his head and laughed. A rich, masculine sound that made her toes curl.

'What do you think?' He was still smiling and she swallowed.

'I don't think you're scared of anything.' She stared down at her feet, mortified by his rejection. 'So it's because I'm not pretty enough.'

There was a long, electric silence and then he slid strong fingers under her chin and forced her to look at him.

'You're beautiful, princess, and you know it.' His voice was soft and he moved his hand and ran his fingers through her blonde hair with the same easy confidence that he applied to everything. 'So beautiful that it hurts to look at you.'

'So why won't you kiss me?'

'Because I'm too old to sneak around kissing children.'

'I'm not a child!'

One dark eyebrow lifted. 'So why were you running away?

Grown-ups don't run away from problems, Katy. They face them. When you've got the courage to kiss me in full view of your father, come back and we'll talk.'

Grown-ups don't run away from problems.

And here she was, running again…

She stared at Jago, thinking that he hadn't changed much. He might be a doctor but it certainly hadn't softened him. He looked tough and uncompromising and totally self-assured. But, then, Jago Rodriguez had always had confidence by the bucketload.

Ironic really, she reflected as she tightened her fists on the sheet. For all her privileged upbringing she'd never managed to achieve much in the way of confidence.

'I'm still waiting for you to tell me what you were running from.'

There was a tap on the door and the nurse opened it warily.

'Miss Westerling's fiancé is here.'

Jago's eyes lifted to Katy's.

There was a long, aching silence and then he stood up, his eyes shuttered. 'Show him in.'

Freddie came striding in, hidden behind a bouquet of flowers the size of Africa. Despite the pain in her head, Katy gave a weak smile. Unlike Jago, Freddie never veered from protocol. He couldn't possibly visit someone in hospital and not take flowers.

Freddie presented the flowers and leaned over to kiss her awkwardly on the cheek. 'Katherine! What the devil happened?'

Katy was hopelessly aware of Jago's dark scrutiny. 'I—I crashed my car.'

Freddie looked perplexed. 'None of us even knew you'd left the party.'

'Nothing changes,' Jago murmured in an undertone, but only Katy understood the implications of his softly spoken words.

'Are you the doctor who sorted her out?' Freddie extended

a hand, his cultured drawl the product of an exclusive public school education. 'Can't thank you enough. Will she be all right?'

'She was lucky. The damage was superficial,' Jago said, his eyes drifting to the dressing on Katy's forehead. 'Stitches out in seven days and the scar will be under the hairline. She'll be modelling again in a few weeks without a mark to show for it.'

Freddie frowned and Katy realised that Jago didn't even know she was a doctor. Especially not a doctor who was going to be working for him in this department in two weeks' time.

Or would she?

Could she really take a job alongside the one man who had the ability to dishevel her otherwise ordered life?

She couldn't believe that fate would do this to her.

On the other hand, working in A and E was what she really wanted, and if she gave up her father would think he'd won and she'd lose the career she loved.

She looked at Jago. For eleven years he'd been haunting her life. In the shadows of everything she did.

Maybe the only way she was going to move on was to face up to the past.

He was just a man after all.

A man who obviously hadn't loved her. *A man who wasn't capable of loving anyone.*

She had more sense than to fall for Jago again.

And she was marrying Freddie.

Conservative, British Freddie who respected convention, could trace his family back six hundred years, spoke with the right accent and always tried to do the right thing.

'How long does she need to stay in?' Freddie glanced discreetly at his watch and Katy almost laughed. He was so transparent. He obviously had a meeting that he was desperate to get to. It was like her father all over again. Only Freddie was much, much nicer than her father.

'You don't need to stay, Freddie,' she said gently, and Freddie gave an awkward smile.

'It's just that I've got dinner with one of the managing directors from Fixed Income and—'

'It's OK.' Her head was throbbing too much to hear about banks. 'I'll be fine. I'll be going home tomorrow. Libby can fetch me. I'll call you.'

'Well, don't worry about the car.' His mind clearly on other things, Freddie leaned forward and gave her another awkward kiss on the cheek. 'I'll buy you a new one as a wedding present.'

Katy's eyes slid to Jago but his face gave nothing away, his thick, dark lashes concealing the expression in his eyes. She remembered her father saying that it had been his inscrutability and cool head that had made him such a fearsome reputation at such a young age.

'I'll be in touch, then.' Freddie slid out of the door, leaving the two of them alone once more.

'So he's the reason you were running.' Jago's voice was even and suddenly Katy felt exhausted.

She just wanted to close her eyes and sleep for ever. She wished her head would stop throbbing.

'Go away, Jago.' *Before she made a total fool of herself in front of him.*

'Your father's choice, I presume. I can't believe you're marrying him,' he drawled softly. 'He's totally wrong for you.'

Weakened by her injury and the shock of seeing him again, Katy roused herself sufficiently to defend herself.

'He's totally right for me. I *want* to marry Freddie.'

'Do you? So, tell me, Katy...' He leaned forward, his voice suddenly soft. 'If it's what you want, why did you just drive your car into a ditch?'

CHAPTER THREE

JAGO strode back to his office, tense and on edge, shaken out of his customary cool by his encounter with Katy.

Why the hell had he gone and seen her personally?

He could have arranged for a more junior doctor to check on her and discharge her, but instead he hadn't been able to resist seeing her one more time.

Some self-satisfied, macho corner of his make-up had wanted to see her awake, to test her reaction to him.

He'd walked away eleven years before, too angry to risk seeing her face to face. Confronted by her after all this time, he'd suddenly wanted to see if there was even the slightest hint of guilt or discomfort in that beautiful face.

There hadn't been.

Oh, she'd been shocked to see him, but she'd met his gaze steadily, without the slightest hint of remorse. A man with less experience than him might have thought she was as innocent as the day she was born, but he knew better.

Katy's innocence was only on the surface.

He opened the door to his office, anger erupting inside him at the memories her presence had reawakened. Until he'd met Katy, he'd always prided himself in his lack of vulnerability when it had come to the female sex. He'd been streetwise and sharp and able to recognise every one of their tricks.

He shouldered the door shut behind him and swore softly in Spanish. Katy was the only woman in his life who'd managed to sneak under his defences. Her fragile innocence and femininity had appealed to everything male in him and he had been totally unprepared for the strength of his reaction to her. She had been so far removed from the type of woman he'd usually spent time with that to begin with he'd avoided her, but her blatant fascination in him had proved impossible to resist.

He tried to ignore her lush curves and told himself that his taste didn't run to innocent schoolgirls, however beautiful. *And Katy was astonishingly beautiful.* An incredible heart-shaped face surrounded by a cloud of silken blonde hair that could make a man lose his mind. At eighteen she possessed a sweetness that had stifled his usually measured reaction to the opposite sex.

There was something about those huge blue eyes, about the way she watched him with a mixture of excitement and longing, that gradually eroded his already severely tested self-control. Given the temptation, maybe it wasn't so surprising that he behaved like a hormonal teenager, allowing the power of sexual attraction to overwhelm common sense.

It amused him to take her out and watch the havoc that her presence caused. She was so dazzling that wherever they went she attracted the maximum amount of male attention, attention that went completely unnoticed by Katy herself because she was never able to drag her eyes away from *him.*

And her blatant and naïve adoration of him was both a source of amusement and smug male satisfaction.

She was his and only his.

Knowing her to be sexually inexperienced, for the first time in his life he was forced to curb his own physical needs until he judged that she was ready. And when that moment came, he derived an astonishing measure of gratification from peeling away the layers of shyness and reserve to reveal the hot, sexual nature that he'd detected from the first time he'd seen her.

He gritted his teeth as he remembered just how passionate a nature his patience had revealed.

Too passionate.

When her father took him to one side and told him the truth about her, he was stunned by the depth of his own disappointment and distaste.

Stunned by the emptiness he felt, he walked away in a state of shock and never contacted her again, grimly aware that he'd let her touch him in ways that weren't exclusively physical.

I love you, Jago.

He tensed, reminding himself of the truth. That her declarations had proved as shallow and fragile as her promises of commitment.

And now she was engaged to be married.

Freddie was so obviously the suitable man.

And Katy would make an excellent businessman's wife.

Jago stared fixedly out of the window, wondering why he wanted to put a fist through it.

'Did you slap his face?' Libby curled up on Katy's bed in the flat that they shared and broke a piece off a bar of chocolate. Her blonde hair showed only the merest hint of strawberry after several washes and was now held in a ponytail with a brightly coloured ribbon covered in cartoon characters. Libby worked on the paediatric ward and instead of uniform they wore practical, colourful tracksuits.

'Hardly.' Katy pulled a face, still hating herself for being so completely tongue-tied when she'd found herself confronted by Jago. 'Lying injured in a hospital bed in a nightie which only has a front to it hardly gives you the confidence to confront your past.'

'Mmm. I see your point.' Libby shook her head. 'I can't believe he's a doctor. I bet none of the female staff get any work done. Is he still fabulous-looking?'

Katy remembered the nurse who'd dropped the chart when he'd walked into the room.

'Spectacular.'

Libby grinned and sucked chocolate from her fingers. 'Oh, boy. What are you going to do?'

Katy lifted a hand and touched the dressing pad on her head. She'd asked herself the same question repeatedly.

'I'm going to start my job and try and ignore the fact that he works there,' she said finally. 'It's a big department and very busy. He's not going to have time to worry about me. It's time I put that episode of my life behind me.'

No more dreams.

'You think you can do that?' Libby chewed slowly, her expression doubtful. 'You were crazy about him, Katy.'

'But he wasn't crazy about me. I was just a conquest. When it came to it, Jago walked away without a backward glance.'

Libby sighed. 'He was a rat, that's true, but, Katy, to be fair to him he never knew about—'

'I don't ever want to talk about that,' Katy interrupted her quickly, and Libby sighed.

'I know, but I think if you told him—'

'It's history.' Katy lifted her chin. 'He left. I'm over it. End of story.'

'Right.' Libby looked at her. 'So you didn't feel a single thing when you looked at him?'

Katy reminded herself of all the reasons she was marrying Freddie.

'No. Not a thing.' She looked at her sister and inhaled deeply. 'I'm not eighteen any more, Lib. Do you really think I'd be mad enough to get involved with him again?'

After all the pain she'd suffered...

'You couldn't help yourself last time,' Libby pointed out gently. 'I saw the way you were with him. He was the one, Katy.'

'I wish you'd stop saying that!' Katy leapt of the bed, her breathing rapid. 'He wasn't the one. *He wasn't!* I was too young and inexperienced to know what I was doing.'

'Not that young.'

Katy shook her head. 'It can't be love if it's one-sided, and Jago never loved me.'

I don't do commitment, Katy.

'OK, calm down.' Libby looked at her warily and stuck out her hand. 'Have some chocolate. It's good for the nerves.'

Katy sighed. 'I'm beyond chocolate.'

Libby looked unconvinced. 'Nothing is ever beyond the reach of chocolate. Well, if you don't want chocolate, we could go shopping. I saw this gorgeous pair of shoes today.'

Katy gave a wan smile. Libby's two big loves in life were chocolate and shoes. 'If you buy any more shoes we'll need a bigger flat.' She bit her lip. 'I can handle him now, Lib. I'm older and more sensible. I *know* he's wrong for me. I don't want a man like Jago. He's ruthless and macho and totally not my type.'

She remembered the careless way that he'd dismissed the nurse. It seemed that, whatever career he pursued, Jago had to be in control.

'He's Spanish,' Libby reminded her. 'These Mediterranean types are all the same. Unreconstructed when it comes to women.'

'Well, I don't want unreconstructed,' Katy said firmly. 'Not any more. That was just a phase I went through as a teenager. Now I'm older and wiser and I want romantic—like Freddie. Did you see the flowers?'

Libby pulled a face. 'I could hardly miss them. Freddie certainly isn't subtle.'

Katy stiffened defensively. 'He's kind.'

'Right.' Libby looked at her. 'So is the mechanic that services my car, but I'm not marrying him.'

'Just drop it.'

'You know I don't think you should be marrying Freddie, and

neither does Alex.' Libby looked her straight in the eye. 'Don't try telling me you're not still affected by Jago, Katy. Look at yourself! You're a nervous wreck. You couldn't resist him before. What makes you think you can do it this time?'

'Because I'm older and wiser and I'm marrying Freddie.'

'Freddie is completely wrong for you.'

Katy gritted her teeth. 'He's very romantic. Something that Jago could never be.'

'But then Jago is one hundred and fifty per cent full-on virile male,' Libby said softly, 'something that Freddie could never be.'

'That's enough!' Katy lifted her hands to her ears but Libby didn't give up.

'You're going to be waking up every morning next to Lord Frederick—that's if he hasn't left early to get to the office before the markets open...'

Katy still had her ears covered. 'I'm not listening.'

'Fine. Don't listen.' Libby sprang off the bed and tossed the chocolate wrapper in the bin. 'But if you think you can work alongside Jago without creating fireworks then you're deluded.'

'I—I can,' Katy stammered. 'He doesn't affect me any more.'

Libby lifted an eyebrow. 'Really?'

'I don't even think about him.'

The heat of his mouth on hers, the erotic sweep of his tongue...

'Right.' Libby looked at her steadily. 'Well, in that case, working with him isn't going to be a problem, is it?'

Two weeks later Katy stood nervously in the A and E department, listening as one of the other consultants showed them round and explained what was expected of them.

A tiny scar hidden in her hairline was the only remaining physical evidence of her accident but emotionally it was a different matter. The shattered pieces of her heart, painstakingly glued back together over the past eleven years, had been torn apart again by just one meeting with Jago.

The air around her felt stuffy and close. *She could hardly breathe.* Just *thinking* about bumping into him made her knees tremble and her palms sweaty.

What had possessed her to think that she could do this?

How would he react when he discovered that she was a doctor and that she was going to be working in his department?

And how was *she* going to react to *him?*

'This is the resuscitation room and it's always kept ready. Basically we divide the department into different areas.' Totally unaware of Katy's inner torment, the consultant smiled at the group of doctors gathered around him. 'For serious injuries we use a team approach in this hospital. It means that different tasks can be performed simultaneously and makes for a more rapid assessment of the patient, and that improves the survival rate.'

Reminding herself that she had a job to do, Katy forced herself to concentrate. It was her first day and at the moment it was quiet, but she'd been warned that there could be an influx of patients at any moment. A group of them had started together and so far everyone seemed friendly enough.

And there was no sign of Jago Rodriguez.

Gradually her knees started to shake a little less and her breathing grew easier.

'How many people make up the trauma team?' A good-looking, fair-haired doctor, who'd introduced himself as Carl Richards, asked the question and the consultant turned to face him.

'We use four doctors, five nurses and a radiographer. One of the doctors acts as team leader, then there's the airway doctor who does the obvious but also checks the cervical spine and inserts any central or arterial lines that might be needed.'

'And the other two doctors?'

'We call them circulation doctors. They help with the removal of the patients' clothes, put up peripheral lines, insert chest drains—that type of thing. The nurses work in much the same way. The important thing to remember is that there should only be six people touching the patient or it leads to total chaos. The others should keep well back.'

'And most of the senior doctors.' It was Carl again. 'Have they done the ATLS course?'

The consultant nodded. 'The advanced trauma life support course was originated by the American College of Surgeons, but we now run something similar over here in the UK.'

Katy spoke up. 'So will we be part of the trauma team?'

The consultant gave a wry smile. 'You're going to be part of everything. The team leader is always a consultant but you'll certainly be working as circulation doctors, obviously operating within your skill level. If certain procedures are unfamiliar, we expect you to say so. Now, I'm going to show you the most important room of all. The staff common room.'

Half an hour later, Katy pushed her bag into her locker, slammed it shut and made to follow the others out onto the unit. They'd had a cup of coffee and now the work was about to start.

Her first day on A and E.

She was the last person left in the common room and she gave a start as the door crashed open and Jago strode in, formidably male, his strong features strained.

'Tell me this is a joke,' he launched, slamming the door shut behind him and keeping a hand on it so that no one could disturb them. 'I've just seen your name on the rota. *Dr* Katherine Westerling?'

If anything, he was even colder than he'd been when she'd been admitted as a patient and Katy closed her eyes briefly.

Maybe it was her fault. She should have warned him, but when she'd been lying in hospital she hadn't even decided whether she was going to be able to do it.

And now she was having serious doubts.

How could she ever have thought that she could work alongside him without a problem?

Connecting with those volcanic dark eyes, she felt an explosion of awareness erupt inside her body and hated herself for
it. It seemed that it didn't matter how indifferent he was to her,
she was still a sucker for his type of raw, masculine sexuality.

'It's not a joke.' Katy's breathing was suddenly uneven as
she struggled to hide the disturbing effect he had on her. At five
feet ten she was used to being at eye level with most men, but
she'd always had to look up to Jago. He was six feet three of
intimidating, angry male, and being in the same room as him
had a seriously detrimental effect on her nerves.

'Why the hell didn't you tell me when you were in here two
weeks ago?'

'I—I didn't think it was relevant.'

Because she'd been shell-shocked to see him again.

Because she hadn't made up her mind whether she would
be able to take the job, knowing that it would mean working
with him.

'Not relevant?' His eyes raked over her in a naked disbelief
that would have offended her if she hadn't become used to it
over the years. People always looked at her in disbelief because
she didn't fit their stereotype of a doctor.

Katy sighed, reading his mind. 'Women become doctors,
Jago. Even blondes.'

He frowned sharply. 'I'm not prejudiced against women doctors.'

'So what's wrong?'

'Seeing you in A and E is what's wrong,' he drawled, his
penetrating dark gaze locking onto hers. 'You were a model. A
woman whose main priority was the state of her nails.'

That wasn't true but she couldn't blame him for thinking that.

At the time she'd been breathlessly aware that Jago had only
dated really, *really* beautiful women and she'd been determined
to be as beautiful as possible to see off the competition. And
that had been time-consuming.

It occurred to her suddenly that she and Jago hadn't ever really talked about anything that mattered. She'd certainly never told him that she'd wanted to be a doctor. In fact, apart from Libby and Alex, no one had known just how badly she'd wanted to be a doctor until the day she'd told her father.

She lifted her chin. 'I gave up modelling when I was eighteen.' *Just after he'd walked out of her life.* 'I—I had a few years off and then I went to medical school.'

He looked at her. 'And did your father approve of that?'

Her heartbeat increased at the memory and her gaze slid away from his. 'No.'

'So you finally stood up to him about something.' He gave a short laugh. 'Good for you. But that still doesn't make you suitable material for an A and E doctor.'

She stiffened, refusing to be intimidated by his disparaging tone. 'I was top of my year, Jago.'

'I never said you weren't bright and I'm sure you'd make an excellent GP,' he said dismissively, his expression hard and uncompromising. 'What was your last job?'

'Paediatrics.'

'Go back there,' he advised silkily. 'Accident and emergency is medicine in the raw. It's a real job. It won't suit you.'

Her heart was thumping so hard she felt dizzy.

'I've done real jobs before.'

'Really?' He lifted an eyebrow, his tone heavy with sarcasm. 'Just how much blood and serious, gut-wrenching trauma have you dealt with in your time, Katy?'

None.

She'd done the required medical and surgical house jobs after she'd qualified, of course, and then she'd done a year of paediatrics before deciding that it wasn't the route she wanted to take in her career.

It had been her consultant on the paediatric ward who'd observed her calm, unflappable nature and suggested that she might like to consider A and E work.

And despite Jago's acid comments, she *knew* she could do it.

'I'll be fine.' She swallowed. If she was honest, she was slightly anxious about how she'd cope with major trauma, but she'd rather stop breathing than admit that to Jago. 'Being a good doctor isn't just about blood and guts. I'm good at communicating with patients and I have good instincts when it comes to judging clinical situations.'

His eyes raked over her from head to foot, taking in every inch of her appearance. 'And do you really think that scraping back that blonde hair, wearing glasses that you don't need and dressing like my grandmother is going to make you seem tougher?'

Katy touched the glasses self-consciously. Having long blonde hair and being considered exceptionally pretty had turned out to be a distinct disadvantage, so over the years she'd adopted a disguise. She'd discovered that if she dressed discreetly then people paid more attention to what she was saying. But not Jago, of course. He saw through the disguise right to her soul. He'd always been razor sharp.

She decided to be honest. 'I wear the glasses because they make people take me more seriously.'

His laugh was unsympathetic. 'And I bet you need all the help you can get, *querida*.'

She bristled at his tone and lifted her chin with an icy dignity that she'd learned from her mother.

'I'm a good doctor, Jago.' She'd had to prove it on umpteen occasions in the past so it was nothing new. 'I'll be fine.'

'Too right you'll be fine.' His voice was lethally soft and contained more than a hint of menace. 'You'll be fine because I'm going to be breathing down your neck every minute of the day. Everything you do, Katy, every patient you see, I'm going to be there, next to you, watching. I do not need another light-weight doctor in this department. If someone is sick on those designer shoes of yours, you're going to have to carry on to the end of the shift. You're going to have to prove yourself to me.

And you don't have to be as good as everyone else, you have to be twice as good. Or you're out.'

Her heart was thumping double time.

'I'm not lightweight. You're making judgements about me—'

'Based on experience.' He moved towards her. 'I know you, Katy. I know how you think. You hate confrontation. There's no way you'll cope with A and E. I guarantee that after one week you'll wish you were back in paediatrics.'

She licked her lips, her whole body pulsating in response to his looming proximity.

'That won't happen and you're totally wrong about me.'

'Yes?' His black eyes were as hard as flint. 'When I knew you, you didn't even have the courage to stand up to your own father. You were terrified that he might find out you were seeing me.'

She tried to back away but there was nowhere to go. The cold metal of the lockers pressed through the thin fabric of her blouse.

It was true that at eighteen she'd been terrified of her father. And as it had turned out, her fear had been fully justified.

But Jago didn't know that, of course. He'd vanished into the sunset before any of it could get ugly, ignorant of the devastation he'd left behind him.

He'd never known what her father was like.

Very few people did.

'Your father was a tough man—probably still is—but he's a walk in the park compared to some of the patients we see in this department on a Saturday night.'

A walk in the park?

Remembering just what had transpired after Jago had left, Katy was shocked into speechlessness.

He stepped closer. 'You don't like disagreements or controversy and you hate all forms of violence. We do violence quite well in A and E, you know.' His tone was smooth. 'Saturday afternoons after football and rugby, nights after the pubs

close. What are you going to do when the department is full of
drunks? What are you going to do when someone turns round
and hits you?'

He was trying to scare her off but it wasn't going to work.

The only thing that frightened her about working in A and
E was being close to *him*.

Especially the way he was acting at the moment.

Like a madman.

*As if he wasn't the man who'd taken her virginity and then
walked away without a backward glance.*

She cast him a confused look. 'Why are you being like this?'

His gaze was hard and unsympathetic. 'Because this is a
horrifically busy department and frankly I don't have time to
nursemaid someone who's main concern in life is whether she
needs to file her nails.'

He made her sound frivolous and shallow, but maybe she'd
seemed that way to him when he'd known her at eighteen. One
thing was sure, if they were ever going to be able to work together effectively, they had to get the past out of the way.

'You don't know me any more.' She kept her tone concilia-
tory, the way she did when her father was in one of his scary
moods. 'It's been eleven years since you last saw me. Maybe
we should talk about what happened, Jago.'

Maybe he could explain why he'd walked away.

Jago's eyes were cold and his broad shoulders were rigid with
tension. 'The past is history. There's nothing that I want to talk
about and if you're trying to convince me that you've changed,
you're wasting your breath. You're forgetting that I met the man
you're engaged to.' He gave a short laugh. 'That in itself was
enough to prove to me that you haven't changed one little bit.'

Maybe *he* had changed, she reflected. Despite his Spanish
ancestry, Jago had always been so emotionally controlled that
in the past she'd longed to do something which would shake
him out of his almost permanent state of indifference. Yet she
sensed that at this moment he was hanging onto control by lit-

tle more than a thread. For the first time she was seeing a hint of that volatility that was supposed to characterise Mediterranean men.

But what she didn't understand was *why*. Something had obviously really challenged his legendary cool and she had absolutely no idea what. And his lack of remorse about the way he'd treated her still puzzled her. He seemed so *hard*.

She forced her mind back to the subject. 'You don't know anything about Freddie.'

'I know he's the man your father's chosen for you.' That burning dark gaze locked on hers with all the lethal accuracy of a deadly weapon. As he stepped even closer to her his voice dropped to a low purr, like a tiger soothing its prey before the kill. 'Does he make you hot inside, Katy? Does he make you so desperate that he has you panting and ripping at his clothes?'

Powerful images exploded in her head and her face burned with shock and embarrassment at his explicit words.

'Have you finished?' Determined not to betray just how uncomfortable she felt, she looked him straight in the eye. It was a mistake.

She tumbled into the fathomless depths of his dark eyes and felt her knees tremble.

He leaned forward. 'That man has no idea how to unlock the real Katy.'

'And I suppose you think you do!'

'Of course.' The lazy arrogance in his voice was the final straw and she lifted a hand and slapped him so hard that the palm of her hand stung.

'Dios mio.' His head jerked backwards and he looked at her with raw incredulity, disbelief pulsating in the depths of his eyes.

Stunned by her own behaviour, Katy opened her mouth to apologise and then closed it again. There was no way she was apologising to him!

'Eleven years is a long time, Jago, and you don't know anything about who I am any more.' Her small hands clenched by her sides and she forced herself to breathe normally. 'I'm more than capable of working in this department and I'm going to marry Freddie.'

They stood, eyes trapped by an invisible force, until the door opened and a male voice said, 'I've found our straggler. She's still in the common room.'

The consultant walked in and gave Jago a nod before turning to Katy. Fortunately he didn't seem to notice the reddened streak on Jago's cheekbone.

'If you've finished in here, I'll take you out and see which member of staff you're allocated to. We find that the new casualty officers settle in quickly if they work closely with another member of staff. I'll just check who that is.'

'You needn't bother.' Jago's voice was soft and his eyes were still fixed on Katy's pale face. 'Dr Westerling will be working with me.'

His colleague looked startled. 'Oh, right—well, you've obviously already met Jago Rodriguez, one of our other consultants. In that case, I'll leave you in his capable hands. I'm sure you're keen to get started.'

Jago's mouth curled into a smile. 'I'm sure Dr Westerling can't wait.'

There was a sardonic gleam in his sexy dark eyes that brought a flush to her pale cheeks and a sick feeling to the pit of her stomach.

Working with Jago wasn't just going to be difficult.

It was going to be a nightmare.

Twenty-four hours later Katy was wondering why she'd ever thought she'd be able to cope with A and E.

She'd seen a never-ending stream of patients, most of them angry at having been kept waiting for hours.

'Can't we see patients any faster?' she asked Charlotte, the sister who had looked after her when she'd been brought in after her car accident. 'I'm fed up with being verbally abused by everyone I see.'

'Welcome to A and E.' Charlotte handed her a set of X-rays to check. 'We make a dent and then an emergency comes in and takes priority. That's the way it works. That's why we have triage. Non-emergency cases go to the bottom of the pile and they stay there until someone has time to see them.' She smiled sympathetically at Katy's drawn expression. 'Don't worry, you get used to people yelling at you after a while.'

'I don't mind people yelling,' Katy lied quickly, not wanting to risk Charlotte telling Jago that she couldn't cope. 'I just wish we didn't have to keep people waiting.'

'At least you're working with Jago. He can be a pretty hard taskmaster, I know, but he's a brilliant doctor. You're lucky.'

Katy kept her mouth clamped shut. Lucky? She certainly didn't feel lucky to be working with Jago. She felt as though she must have done something seriously wrong in a previous life to have deserved such punishment.

Realising that Charlotte was looking at her oddly, she managed a smile.

'I'm sure you're right,' she replied smoothly. 'I'm looking forward to learning from him.'

'As a doctor he's staggeringly gifted,' Charlotte went on. 'He has this uncanny ability to spot things that other people miss, but sometimes he forgets that the rest of us are human. Don't let him get to you.'

He *was* getting to her.

He made it perfectly obvious that he didn't think she had what it took to work in A and E and he was watching her every move, waiting for her to make a mistake.

Why did he hate her so much?

All she'd ever done had been to fall in love with him, and surely that was her problem, not his.

They hadn't really talked about what had happened in the past. Maybe she should bring it up. Clear the air.

Feeling totally miserable, Katy sighed and reached for the X-rays but at that moment Annie, one of the staff nurses, rushed up.

'Ambulance Control just rang. They're bringing in a forty-year-old man who's had an accident in a warehouse. He got caught by a forklift truck. Apparently he's in a bad way. Very weak pulse and virtually no blood pressure. They should be here in less than five minutes.'

'Find Jago,' Charlotte said immediately, but his voice came from behind them.

'I heard. Annie, get the trauma team together in Resus and make sure we have a radiographer. I don't want to be hanging around for X-rays.' His gaze flickered to Katy. 'You can join us in Resus and act as one of the circulation doctors. You saw us in action yesterday—do you think you can cope?'

Katy's stomach lurched and her pulse rate quickened, but she met his gaze without flinching.

'Of course.'

She'd cope or die in the attempt.

'Good.' His dark eyes locked on hers moodily and then he strode off towards Resus, leaving her to follow.

Charlotte alerted the nursing team and one of them was given the task of informing people in the waiting room that the waiting time was likely to be increased because a major injury was coming in.

'There'll be a riot,' Annie predicted gloomily, and Harry, one of the other consultants, nodded.

'Very probably, but there isn't much we can do about it except mop up the blood afterwards.'

Jago was prowling around Resus, checking that the right equipment was ready and everything was where he wanted it.

Moments later the doors crashed open and the paramedics hurried in with the stretcher.

'This is Dan Walker. He's a warehouse supervisor. He was caught under the ribs by a forklift truck. No obvious injury but he's shocked and his pulse is thready. We've given him high-flow oxygen and we managed to get a line in at the scene...'

The paramedic outlined the care they'd given and Jago moved to the head of the trolley.

'OK, let's move him across, on my count—one two three.'

They lifted the man carefully and he groaned slightly, his skin pale and clammy.

Katy's blood was pounding in her veins. This was her first real trauma case. What if she did something wrong?

But it soon became clear to her that she couldn't possibly do anything wrong because Jago was directing the entire operation with an air of cool command which left no doubt in anyone's mind who was in charge.

Having secured the man's airway and satisfied himself that there was no damage to the cervical spine, he turned his attention to the work of the rest of the team.

'Get another line in. I want vital signs recorded every five minutes and get his clothes off fast—I want every inch of him examined.'

Using sharp scissors, they cut off his clothes and Katy reached for the man's wrist to insert another line. One of the nurses handed her a swab and venflon and she searched frantically for a vein.

'Everything's shutting down,' she murmured, her fingers slipping on the man's skin as she nervously tried to find a vein.

'Let Harry try,' Jago said sharply, and she gritted her teeth and felt around again for a vein.

'Give me one more go—I think I felt something then.'

Please—*please*...

Something moved under her fingers. Was that it?

She slid the needle through the skin and breathed a sigh of relief as blood came back into the venflon.

'I've done it. I'm in.'

'Well done.' Harry gave her an encouraging smile but Jago merely barked out more instructions.

'Take blood for group and cross-match, full blood count, urea and electrolytes, and get a catheter in so that we can assess his fluid output. What's his blood pressure doing?'

'It's falling.' Annie checked the reading and recorded it on the chart.

'Remember that there is a consistent fall in the systolic blood pressure only after 30 per cent of blood volume is lost,' Jago said, his tone cool. 'Get him attached to an ECG monitor and let's give him a bolus of fluid. Start with a litre of warm colloid and then we'll reassess.'

There were so many questions that Katy wanted to ask but she knew they were going to have to wait until the patient was stable.

She watched while Jago examined the patient's abdomen, his hands moving skilfully as he looked for signs of tenderness.

'There's bruising and tenderness under the ribs,' he murmured, and then glanced at Annie. 'Phone down and see if they've confirmed the blood group yet. It's been ten minutes so they should have. Once they have, get some blood up here,' he ordered sharply, and Annie hurried to the phone just as another nurse popped her head round the door.

'His wife is in the relatives' room. Is there someone who can see her?'

Jago glanced at Charlotte. 'Can one of your team go to her until we've stabilised him? Tell her we'll be with her as soon as we have some news.'

Charlotte moved towards the door. 'And if she wants to come and see him?'

Jago didn't hesitate. 'Then let her.'

Katy frowned and Jago raised an eyebrow in her direction.

'Something wrong, Katy?'

At least he was calling her by her first name now, instead of referring to her as 'Dr Westerling'. 'I just thought it might be distressing for her to see him like this.'

'It is distressing...' Jago glanced across to check the ECG

and the blood-pressure reading '…but studies have shown that on balance it's probably better for the relatives to see the patient in Resus than not to see them.'

Annie looked up. 'His blood pressure is falling, Jago.'

'He needs blood and we need to call the surgeons and warn them that he's likely to need a laparotomy.'

Jago looked impatiently towards the door and at that moment one of the nurses came hurrying in, carrying the blood bags.

'At last.' Jago reached out a hand and took one of the blood bags, attaching it quickly to the giving set. 'Open the tap and let's see if that helps.'

They worked to stabilise the man but the blood transfusion seemed to have no effect.

'Still no improvement. OK, that tells us one of two things.' Jago's expression was grim. 'Either the shock isn't caused by bleeding, or he's bleeding faster than we can infuse the blood— my money's on the latter. He needs urgent surgical intervention. Has someone bleeped the surgeons?'

Charlotte nodded. 'Mr Hart is on his way.'

'Well, he'd better be quick.' Jago turned his attention back to the patient, who was deteriorating by the minute.

'His blood pressure is still falling.' Annie looked at Jago expectantly and his mouth tightened.

'Push that blood through faster.'

At that moment the door swung open and a tall, blond man strode into the room. 'Jago?'

Jago gave a succinct report on the man's condition and the surgeon examined him briefly.

'You're right. He's bleeding. Let's take him straight to Theatre.'

There was a flurry of activity and the man was transferred to the operating theatre for a laparotomy which would allow the surgeons to assess any internal damage.

Katy found herself alone in Resus with Charlotte. 'Phew,

what a mess!' She glanced around the room, taking in the discarded blood bags, needles and other equipment.

'What happens now?'

'We clear it up ready for the next patient,' Charlotte said immediately, thrusting needles into the sharps bin and scooping up soiled dressings. 'Jago's gone to talk to the relatives with Annie. Can I ask you something?'

'Of course.' Katy checked the intubation tray and ran another bag of saline through a giving set.

'How do you two know each other?'

Katy's eyes flew to hers and she thought about denying their past acquaintance, but Charlotte's next words made her realise the futility of that approach.

'When you were brought in here two weeks ago, he was the one who identified you.'

'Oh.' Katy concentrated on the equipment she was checking, wondering what Jago had felt when he'd seen her lying on the ambulance stretcher. Had he felt any guilt at all? 'We knew each other years ago. He used to work for my father.'

'In the bank?' Charlotte's eyes widened. 'He's filthy rich and we've all been dying to know how he made his money. I suppose that answers the question.'

'I suppose so.'

Katy moved away, hoping that was the end of it. She hated gossiping about people.

Charlotte was still looking at her in fascination. 'Did you know him well?'

Katy shook her head and avoided eye contact. 'Not that well.' *She'd thought that there had been gentleness under the strength but she'd been wrong.*

Charlotte gave a wistful sigh. 'He's the hospital heartthrob.'

Katy kept her eyes fixed on the intubation tray. Of course he was. Jago Rodriguez was seriously rich, stunningly good-looking and single. A prime target for every woman on the planet.

Except her.

She'd learned her lesson the hard way eleven years ago and she wasn't that innocent, naïve girl anymore.

Charlotte sighed. 'Every available woman in the hospital dreams of being the one to tame him and marry him.'

Katy looked up at that, unable to hide her incredulous expression. 'Marry him?' Well that showed how well they knew Jago. *I don't do commitment, Katy.* 'If you know him then you'll know he isn't the marrying kind.'

Charlotte shrugged. 'Everyone's the marrying kind if they meet the right person.'

'I don't think so.' Katy's voice was soft and thoughtful. 'I think some people just can't allow themselves to be that vulnerable.'

And Jago didn't have a vulnerable part to his make-up.

At one point she'd thought he had. He'd fooled her with a display of gentleness that had turned her insides to jelly but she knew now that that was just part of his superior bedroom technique.

'You've obviously thought about it a lot.' Charlotte hung the giving set over the stand and looked at her quizzically. 'But you're getting married so you must believe in love and commitment.'

Did she?

Katy turned her attention back to the intubation tray, not wanting to shatter Charlotte's romantic illusions.

She certainly wasn't in love with Freddie.

And she didn't feel guilty about it because she knew that Freddie wasn't in love with her either. He was marrying her because she was the right sort of girl with the right sort of connections and that suited her fine. She didn't want love.

Her one experience of love had been a shattering, all-consuming experience that had threatened her very existence.

I don't do commitment, Katy.

'Not that we hospital staff really get a look in,' Charlotte said gloomily, tearing off her plastic apron and lobbing it in the bin.

'He's dating a stunning Brazilian model at the moment. The real woman type. Legs up to her armpits and boobs to make a man drool. She's a very lucky woman.'

Katy clenched her fists and told herself firmly that she didn't care who Jago was dating. It was none of her business.

And she wanted to end the conversation.

'I'd better get back to the main area and see some more patients,' she said quickly, anxious to get away from Charlotte. She was nice but she didn't need to talk about Jago. Working with him and seeing him every day was bad enough without talking about him as well.

CHAPTER FOUR

KATY'S first week passed quickly and every time she looked up Jago seemed to be there, challenging her, asking questions, his handsome face inscrutable.

Determined not to make a mistake, she examined every patient meticulously, made sure that her questions were detailed, never took anything at face value. And in her opinion she'd performed well. But Jago hadn't uttered a single word of praise and she was starting to feel the strain.

Was he going to keep this up indefinitely?

Did he really think that she wasn't up to the pressures of A and E or did he have another reason for not wanting her in his department.

A more personal reason perhaps?

On her first Saturday night working on A and E a fight broke out in the street behind the hospital. They heard the sound of police sirens and a few minutes later a group of drunks staggered through the door that led to the ambulance bay, half-supporting a man who seemed barely conscious.

'Hey, you!' One of the drunks waved a hand at Charlotte who frowned with distaste.

'You can't come in through that entrance,' she said tightly. 'It's reserved for emergency vehicles. You need to—'

'Don't tell me what I can and can't do,' the man slurred, his eyes flashing angrily at Charlotte as he struggled to remain upright and focus. 'Get me a bloody doctor. *Now!*'

Charlotte stiffened and turned to Jago expectantly.

'This is one for Katy,' he delivered softly, his dark eyes connecting with Katy's in unmistakable challenge.

There was no missing the message in his gaze. This was one of the situations he was convinced she'd never be able to deal with, and he was testing her.

She almost laughed. She'd probably had more experience with drunk, violent men than he had.

Ignoring Charlotte's shocked murmur of protest, Katy stepped forward, her manner calm and professional.

'That looks like a nasty cut.'

She addressed her remarks directly to the injured man, who barely acknowledged her presence.

His head rolled onto his chest and his expression was glazed.

Was he drunk or was he suffering the consequences of a head injury?

She'd read enough to be aware of the potential pitfalls of dismissing someone as drunk. There were plenty of horror stories about people who'd been discharged from Casualty only to die the next day as a result of a head injury that no one had taken seriously. Drink could mask a number of symptoms and she had no intention of missing anything.

She turned to his friend, who was clearly having trouble staying upright. 'What's his name?'

'James.'

'And what happened?'

The man swayed slightly. 'He fell over and banged his head.'

He was slurring his words so badly that it was difficult to understand him, but Katy knew how important it was to obtain some sort of history. 'And did he knock himself out?'

The man shrugged, his eyes glazed. 'Dunno.'

Great. Some history.

'All right.' Katy's tone was brisk. 'Well, I need to take a look at his head. Why don't you sit him over there and then go and give his details to Reception?'

The man didn't answer, his body swaying as he watched her. 'I asked for a doctor. You're never a doctor.'

Katy gave a calm smile. The same smile she'd used on her father time and time again.

Don't antagonise him, Katy.

'I'm a doctor.' She spoke quietly, knowing better than to joke or argue with him or enter into any conversation that wasn't necessary. She could see that the man was very drunk and suspected that he was only too keen to pick a fight. 'Now, if you'll just sit him over here, I can take a look at his head.'

Without giving the man time to argue, she took charge and helped the injured man onto the couch in the first cubicle, half-drawing the curtain around him.

She looked at Charlotte. 'Would you mind showing his friend the way to Reception so that he can give some details, please?'

Charlotte nodded, her eyes wide with admiration. 'Of course.'

Jago said nothing. He just leaned broad shoulders against the wall, his eyes narrowed as he watched Katy.

Trying to hide how much his presence affected her, Katy reached for an ophthalmoscope to examine the patient's eyes, but as she put a hand on the man's head, he gave a groan and lurched towards her. She sidestepped neatly and he vomited over the floor.

Katy reached for a bowl and held it for the man while he retched and mumbled incoherently.

Charlotte, back from Reception, rolled her eyes in disgust. 'It's on your shoes,' she muttered, and Katy shook her head dismissively.

'I'll sort that out later.' She didn't care about her shoes but she was seriously worried about her patient. Were the symptoms he was displaying the result of alcohol or the bang on the head he'd received? It was such a difficult decision.

If she admitted a patient who was perfectly healthy, she'd be wasting precious hospital resources. On the other hand, if she discharged him and his symptoms were the result of a serious head injury, she would have failed in her duty as a doctor.

Medicine had never seemed so complicated.

She knew that she could ask Jago for advice but she didn't want to. He might take it as a sign of weakness on her part and she was determined to prove to him that she was more than capable of doing the job without constant supervision.

'Can you hear me? Can you tell me your name?'

She spoke clearly and the man groaned and mumbled something unintelligible.

'Do you know what day it is?'

She continued to question the man but was far from satisfied by the results.

Jago stepped closer to her. 'He could just be very drunk,' he said coolly, and she knew he was testing her again.

'Or his symptoms could be the result of his head injury.' She tried to ignore the explosion of heat that consumed her body as he moved closer still. Breathing in his warm, familiar, male scent, she felt her head swim.

'So which is it, Dr Westerling?'

She made the mistake of looking at him and his eyes locked onto hers with the power and force of a missile attack.

The mood was suddenly electric and Katy found herself mesmerised by the look of raw, sexual intimacy in his eyes.

Suddenly her breathing was suspended and she struggled to find her voice.

'I—I need to finish my examination before I can answer that question.'

He dealt her a slanting smile. The same smile that she'd

found totally irresistible at the age of eighteen. 'Then finish it, Doctor.'

Cursing her own weakness and the effect he had on her, Katy turned her attention back to the patient.

She asked more questions, checked the patient's reflexes and only after completing an exhaustive examination did she make her decision.

'I'm sending him for a CT scan and then I'm admitting him,' she said firmly, and Jago lifted an eyebrow.

'And why is that?'

'He's showing symptoms of a serious head injury. Headache, vomiting, disorientation. I'm not prepared to discharge him.'

Confident in her decision, Katy looked straight at him, her heart lifting as she saw the glimmer of respect in his dark eyes.

Finally.

After a week of concentrated hard work.

'Good decision,' he said smoothly. 'Make the arrangements and then come to my office and we can talk about it further.'

Light-headed with relief that she'd done the right thing, Katy suddenly wanted to smile. *He'd praised her.* He thought she'd done a good job.

But there was no way she was going to his office.

The effect he had on her was just too powerful and if she couldn't control her reactions she needed to avoid him.

She lifted her chin, her confidence increasing by the moment. *She'd done a good job.* 'Can we talk about it tomorrow, please? I was supposed to be off duty an hour ago and I'm going out so I need to go and clean the vomit off my shoes and—' her eyes challenged his and a small smile touched her mouth '—file my nails.'

And remind herself that dreaming of Jago was a fast route to a miserable life.

Jago looked taken aback. Then to her surprise he threw back his dark head and laughed. 'Tomorrow will be fine.' He turned

to Charlotte, who was gaping at the scene being played out
before her. 'I'm out of here. If you need me, call my mobile.'

Charlotte watched him stride away and looked at her with
awe. 'Would someone mind telling me what's going on here?
You answered him back and he just laughed,' she muttered,
reaching for the notes so that she could make the arrangements
for the CT scan. 'And I can't believe he let you deal with those
drunks. I've never known him to act like that before. Normally
he's very protective of the female staff, to the point of chau-
vinism. I mean, we all ought to deal with the same patients but
the truth is when you're built like Jago you stand more chance
with a violent drunk than someone who is built like you. I don't
know what he was playing at.'

Katy gave a weak smile. She knew exactly what he'd been
playing at. He'd been waiting for her to fail.

He'd wanted her to fail since the day she'd started.

What she didn't understand was why.

A pleasant warmth spread through her veins. His reasons
didn't really matter. *She hadn't failed.* She'd managed fine, she
knew she had. She'd made all the right clinical decisions and
she hadn't needed his help.

She straightened her slim shoulders and gave a small smile,
suddenly feeling more confident.

He'd tested her and she'd passed with flying colours.

So now what would happen?

Jago closed the door of his office and ran long fingers through
his cropped hair.

What the hell was the matter with him?

He'd sent a woman to deal with a bunch of drunks.

And not just any woman, he'd sent Katy. Katy, who was
about as robust as a spring flower.

What had he been thinking of?

But he knew the answer to that, of course.

He'd been trying to prove that she couldn't cope with the rigours of practising medicine in the A and E department. He'd been trying to scare her away.

Because he didn't want her here, on his territory, looking at him with those wide violet-blue eyes.

Just thinking of her exceptionally beautiful, heart-shaped face made him harden in an instinctive and powerful male reaction, and he gave an exclamation of disgust.

Hadn't he learned anything? Was he really that basic that he could forget everything just to satisfy the most primitive of male urges?

What was it about Katy Westerling? True, she was astonishingly beautiful but he met beautiful women all the time and they didn't make him abandon his usual caution towards members of the opposite sex.

He had to keep reminding himself that she wasn't what she seemed.

That the innocent aura that aroused a man's most fiercely protective instincts was actually just an act.

His hands tightened into fists and his hard jaw clenched as he remembered the photographs her father had shown him.

She might have been a virgin when he'd first slept with her, but less than four weeks later she'd slept with another man.

I love you, Jago.

Remembering the incredibly intimate pictures he'd seen, he growled low in his throat and strolled across to the window of his office which looked out on the ambulance bay.

It was eleven years ago, he reminded himself. And eleven years was a long time. Enough to change a person, and Katy had obviously changed.

The old Katy had been deliciously shy and tongue-tied but the Katy he'd seen in action today was very different from the girl he'd made love to so long ago. Far from buckling under the challenge he'd set her, she'd coped well.

In fact, she'd handled those drunks with an admirable level
of skill and tact. There had been every sign that they could have
become violent at any minute but she'd reacted with textbook
efficiency and had successfully defused any suggestion of ag-
gression on the part of the patient and his friends.

She'd behaved as though she'd been operating totally within
her comfort zone, which didn't make a scrap of sense. When
would Katy Westerling, with her over-privileged, protected
upbringing, ever have been exposed to drunk, violent men?

His dark brows locked in a frown as he puzzled over her
complete lack of concern. She hadn't even seemed to notice
the danger. But some deep-seated instinct told him that she had
been all too aware and had known exactly how to cope with it.
She'd stood up to them and she'd stood up to him.

He allowed himself a brief smile of admiration as he remembered her gutsy response to his command that she meet
him in his office.

She'd remembered his caustic remark about her filing her
nails and she'd thrown it back at him.

No, Katy had definitely changed. She'd dropped the innocent
act—and they both knew that it had been nothing more than
an act—and she was showing a level of courage that frankly
surprised him. There were still hints of the feminine fragility
that she'd shown at eighteen, but he sensed a strength and determination that hadn't been there before.

Suddenly he was intrigued.

And he was also impressed. He'd seen numerous colleagues
make the mistake of dismissing a patient who was drunk. She
hadn't made that mistake. Even when the patient had vomited on
what he assumed to be a frighteningly expensive pair of shoes,
she hadn't allowed it to cloud her decision-making.

She was a good doctor.

And he had to face the fact that the reason he was being so
hard on her had absolutely nothing to do with her clinical abilities and everything to do with his own emotions.

* * *

Katy was nearly at the end of her shift the following day when a call came through requesting a medical team to attend an accident.

'They've got a man trapped in a car and they're worried about his leg. I'm the duty consultant so it's mine,' Jago said immediately, reaching for high-visibility jackets and the equipment they'd need at the roadside. 'I'll take Charlotte and Katy.'

Katy felt the adrenaline rush through her veins.

She knew that immediate care—tending to the patient at the scene of the accident—was very different from looking after someone in the A and E department where they were surrounded by equipment.

Was he expecting her to take the lead as he had with the drunken head-injury patient the previous day?

'I'm taking you as an observer,' he said smoothly, evidently reading her mind, 'and an extra pair of hands if we need one. I'll be right by your side all the time.'

And she was supposed to find that reassuring?

But Katy didn't have time to reflect on Jago's reasons for taking her because they were soon in the car, travelling at high speed towards the scene of the accident.

The roads were slick with rain and Jago drove fast but carefully, the powerful headlights cutting through the darkness.

They arrived to find the fire crew cutting one of the occupants of the car out of the vehicle.

Jago retrieved several rucksacks from the car and checked that she was wearing the correct protective clothing.

The darkness and the foul weather were clearly hampering the rescue efforts.

Responding to a shout from one of the paramedics, Katy hurried across to one of the stretchers.

'We've got him on a spinal board and he's conscious but his leg's a mess. It needs attention before we transfer him.' The paramedics addressed her directly and Katy looked frantically around for Jago but he was speaking to a member of the fire crew.

Which meant it was up to her.

A blanket was covering the injured man and Katy lifted it gently, feeling the colour drain out of her face as she saw the extent of the man's injuries. The leg was severely deformed and she felt a cold rush of panic in her chest. *Where should she start?* She could see that there was an open fracture, with part of the bone exposed to the air, as well as a severe laceration. She knew that it was important to cover it to try and prevent infection but the leg was so badly damaged that she was afraid of making the damage worse.

Aware that she was well outside her own realms of experience, she looked over her shoulder for Jago and to her relief he was there, his powerful presence reassuring in the chaos of the accident.

'What have we got?'

Unlike her, his expression didn't flicker as he saw the state of the man's leg. He merely pulled on a pair of sterile gloves, and turned to the nearest paramedic and quietly listed the equipment he needed.

Katy took a deep breath to steady her stomach and those sharp dark eyes settled on her face.

'Are you OK?' He frowned sharply as he scanned her pale face. 'You can wait in the car if you like.'

And give him more ammunition for accusing her of not being able to cope? No way!

'I'm fine,' Katy replied sickly, hoping that he couldn't see just how much she was shaking.

'As long as you're sure.' His voice was surprisingly gentle. 'If you change your mind, let me know.'

The rain had plastered his jet-black hair to his face and trickled off the dark stubble on his hard jaw.

He was breathtakingly handsome and very much in control of the situation.

Which was a relief because she felt completely and totally out of her depth.

He kept his voice low, explaining what he was doing as he worked. And he worked quickly.

'Normally we wouldn't handle the injured part without splinting,' he told her after they'd given the man drugs to control the pain, 'but in this case there's severe deformity and the blood supply is compromised.'

'So that could damage the soft tissues?'

'Exactly. A good blood supply is vital to limb survival. So in this case I'm going to apply gentle traction to restore the alignment of the bones. Then we'll splint.'

Katy blinked in surprise as one of the paramedics took a Polaroid photograph of the wound before covering it with a sterile dressing.

'Why did he do that?' She spoke in a low voice even though the patient was drifting in and out of consciousness, barely aware of what was happening.

'Because exposing the wound again in the A and E department will increase the risk of infection, so if we can we take a photo at the roadside before we cover it,' Jago explained. 'No one will disturb the dressing now until this chap reaches Theatre.'

Katy watched while he reduced the fracture and then checked the pulses in the limb.

'OK.' He glanced up at the paramedics and ran a hand over his face to clear his vision, his thick, dark lashes clumped together in the rain. 'I need a long leg splint.'

They produced one immediately and Jago immobilised the leg with help from Katy and one of the paramedics.

'Splinting the leg will help control the pain but we need to get him to hospital fast. Blood loss from limb wounds and internal bleeding from fractures contribute to shock so we need to resuscitate him carefully.' His eyes flickered to Katy. 'Don't forget that blood loss from open fractures can be two or three times greater than that from closed fractures.'

Katy listened, taking in everything he was saying, totally in awe of his amazing calm and the amount of knowledge he displayed.

He seemed totally indifferent to the rain and darkness, acting with the same degree of supreme self-confidence that he displayed in the well-equipped A and E department.

He was talking again. 'One of the advantages of attending the scene of the accident is that you get a real picture of what happened and that helps you assess the possible injuries.'

She was eager to learn from him and for a brief moment their past history was forgotten, the tension between them easing as they concentrated on the patient. 'And that's why you always question the paramedics about whether the patient was a passenger or the driver?'

Jago nodded, his attention fixed on the patient. 'It's important to know whether they were in the vehicle or a pedestrian. Whether they were restrained by a seat belt. The direction of impact and the degree of damage to the car.'

'So if you know that someone was thrown from a vehicle—'

'Then you know that you're dealing with potentially fatal injuries,' he slotted in, nodding to the paramedics to indicate that they could load the patient into the ambulance. 'It's one of the reasons we always make you undress trauma patients in the A and E department. You never know what injuries may be hiding and clinical signs may be subtle, particularly in the unconscious patient.'

He directed operations as the patient was carefully lifted into the ambulance and then sprang into the vehicle, his movements swift and athletic.

'You and Charlotte bring the car. I'll see you back in A and E.'

She turned back to the car feeling a huge range of emotions. On the one hand she felt that she'd learned a lot but on the other she felt helpless and cross with herself, knowing that she hadn't dealt with the situation well.

The truth was, she'd been horrified by the extent of the injuries she'd seen and too panicked to know where to begin.

Was that normal?

Had other doctors found themselves in the same situation?

Charlotte walked up to her, carrying some equipment. 'Slick, isn't he?'

Katy helped her lift it into the boot of the car. 'He's very confident.'

'Well, that's because he knows what he's doing.' Charlotte slammed the boot shut. 'He's ferociously intelligent and he never loses his cool.'

Except with her.

Katy walked round the car and slid into the passenger seat, relieved to get out of the rain.

What would happen now? He'd been waiting for signs that she couldn't cope with trauma work and unfortunately she'd now given him all the ammunition he needed. The way he'd looked at her had left her in absolutely no doubt that he'd noticed her horrified reaction. Hardly an impressive response for a doctor who was beginning a career in accident and emergency medicine, she thought, frustrated beyond belief by what she perceived as her own weakness.

Her first experience of on-scene trauma and she'd panicked and behaved like a frightened rabbit.

He had every right to be impatient with her.

As she and Charlotte drove back towards the hospital, she pondered on the outcome of the inevitable encounter. He'd said that if she couldn't prove herself then she'd be out.

So what would happen now?

CHAPTER FIVE

JAGO heard the tap on the door of his office and looked up from his computer with a frown.

He'd had a long and trying day and technically he was now off duty so he hadn't been expecting visitors.

Katy stood in the doorway, her blue eyes wary as she watched him from the doorway.

She looked tired and incredibly nervous.

He sat back in his chair, his eyes suddenly watchful, his senses on full alert. Why was she nervous? She was looking at him the way a baby impala looked at a hungry lion at lunchtime.

She closed the door behind her and cleared her throat. 'I didn't mean to disturb you.' Faint streaks of colour touched her cheekbones and for a disturbing moment he had an all too clear recollection of the way she'd looked after he'd finally made love to her the first time.

Flushed, round-eyed, softly feminine and in awe of him—much the way she was looking right now.

He felt his body harden in response and he felt a rush of anger at his own inability to control his reactions around her.

'I'm in the middle of something so I'd appreciate it if you could make it quick.'

He saw her flinch but steeled himself against feeling sympathy, reminding himself that she wasn't as gentle and innocent as she seemed.

As he'd discovered to his cost.

'I just wanted to apologise for earlier,' she said quietly, her fingers digging into her palms. 'I was useless out there. I don't know what happened. I'm sorry...'

He was so utterly captivated by her soft mouth that it took him a moment to understand what she was talking about.

The accident. He shook himself slightly. She was talking about the accident.

'You weren't useless.' He resolutely pushed away memories of all that stunning blonde hair spread over the soft grass as he'd rolled her underneath him on a baking summer's day eleven years earlier.

'I wasn't prepared for the injury to be so severe,' she confessed shakily. 'I—I've never attended the scene of an accident before. I didn't know what to do, and I'm sorry.'

He sat back in his chair, suddenly understanding why she was so nervous. Hadn't he warned her on her first day that if she didn't perform she'd be out? She was afraid that her shocked reaction to her first exposure to major trauma at the roadside would count against her.

She was afraid that he was going to get rid of her.

And that had certainly been his intention when he'd first realised that she was going to be working in his department.

He hadn't thought she'd last five minutes.

He hadn't *wanted* her to last five minutes.

And he'd been incredibly hard on her. Harder on her than any other doctor in his team.

And she'd surprised him. So far she'd proved herself to be thorough and competent, and he'd observed on several occasions that her warmth had a calming influence on the most fractious patient.

He felt an unaccustomed twinge of guilt as he reflected on the way he'd treated her since she'd arrived in the department.

'I took you along because I thought you might learn something and because every A and E doctor should have an idea of what the paramedics deal with on a daily basis.' He saw her soft lips part and was suddenly glad that he was sitting behind the desk. At least she wouldn't be aware of the effect she had on him. 'You were there as an observer. I had no expectations of you as a doctor.'

She stood in silence, watching him warily. She was obviously still expecting an explosion. 'I shouldn't have reacted like that, but I just wasn't prepared for how scary it would be, dealing with a patient at the scene of the accident. I'm used to having masses of medical back-up.'

She obviously felt she'd let herself down badly, which wasn't true at all. He'd seen doctors with many more years' experience than her suddenly freeze at the scene of a serious accident.

It was something to do with the almost overwhelming sense of responsibility that came with being first on the scene.

'Just stick to A and E and don't become a paramedic,' he suggested dryly, and then turned back to his computer, hoping that she'd take the hint and leave him alone.

She didn't. Instead, she took a deep breath, steeling herself to ask the question that had clearly been worrying her. 'You said I ought to be a GP or go back to paediatrics. Do you still think I'll make a bad A and E doctor?'

He felt another twinge of guilt. It was his fault that she was asking the question.

'No. You're a good A and E doctor.'

Surprisingly good.

'But you said—'

'I know what I said. I was angry with you.'

His blunt admission didn't evoke the response he expected. Instead of signs of guilt, she looked confused and taken aback. As if he had no right to be angry.

He had to hand it to her, she was an excellent actress.

She was starting to make *him* feel guilty.

Her blue eyes were suddenly huge and she looked more like a little girl than a fully qualified doctor. 'Why were you angry with me? Because of our...relationship?' She stumbled over the word, looking bemused, and Jago's lean hands curled into fists.

'I thought I had already made it clear that the past is history.'

'But it isn't, is it, Jago? It's there between us the whole time.'

'Let's just say that I have a long memory for certain events.' His tone lethally smooth, he leaned back in his chair and surveyed her with the cool intent of a predator poised for the kill. It really was time for her to drop the innocent act. At least then they'd both know where they stood.

'It must have been extremely challenging for you to keep two men running at the same time with such a limited amount of experience on your part. You must have been very nervous that one of us would find out about the other, and yet it never showed,' he mused, his dark eyes resting on her soft mouth. 'I'm filled with admiration as to how you managed it so skilfully. Tell me, Katy, did you tell him that you loved him, too?'

The air around them throbbed and she stood, frozen to the spot, staring at him with a blank expression.

'I really have no idea what you're talking about.'

She was incredibly beautiful and incredibly dignified. If he hadn't seen the evidence with his own eyes it would have been so easy to believe in her innocence.

'Let's just say that when I enjoy a relationship with a woman, my absolute minimum requirement is fidelity,' he informed her, wondering how she'd cope with being forced to confront her sins. Because he'd made up his mind that she was going to confront them. 'Foolishly, I assumed that as I was your first lover, I didn't need to explain that fact.'

She was still staring at him. 'I still don't know what you mean.'

His gaze hardened. 'I mean that, having been introduced to

the joys of sex, you then couldn't wait to spread your wings and sample variety. So tell me, *querida*, was it different with him? Was it worth it?'

She looked startled at his words, hot colour touching her beautiful heart-shaped face, and he was reminded of just how shy she'd been about sex. The product of strict parents and a single-sex school, until she'd met him she'd had virtually no experience of men. He gritted his teeth. Something she'd corrected as quickly as possible.

'Are you saying what I think you're saying? You think that I—' She broke off, her colour deepening, and he gave a wry smile.

'Perhaps you should drop the innocent virgin act now,' he advised. 'I think we've both moved beyond that.'

The colour drained out of her face and she swayed slightly. He felt a flash of concern and then reminded himself that he was dealing with a woman who could sleep with two men at the same time without displaying the slightest flicker of conscience. Now she'd finally been found out he fully expected her to seek refuge in that most female of pastimes. Tears.

'Is that why you left without even a word? Because you believed I was having an affair with someone else?' Her tone was flat and lifeless, her normally sparkly blue eyes dulled with shock and distaste. 'Couldn't you have at least have asked me about it?'

He shrugged a broad shoulder dismissively, his expression sardonic. 'I didn't need to. I had all the evidence I needed. An encounter between us would have been—' He broke off, remembering the searing anger and hurt that he'd felt on discovering her duplicity. His mouth tightened. 'Let's just say that I felt it would be better for both of us if we had no more contact.'

'Evidence?' Her voice was croaky, like someone who hadn't drunk for a week. 'This evidence—who gave it to you?'

He frowned. Surely she should have been asking what the

evidence was? Or was she trying to cover her tracks? 'I don't see the relevance—'

'It was my father, wasn't it?'

So she'd known all along that her father had had incriminating photographs.

'Don't blame him. For once your father was acting honourably. He thought I should know the truth.'

Especially given that ten minutes earlier he had announced his intention of marrying Katy.

Thanks to her father, he'd had a very narrow escape. He owed him a debt.

'Honourably?' Her voice shook and she sank onto the nearest chair, her breathing shallow. She looked terrible. Her cheeks were pale and her slim fingers shook as they clutched the seat of the chair. 'My father has never behaved honourably in his life. He sees what he wants and he goes for it, no matter what obstacles stand in his way. No doubt he manipulated you the same way he manipulates everyone.'

Jago frowned, disconcerted by her unexpected reaction. He'd expected hysterics and denials about the affair. Instead, they seemed to be having a conversation about her father. 'What are you suggesting?'

Katy lifted her head, her eyes dull. 'Show me the photographs.' Her chest rose and fell and she appeared to be struggling to breathe. 'I want to see those photographs. Do you still have them?'

Slight colour touched his cheekbones. 'I don't understand what purpose it would serve—'

'Show me!'

After only the briefest hesitation he reached into his desk and withdrew a large envelope, thoroughly discomfited by the fact that he still had the photographs to hand. It raised questions that he'd never wanted to address before.

But Katy didn't ask questions. She didn't even seem to find

it strange that he had the photographs in his desk eleven years later.

She just ripped at the envelope with shaking hands and emptied the contents onto the desk.

As the glossy prints emerged from the envelope, Jago felt the tension rise in his body. His lean hands fisted and he felt the same sickness he'd felt when he'd first seen them. 'I warn you—they're very revealing.'

She gave an uneven laugh. 'I'm sure they are.' She lifted the photographs, suddenly in possession of an icy control that he'd never seen before.

He frowned slightly, puzzled by her reaction. She certainly wasn't behaving like a woman with a guilty conscience.

As her eyes dropped to the first photograph he averted his eyes. He still wasn't able to look at pictures of her entwined so intimately with another man without wanting to commit grievous bodily harm. *Why the hell had he kept them?* He should have burned them years ago.

She flicked steadily through the pictures, her beautiful face blank.

Then finally she dropped the last one on the pile and lifted her eyes to his. 'I always wondered what made you leave.' Her tone was flat and suddenly all his senses were on alert. Alarm bells were ringing but he didn't know why. She lifted her chin, her eyes glistening with unshed tears. 'You didn't think to ask me about them?'

He was watching her warily now, totally confused by her reaction. Instead of guilt and apology, her blue eyes were full of hurt and accusation.

And disappointment.

Was he missing something here?

'They appear to speak for themselves,' he observed, and she nodded slowly.

'But not when you look at all the facts together.' She turned away from him and walked over to the window, staring out across the courtyard. 'I always wondered what my father said to make you walk away. I knew it had to have been him that ended our relationship. Nothing else made sense.'

Jago was suddenly very still. 'Your father had nothing to do with it. It was my choice to walk away—'

'Yes. You were to blame too, for believing him.' She turned to face him and her eyes were sad. 'He played you like a master, Jago. He did what he does with everyone. He looked for your weakness and then he moved in for the kill.'

Disconcerted and not used to the feeling, Jago stiffened. 'And what was my weakness?'

'Your pride,' she said simply. 'You are, by nature, proud and possessive and my father knew that the one thing that would drive you away from me was finding me with another man. So he made it happen.'

There was an uncomfortable silence while Jago digested her words. 'You're saying that he somehow manufactured these photographs?' He waved a lean brown hand across his desk. 'That they aren't really you?'

'Oh, yes, they're me.' Katy walked back to the desk and picked up the photograph at the top of the pack. 'Good, aren't they? They were taken in a studio in North London when I was modelling. One of the teenage mags wanted some shots to illustrate an article they were doing on safe sex. Aiden and I were supposed to look as though we were in love. Funnily enough, I was more relaxed than I would normally have been because I *was* in love.' Her eyes lifted to his and there was more than a hint of accusation in her clear blue gaze. 'I was in love with *you,* Jago.'

Modelling photographs?

Jago was struggling hard to get a grip on the facts. It hadn't even occurred to him that the photos could have been part of her modelling life.

No. They couldn't be.

Shielding his emotions from her, he glanced at the one on

the top of the pile, noticing for the first time all the hallmarks of a professional photographer.

Feeling as though he'd just taken a cold shower, he suppressed a groan. How had he managed to miss that possibility? But he knew the answer, of course. He'd been so furiously angry at what he'd seen as her betrayal that he'd reacted with raw, naked emotion. Had he employed some of the intellect in his possession he might have reached a different conclusion.

But Katy's father had been completely correct in his reading of his character. He'd gambled on the fact that Jago's Spanish pride would prevent him from wanting to contact her again. And the gamble had paid off. He'd walked into the sunset and left her.

He stilled, unable to grasp the fact that he could have made such a colossal misjudgement. 'You never slept with him?'

'No. He's also gay.'

Her tone was flat and Jago tensed, struggling with the appalling reality of having been thoroughly manipulated. 'I thought—'

'I can see what you thought. Please, don't spell it out any further. I find your suppositions totally offensive.' She gathered up the photographs and he reached out and grabbed her wrist, preventing her from leaving.

'Wait.' His fingers tightened. 'If you suspected that your father was responsible, why didn't you come after me?'

She looked at him sadly. 'Because I believed in you. I never knew what made you leave, but I guessed that my father was behind it and for months I held onto this childish dream that our love would prove stronger than my father had anticipated and that you'd come back and at least talk to me. But you never did.'

He flinched at that but his fingers tightened on her wrists. He needed answers. 'Why would your father do that to you? *To us*?'

'Surely that's obvious. He didn't want us together.' She lifted her eyes to his. 'He found out and he wanted to end it so he bided his time until he found the most effective way. I warned you that we should keep our relationship a secret, but you insisted that you wouldn't creep around.'

Jago's broad shoulders tensed. 'I wasn't afraid of your father.'

'No,' she said quietly. 'But I was. And I was the one left to deal with him after you walked off, Jago. My father didn't know that you had no intention of committing to anyone. For some unfathomable reason he thought you were serious about me and that was the last thing he wanted.'

Jago almost groaned aloud. He *had* been serious.

And he'd made the fatal mistake of telling her father.

Understanding just what had caused her father to take such dramatic steps, Jago ran a hand over his face, lost for words for the first time in his life.

Katy watched him for a long moment and then, with a final pitying look, she tugged her wrist away from his grip, picked up the photographs and left the room without a backward glance.

'Oh, my God.' Libby stared at the photographs in horror. 'Dad gave him these? Well, no wonder the guy walked out. They're very incriminating.'

'I can't believe you just said that!' Katy stared at her in disbelief. 'You're supposed to be on my side.'

'Oh, come on, Katy!' Libby held one of the photographs up and shook her head. 'For crying out loud, you're naked in bed with a man and you're laughing.'

'So? I always liked Aiden,' Katy mumbled, and Libby shook her head.

'Sweetheart, I'm always on your side, you know that, but for a man as fiercely proud as Jago, these would have seemed like the ultimate insult to his manhood. It's the male ego thing. Can't you see that?' She narrowed her eyes. 'I must admit they're bloody good. You look stunning in this one.'

Katy ignored her. 'But I wouldn't *do* a thing like that. *He should have known* I wouldn't do a thing like that. Instead, he assumed I went from virgin to slut faster than you could say broken heart.'

'I know, and deep down I suspect Jago knows, but love must have clouded his judgement.'

Katy stiffened. She was singularly unimpressed by Jago's judgement. Or rather lack of it. 'We both know that Jago never loved me.'

If he'd loved her, he wouldn't have been so quick to believe the worst of her.

'I certainly didn't think he did,' Libby mused, still leafing through the photographs, 'but now I'm changing my mind.'

'Based on what?'

'Think about it. Think about the way he's been behaving since you walked back into his life—or rather since you arrived on a stretcher. He is *seriously* bothered by you. Also, we both know that Jago is Mr Super-Bright. Nothing gets past him in the intellectual stakes, which can only mean one thing...'

Katy stared at her stupidly and Libby rolled her eyes and dropped the offending photographs on the table.

'He was so blinded by love that he didn't bother examining the facts. His reactions were totally emotional, which was what Dad was banking on when he set it all up.'

'You're being ridiculous,' Katy said. 'Jago couldn't have been in love with me.'

'Why?'

'Well for a start because he never mentioned it,' Katy said caustically, and Libby rolled her eyes to the ceiling.

'So? You're twenty-nine, Katy. When are you going to realise that not everyone is as honest and straightforward as you are? I suspect Jago had never said those three little words in his life before. You'd only been together for a month and you were only eighteen. Maybe if you'd had longer—'

'Well, we didn't,' Katy said flatly, 'and it's history now.'

Libby put the photographs on the table. 'I'd be very surprised if it's history.'

'Meaning?'

'A man like Jago isn't going to let it end there.' Libby's eyes narrowed thoughtfully and the hint of a smile touched her soft mouth. 'And if I were Dad, I'd be shivering in my bed.'

'Yes, well, we both know that nothing disturbs our father's sleep,' Katy said bitterly, not wanting to think about how his interference had affected her life. She didn't know who angered her more. Her father for inventing his lies or Jago for believing them.

And he still didn't know the whole story.

Libby looked at her. 'What if he wants you back now he knows the truth? At the very least he's going to want to talk to you again.'

'There's nothing to talk about,' Katy said flatly. 'It was eleven years ago and in two months' time I'm marrying Freddie. Jago Rodriguez is nothing but a painful part of my past. I know that Dad was responsible, but Jago should have believed in me, Libby. He didn't trust me and I can't be with a man who doesn't trust me.'

'Jago, can you concentrate?'

Jago shook himself and stared at Charlotte. 'Did you say something?'

'Yes.' She put her hands on her hips, her expression frustrated. 'I've been talking to you for the past five minutes and you haven't been listening to a word I've been saying. What's the matter with you?'

'Nothing.' Jago's insides were raw.

After Katy had walked away from him the day before, he'd spent a sleepless night coming to terms with the fact that he'd been successfully manipulated by a master.

He'd always known that Sir Charles Westerling was utterly ruthless, but when that ruthlessness had been turned on him, he hadn't spotted it.

He was also extremely disturbed by Katy's quiet statement that she'd been the one left to deal with her father.

What exactly had she had to deal with?

Had her father been violent?

He was suddenly forced to face the uncomfortable truth that he'd misjudged her appallingly and at the moment he had absolutely no idea how to go about making amends.

He couldn't believe that he'd been so quick to pass judgement on her. Hadn't he seen with his own eyes how shy she was? For goodness' sake, it had taken him *weeks* before he'd even attempted to take things further than a kiss. How could he have believed that she would have been so uninhibited as to dive into another man's bed so quickly?

And she'd loved him. He gritted his teeth. She'd told him so again last night.

She'd loved him with an uncritical devotion that had given him a bigger high than the most lucrative deal he'd ever closed on the stock market.

And he'd managed to kill that love.

'I don't know who's made you angry, but I feel sorry for him,' Charlotte announced, giving up on communication and pushing a set of X-rays in his hands. 'When you've finished plotting revenge, can you check those for me, please? The lady is waiting in cubicle 3.'

Plotting revenge?

He wasn't plotting revenge, there would be time enough to deal with her father later. At the moment he was using every ounce of intelligence at his disposal to try and work out how to manoeuvre his way back into Katy's good books.

And it was going to be tough.

Pulling himself together, he checked the X-ray, reassured the patient and then prowled through A and E, looking for Katy.

She was working in the paediatric area, seeing a child who had fallen awkwardly on a bouncy castle.

The mother was a bag of nerves and the child was cranky and irritable.

Unobserved, he stood in the doorway watching Katy, noticing the way her eyes softened as she spoke to the child and the way she reacted so sympathetically to the mother's endless questions and worries.

Everything about Katy was gentle and giving. She opened windows to let wasps out and lifted spiders out of the bath instead of turning on the taps like most other people. How could he ever have thought she'd have betrayed him with another man?

He watched as she soothed the child and examined the arm, her lower lip caught between her teeth as she ran through the possibilities in her mind.

She was an incredibly thorough doctor.

And he'd treated her shockingly.

'I think she might have fractured a bone, Mrs Hancock,' she said finally. 'She's very tender just here and there's some swelling. I'd like to send her for some X-rays so that I can have a proper look.'

The mother looked guilty. 'It was such a busy party—I didn't even see her fall. I just heard her screaming.'

'How awful for you.' Katy sympathised immediately, her manner completely non-judgmental. 'Try not to blame yourself. These things happen with small children. You can't be everywhere all the time.'

She reached for a form, scribbled on it and handed it to the mother, the lights catching her blonde hair and making it gleam. 'If you follow the yellow line, that takes you straight to X-Ray. Come back here afterwards and I'll look at the films.'

Jago felt something burn deep inside him.

He still wanted her.

He didn't deserve her but he still wanted her, and all his instincts told him that part of her still wanted him, too. He didn't believe for a moment that she was in love with her fiancé.

If she *had* been, he told himself that he'd have walked away without bothering her, but he'd seen something in her eyes when she'd looked at him.

He'd seen the same hunger that he felt when he was confronted by her every day.

No matter how badly he'd hurt her, physically at least, she still wanted him.

And he intended to use that to his advantage.

Katy finished filling out the notes and then glanced up, the colour fading from her cheeks as she saw Jago watching her.

Her stomach did a somersault.

'Did you need me for something?'

His gaze never flickered from hers. 'We have things to talk about.'

Just as Libby had predicted, he wasn't prepared to leave things as they were.

She straightened. 'We have absolutely nothing to talk about, Jago.'

'I disagree.'

Her eyes slid self-consciously around her, checking that no one was within earshot. 'It's all history, Jago. In the past. Finished.'

'We both know it's far from finished,' he said smoothly, and she tensed.

Surely he wasn't suggesting…?

Just in case he was, she thought she'd better set him straight. 'Jago, you thought I'd given my…' She glanced furtively around again and lowered her voice to little more than a whisper. 'Given my virginity to you and then slept with another man at the same time.' She brushed a strand of hair away from her eyes with shaking fingers, totally unable to comprehend that he'd had such a low opinion of her. 'You obviously didn't know me at all.'

His wide shoulders stiffened defensively. 'I thought I did but all the evidence pointed to the contrary. Surely you can see that.'

She shook her head. 'Jago, I couldn't ever be with a man who believed I was capable of that. I don't know what sort of women you mix with normally but if that's the sort of behaviour that you've come to expect then I feel sorry for you.'

Jago compressed his mouth. 'It does happen.'

She shook her head in disbelief. 'But not with me. I don't *do* things like that,' she said, hating the fact that there was a quiver in her voice. She wanted so badly to match his cool indifference. 'You didn't even have the decency to ask me about it.'

'My only defence is that my pride was very hurt.' He lifted his dark head and looked at her steadily. 'After I left, why didn't you try and contact me? To explain?'

She gaped at him. 'Are you really trying to suggest that any of this is my fault? *You left*—and you didn't even do me the courtesy of telling me you were going, let alone give me the reason for your sudden departure. I was so naïve that I actually believed that you'd come back. That there was nothing on earth that could keep us apart.' She saw him flinch slightly and felt the anger burn inside her. 'But you didn't and I had no idea how to find you. All I knew was that you no longer worked for my father's company. Even when I discovered that I was—'

She caught herself in time and broke off, heart thumping, horrified by what she'd so nearly revealed.

There was a pulsing silence.

'What did you discover, Katy?' He was suddenly incredibly still and his dark eyes were watchful.

'Nothing.' Her voice was a strangled croak and he muttered something in Spanish and moved towards her.

But whatever he'd intended to say, the opportunity was lost as the mother and toddler returned with their X-rays.

Filled with relief at the reprieve, Katy checked them carefully, aware that he was standing close behind her, feeling his warm breath on the back of her neck.

'She's fractured her radius.' Trying to ignore the tense atmosphere, Katy squinted at the X-ray, visually tracing the cortex of each bone as she'd been taught, looking for irregularities. 'There's a slight displacement,' she murmured, 'but that shouldn't matter in a child this young so I'll just give her painkillers and immobilise it in a cast.'

Jago's eyes flickered to the X-rays. 'Have you checked for a second fracture?'

Katy frowned. Was he still trying to catch her out?

'Yes.'

'So what makes you so smart, Dr Westerling,' he muttered under his breath, and she gave a slow smile, ridiculously pleased by the veiled praise.

'I worked in paediatrics,' she reminded him lightly, tugging the X-ray out of the light-box and returning it to the folder.

From a professional point of view, working with him was definitely getting easier. He no longer made her feel as though she should be back in medical school.

Unfortunately their personal relationship was much more complicated.

Katy discussed the management of the fracture with the mother, all the time aware that Jago was standing there, biding his time.

Suddenly she felt hideously nervous and she was desperately searching for an excuse to escape from him when Charlotte hurried down with the news that Ambulance Control had rung to say that they were bringing in a nasty head injury.

With a look of savage frustration on his lean, handsome face, Jago departed, leaving her in no doubt whatsoever that the subject wasn't closed.

CHAPTER SIX

JAGO rang the bell of the flat with impatient fingers and proceeded to pace up and down like a caged tiger.

Ever since their totally unsatisfactory, interrupted conversation, he'd been filled with a rising tension and foreboding.

What had Katy been about to say when she'd stopped in mid-sentence?

Obviously something that she would rather have kept a secret, he reflected grimly, remembering the sudden pallor of her cheeks.

The door suddenly opened and Libby stood there, her blonde hair tumbling over her shoulders, a defiant gleam appearing in her eyes as she recognised him.

'Yes?' Her tone was decidedly unfriendly and he tensed. He wasn't accustomed to receiving such a complete lack of response from a woman.

Obviously he had some serious fence-mending to do with the sister as well as Katy.

'I need to talk to your sister.'

'She's got a date with Freddie tonight,' Libby announced smoothly. 'He's the man she's marrying in two months' time.'

Seeing that she was about to close the door in his face, Jago planted a powerful hand in the middle and pushed it open.

'She won't be marrying him.'

Given no choice but to let him in, Libby backed away from the door and glared at him. 'It took years for her to recover when you walked out last time,' she said frostily. 'Because of what you did she's avoided men like the plague. Don't think Alex and I are going to stand by and let you do it again.'

'I'm not going to hurt her.' Jago stood still, wondering why he felt the need to explain himself to Katy's sister. He wasn't in the habit of explaining himself to anyone. 'I came to finish a conversation. She finally told me everything this morning.'

Libby's blue eyes were suddenly wary. 'What do you mean, *everything*?'

Pushing away the slight niggle that he wasn't playing fair, Jago took instant advantage. He needed the information. He needed to *know*.

'Everything. I know about the baby.' It was no more than an educated guess but he could see from the look in his eyes that he'd hit the jackpot.

'She told you that?' Libby's eyes narrowed. 'She didn't mention it to me this evening.'

Jago's fabled intellect was working overtime, trying to map out a conversation that would give him the information he needed without revealing that there had been no confession.

'Let's just say we've finally started talking about things we should have talked about a long time ago. It must have been terrible for her.'

'It was terrible for all of us. We thought she was going to die for a while,' Libby said softly, her eyes clouded by unpleasant memories. 'She was devastated when you left, but then to lose the baby was the final straw. And she was *so* ill.'

She *lost* the baby?

His baby?

Stunned by the news, Jago masked his expression, determined to elicit all the facts. 'She was in hospital?'

'Of course.' Libby frowned, as if surprised that he should

ask such a strange question. 'It was such a bad fall they were really worried about her.'

Jago was battling with the shock of discovering that Katy had been pregnant when he'd left her and had then lost the baby. He was utterly appalled by the notion that he'd somehow failed to protect her. And confused. How could she have become pregnant?

His hard jaw clenched. Had her father known she was pregnant? And why had she fallen?

His brain was still scanning through a variety of equally distasteful scenarios when the door opened and Katy walked into the room.

Dressed for an evening out, she looked incredibly beautiful in a silky black dress and he felt his body tighten in the most basic of male responses. He adored her curves. Like most men, his preference was for women to be shaped like women rather than sticks, and Katy was every inch a woman. The only thing that was wrong with her appearance was her hair.

His mouth tightened as he saw how carefully she'd styled her hair, twisting it and taming it until it lay subdued on top of her head.

She had fabulous hair. Left loose, it fell like a sleek gold curtain almost to her waist and he'd spent hours smoothing his fingers through it, enjoying its amazing scent and texture. But she'd only ever worn it loose when he'd forced the issue. The rest of the time she'd twisted it into submission on the top of her head.

It was the style she always wore for her parents and he hated it. It was restrained, dignified and repressed. All the things that she thought she ought to be. How many times had he ripped the pins out of her hair when they'd been together?

It was as if she was locking an important part of herself away.

He wondered briefly if her fiancé knew what she was really like underneath that elegant, contained exterior and then almost growled with anger at the thought of another man touching her.

She was his.

She'd always been his.

The thought made him catch his breath.

'Jago!' Her startled gaze slid between him and her sister and Libby pulled an apologetic face and backed towards the kitchen.

'Sorry, he forced his way in.' She glared at Jago and then looked pointedly at her sister. 'I'll be making coffee if you need me.'

'Libby—wait!' Katy's plea was ignored and the kitchen door closed firmly behind Libby.

Jago derived some comfort from the fact that Katy hadn't wanted to be left alone with him.

She didn't trust herself.

It gave him a primitive type of male satisfaction to note the way her soft lips parted and her pupils dilated when she looked at him.

He gave a soft smile and stepped towards her.

Katy's eyes locked on Jago's powerful frame and she felt a rush of panic.

He'd come after her.

And hadn't she guessed that he would? Ever since her thoughtless, unguarded comment spoken in the heat of the moment, she'd known that he wouldn't let it go.

His dark gaze locked on hers with the deadly accuracy of a heat-seeking weapon and she felt something unravel deep within her stomach.

It appalled her that he could still make her feel this way. All right, so he was gorgeous, but he was also the man who'd thought her capable of sleeping with two men at the same time. They clearly didn't share the same moral values. How could she still find him even remotely attractive?

But she did. One look at his hard mouth made her skin tingle and her breasts ache.

She felt *hot* all over.

Shocked by the depth of her reaction, drowning in her elemental response to him, Katy sucked in a breath and tried to apply logic to the situation.

Of course she found him attractive. What woman wouldn't? Jago Rodriguez was as sexy as sin. Her reaction didn't mean anything. It was something she could control.

Furiously denying what she was feeling, she reminded herself that she was marrying Freddie in two months' time, and if a tiny voice pointed out that Jago could arouse a response at a distance of metres that Freddie couldn't match even when they were touching, then she chose to ignore it.

There was no way she'd be so foolish as to resume a relationship with Jago again.

Whatever she felt for him, she couldn't be with a man who didn't trust her. And Jago hadn't trusted her.

Having reminded herself firmly of that fact, she tried to match his attitude of cool indifference. 'What are you doing here?'

'Finishing our conversation.' His eyes rested on her mouth with blatant fascination and then slid down her body, his intense scrutiny making her relieved that she was wearing a very modest silk dress. At least he couldn't *see* what she was feeling.

Or could he?

'The conversation was finished, Jago.'

'I don't think so. We'd just reached the part where you were telling me about the baby.'

She was shaken into silence by his smooth declaration and panic clawed at her stomach. 'I didn't say—'

'It was more what you left unsaid,' he finished softly, stepping closer to her. 'Finish the story, Katy.'

She turned and fled towards her bedroom but he was right behind her, closing the door and isolating them together in the confines of the cosy room. Instantly she realised her mistake.

The large, elegant hallway was impersonal whereas everything about her bedroom was soft and intimate. *Personal.*

The last place in the world she'd have chosen to be alone with Jago.

In the hallway of her apartment she hadn't found him particularly intimidating, but in her bedroom she couldn't help but be aware of his superior height and strength. He dominated the room, overwhelmingly male and unshakably confident. And he was looking for answers.

'When did you find out that you were pregnant?'

'After you left.' What was the point in denying what he clearly knew? She walked over the far end of her bedroom, wondering how a room that she normally regarded as a sanctuary could suddenly seem so claustrophobic.

He frowned. 'You didn't find out until after I left?'

She swallowed. 'I suspected…'

'But you didn't say anything?'

'I panicked.'

'I can imagine.' He ran a hand over his jaw, visibly tense. 'Katy, you told me you were protected.'

His voice was surprisingly gentle and her heart missed several beats. If she was vulnerable to his macho, dominating male side, she was even more vulnerable to his gentle side. She wished he'd kept it hidden.

She felt the colour touch her cheeks. 'There really isn't any reason to talk about this.'

'Your sister clearly blames me for making you pregnant,' he pointed out, and she sat down on the edge of the bed because standing suddenly seemed too much like hard work.

'That's not true. I *told* Libby it was my fault.'

He inhaled sharply. 'I was older than you and more experienced. It was my responsibility but you *definitely* told me you were protected.' He stepped forward and hunkered down next to her, his dark gaze fixed on her pale face, his eyes tormented. 'Have you any idea what it does to me to know that I left you pregnant? You lied to me, *querida*. Why?'

'Because I was eighteen and stupid,' she muttered, her cheeks hot with embarrassment. 'And desperate.'

He frowned with an unusual lack of comprehension. 'Desperate?'

'To go to bed with you.'

She looked away from him, instantly regretting her honesty, but strong fingers caught her chin and forced her to look at him.

Connecting with those stunning dark eyes, she suddenly understood with appalling clarity how she could have made such a serious error of judgement at eighteen. Jago was so staggeringly sexy that exercising common sense would have been as unlikely as a snowstorm in summer.

He said something under his breath in Spanish and then switched to English. 'I can't believe I let that happen,' he muttered, and her eyes slid away from his.

'I've never blamed you.'

'You should have told me you were pregnant.'

'I had no idea where you were,' she pointed out, struggling to control the traitorous reaction of her body. He was so close to her. She curled her fingers into her palms in case she gave in to the temptation to slide them into his silky black hair. 'And, anyway, you'd rejected me.'

He gave an agonised groan. 'Don't remind me. If I'd known...' His face was unusually pale, the skin stretched taut over his cheekbones. 'And then you lost the baby. How did you fall? Tell me what happened.'

Shaken by a question that she hadn't been anticipating, she stared at him. 'How did you know I fell?'

'I'm afraid I took advantage of your sister,' he muttered, and she stood up and moved over to her bedroom window.

He was being too nice to her. The only way she could keep him at a distance was if she reminded herself that he was an uncaring, unfeeling monster who hadn't trusted her, and it was very hard to do that convincingly when he was working overtime on demonstrating his sensitive side.

She desperately wanted him to leave.

Unfortunately Freddie wasn't due for another half-hour so there was no hope of a reprieve from that direction.

'Katy?' Eyes narrowed, Jago rose to his feet in a fluid movement and she stopped to pick up a towelling robe, which lay discarded on the floor, and draped it over the back of a chair.

Anything to avoid that penetrating gaze. He saw too much.

'I tripped—it was just one of those things.'

There was a long silence. 'You *tripped*?'

She licked her lips, hearing the surprise and disbelief in his tone. 'That's right. And now can we change the subject?' She looked at him and managed something resembling a smile. 'As you're always saying, it's history now and I certainly don't blame you for the baby.'

His powerful body radiated tension. 'But you blame me for everything else.'

'You should have trusted me, Jago,' she said simply. 'I was completely in love with you and a man as experienced as you should have seen that I couldn't see straight enough to focus on another man.'

A muscle moved in his cheek and she watched him dealing with the unfamiliar experience of being in the wrong.

For a man with his pride she knew it would be hard and she certainly wasn't expecting an apology. Jago had probably never apologised for anything in his life.

'You have to admit I had reason—'

'You ignored what you knew about me and judged me on the evidence of someone who had every reason to destroy our relationship,' she said quietly, holding onto the fact that he'd behaved with such totally predictable male arrogance. Only by remembering that would she be able to keep him at a distance. 'I still can't quite believe you did that. And now you have to go, Jago. Freddie will be here any minute.'

'Call him and cancel.'

He moved towards her with deliberate intent and she found herself backing against the wall of the bedroom.

'He's booked a table.'

'Cancel.' His eyes dropped to her mouth and she felt her heart rate increase with startling rapidity. 'You're not going to marry him, Katy.'

The atmosphere in the room was suddenly charged with tension and she felt frighteningly out of control.

'I *am*, I'm—'

'Call him and end it. We both know you're not in love with him. So why are you marrying him?'

Because she didn't *want* love.

Jago stepped closer still and she felt sensation knife through her pelvis. She was breathlessly aware of him, of the blue-black stubble on his jaw, of the slumberous dark eyes probing hers with relentless intent, of his wide shoulders blocking her escape.

'You're dating a Brazilian model,' she reminded him desperately, and he gave a groan of denial.

'Not any more.'

Trapped by his ferocious masculinity, she felt the tension in the room rise to an almost unbearable degree.

'End it,' he instructed softly, his eyes dropping to her parted lips and clouding hungrily, 'or stop looking at me like that.'

She couldn't get the air into her lungs. 'I'm not looking at you—'

'Yes, you are.'

Without warning he took her mouth in a kiss so explicit in its intent that her senses went into freefall. With a rough exclamation he hauled her against his powerful body, the sensual onslaught of his kiss creating an excitement so wild that she couldn't help but respond. Fevered by his touch, she kissed him back, locking her arms around his strong neck, feeling the heat of his body pressing through the thin fabric of her dress.

His breathing fractured, he lifted a hand and tugged roughly at her hair, discarding the clips impatiently until it tumbled in a silken mass over his arm and down her back.

With a groan of satisfaction he sank both hands into the soft waves that he'd released, anchoring her head against the relentless onslaught of his skilled mouth.

'I love your hair.' He muttered the words against her mouth, moving his lips over hers, exploring suggestively with his tongue until she went up in flames.

How could she have forgotten what it felt like to kiss Jago?

Instead of pulling away, she pressed herself closer to him, quivering with response as he kissed her senseless.

Her body softened under the hard possession of his mouth, her insides melting as his tongue probed and teased in an erotic reminder of more intimate moments.

'Jago, *please…*' She was out of her mind with excitement, her whole body consumed by a wild hunger that was totally outside her control.

She needed him so badly.

It had been so long.

The hot demands of his mouth intensified and she started to shiver, held in the grip of an electrifying force so powerful that that she thought she might explode.

She felt frantic.

Desperate.

When Jago finally dragged his mouth away from hers, she staggered slightly, grateful that his fingers were gripping her arms so tightly. If they hadn't been, she would undoubtedly have fallen.

Aghast and embarrassed by the uninhibited way she'd responded to him, she freed herself from his grip and backed away, deriving some small satisfaction from the fact that Jago looked as stunned as she felt.

Maybe he wasn't quite as cool and in control as he liked to pretend.

He sucked in his breath and took a step backwards, reaching out to steady himself as he almost tripped over the chair.

His dark eyes burned into hers. 'You *definitely* need to call Freddie.'

With that parting shot he turned and strode out of the room, leaving her staring after him in trembling disbelief, feeling intensely vulnerable.

What had she done?

She'd kissed Jago.

And that hadn't been any old kiss. That kiss had been as close to sex as it was possible to get without removing clothing.

She groaned in mortification. Knowing Jago, he wasn't going to let her forget it. He was self-confident and arrogant enough to have taken that response as a green light. From now on he'd be pursuing her with all the subtlety of a herd bull.

Shocked and confused, she sat on the edge of the bed until the sound of the doorbell disturbed her.

It would be Freddie. What was she going to do?

She stared at the closed door with something close to desperation.

She was engaged to Freddie but she'd kissed Jago. And kissing Jago had exposed her to a level of excitement that she'd denied herself for eleven years. Intense, toe-curling excitement that could so easily become addictive.

Lifting a hand, she touched her lips, still able to feel a slight tingling where he'd plundered her mouth with his.

No one but no one kissed like Jago. Jago had cornered the market in sexual excitement.

Hearing Freddie's voice in the hallway, she closed her eyes, knowing that she needed to make a decision.

Fingers shaking, she stood up just as Freddie tapped on the door and walked in. He stopped in surprise, visibly taken aback by her appearance.

'Goodness, Katherine, what have you done to your hair?' His frown was faintly disapproving. 'The Fletcher-Gibbs are quite formal usually and this evening is very much a business dinner. There'll be clients there. You might want to wear it up.'

Katy blinked, suddenly realising that she'd forgotten to redo her hair after Jago had strode like the conquering male out of her bedroom, having kissed her to the point of total surrender.

She lifted a hand and realised that her long blonde hair, normally fiercely restrained, was flowing loose over her shoulders.

'I—I—' She broke off, suddenly needing to ask him a question. 'Freddie, do you like it like this? If we weren't dining with the Fletcher-Gibbs, would you prefer that I left it down?'

He looked at her with the expression of a man who knew he was on dangerous ground. 'You look lovely,' he said tactfully, 'but generally speaking I prefer it up. It projects the right sort of image, don't you agree?'

And that was what Freddie cared about, of course. Image.

Katy looked at him thoughtfully. Jago didn't prefer it up. Her hair had always driven him wild. But, then, as Libby had pointed out, Freddie wasn't the sort of man to be driven wild by anything except stocks and shares.

And that had been one of the reasons she'd agreed to marry him.

But what was she going to do now?

Could she ever be satisfied with the blandness of Freddie after experiencing the heat and colour of a man like Jago?

CHAPTER SEVEN

JAGO strode through the A and E department the next morning, satisfied that he'd successfully salvaged what could have been a difficult situation.

All right, so he'd made a mistake about Katy, but her response to his kiss had more than convinced him that she'd forgiven him for not trusting her. After the kiss they'd shared the night before he was supremely confident that she would have ended her engagement to Freddie.

Which meant that they could resume their relationship.

And he had every intention of doing exactly that.

He loved her.

He'd always loved her.

Convinced that he had the situation well in hand, it came as an enormous shock to see her clutching a huge hand-tied bouquet of flowers as she walked along the corridor towards him.

Instinct told him that they had to be from Freddie and he tensed in stunned disbelief. What sort of guy sent flowers after he'd been dumped only a few months before the wedding?

Unless she hadn't dumped him.

Maybe his plan wasn't going quite as smoothly as he'd anticipated.

'You didn't do it?' He glowered at her, disconcerted by the feeling that tore through him. The feeling that he only ever seemed to experience when he was around Katy. 'I can't believe you still intend to marry that man. How can you marry him after the way you kissed me last night?'

'*You* kissed *me*, Jago,' she pointed out calmly. 'And please don't criticise Freddie. He's romantic and kind.'

Romantic?

She thought Freddie was romantic?

He stiffened, offended by the implication that he was somehow lacking in that direction. 'You don't think I'm romantic?'

'You?' She looked startled at the question, as if the thought genuinely hadn't occurred to her before. 'You don't have a romantic bone in your body, Jago.'

Rocked from his unshakable conviction that he was the only man she'd ever wanted, Jago was completely wrong-footed. 'This isn't the place to have the type of conversation we need. I'm taking you to dinner tonight. I'll pick you up at eight-thirty. We can talk then.'

'And you think you're romantic?' She shook her head, her expression sympathetic and slightly amused. 'Sorry. I'm already going out.'

With Freddie no doubt.

His lean hands curled into fists. 'You still want me, Katy, and I want you.'

Having laid most of his cards on the table, Jago watched her warily, trying to gauge her reaction. Normally he prided himself in his ability to understand and outsmart the most devious member of her sex, but Katy didn't play any of the games that women normally played. Whatever reaction he was expecting to that declaration, it wasn't the one he received.

Instead of falling into his arms and treating his announcement with the misty-eyed delight that he'd expected, she merely looked at him, visibly unenthusiastic at the prospect of resuming their relationship.

Uncomfortably aware that nothing was going according to plan, Jago suddenly found himself in the novel position of not knowing how to handle a woman. After that kiss he'd assumed that they'd be resuming their relationship as soon as she'd ended her engagement to Freddie. But there was something disturbingly discouraging about the expression in her blue gaze.

'Up until twenty-four hours ago you believed me capable of sleeping with another man, even though I'd told you that I was in love with you.' Her tone was cool and controlled. 'You told me yesterday that your barest minimum requirement in a relationship is fidelity. Well, mine is trust, Jago. I absolutely cannot be with a man who doesn't trust me.'

Jago sucked in a breath. 'I already explained what happened.'

'And that's supposed to make it OK?' Her voice shook slightly and he realised that she wasn't quite as cool as she was making out. 'You didn't trust me, Jago. I doubt that you've ever trusted anyone. You move on before you can get close to a woman.'

Thoroughly discomfited by her blunt appraisal, he took refuge in attack. 'You still want me, Katy. Do you think I didn't feel it when we kissed last night?'

'A relationship has to be based on more than kissing. I'm not interested, Jago.' Her grip on the flowers tightened. 'We might have to work together, but I don't want anything else.'

And with that parting shot she walked off, leaving him to come to terms with the fact that for the first time in his thirty-five years, a woman had chosen to walk away from him.

He wanted her back.

Katy stuffed the flowers in water so that they didn't die before the end of her shift and slipped the card into her pocket with shaking fingers.

She wondered what Jago would have said had he known that they weren't from Freddie at all but from Alex, whom she'd spoken to on the phone the night before. And it was Alex she was having dinner with. Alex and Libby.

In fact, his hasty assumption that she hadn't broken up with Freddie was yet another indication of Jago's jaundiced view of her sex. He was assuming that, despite the kiss they'd shared, she was still going ahead and marrying another man.

She wondered what had happened in his life that made him so cynical about women.

It showed that he still knew very little about her. She would never do a thing like that.

She would never kiss one man and then marry another.

And that was the reason she'd ended her engagement to Freddie the evening before.

She felt slightly guilty about not telling Jago but she hadn't actually lied, she reassured herself. She just hadn't told the whole truth.

And why should she?

Jago didn't love her. All he wanted was a physical affair and she knew that pursuing a relationship with Jago would be a quick route to another broken heart. They just didn't want the same things in life. So surely she was right to protect herself?

She walked out of the staffroom, reflecting that breaking up with Freddie had been surprisingly painless. Even though initially he'd seemed a little startled by her announcement that she couldn't marry him, he'd accepted it with a readiness that suggested that he'd been having second thoughts about the wedding himself. She just wished that telling her parents would prove as easy.

She needed to pick the right time to do it but it had to be soon, otherwise they'd hear from other sources.

The morning was incredibly busy but she successfully avoided Jago until lunchtime when the doors to the ambulance bay crashed open and the paramedics rushed in with a small girl on the stretcher.

'This is Molly Churchman. She's two years old and she fell

out of the bedroom window,' the paramedic told them, his expression tense and anxious. 'Bedroom on the first floor—the mother is hysterical.'

Jago reached for the oxygen mask and positioned it carefully over the child's mouth and nose. He watched carefully, nodding with satisfaction as he saw the mask fog.

'Her airway is patent and she's breathing by herself,' he growled. 'I want two lines in and I need an estimation of her weight.'

Katy wondered whether it was the sick child or their earlier confrontation that was responsible for the grim expression on his handsome face and the tension in his broad shoulders.

It was probably the child, she decided. Their relationship couldn't possibly be that important to him.

Charlotte looked up. 'I asked the mother about her weight but she was too upset to give me a lucid answer.'

'In that case, use the Oakley Paediatric Resuscitation chart on the wall,' Jago instructed, and one of the other nurses hurried to do that while he carried on assessing the child. 'Cervical spine injury is rare in a child of this age but we'll keep the spine immobilised until we've ruled it out.'

There was a flurry of action and Annie came back from examining the chart on the wall. 'Estimated weight is about 12 kilograms.'

'Right. Charlotte, make a note of that. Annie, go back to the mother,' Jago ordered, 'find out if the child cried immediately—I need to know whether she was unconscious for any time. And get me details of allergies, medications, past medical history and when she last ate or drank. And try and get a more precise account of the accident. What surface she landed on, how she was lying—that sort of thing.'

Annie hurried off to do as he'd instructed and Jago spoke quietly to the little girl, reassuring her in a gentle voice as he worked.

Charlotte was visibly upset as she undressed the child so that they could make a more accurate assessment of her injuries.

'She's so tiny. That poor mother.'

'Lose the emotion,' Jago said harshly. 'We've got a job to do. Finish undressing her and get some overhead heaters and warming blankets—a fall in body temperature causes a rise in oxygen consumption.'

Charlotte swallowed and looked at him, startled by the sharp reprimand.

Katy felt a flash of empathy for her colleague but she knew that Jago was right.

It wouldn't help the child if they let emotions get in the way of their work. The child needed them to be professional.

But there was no doubt that Jago was unusually tense.

They removed all her clothes and then covered her in warm blankets and adjusted the heaters so that she wouldn't become cold.

With the minimum of fuss, Katy found a vein and slipped in the cannula.

'Her blood pressure is slightly down,' one of the nurses said, 'but not dramatically.'

'Check her capillary refill time,' Jago ordered, and Katy finished taping the first IV in place and glanced up at him.

'Is that significant?'

He gave a brief nod. 'A child can suffer considerable blood loss without a significant change to the vital signs,' he told her, his eyes fixed on her fingers as she searched for another vein. 'When we diagnose shock in children we rely on other signs, like capillary refill time, the appearance of the skin, the temperature of the extremities.'

'Based on those criteria, this child is in shock,' Katy murmured, pausing as she located what felt like a vein.

Without hesitating, she inserted the cannula smoothly and watched as the blood flowed backwards.

'Both lines are in,' she said quickly, relieved that she'd managed what had proved to be a difficult task. Finding veins in a child that small was difficult at the best of times and sometimes they had to give an infusion directly into the bone.

The child had barely protested, which was another indication of how ill she was.

'That was a tricky job.' Jago's voice was gruff. 'Well done.'

For a brief moment their eyes met and he gave a slight smile. The tension in the room seemed to ease slightly but there was a hint of challenge in that smile that made Katy breathless.

The subject of their relationship was obviously far from closed.

She picked up a selection of blood bottles. 'I'll take bloods for group and cross-matching, blood-glucose estimation and request a full blood count and biochemistry. Anything else?'

Jago shook his head. 'No, but we need to get her some pain control.'

'Her skin is very cold and clammy and her capillary refill time is prolonged,' Charlotte said quietly, and Katy bit her lip as she took the bloods and administered the pain relief that Jago had ordered.

'She's very lethargic,' Jago murmured, his eyes never leaving the child as he worked. 'She's showing all the features of class III shock. I want to give her 20 milligrams of crystalloid per kilogram. Do the calculation, Katy.'

Katy did as he ordered and warmed the fluid before injecting it into the child's vein.

Jago carried on examining the limp, unresponsive body of the toddler. 'She's bleeding from somewhere and we need to find out where. Check her pulse and blood pressure again,' he ordered, glancing at Charlotte as he spoke. 'I've got a bad feeling about this. Bleep the surgeons and get me some blood up here fast. If her vital signs don't improve in the next few minutes I'm going to transfuse her. Can we get a nasogastric tube down, please? And I want X-rays of her chest and pelvis.'

* * *

Katy looked at the tiny body on the trolley and, despite Jago's warnings about becoming emotional, she felt a lump in her throat.

The little girl was so tiny and helpless. No wonder the mother was hysterical. She would have been hysterical if it had been her child who was lying there injured.

They had to save the child. They just couldn't let her die.

A niggling suspicion entered her head and she opened her mouth to speak and then closed it again.

'What?' Jago's tone was sharp. 'You were going to say something.'

Katy hesitated. 'I was wondering whether it could be her spleen,' she said quietly, 'but there's no clinical reason to imagine that it could be. Just a gut feeling.'

'Never dismiss gut feelings.' Jago looked at her and then returned his attention to the child, his expression thoughtful. 'It would explain the degree of shock in the absence of visible injury.'

Annie returned, having interviewed the mother in more depth, and she gave a full report to Jago who had examined the X-rays and now had his eyes fixed on the abdominal ultrasound.

'She's bleeding into her abdomen,' he muttered, and Carl, one of the other junior doctors, looked at him questioningly.

'But her abdominal wall is barely bruised.'

'That isn't a reliable sign in children.' Jago didn't look up. 'She's showing signs of abdominal injury. I think Katy is probably right. It's her spleen.'

Carl rubbed a hand over the back of his neck. 'So we need to get her to Theatre urgently?'

'Not necessarily.' Jago shook his head. 'We tend to avoid surgery and adopt a conservative approach where possible. The spleen is the most commonly injured organ following blunt trauma to the abdomen, then the liver and kidneys.'

'If it is her spleen, will they try leaving it to heal by itself?'

Katy frowned, racking her brains to recall the detail of something she'd seen in a medical journal. 'Didn't I read something recently that suggested that removing the spleen can result in significant long-term health problems?'

'That's right.' Jago nodded. 'It's very unusual to remove the spleen these days.'

Charlotte checked the child's vital signs again. 'I think she's improving. That fluid is helping.'

At that moment the doors opened and the surgical team swarmed into Resus.

They conferred with Jago, checked the abdominal ultrasound and examined the child carefully.

'I think you're right,' the consultant said finally, glancing at Jago with a slight smile. 'I'd say she has a small tear in her spleen.'

Jago glanced at Katy and a slight smile touched his firm mouth. 'It was Dr Westerling's diagnosis,' he said softly, and the consultant gave her an approving nod.

'In that case, well done to you, Dr Westerling. We'll get a CT scan and take it from there. If her signs continue to improve, we'll manage it conservatively. Are the parents with her?'

'The mother's in the relatives' room,' Jago said, ripping off his gloves and dropping them in the bin. 'I'm going to speak to her now. Katy, you can come with me as this seems to have turned into your case.'

Warmed by his approval, Katy blushed slightly. Despite his encouraging comments, she was well aware that it was he who had saved the child.

'Do you think she's going to live?' Katy quickened her stride to keep pace with him as he strode out of Resus and made for the relatives' room. She'd never been assigned the task of talking to relatives before, and was relieved that he was there to do it with her.

Jago pulled a face. 'Because children are so small, a fall like that can cause multisystem injury. You have to assume that they have multiple injuries until proved otherwise. If it's just a small tear to her spleen, she should recover fully.'

'You were so calm.'

He cast her a wry smile that was thoroughly unexpected. 'Not that calm.' He paused for a moment, his dark eyes resting on her face. 'I have feelings, too, you know.'

She looked at him, breathless, wondering whether he was just referring to Molly.

'But you don't show them.'

He lifted a broad shoulder in a shrug. 'How would that help the child? The patient needs me to be detached and efficient. Emotion clouds judgement, Katy. Remember that.'

He gave a twisted smile and suddenly she knew what he was thinking.

That emotion had clouded his judgement eleven years ago when he'd seen those photographs.

And in a way, wasn't it the same for her?

She knew that loving Jago was a quick road to heartache but she just couldn't help herself. He was drop-dead gorgeous and seeing him save a child's life with such impressive skill and supreme coolness made her want to surrender to him on the spot.

She studied him helplessly.

Everything about him was just so masculine. From his straight, aristocratic nose and perfect bone structure to the blue-black stubble beginning to show on his hard jaw, he was one hundred per cent red-blooded male and she realised with a sinking heart that she'd never stopped loving him.

Realising that they'd reached the relatives' room, she jerked her eyes away from his sinfully sexy mouth and tried to concentrate.

'Don't you usually take a nurse with you to do the gentle, caring bit?'

He dealt her a sizzling smile that cranked her pulse rate up still higher. 'Why do you think I've brought you along?'

Without waiting for her reply, he pushed open the door with

his shoulder and extended a hand to the woman sitting slumped in one of the armchairs.

'Mrs Churchman? I'm Mr Rodriguez, one of the A and E consultants. This is Dr Westerling. We looked after Molly in the resuscitation room.'

Katy closed the door behind them and went to sit beside the mother, concerned that she looked so distraught. Annie had told them that she hadn't even wanted to see her daughter in the resuscitation room.

'I've killed her. I know I've killed her.'

She started to sob hysterically and Katy glanced at Jago, expecting to see him tense and uncomfortable in the face of such hysterics. Instead, he frowned in concern and hunkered down next to the sobbing woman, taking her hand in his.

'You haven't killed her, Mrs Churchman.' His voice was warm and firm. 'She had a bad fall and she is suffering from some internal injuries but she is doing very well at the moment. We've transferred her to the children's surgical ward for some more tests and observation.'

The young mother looked at him, her chest jerking as she tried to hold back the sobs. 'She climbed out of the window.'

Jago nodded. 'So I understand.'

'I didn't even know she could reach the window,' Mrs Churchman whispered, horror in her voice as she related the tale. 'She pulled up a chair and climbed onto the window-sill. I was changing her bed at the time and I'd only nipped out for a moment to fetch a clean sheet. I must have been out of the room for less than thirty seconds, no more.'

She gave another sob and Katy reached for a box of tissues. 'Being a parent is the most difficult, responsible job in the world,' she said quietly. 'What Molly needs now is not for you to feel guilty but for you to be there for her. She needs her mother.'

Mrs Churchman blew her nose and nodded. 'You're right, I know you're right. But seeing her lying there as if she was dead just upset me so much.'

Jago frowned. 'She isn't dead, Mrs Churchman.' He went on to outline Molly's injuries and treatment in a cool, factual way and eventually the young mother seemed to gain some measure of control.

'Can I see her now?'

Katy nodded. 'When you're ready, one of the nurses will take you to the children's ward and you'll be able to stay with her. Is there anyone you'd like us to call to be with you?'

Mrs Churchman shook her head and reached for her bag. 'No. Her father is away on business and I don't want to worry my parents with it. I'll be fine now.'

Looking at her pale face, Katy wasn't so sure and she made a mental note to check on her later.

Leaving Mrs Churchman to gather her belongings together, they left the room and Katy arranged for a nurse to escort her to the ward.

'I'm glad you were there,' Jago said dryly as they walked back towards the main area of the A and E department. 'Dealing with hysterical females is not my strong point.'

She smiled at him. 'I thought you were brilliant.'

'Well, thank you,' Jago drawled softly, pausing as one of the other casualty officers waylaid him to ask his opinion on an X-ray.

Jago took the film in question and pushed it into the nearest light-box, his gaze fixed on the X-ray in front of him. 'There's a hairline fracture on the anterior view.'

The doctor muttered his thanks, looked slightly embarrassed that he hadn't spotted it himself and then hurried off to manage the patient accordingly.

Katy staring at Jago with a mixture of admiration and frustration. 'You never miss anything, do you? Has anyone ever told you that you set impossibly high standards?'

'This is an A and E department,' Jago reminded her with a careless lift of his broad shoulders. 'How can standards ever be too high? If we get it wrong, people die. And in this wonderful age of litigation, if we were even remotely to blame, we're sued.'

They walked on down the corridor and Katy bit her lip, knowing that there was some truth in what he said.

People *were* much quicker to apportion blame these days.

'Well, I for one am glad you have high standards. You were great with Molly,' she said softly, and he glanced towards her.

'So were you,' he said equally softly, a wry smile pulling at the corners of his mouth. 'You're a good doctor, Katy. You have good instincts.'

She looked at him and found her gaze trapped by his. The tension pulsed between them and she took a step backwards, stunned by the intensity of the attraction.

Breathing hard she tried to pull herself together.

He hadn't trusted her.

She had to keep reminding herself of that fact.

'I hope Molly will be all right.'

The faint amusement in his dark eyes indicated that he was well aware of her internal struggle. 'She was lucky,' he said smoothly. 'That mother should have had locks on the upstairs windows.' With a last lingering look at her mouth he turned away from her and walked back towards the main area of the A and E department, obviously expecting her to follow. 'She was totally negligent.'

Katy was taken aback by his sharp comment. 'Children move so fast—'

'And it is a mother's job to be one step ahead of them,' he shot back, his expression disapproving. 'A two-year-old girl should *not* be falling out of windows, no matter how hot the weather.'

'Accidents happen,' Katy reminded him gently. 'People make mistakes. You're very judgmental.'

'And you're very forgiving, *querida*,' he observed, stopping dead in his tracks, his dark lashes hiding his expression from her, 'except, it would seem, when I'm the culprit.'

Heat rushed to her face and she bit her lip, flustered by the hint of a smile pulling at the corners of his firm mouth.

'Jago—'

'Tell me, Katy.' He stepped closer to her and lowered his voice. 'How long are you going to keep up this pretence?'

She licked dry lips and then immediately wished she hadn't as his dark eyes lasered in on the gesture with visible hunger. 'What pretence?'

'The pretence that there's nothing between us.' With obvious reluctance his eyes lifted to hers, holding her captive. 'What does a guy have to do to get you to forgive? Send flowers? Beg?'

Her body slowly heated up under his gaze, sexual excitement burning low in her stomach. Why did being close to Jago *always* have this effect on her?

'I—I forgive you,' she stammered, backing away slightly from his powerful presence. 'But it doesn't mean I want a relationship. We're too different, Jago. We want different things.'

He gave a smile that was pure predatory male. 'I don't think so.'

'That's just sex!' She said the words without thinking and then looked round in embarrassment, realising that any of the staff could have been within earshot. Fortunately they weren't. 'You left me, Jago. You left me without a backward glance. Give me one instance that proves that you cared about me and not just the sex.'

'I kept the photographs,' he reminded her simply, a smile of satisfaction appearing in direct response to her shocked expression. 'Think about that, *querida*.'

With that he touched her on the cheek and walked away, leaving her staring after him.

He'd almost told her about the ring.

Jago stared at a conference programme, bombarded by totally alien emotions. He sensed that whatever he said at the moment, it wouldn't be enough. Katy was incurably romantic. As a child she'd played with dolls and dreamed of princes. And none of those dreams had included a prince who left her when the going got tough. It was going to take some very fancy foot-work on his part to convince her that he loved her.

He'd always loved her.

And eleven years before she'd been madly in love with him, and he'd killed that love with his lack of trust.

Somehow he had to win that love back.

But how?

Despite her passionate response to his kiss and the fact that her whole body reacted when he walked into the same room as her, Katy wasn't showing any signs of wishing to renew their relationship.

Remembering the way she'd clutched the flowers that morn-ing, his fingers tightened on the programme.

She'd been delighted with them. And she clearly hadn't bro-ken off her engagement to Freddie.

With a muttered curse he ran a hand over the back of his neck, acknowledging with unusual insight that it was going to take more than an exotic bunch of flowers to redeem himself in Katy's eyes.

Thanks to a major overreaction on his part over the photo-graphs, she was now completely convinced that he didn't pos-sess a sensitive side.

With a groan of frustration he tossed the programme onto the desk and applied his brain to the intellectual challenge of how to convince Katy he was as caring as the next guy.

He was absolutely sure about one thing—their relationship was never going to progress unless he got her away from the hospital and away from Freddie.

With a complete lack of vanity he recognised the fact that she was marrying Freddie because she was afraid of the feel-ings she had for *him*.

Katy was soft-hearted and loving and he'd hurt her badly. She didn't want to be hurt again and he'd seriously underestimated her strength of will. Once he'd apologised for having misjudged her, he'd stood back and waited for her to fall back into his arms.

But instead she'd walked away and now he found himself in the unique position of having to chase after a woman he wanted.

He looked at the conference programme again and an idea suddenly formed in his mind.

He was due to present a paper at a major medical conference in Seville at the end of the week and he'd arranged to visit his family afterwards.

He had space for one other doctor.

'Have you heard there's a place for a doctor to go to the conference in Seville at the end of the week? Apparently Harry was due to go but had to drop out at the last minute.' Several of the casualty officers were gathered around the noticeboard in the staffroom when Katy walked in and pushed her bag in the locker. Her mind was still on the confrontation she'd had with her parents the night before.

Her mother had been hysterical at the news that the wedding was off and her father had refused to accept that she was no longer marrying Freddie.

All in all it had been an extremely unpleasant evening.

Her colleagues were still looking at the noticeboard and chatting. 'Mr Rodriguez is presenting a paper and he's allowed to take someone with him. If you want to go you have to sign your name and then they're going to put the names in a hat.'

'Very scientific.'

Only half listening to the conversation, Katy checked that her hair was neatly tied back and walked onto the unit without signing her name. She was struggling to cope with Jago in the impersonal atmosphere of the A and E department without subjecting herself to the intimacy of a foreign trip.

As far as she was concerned, one of the others was more than welcome to go.

The waiting room was crowded with people and Katy didn't have time to give the trip another thought until one of her colleagues approached her at lunchtime with a rueful smile.

'Well, you're the lucky one.'

Katy stared at him blankly. 'I am?'

'Your name was pulled out of the hat. You're going to Seville with the boss.'

Katy put her sandwich down untouched. 'That's not possible.' She hadn't even put her name on the board.

'Finding it hard to believe your luck?' The other doctor grinned at her. 'You shouldn't feel guilty. It was all done fair and square. I was the one who pulled your name out of the hat.'

But her name shouldn't have been *in* the hat.

Totally appalled by the prospect of attending the conference with Jago, Katy got to her feet and knocked the chair over.

'Hey, steady on.' Her colleague looked at her in amusement. 'I know you're excited but you don't want to injure yourself before you go.'

She didn't wait to hear the rest of what he had to say. She needed to see Jago.

He was in his office, working on the computer, and she marched in without knocking.

'How did my name get in that hat, Jago?'

She glared at him angrily, her irritation increasing at his total lack of reaction.

'What hat?'

'Don't pretend you don't know what I'm talking about.' Suddenly aware that they could be overheard, she closed the door firmly and stalked across to his desk. 'I understand my name has been pulled out of the hat to go with you to Seville.'

'Has it?' His voice was a low drawl and he didn't lift his eyes from the spreadsheet he was working on. 'Don't complain. That place was very much in demand.'

'But not by me.' Frustration bubbled up inside her. 'You're not listening to me!'

Finally he looked at her, his gaze cool. If he was playing games then there was certainly no sign of it.

She took a deep breath and tried again. 'I didn't put my name on that list. I don't *want* to go with you to Seville.'

One dark eyebrow lifted. 'It's a first-class meeting with some excellent speakers,' he said calmly. 'You'll find it very informative and useful.'

'I'm sure the meeting will be great. This isn't about the meeting.'

'So what's bothering you?'

He was bothering her. And he knew it.

She licked her lips. 'Jago, I can't go with you.'

He sprawled back in his chair, his expression mocking. 'Am I that dangerous?'

Yes.

He gave a slow smile. 'It doesn't say much for your relationship with Freddie if you can't trust yourself to be alone with me,' he observed softly, and she coloured slightly, uncomfortable with the fact that she hadn't corrected his assumption that her wedding was still going ahead.

Why hadn't she?

Because she'd hoped that his belief that she was still engaged would encourage him to back off.

But she could see from the look in his eyes that he had no intention of backing off. He wanted her and he was going after her with all the ruthless determination that was so much a part of his character.

'Let yourself go, Katy,' he advised. 'Be yourself. Stop trying to be what your parents want you to be.'

Wasn't that what Libby and Alex were always saying?

'I am myself,' she said finally, her mouth dry and her heart pumping hard at the mere thought of being alone on foreign soil with Jago.

'Then, in that case, there isn't a problem, is there?' With a cool smile he reached across his desk and handed her a file.

'The flights and accommodation are all arranged and the programme is in there—you might like to look at it. I'm presenting on the first day but it runs for four days in total.'

Four days in Jago's company?

Her mind numb, she took the file, still wondering how her name had come to be added to the list. Jago hadn't admitted that he'd been responsible but he hadn't exactly denied it either. And the question was academic now. She could hardly refuse to go without drawing attention to herself. The other doctors saw it as a fantastic opportunity to catch up on the latest developments in the field of emergency medicine and if it had just been about the conference she would have been excited, too.

But it wasn't about the conference.

It was about being alone with Jago. Jago, who wanted nothing more than to resume their physical relationship—something that would lead to yet more heartbreak.

Would she have the willpower to resist him?

CHAPTER EIGHT

EXACTLY three days later Katy found herself standing on the balcony of a hotel in the Spanish city of Seville.

The heat of the summer sun, even so late in the afternoon, was almost unbearable and she retreated into the welcome cool of her suite.

Stepping away from the balcony, she stared in awe at the room again, wondering how she could possibly have been booked into anything so sumptuous.

This was the first time she'd attended a medical conference in her career, but she'd assumed that relatively junior doctors like herself usually had to make do with pretty humble accommodation.

But there was nothing humble about her room. It reflected the Moorish influence on the city, with a décor so opulent that it made her feel as though she should be dressed in seven veils and prepared for a harem.

As she reached for her suitcase, there was a knock on the door and one of the hotel staff delivered her a letter.

Surprised, she tore it open and immediately recognised the bold, black scrawl.

'Be ready at 7. Jago.'

Her fingers tightened on the note and her heart rate sped into the distance. It was typical of Jago to arrogantly assume she'd be willing to spend an evening with him. And equally typical for him not to disclose what he had in mind.

The conference didn't officially start until tomorrow, but she knew that there was a welcoming dinner for the delegates.

He must be planning to escort her to that.

Suddenly she had butterflies in her stomach. She shouldn't go with him. She really, really shouldn't...

But she'd been planning to attend the dinner anyway and it would certainly be more relaxing to be with someone she knew, she reasoned. And they'd be surrounded by other delegates. What could possibly happen?

Helplessly acknowledging just how much she wanted to spend an evening with Jago, she gave a sigh.

Why not?

Just one evening and she'd make sure that she slept in her own room at the end of the night.

Not wanting to dwell on her decision for too long, she glanced at her watch.

If he was collecting her at seven then she had less than two hours to find something suitable to wear and get ready for the evening, and she hadn't even had time to unpack yet.

She opened her case and gave a gasp of surprise.

Instead of the businesslike dresses and co-ordinates that she'd packed in blacks and other muted colours, the case contained what appeared to be an entire summer wardrobe in vibrant, eye-catching colours and designs.

At first she thought that there'd been a mix up with her luggage but then she saw the note attached to the inside of the case.

'Time to stop locking yourself away. Enjoy. Love, Libby and Alex.'

She sat down on the bed with a plop. Somehow Libby had managed to switch the entire contents of her case without her noticing. Instead of her usual safe, understated wardrobe, she was confronted by a rainbow of bright, sexy clothing.

She swallowed as she fingered the first item of clothing that came to hand. It was a strappy top in aquamarine, which came with a silk skirt in myriad complementary colours.

Rummaging further into the case, she found a selection of similar clothes. Short, flirty summer dresses, skirts, T-shirts, even a very brief bikini.

Spreading them out on the bed, Katy stared at them helplessly. They were the sort of clothes she would never have selected for herself. The woman who wore them would be confident of her feminine appeal and happy to flaunt it. *But she wasn't that sort of woman.*

Or was she?

Without intending to, she found herself picking up the strappy top and holding it against her as she looked at herself in the mirror. The colour seemed to intensify the blue of her eyes and the soft blush of her complexion.

She smiled, suddenly feeling like a little girl dressing up.

Why shouldn't she wear it? She wasn't speaking at the conference. In fact, she wasn't doing anything except listening to other people and learning. Apart from Jago, no one knew who she was. She didn't have to create an impression. She didn't need to worry about being taken seriously.

Telling herself that wanting to look good had absolutely nothing to do with the fact that she was spending the evening with Jago, she tugged the top over her head and frowned as she noticed the way it clung to the roundness of her breasts. For someone who usually wore loose shirts in nondescript colours it seemed incredibly daring.

Feeling ridiculously light-headed, she pulled on the skirt and rummaged for something to put on her feet, smiling as she found a pair of Libby's favourite designer shoes at the bottom of the case.

The heels were ridiculous and she'd probably break an ankle, but they matched the outfit perfectly.

Having brushed her hair until it poured down her back in a silken curtain, she risked a glance in the mirror.

She looked…different.

Bold. Feminine.

Sexy.

Not at all the way she'd have chosen to look for an evening out with a man as lethally attractive as Jago Rodriguez.

What was she doing?

Jago strode into the hotel lobby at five minutes to seven and made straight for the lifts.

When he'd written the note he'd been banking on the fact that Katy would be feeling vulnerable in a strange city. He was acutely aware that nothing else would have induced her to spend an evening with him so he was bracing himself for yet another rejection when he rapped on her door.

The door opened and he found himself frozen into immobility.

She looked stunning.

She was wearing something stretchy and blue that brought out the colour of her eyes and clung provocatively to the soft curve of her breasts. Her skirt was long enough to be decent but short enough to reveal a tempting expanse of her perfect legs. And as for her hair…

Feeling himself harden in an instinctive male reaction, Jago fought the temptation to power her back inside the bedroom and lay her down on the nearest suitable surface.

Conscious that he was staring, he made a supreme effort to pull himself together, wondering what had happened in the few hours since he'd last seen her.

As long as he'd known her, Katy had always tried to conceal her looks. *But not tonight.* Tonight for some reason she'd chosen to put her incredible beauty on display.

'You're staring.'

Her husky tones penetrated the haze of lustful male appreciation and he jerked his eyes to hers, noticing with no small degree of satisfaction that she was trembling.

'And who can blame me? You look stunning, *querida.'*

'Do you think so?' She glanced at him and then looked down at her feet. 'To be honest, I'm not sure if I can even walk in these. They were Libby's choice. The minx switched the contents of my suitcase.'

'Did she now?' Jago's eyes narrowed as he contemplated the meaning behind those words.

So he wasn't the only one who was trying to unveil the real Katy.

Her cheeks were pink and she smiled apologetically. 'I don't usually wear heels. I dwarf whoever I'm with.'

'Then it's fortunate that I'm tall,' he said with amusement, extending an arm. 'For the record, I'm glad you've left your hair loose.'

She gave a wry smile. 'I thought it would save you the trouble of pulling it down.'

'Very wise.' His eyes gleamed. 'Shall we go?'

She locked the room and followed him into the lift. 'Are we going to the conference dinner?'

'No.' He could see the taut outline of her nipples under the clinging fabric of her top and he had to stop himself pushing her against the side of the lift and taking her in the most primitive way possible. His whole body ached with the strength of his arousal and he closed his eyes and tried to apply logic to the situation.

He was about to walk across a hotel lobby in full view of a large number of staff, not to mention guests, and if he didn't think about something other than Katy spread beneath him then he was going to be arrested.

'So where are we going?'

How could she be so totally unaware of the effect she had on him? Was she really still as innocent as she'd been at eighteen? Jago gritted his teeth and concentrated hard on the buttons of the lifts. Surely they were suitably boring?

'I'm taking you to see the real Seville.'

The lift doors opened and Jago ran a hand through his dark hair, feeling thoroughly out of control. His feelings intensified as he intercepted the appreciative male stares that Katy received as they walked out of the hotel. Growling under his breath, Jago took her hand possessively.

The down side of her looking so stunning was that everyone else thought she looked stunning, too. For the first time he had some understanding as to why she chose to conceal her beauty. Katy could stop traffic in the dark.

They walked for a short distance and then he pushed open the door of a well-known bar.

Katy looked at him in confusion. 'Are we eating here?'

Jago laughed. 'This is a tapas bar, *querida*. In Spain we eat dinner late in the evening. Tapas is a way of preventing us from dying of hunger. It's an integral part of Spanish culture.'

'Oh.' She looked interested and pleased and settled herself on a stool by the bar, looking round her with wide-eyed enthusiasm. 'I've had tapas in London but I don't suppose it's the same thing.'

'Similar, but each bar here will have its own speciality,' he told her, gesturing to some of the dishes that kept appearing.

'Translate, please.' She looked at him expectantly and he fought the impulse to kiss her.

That was going to have to wait until they were back in the privacy of their hotel.

With considerable difficulty he turned his attention to the food. 'Do you trust me to order?'

She nodded and he spoke in rapid Spanish, selecting a number of dishes that he thought she'd enjoy.

'This is a variety of olive grown in Seville,' he told her, lifting an olive towards her soft mouth. 'It's called Manzanilla.'

She tasted it and smiled. 'It's delicious.'

'And this is Chorizo—a spicy sausage.'

Katy nodded. 'I've seen it in the supermarket at home.'

'Not the same,' Jago assured her with an exaggerated shudder. 'This is fat and juicy, try it.'

She chewed slowly and he suppressed a groan as he watched her lips move. Food became unbearably erotic when Katy was involved.

'You look great in that outfit,' he said gruffly, helping himself to some food. 'Libby knows what will suit you.'

'She also knows that I never wear this sort of thing,' Katy confessed, glancing down at herself with a rueful expression. 'I feel...conspicuous. As if I'm shouting, "Look at Me," at the top of my voice.'

'Katy, you're the most beautiful woman I've ever seen,' he said dryly, 'and the same goes for every man in this room. You could be wearing a bin bag and people would stare.'

She looked shaken by his compliment and he resisted the urge to yank her off the bar stool and carry her back to the hotel.

For a minute she didn't reply and then she lifted her eyes to his and he saw the sadness there.

'But sometimes people don't see any further than the way I look.' Her voice was so soft he had to strain to hear her.

'It's true that the human race has an uncomfortable tendency to judge on appearances,' he agreed, forking another morsel into his mouth. 'But being beautiful must surely work to your advantage.'

She shook her head. 'Not always. Take being a doctor. To begin with, all anyone sees is my blonde hair and the fact that I'm so tall. That's why I wear flat shoes—'

'And glasses,' he finished, and she nodded.

'The glasses were Alex's idea. He has this thing that women look more academic if they wear glasses, and I think he's right. If I scrape my hair back, wear something sober and put on my glasses, people take me more seriously.'

Jago decided against confessing that he wanted to drag her into bed whatever she was wearing. He found her naïvety incredibly sweet.

'Is that why you gave up modelling?'

'Partly. It was so shallow. And incredibly boring.' She pulled a face. 'And I hated the falseness of it all—people just wanting to be seen with you because you were a model.'

Thinking about it, it didn't surprise him that she'd given it up. He'd been out with enough models in his time to know that she was much too gentle and sweet to survive long in such a cut-throat profession.

Suddenly he found himself fascinated by every tiny detail of her life and he realised that they were talking about things they'd never talked about before. Eleven years ago their relationship had been based on a searing mutual attraction that had pretty much eclipsed all other aspects of their relationship. Which was why he'd been so hasty to believe her father. If he'd known more about her thoughts and feelings, he would have known that such an action would have been totally out of character.

'So when did you decide on medical school?'

'When Alex started talking about it.' She took a sip of her drink. 'It sounded so exciting and my exam results were almost as good as his so I didn't see why I couldn't do it, too.'

'But your father objected.'

Her face lost its colour and he felt his shoulders tense. Was she really so afraid of her father?

'He had other plans for me.'

'And he didn't think that you should be allowed to decide your future for yourself?'

'That isn't the way my father works, as you should know by now. He's very controlling.'

Jago frowned. 'Is he the same with Alex?'

'He's the same with everyone, but he has absolutely no influence over my brother.' She gave a wry smile. 'My father has met his match in Alex. They clash like herd bulls fighting over territory.'

'And Libby?'

Katy gave a rueful smile. 'We each handle him in a different way. Libby takes the confrontational approach and provokes him constantly so the atmosphere is pretty charged when they're together.'

'Whereas you go for the path of least conflict?'

She hesitated. 'Let's just say that over the years I've learned that it's better not to antagonise him. But that doesn't mean that I don't stand up for myself on the big issues.' She tilted her head to one side and her blonde hair shone under the lights. 'What about you? Why did you go into medicine?'

Jago made a huge effort and dragged his eyes away from her hair. It was confession time. Just how honest did he dare be with her? For the first time since they'd met again, she seemed to be relaxing with him and he certainly didn't want to destroy that. On the other hand, he was rapidly coming to the conclusion that having secrets definitely didn't work. Especially not with someone as honest as Katy. 'I'd been thinking about it for a while,' he hedged, and then he caught her puzzled glance and let out a long breath. 'You're not going to like what I tell you, *querida*.'

Her blue eyes widened, and he reflected grimly that telling the truth certainly wasn't the easy option.

'After he showed me the photographs, your father suggested that it would be better for everybody if I left the company and started afresh somewhere else,' he said curtly, aware that the facts looked uncomfortably incriminating. 'You have to understand I was very hurt by the photographs. Had I stayed with the company it was inevitable that we would have run into each other again. I was only too pleased when your father encouraged me to leave.'

There was a long silence as she made the connection.

'He paid you off, didn't he?' Her voice was little more than a whisper. 'He showed you the photographs and then he paid you to leave.'

She was obviously more attuned to her father's tricks than he'd been.

'At the time I thought of it as a generous severance package,' he admitted not quite levelly, all too aware of the interpretation she would put on the facts.

Pale and taut, she slid off the bar stool and looked at him blankly.

'I'd already decided to train as a doctor and he offered me a good package,' Jago said, feeling the tension spread through his shoulders. 'It's standard practice in many companies. At the time I didn't think it had anything to do with my relationship with you. It was a business issue.'

'Not to my father. He didn't dare risk having you anywhere near me because he knew you'd find out what he'd done.' It was almost as if she was talking to herself and he felt maximum discomfort for the part he'd played in the destruction of their relationship eleven years previously. 'He was determined to keep us apart.'

Jago found himself unable to argue with that. Even he was stunned by the level of manipulation to which her father had stooped and he thought of himself as a fairly cynical guy.

Katy stared at him in disbelief. 'You accepted money from him in return for an agreement not to see me again.'

He stiffened. 'That's not true. Your name was never mentioned in connection with the money. That was a business issue.'

'You're deluding yourself.' Her eyes glistened with hurt. 'He paid you off, Jago. And you took the money.'

'There seemed no reason not to.'

'You were already rich, Jago. I know that. How much money was enough?' she said shakily. 'How much did it cost him to get you to walk away from me?'

Jago swore softly in Spanish. 'It wasn't like that.'

'My life fell apart when you left but you were so self-absorbed, so wrapped up in your own emotions and feelings that you didn't stop to think about me even for a minute. You took the money and ran. Literally.'

Aware that the warmth of the atmosphere had plunged several degrees below zero, and extremely disconcerted by her less than flattering interpretation of the facts, Jago attempted to salvage the situation.

'We were having a pleasant evening before we started talking about your father,' he said calmly. 'Can we just forget it?'

'I don't think so.' Her breathing was rapid and she lifted her chin. 'You've just reminded me why I shouldn't have said yes to going out with you tonight. You are arrogant and selfish and we don't share the same beliefs and values. Goodnight, Jago.'

Reaching the frustrating conclusion that women were definitely from another planet, Jago made an abortive attempt to prevent her from leaving but she was too quick for him, heading for the door as fast as she could reasonably manage in Libby's ridiculously high-heeled shoes.

CHAPTER NINE

STILL sniffing back tears, Katy slid out of her skirt and dragged off the clingy blue top that she'd put on with such breathless anticipation. Feeling in need of a warm drink, she ordered from room service and then padded into the bathroom in her underwear to run herself a bath.

Of all the men on the planet, she'd chosen to fall in love with someone so totally wrapped up in himself that he didn't even know there was a world around him.

She emptied the entire contents of the miniature bubble bath bottle into the water and watched while it frothed.

Jago could be so charming when he wanted to be, but it was all part of his strategy for getting her back into his bed. And she'd nearly fallen for it.

Removing her underwear, she stepped into the water, reflecting that the sooner she learned to apply cynicism to her judgement of people, the happier she'd be. For a short time she'd been fooled by his trick of seeming so interested in her family and her feelings, and it had only been the shocking discovery that he'd actually accepted money from her father to remove himself from her life that had reminded her that this was the man who'd given absolutely no thought to her feelings whatsoever.

They said that everyone had their price, but it was agonising to realise that it was true.

In his own way, Jago shared many traits with her father. He was driven and ruthless and all he thought about was money.

It didn't matter how much she loved him. She'd be crazy to start a relationship with him again.

Hearing a knock on the door, she stepped out of the bath and wrapped herself in a fluffy white bathrobe. She opened the door to receive the drink she'd ordered and found Jago lounging there, his expression hidden under lowered lashes.

'I've come to the conclusion that we should both stop talking, *querida*,' he drawled, planting a lean brown hand in the middle of the door to prevent her shutting it in his face. 'Words can so easily be misinterpreted, which is why we're moving on to actions.'

She backed away from him, acutely conscious of her still damp, naked body underneath the softness of her white, fluffy bathrobe.

'I was having a bath.'

'I can tell. The ends of your hair are wet,' he murmured, his dark gaze roaming with appreciation over the golden strands.

Without her even being aware of how it happened, he was inside her room with the door firmly locked behind him.

Paralysed by the hot, quivering excitement that erupted inside her, she reminded herself repeatedly that he was a selfish, egotistical, thoroughly objectionable male who would break her heart again if she were to be so stupid as to let him.

'There is just no way you're marrying Freddie,' he imparted thickly, hauling her against him with all the finesse of a wild animal. In fact, she realised with some considerable degree of shock, Jago didn't seem controlled at all. The hand that brushed her damp hair away from her brow was decidedly unsteady, and his breathing was far from even.

His mouth fused with hers, his kiss rough and demanding, and despite all her resolutions Katy just melted.

She kissed him back, her fingers resting on the hard muscle of his chest and then sliding upwards round his strong neck. Wild excitement exploded inside her. He felt *so* good.

He cupped her face, his tongue teasing hers, exploring every part of her sensitive mouth, and suddenly she found she was shivering.

He lifted his head with a reluctant groan, and hugged her close. 'Are you cold?'

'I'm not cold.' She looked at him with helpless longing, knowing that she ought to tell him to leave, but totally unable to do it.

His mouth descended to hers again and this time she felt his hands on her shoulders, divesting her of her fluffy bathrobe with electrifying efficiency.

'Jago!' Suddenly aware that she was naked and he was still fully clothed, she pulled away from him, but he swept her into his arms and deposited her on the bed before she could even consider covering herself.

'You have the most incredible body,' he muttered, fumbling with the buttons of his shirt with considerably less finesse than he'd shown when he'd undressed *her*.

His shirt hit the floor and she stared, feasting on the sight of his muscular chest and flat abdomen.

'You could help me,' Jago suggested huskily, but Katy found she couldn't move.

She just lay there, watching him, flattened to the bed by an excitement and anticipation so intense that it was almost painful.

She wanted him. *Badly.*

Every single part of her body ached for him to possess her.

Gloriously naked, Jago moved over her with the lithe movement of a jungle cat and all the confidence of a male with the upper hand.

'Are you going to speak, *querida*?' His soft, teasing tone

made her insides melt and she shook her head, her eyes dropping to his incredible sexy mouth.

She was beyond speech.

With a soft laugh he lowered his head to within an inch of her mouth, hovering tantalisingly close, allowing their breath to mingle but still not touching her.

A slow burn began inside her and she shifted her hips, desperate to relieve the tension.

His attention drawn by her wanton movements, he gave an earthy groan and crushed her mouth under his.

His kiss was hot and hard and intensely sexual and she clutched at him desperately, writhing against him in an attempt to get closer still.

Breathing hard, he detached himself and worked his way down her body, using his incredibly skilled fingers to torment the hardened peaks of her full breasts.

She arched and cried out in desperation and his mouth replaced his clever fingers, his tongue teasing the damp tips with an erotic expertise that made her squirm.

She could feel his breath warming her and then he sucked her into the darkness of his mouth and she gasped in disbelief as she felt the sensation deep in her pelvis.

Instinctively she parted her thighs and immediately his fingers were there, exploring and teasing her in the most intimate way possible. He knew exactly how to touch her to create maximum sensation and soon she was beyond modesty or control.

She felt totally wanton, agitated and feverish, and he continued to torture her with pleasure, teasing her until she gasped his name in an agony of longing, desperate for him to give her the fulfillment she craved.

Driven totally wild by his leisurely exploration of her body, she twisted under him in a frenzy of almost unbearable anticipation, but he shifted his weight and held her still, refusing to give her the satisfaction she sought.

'Jago, *please*...' Her whole body was burning with erotic

sensation and she was sobbing now, begging for him to stop
tormenting them both. The excitement was intolerable, a fiery
ache deep inside her that threatened to consume her whole
being with its intensity.

He stared down into her flushed face, his eyes dark with a
depth of arousal that made her catch her breath.

'Jago…'

'*Tell me you want me,*' he said thickly, stroking her silken hair
away from her damp skin. 'I need to hear you say it, *querida*.'

Trapped by the raw emotion she saw in his eyes, she could
barely speak.

'I want you—*now.*'

He muttered something in Spanish and slid a strong arm
under her hips, moving her under him. Her breath came in
pants as she felt the silken thrust of his arousal against the very
heart of her and then he drove into her with a hard thrust that
brought a gasp of ecstasy to her lips.

She cried out his name and he plunged deeper still and suddenly all she could feel was heat.

The scorch of his mouth as it covered hers.

The burn of his body as he moved with a pagan rhythm that
drove her to a level of excitement that she'd never experienced
before.

And the fire within her.

Desperate to be closer still, she arched against him and he
gave an earthy groan and withdrew before sliding into her again
with a force that made her sob with ecstasy.

She was no longer in control of anything. She wasn't aware
of anything except the explosive excitement that consumed her
body as he thrust hard into her with a rhythmic force that drove
her to a state of such intense arousal that it seemed too much to
bear. Arching against him, she slid her hands over the smooth
muscle of his back, urging him closer still, her body screaming
for completion. And then suddenly, when she thought she could
bear it no longer, he sent her flying into a shattering climax

which seemed to last for ever, her whole body unravelling in an ecstasy intensified by the shuddering throb of his own release.

Completely wiped out by the experience, Katy lay still, aware of the pounding of his heart against hers, of the damp warmth of their bodies as they clung together so intimately.

His breathing still uneven, he shifted his weight and rolled onto his back, taking her with him, and suddenly she was hideously aware of just how out of control she'd been.

She squeezed her eyes tightly shut in a rush of embarrassment.

What had happened to her?

For goodness' sake, she'd virtually begged the man!

Mortified by the intensity of her response to him, she rolled away from him, only to find herself dragged back against his hard, muscular body.

'*Stop* trying to create distance between us,' he murmured huskily, sliding his fingers through the length of her hair with all the smug satisfaction of a man who'd just got exactly what he'd wanted.

Desperation spread through her body like a flood. Would she always be this vulnerable to him?

'Sex doesn't change anything between us.'

'Shut up,' he groaned, rolling her under him and proceeding to kiss her again. 'You *definitely* talk too much.'

So instead of talking, she found herself kissing him back and this time he took her with agonising slowness, each slow, deliberate thrust designed to drive her to the very heights of desperation. Unable to believe that he could arouse her again so quickly, Katy closed her eyes and gave herself up to sensation, totally unable to control her response.

'You feel so good,' Jago groaned, and her eyes flew wide and clashed with his as he thrust into her with surprising gentleness.

Transfixed by the look of male appreciation that she caught in his eyes, her stomach tumbled over itself and she felt swamped with love. He was just so amazing in bed. It would have been so very easy to believe that he loved her.

She felt her body tingle as he aroused her yet again to a state of mindless abandonment, but yet again he chose to delay satisfaction until their bodies were both screaming with unfulfilled excitement before driving them both, gasping, to a ferocious climax.

The first shafts of morning sunlight were fingering their way through the open window when she finally fell asleep, and when she awoke he was gone.

After a day of back-to-back presentations and discussions, during which she'd watched with helpless hunger as Jago had wowed the extremely high-powered audience with his cool intellect, Katy returned to the hotel and opened the door of her room.

She was immediately assaulted by the powerful scent of flowers. And not just one bunch of flowers. Her room seemed to contain the entire year's stock of an average florist.

Taken aback, she walked into the room, her eyes focusing on a card which had been left on the table.

She picked it up and read it.

'You look very beautiful when you're asleep. J.'

They were from Jago.

Jago, who'd never sent her flowers before.

Still reeling over the sheer volume of blooms, she heard the door of her room close suddenly and turned to find him standing there.

Her heart stumbled in her chest and she felt her whole body react to his powerful presence.

He was staggeringly good-looking.

To even *think* that she could resist him was to totally underestimate the impact of his explosive brand of sexuality.

He removed his jacket with a shrug of his broad shoulders and jerked off his tie. 'It's been a very long and very boring

day, *querida*,' he murmured huskily, dropping the tie on the bed
with careless disregard for its future appearance. 'Concentrating on my slides was a formidable challenge. All I could think
of was getting back to the hotel and being with you.'

Katy stared at him helplessly.

All he could think about was sex. He was just *so* basic and
she really ought to be protesting, but already he'd undone the
buttons on his shirt and her mouth dried as the fabric fell apart
to reveal a tantalising glimpse of his tanned, muscular chest.
Unable to help herself, her eyes traced the dark hairs as they
travelled down and into the waistband of his trousers.

'If you want to help, please, feel free,' he teased her gently,
and she felt the colour touch her cheeks.

'Jago, we ought to talk.'

They hadn't resolved anything and she just *knew* he was
going to hurt her again. After all, never, despite all his com-
mands that she give up Freddie, had he once implied that he
felt anything for her other than lust.

She had to tell him that, despite what had happened between
them the night before, nothing had changed.

She still had no intention of renewing her relationship with
him in the long term.

'Talking never seems to clear the air between us,' he pointed
out thickly, moving towards her with effortless elegance and
tipping her backwards onto the bed.

He came down on top of her, confident and fully in control,
and she realised helplessly that he was fighting the battle with
the strongest weapon in his armoury. His ability to excite her
to a state of mindless desperation.

And he was winning. Despite all her reservations about the
future, the truth was that this was *now*, and she wanted him
so much.

Suddenly losing her natural shyness, she stroked her fingers
through the curling hair on his chest, loving the feel of his hard

muscles. He was just so strong. Her breathing jerky, she followed the line of silky dark hair with the tips of her fingers, pausing as it vanished into the waistband of his trousers. She felt him suck in a breath and realised that for once he seemed uncertain.

With a smile that was pure female seduction, she dealt with the rest of his clothing, and if it wasn't done with quite the finesse he'd managed, neither of them seemed to notice.

Certainly not Jago, whose shocked exclamation had turned to a groan of earthy satisfaction as she explored him with incredible intimacy. Aware of the reaction of his body, she drove him wild with her mouth and tongue until he dragged her away from him with a rough groan.

He looked at her with a glazed expression and she derived considerable satisfaction from the look of stunned amazement on his handsome face. He looked positively shell-shocked. Feeling immensely satisfied that she'd finally managed to make him lose control, she leaned forward to kiss him and he caught her in lean, strong hands and moved her so that she was straddling him.

Still breathing heavily, he slid her flimsy dress up to her hips and moved the dampened silk of her panties to one side with lean fingers.

Shocked by the revelation that he didn't even intend to undress her, Katy trembled with anticipation, a gasp of helpless excitement wrenched from her as she felt him position her to receive him.

She felt the silken throb of his erection against her and then her eyes flew wide as he slid into her, hard and strong, holding her writhing hips still as he ground deep inside her.

Cheeks flushed, lips parted, Katy moaned as she felt him move, unbelievably aroused by the force of his possession.

It was over quickly, both of them reaching a climax of such unbelievable intensity that they clung together for endless mo-

ments before Jago smoothed her tangled blonde hair away from
her face and snuggled her in his arms.

She closed her eyes in disbelief, hardly knowing herself.

'You've never done that before,' he said softly, shifting
slightly so that she was forced to look at him. 'You were always much too shy.'

She knew it was true and felt hot colour touch her cheeks.
Somehow making love with Jago felt different now that she
was older.

At eighteen she'd been hideously self-conscious and gauche
and she was only now beginning to realise how careful he'd
been with her, how much he must have been holding back. Their
love-making had possessed none of the wildness that he'd displayed in the last twenty-four hours.

He touched her cheek with gentle fingers, his expression
thoughtful. 'We will be checking out tomorrow,' he told her.
'We're visiting my family.'

She stilled in his arms. His family?

Jago always avoided questions about his family and she knew
better than to ask.

Why was he taking her to meet them?

And why was she excited at the prospect?

This wasn't what she wanted, was it? Whatever she felt for
him, she didn't *want* to renew her relationship with Jago.

She closed her eyes tightly, knowing that she should send
him back to his room and go straight home to England without meeting his family.

But how could she when she was loving every minute of
their time together?

Why shouldn't she just enjoy herself for now? Why shouldn't
she just make the most of this time in Spain, she reasoned, ignoring the tiny voice in her head that warned her this wasn't
real.

She'd have plenty of time to face reality when they returned
to England.

* * *

They left the following afternoon, immediately after the last lecture.

Having cleared her room and packed, Katy made her way to the foyer of the hotel, intending to check out before going with Jago.

The hotel manager met her at the marble reception desk. 'Everything has been taken care of,' he said in heavily accented English.

Katy stared at him in confusion. What did he mean—taken care of? How could her bill have been taken care of?

The hotel manager suddenly looked over her shoulder and smiled warmly. Following his gaze, Katy turned to find Jago approaching. Just looking at him made her legs turn to jelly. He was so good-looking it was almost indecent. Surely no one man should be blessed with such incredibly good looks, she thought helplessly. Didn't he have a single flaw? He was wearing jeans and a black polo shirt that emphasised his dark, exotic brand of masculinity.

Reaching her side, he gave her a brief smile and then turned his attention to the hotel manager, conversing in rapid Spanish which she found totally incomprehensible.

The two men obviously enjoyed a good relationship and suddenly they were descended on by staff who carried her luggage towards the door of the hotel, leaving them to follow.

'You shouldn't have had to carry your case downstairs,' Jago muttered as he strode towards the entrance of the hotel, leaving her struggling to keep up with him.

She looked at him with some amusement. 'Jago, I can carry my own case!'

'Not in this hotel,' he growled, pushing open the swing doors and snapping his fingers.

Katy's mouth fell open as a stunning black Ferrari pulled up at the entrance.

Accepting the keys with a nod of thanks, Jago shot her a sat-isfied smile. 'Your carriage, *senorita*.'

In awe of the sleek lines of the beautiful car, she slid inside, feeling herself enveloped by the sumptuous leather interior.

'Wow...'

He slid into the driver's seat next to her and smiled at her childish exclamation.

'I agree,' he said, laughter in his voice. 'This car is defi-nitely "wow".'

She couldn't resist teasing him. 'Boys with toys, Jago?'

'Of course.'

'Everyone's staring,' she muttered, clearly conscious of the looks they were receiving.

'That's why I bought the car,' he drawled. 'It increases my street cred no end.'

He pulled out into the traffic and she looked at him curi-ously. 'It's yours?'

'It is mine. I keep it here for my trips home.'

He kept a Ferrari just for his trips home. She couldn't contain her questions any longer. 'Do you often come home?'

'As often as I can.'

She rolled her eyes at his answer, which was typical Jago. 'Do you ever give anything away?'

His smile was totally unapologetic. 'As little as possible.' There was a silence as he negotiated a particularly busy junc-tion and then he spoke again. 'I come back to Spain about once every two months—sometimes more if I have to.'

'To stay with your family?'

He hesitated. 'I have business interests in Seville.'

'But you're a doctor.'

He smiled. 'How can you be the child of Charles Westerling and be so totally lacking in commercial awareness?'

She blushed and looked away. She hated business and found her father's approach to business ruthless and distasteful.

'Working with your father taught me just how fragile financial success can be,' Jago said quietly. 'After I left his company I used the money I'd made to invest in various business ventures in Spain. I own the hotel where we just stayed.'

He owned it?

Katy's head spun round and she stared at him. 'Is that why I had such a fabulous room?'

'You liked it?' He gave her a smile that was thoroughly male. 'Good. I thought you would enjoy it.'

'And somebody had settled my bill.'

'There was no bill, *querida*,' he said smoothly. 'You were my guest.'

She digested this information. 'Where did the other delegates stay?'

He gave a careless shrug. 'At various hotels around the city.'

So he'd made sure that they were staying separately from the others.

She took a deep breath. 'The money you invested—'

'Was not the money your father gave me as a severance package,' he drawled, his voice low and deep. 'I can read you like a book. I used that for something entirely separate, as I hope to show you in a few hours.'

Not wanting to threaten the delicate truce between them, Katy relaxed back in her seat and enjoyed the Spanish countryside.

They drove along dusty roads, passing olive groves and almond trees, and Katy suddenly felt happier than she had for ages.

Whatever he'd done in the past, she couldn't help loving him and just being with him made her feel good.

They'd been driving for about an hour when they approached a small village and Katy noticed a crowd gathered by the side of the road.

'Stop, Jago!' she cried out, and put a hand on his arm. 'Something's wrong. Someone's on the ground—there must have been an accident.'

Jago responded immediately, pulling into the side of the road. In an instant Katy was out of the car.

A young woman was lying on the pavement, clutching her throat, struggling for air.

Her heart thumping frantically against her chest, Katy dropped to her knees, making a diagnosis without even the briefest hesitation. She knew instantly what she was seeing.

She'd seen it before.

'Get away from her and give her some air,' she said, aware that they were looking at her blankly. Fortunately, at that moment Jago appeared by her side and spoke in fluent Spanish. The crowd parted instantly.

'She's in anaphylactic shock,' Katy muttered. 'Her lips and tongue are swollen and she's wheezing badly. Ask them what happened. Has she been stung?'

There was a rapid exchange of Spanish and then Jago hunkered down beside her. 'They say that she was stung by a bee a few minutes ago.' He sucked in a breath as he looked at the young woman. 'She's bad and I don't have anything in my car.'

'My handbag.' Katy looked up at him, her blonde hair flopping over her face. She scraped it away with an impatient hand. 'Get my handbag, quickly.'

Without arguing, Jago did as she requested, returning in seconds with the bag she'd left in the footwell of the car.

She snapped it open and rummaged to find what she needed.

'Where was she stung?'

She addressed her question to Jago, who translated quickly and then turned back to Katy.

'Above her eye.'

'We've got to get that sting out.' Katy located the sting and then removed it quickly with some forceps that she always kept in her bag.

'We need to give her some adrenaline.' She reached into her bag again and removed a small box that she always carried. 'I presume someone has called an ambulance?'

'It's on its way,' Jago said, looking at her in stunned disbelief. 'What have you got there?'

'Adrenaline and hydrocortisone,' Katy muttered. 'I always carry it.'

Aware of the horrified murmurings of the crowd, she jabbed the woman in the arm and delivered the adrenaline as fast as she could. Then she picked up the other syringe, brisk and competent.

She knew exactly what needed to be done and she knew that it needed to be done quickly.

'Can you squeeze her arm for me?'

Jago obliged and Katy searched for a vein and then injected the hydrocortisone.

Dropping the empty syringe back into the box, she then moved the woman into the recovery position with Jago's help.

'Her breathing's improving, but just to be on the safe side I'm going to give her some chlorpheniramine as well.' She rummaged in her bag again, aware that Jago was watching her with amazement.

'She's starting to recover.' He checked the woman's pulse. 'This is unbelievable. Do you carry an entire drug cabinet in your handbag?'

Despite the seriousness of the situation, she managed a smile. 'I happen to be an expert in this particular emergency. There's nothing else we can do now. She needs high-dose oxygen. I wish that ambulance would hurry up.'

Even as the words left her mouth they saw the ambulance approaching.

'She needs to be admitted,' Katy said, dropping the remains of the injections back into the box and returning it to her handbag. 'Twenty per cent of patients relapse within eight to twelve hours. Better make sure they know that.'

The moment the words left her mouth she coloured. Why was she telling him that? Jago would almost certainly be aware of the fact.

Jago was speaking to the ambulance crew in Spanish and suddenly an oxygen cylinder appeared.

By now the young woman was sitting up, looking decidedly shaky and pale but very much alive.

An older woman burst into tears and flung her arms around a startled Katy.

'She's the woman's mother,' Jago said softly, a strange expression in his dark eyes. 'She says that you saved her daughter's life and she will always be in your debt.'

He spoke to the woman and she nodded and gave Katy a final hug before releasing her.

Suddenly the whole crowd was swarming round her and Katy looked at Jago in mute appeal.

He grinned and shouldered his way through to her. 'You're a bit of a heroine.'

'I just did what anyone would have done,' she mumbled, and he lifted an eyebrow.

'Most people don't carry an entire drug cabinet around with them.'

She smiled self-consciously and watched as they loaded the woman into the ambulance. 'Can we go now?'

'If that's what you want.'

He took her hand and led her through the crowd and she slid into the Ferrari with relief, feeling her limbs start to shake.

'Are you all right?' He settled himself in the driver's seat and frowned at her. 'You look very pale all of a sudden.'

She took a deep breath and gave him a wobbly smile. 'I think it just hit me that it could have had a different ending. She had a very severe reaction.'

'She would have died if it hadn't been for you,' Jago said roughly, rubbing a hand over his face and letting out a long breath. 'All right. Enlighten me. Why the hell do you carry all those drugs in your handbag?'

'Because of Libby.'

His eyes narrowed. 'Libby?'

'My sister is severely allergic to bee stings,' Katy told him. 'She carries adrenaline herself but I've got so used to worrying about her whenever we're out together in summer that I've just got used to carrying a stock of drugs. Alex does the same.'

Jago shook his head. 'Unbelievable.' He surveyed her with amusement and no small degree of admiration. 'I thought you were no good at immediate care?'

A warm feeling spread inside her and she flushed, pleased by his praise. 'I just happened to know about anaphylactic shock because of Libby.'

'Well, you undoubtedly saved that girl's life,' he said softly. 'I certainly don't carry adrenaline in my boot, although from now on I think I might do just that.'

Two hours from Seville, Jago turned down a dusty track and Katy saw a beautiful traditional Spanish farmhouse.

'Oh—it's beautiful.' The dusty bricks were a warm shade of apricot and the dwelling was surrounded by a terrace shaded by vines.

The front door opened and she recognised Jago's mother Maria, the woman who had been her parents' housekeeper for several years.

She stood back while they greeted each other, wondering what Maria would make of her presence.

Would she be surprised to see her?

Releasing Jago and wiping her eyes, Maria caught sight of her and her face brightened. She said something to Jago in Spanish and then stepped forward and embraced Katy affectionately.

'As beautiful as ever.' She reached up a hand and touched Katy's cheek. 'You are so very fair.' She frowned at her son. 'You must be careful not to let her burn in this hot sun.'

Touched by the warmth of her welcome, Katy followed them inside the spacious farmhouse, through a traditional kitchen and out onto a large terrace shaded by vines. Sunlight dappled the long wooden table, which was laid for dinner.

A couple were seated at the table and Jago greeted them and introduced them to Katy.

'Juan and Rosita Ruiz.' He took Katy's hand and pulled her forward. 'My aunt and uncle. I'm afraid they speak very little English.'

'Hola.' Katy returned their greeting shyly, using her very limited Spanish, and soon she was seated at the table, enjoying the warmth of their hospitality.

They ate plump olives and lamb roasted in herbs, and drank the warmest, most delicious red wine she'd ever tasted, and soon she found herself relaxing.

Totally at home in her new surroundings, Katy found herself sneaking looks at Jago, marvelling at the change in him.

He lounged in his chair, long legs stretched out in front of him, more relaxed than she'd ever seen him, switching smoothly between Spanish and English so that he could communicate with everyone.

By the time they'd finished dinner it was late and Katy fell into bed exhausted.

She awoke the next morning and found Jago already in the kitchen, drinking coffee.

'Good morning.' He rose to his feet and gestured to the food on the table. 'Toasted bread, home-made jam and *café con leche*—milky coffee. Help yourself.'

She settled herself at the table, trying not to look at the dark shadow of his hard jaw. Her constant awareness of him was so intense that it was making her jumpy.

'I missed you last night.' He put a hand over hers and suddenly she had butterflies in her stomach.

'Jago—'

'My family are very traditional and I would in no way offend them by broadcasting our relationship,' he said quietly, pouring her coffee and handing it to her. 'On the other hand, if you are going to carry on looking at me with that totally dizzy expression on your face, we're going to have to go and find ourselves a barn, *querida*.'

She blushed hotly at his teasing reminder of their relationship eleven years earlier. After that first encounter they'd continued to meet in the barn and the surrounding fields, often spending the entire night entwined together.

She had too many knots in her stomach to eat and he shot her an amused look and stood up.

'If you've finished, go and put a hat on. We're going for a walk and my mother is worried that you'll damage that delicate English skin of yours.'

Wondering where he was taking her, Katy found the pretty hat that Libby had tucked into her case and joined him on the terrace.

There was no sign of Maria or Jago's aunt and they left the farmhouse and walked along a dusty track that eventually led to a river. In the early morning sunlight it glistened and danced over boulders and Katy smiled with delight.

'It's beautiful.' It was the clearest water she'd ever seen and she watched it with fascination. 'What a lovely place.'

'The river marks the boundary of our property,' Jago told her, stooping to pick up a stone and tossing it in the water.

She glanced around her, screwing up her eyes against the sun. It was still quite early and yet already she could feel the heat on her skin.

'I love it here.'

'Do you?' He turned her to face him, his eyes suddenly intent. 'I bought it with the money your father gave me when I left the company.' Suddenly his eyes were hard and his fingers tightened on her arm in an almost painful grip. 'When he suggested that I leave, he also made Maria homeless and jobless.'

Shocked by that sudden revelation, Katy felt her mouth dry. At the time she'd been so distraught about her own situation she hadn't thought to question what had happened to her parents' housekeeper. She'd known that her leaving had coincided with Jago's but she'd just assumed that it had been coincidence. How could she have been so naïve?

Suddenly she felt horribly sick. 'My father fired her?'

Jago's eyes were as hard as flint and his mouth tightened. 'Let's just say he made it impossible for her to stay.' He released her and turned to stare at the river. 'Your father was in possession of some information which he knew would hurt my mother.'

Katy's knees were trembling. 'What information?' It was a favourite trick of her father's. He somehow managed to find something on everyone.

Jago didn't respond immediately and the silence seemed to stretch into infinity.

Katy felt her heart plummet uncomfortably. Part of her didn't even want to know what her father had done, but she knew that there had been too many secrets between them already.

'Jago?'

'Maria isn't my mother.' He made the statement in a matter-of-fact voice. 'My real mother had me at nineteen, was married immediately and then proceeded to have affairs with anyone that crossed her path.'

Katy stared at him, mute. Maria wasn't his real mother? His mother had had affairs?

'The people of Andalucia are very traditional. In some ways quite backward,' he said dryly. 'Machismo still rules in this part of Spain.'

Katy found herself holding her breath, knowing that there was more to come.

'My father eventually heard of one of her affairs and he shot her.'

Katy gasped and lifted a hand to her mouth. 'Jago—no!'

'No one thought he meant to do it,' Jago said, his voice strangely flat. 'He was just so crazed with grief that he wasn't rational. When he realised that he'd killed her he turned the gun on himself.'

Shocked into silence, Katy sank down onto a rock and stared at him.

'It created a huge scandal, of course,' Jago said in a lifeless voice. 'I was six years old so I wasn't aware of much, but I realised that suddenly no one seemed to want to play with me.'

She licked her lips. 'So what happened?'

'Fortunately for me, my mother had two sisters who realised that I needed to be taken away if I was ever going to be able to lead a normal life. People in Andalucia have very long memories. Maria moved to England with me and took a job as a housekeeper. It was very brave of her. At the time she spoke hardly any English, but she thought her secret was safe in England.'

'But my father knew about it?'

'Of course.' Jago's mouth tightened and a muscle worked in his lean jaw. 'As you've pointed out before, your father knows everything. He kept the information to himself in case he ever needed it. And, of course, once I showed interest in his daughter, he knew that that time had come. There was no way he wanted that sort of scandal attached to his family.'

'Oh, my God.' Katy stared at him, understanding more clearly why her father had been so determined to keep them apart. A high-profile figure, her father only ever wanted to read good things about himself in the press. At the time she'd thought that his objection had stemmed from the fact that Jago wasn't English and didn't have the right pedigree, but obviously there had been so much more to it than that.

Jago was still talking. 'Once he successfully removed me from your life, he knew that he had to get rid of Maria too or he'd risk me running into you when I visited her.'

Katy shook her head and swallowed hard. 'I never knew. I never knew that Dad made her leave. When I came out of hospital she was gone and I was just told that she'd decided to go back to Spain. I'm so sorry.'

He shrugged dismissively. 'Not your fault and, to be honest, Maria was ready to leave. She wanted to go back home but didn't really have the means.' He gave a short laugh. 'Fortunately, those years working for your father in the bank gave me the means. I bought her this place and she lives here with her other sister and brother-in-law.'

'And the locals?'

'They were apparently impressed with the way she sacrificed her homeland to care for a small, vulnerable child. She's been accepted back into society and lives very happily here.'

Katy was digesting the full implication of his words. 'No wonder you were so upset when you thought I was having an affair.'

He gave a wry smile. 'As I said, *querida*, for me faithfulness is the minimum requirement in a relationship.'

And she could understand why.

He'd grown up with the knowledge that his whole family had been destroyed by the actions of his mother.

For the first time she saw those photographs as he must have seen them.

As the ultimate betrayal.

For a man with such a shocking secret buried in his past, was it really surprising that he'd overreacted?

'I'm sorry,' she whispered. 'I understand now why you reacted so strongly when you saw those photographs.'

He gave a twisted smile. 'As you pointed out, your father was a master at manipulation. He knew exactly how to extract the maximum response from me.'

Numb with despair, Katy looked around her, aware of the calm beauty of her surroundings and yet barely seeing it. 'I'm really so very sorry about everything. And I'm sorry about what my father did to your mother.'

She felt mortified. Embarrassed and horrified at this latest example of her father's utter ruthlessness.

'Your father was very thorough,' Jago observed, the expression in his dark eyes veiled by thick lashes. 'He didn't want me

involved with you and he was prepared to go to any lengths
to prevent it.'

'He succeeded,' Katy said sadly, reflecting on the utter devastation that his actions had caused.

'Maybe not. We seem to have found each other again.' Jago
stepped towards her and cupped her face in his hands. 'You
know that you can't marry Freddie. He is wrong for you, and
if you'd loved him you never would have slept with me.'

Katy almost smiled at the irony of that self-satisfied statement. Only a week ago he had believed her capable of exactly
that. But now she understood his sensitivity in that area.

'I'm not going to marry Freddie,' she said quietly. 'I ended
it that night you came to the flat.'

There was a long silence and when he finally spoke his voice
was hoarse. 'You *did* end it? But you didn't tell me—you let
me think…' He broke off and dragged a hand through his dark
hair. *'Why?'*

She swallowed. 'Because I wanted to keep you at a distance.'

He gave a groan and hauled her against him. 'Have you any
idea what I went through, thinking that you were still going
to marry him? It was torture. And it's never going to happen
again.' He let go of her suddenly and cupped her face in his lean
hands, his eyes fierce. 'I want you to marry *me*.'

Katy stilled, convinced that she must have misheard him.
'Pardon?'

'Perhaps I'll rephrase that.' His voice was low and velvety.
'You are going to marry me.'

Her heart stampeded against her chest wall. 'But why? Why
would you want to marry me?'

There was only the briefest hesitation on his part. 'Because
you and I are good together.'

Katy swallowed back her disappointment. He'd made no
mention of love. Clearly what he'd meant had been that they
were good together in bed.

'Good sex doesn't guarantee a good relationship, Jago.'

He frowned. 'I'm not just talking about the sex. There has always been something between us.' He looked at her warily, clearly out of his depth and struggling to express himself, and she loved him all the more for it.

He was so utterly hopeless at talking about his feelings. And perhaps that was understandable. After such an awful childhood it was hardly surprising that he'd come to rely very much on his own resources.

And he might not love her but *she* loved him.

Couldn't that be enough?

After all, she'd been prepared to marry Freddie without love on either side. Why shouldn't she marry Jago when she loved him so desperately?

She knew that she could never be happy with any other man.

She looked at him shyly. 'You're serious? You really want to marry me?'

In answer Jago lowered his head and kissed her thoroughly.

'I'm going to marry you,' he muttered against her lips. 'As soon as we get back to England. And this time we're going to just do it and not tell your father.'

She opened her mouth to point out that her father was bound to find out at some point, but he hauled her into his arms and all rational thought vanished into the Spanish sun.

CHAPTER TEN

THEY flew home the following day and Katy returned to work that afternoon feeling as though she was walking on air.

She was marrying Jago.

She still couldn't quite believe it.

They'd agreed to keep it quiet until Jago could make the arrangements and she'd readily agreed. After all, she hadn't advertised the fact that her relationship with Freddie had ended and she was more than a little uncomfortable about announcing that she was marrying another man so quickly.

She was checking a set of X-rays when Jago strolled up, dressed in a light grey suit that emphasised the width of his shoulders and the golden sheen of his skin. He looked incredibly handsome and thoroughly fed up.

'I have a meeting with the hospital management about staffing levels,' he murmured grittily, glancing at his watch with obvious irritation. 'I have only one thing to say to them and that is that I need more staff, but doubtless they'll make me sit there for hours, listening to arguments for reducing manpower to skeletal proportions.'

She smiled and then remembered that she had something to tell him. 'I just rang the paediatric ward to check on Molly. Libby says she's doing really well.'

A smile touched his firm mouth. 'That's good news. I'll try and see her on my way to this meeting.'

Katy gazed at him longingly and he gave a low growl and stepped closer.

'Stop looking at me like that or I'll forget where we are and commit an indecent act in a public place.'

She chuckled and pushed him away, glancing round quickly to check that no one had seen them.

'I'll be back as quickly as I can,' he muttered huskily, his mind very clearly not on his work. 'If there's a crisis, call me.'

With a last lingering look at her mouth he strode off down the corridor like a man on a mission, as lithe and agile as a panther and totally back in control.

Katy forced her mind back to work, finished checking the X-rays and then returned to the patient.

'These X-rays are fine, Mrs Maxwell,' she said, reflecting on how much her confidence had grown since she'd started working with Jago. Because he had such high standards, knowing that he believed her to be a good doctor meant so much more.

She saw a series of minor injuries and then, about an hour into her shift, Ambulance Control called to say that they were bringing in a patient with chemical burns.

Three of the other senior doctors were already dealing with a man who'd come off his motorbike and Katy was forced to call Jago's mobile. She was reluctant to disturb him but knew that she was going to need his help. The other doctors were already pushed to cope with the volume of emergencies that had bombarded the department all morning.

'He works in a glass factory but I have no idea what the chemical is,' she told him, trying to sound calm. 'I'm guessing it could be hydrofluoric acid.'

'You're probably right.' Jago's reply broke up slightly as the signal on his mobile faltered. 'Get him into Resus and irrigate it with lots of lukewarm water. I'll be right down. And, for goodness' sake wear gloves before you touch him.'

She heard the ambulance siren as she replaced the phone and dragged on a pair of gloves before hurrying to meet the paramedics as they pushed open the doors and wheeled in the stretcher.

The man was writhing on the trolley, groaning in agony from the severity of the burns inflicted by the chemical.

'He had an accident with hydrofluoric acid. It's over both legs. We irrigated it with copious volumes of water while we were at the factory,' the paramedic informed them, 'but we wanted to transfer him as fast as possible.'

As they moved him into Resus Jago appeared at Katy's side.

'Keep irrigating it,' he ordered immediately, seeing just how badly the man was burned. 'Get both legs under a tap and then rub in some 2.5 per cent calcium gluconate gel.'

He reached for a pair of gloves and tugged them on with grim-faced efficiency.

'Did someone call for calcium gluconate gel?' Like a miracle of efficiency and teamwork, Charlotte appeared beside them and they washed the burn repeatedly and then finally applied the gel to the burns.

'What exactly does this gel do?' Charlotte asked as they worked.

Katy glanced at her. 'In this case calcium gluconate acts as a neutraliser but you have to be careful with some chemical burns. If you attempt to neutralise the chemical you can create heat and make the burn worse. Hydrofluoric acid is the exception.'

'Really?' Charlotte looked at her in admiration and Jago smiled.

'Chemistry was obviously your thing, Dr Westerling.'

'I was always quite good at chemistry,' Katy said modestly, concentrating on trying to stabilise the patient, who was still howling in agony.

'Charlotte, call the plastic surgeon,' Jago instructed. 'He needs more pain relief so we'll give him an injection of calcium gluconate. And then we need to take some bloods. Fluoride ions are absorbed by the skin.'

'Even when it's only damaged a small surface area?' Katy gave the injection under the skin and then started to search for a vein.

'You can get problems with as little as a two per cent body surface area burn when the chemical is concentrated 70 per cent hydrofluoric acid. Fluoride ions end up in the circulation and produce a variety of systemic problems. We'll check his calcium and magnesium levels and his U and Es,' Jago told her, nodding approval as Charlotte appeared with a cardiac monitor. 'Good. We need to get him wired up so that we can keep an eye on his ECG.'

As Charlotte connected the machine to the patient, Katy watched the wavy line on the screen, seeing that it was showing a normal heart rate.

They waited for the results of the blood tests and in the meantime the plastic surgeon arrived to assess the burns.

'Hmm. Nasty.' He examined them closely and pulled a face. 'Some of those burns are full thickness. There's a bed on the ward so I'll admit him and take it from there.'

Jago gave a full handover and Charlotte arranged for the patient to be transferred to the ward.

'What will happen now?' Katy asked, after they were finally left on their own.

'Well, he's probably going to need skin grafts to at least some of those burns,' Jago said, finishing off the notes and sliding his pen back in his pocket. 'Now, on to more important matters. What are you cooking me for dinner?'

Katy worked through to the end of her shift and made her way home via the supermarket where she picked up some food for supper.

Realising that she'd never actually cooked a meal for Jago before, she felt a smile touch her lips. She was looking forward to it.

Chopping onion and garlic, she suddenly heard the sound of a key in the door.

Expecting to see Libby, she turned with a smile on her face, excited at the prospect of confessing that she was going to marry Jago.

Her father stood in the hallway.

The smile on her face died. Katy felt her heart rate double and suddenly her palms were damp.

Reminding herself that she was twenty-nine years of age and that he couldn't touch her any more, she dropped the knife she was holding and tried to control her shaking legs.

'Dad! How did you get in?'

'I've got a key.'

Well, of course he had, Katy thought dully. Somehow, somewhere her father had managed to obtain a key to her flat. And now he was inside. And she was in trouble.

'Did you want something?'

He moved towards her, his powerful bulk blocking the doorway of the kitchen, his expression ugly. 'You're seeing Rodriguez again.'

Her heart lurched and she fought the impulse to take several steps backwards. 'That's none of your business.'

She didn't even question how he knew. Her father knew everything.

'I wondered why you made that nonsensical speech about breaking off your engagement,' he growled. 'I should have guessed it was Rodriguez. And don't try denying it. I had a call from a journalist today. They've got pictures of you together.'

Katy stared at him blankly. Pictures?

How?

They'd been in Spain, for goodness' sake. Who on earth had managed to take a picture of them?

'Some nonsense about you saving a life in Spain.' Her father gave a dismissive snort. 'It's everywhere. Take a tip from me—next time you want to run away with your boyfriend, be more discreet.'

'And leave someone lying by the roadside?' Katy looked at him with incredulity, registering just how callous he was. 'And for your information, I wasn't running away with anyone.'

'But you're seeing him. I can't believe you'd be stupid enough to see Rodriguez again. I thought I'd managed to get rid of him eleven years ago,' her father said nastily, taking another step into the room.

Suddenly realising that she could smell alcohol on his breath, she felt her stomach lurch with fear. 'I want you to leave,' she said quietly. 'We can talk about this another time.'

'There's nothing more to talk about.' He lifted a hand and stabbed a finger towards her. 'You're marrying Freddie, my girl, and that's the end of it.'

'I'm marrying Jago!'

The moment the impulsive declaration left her lips she knew she'd made a mistake and she closed her eyes briefly, cursing her stupidity.

Dear God, she never should have said that.

In his current mood, goodness only knew what her father was capable of.

He stared at her for a moment, stunned into silence by her passionate announcement, swaying slightly as he stood. 'You're marrying *Rodriguez*?'

Katy stood still, frozen to the spot, hardly daring to breathe.

Her father gave a short laugh. 'Then you're more of a fool than I thought you were. Do you really think he loves you?' He gave a derisive snort. 'Of course he doesn't. He's just using you. He wants your name, your reputation and your money. But most of all he wants revenge.'

Revenge?

She knew Jago wasn't interested in any of the first three things, but revenge? Was it possible that her father was right?

After all, she knew that Jago didn't love her.

Was that why he'd asked her to marry him? Because he knew that it would be the ultimate revenge on her father?

Filled with doubts, she suddenly wanted to be on her own.

She lifted her head and looked at her father. He'd done it again. Put doubts in her mind. Tried to ruin everything.

'Go away.' She couldn't keep the choke out of her voice. 'Just leave me alone. This is my life. *My life.*' She never raised her voice but she was shouting now, the frustration of years of dealing with her father's bully-boy tactics coming to a head. 'I don't ever want to see you again.'

Infuriated by her unusual attitude, her father stepped towards her.

'You'll marry Rodriguez over my dead body,' he roared, and then staggered as a powerful arm clamped itself like a vice around his throat and pulled him away from her.

Jago's tone was ice cold. 'If you ever lay a finger on Katy, that's exactly what's going to happen.'

Charles Westerling gave a grunt of anger and tried to free himself, but Jago powered him against the wall and held him easily, the muscles of his shoulders bunched as he used his strength to subdue the older man.

'When you agree to behave like a decent human being I'll let you go.' He spoke to Katy over his shoulder. '*Querida*, did he hurt you?'

Katy shook her head. 'No. Let him go, Jago. Please.'

She just wanted him out of the flat so that she could think.

Was Jago really just marrying her to get revenge?

As usual, her father had managed to destroy her fragile happiness with a few well-chosen words.

Jago frowned slightly and turned back to her father, his expression menacing. 'It is time we got a few things straight.' His voice was raw and angry and his Spanish accent was more pronounced than usual. 'I am marrying Katy with or without your approval. Your wishes are of absolutely no interest to us whatsoever. As you quite clearly cannot behave yourself you won't be invited to the wedding, and in future if you wish to see Katy you can only do so when I'm present.'

Her father gaped at him, stunned that anyone would dare to speak to him like that. 'You can't dictate when I see my daughter!'

'I just did.' Jago's eyes were as hard as flint. 'Understand that the first duty of a Spanish male is to protect the woman he loves. I repeat—you won't be seeing her unless I am present. Do you understand?'

Loves?

Katy heard the word and clung to it, desperate for any scrap of reassurance that came her way.

'That's outrageous.' Charles struggled against that vice-like grip but Jago refused to release him.

'No.' Jago's voice was ice cold. 'It's just the way it's going to be. Your chauffeur is outside. Better not keep him waiting.'

Her father staggered slightly as Jago released him and made a move to approach Katy, but Jago stepped in front of him, preventing access.

With a last furious grunt her father turned and strode out of the flat, past Libby who'd just returned from work.

Libby flinched as the door crashed shut and she shot Jago an apologetic look.

'It's a wonder we're even vaguely normal, isn't it?' she delivered calmly, dropping her bag on the floor and strolling into the kitchen. 'Always such a pleasure to have a visit from one's parents.'

Katy sank down on one of the kitchen chairs, her legs still shaking.

'He said that we're in the papers. Someone took a picture of us together when we stopped to help that girl.' She looked at Jago blankly. 'I didn't even notice anyone.'

'That's always the trouble with the paparazzi,' Libby grumbled, reaching into the cupboard for a jar of peanut butter. 'If you don't notice them you can never give them your good side.

Not that you have anything but a good side, it has to be said. I just hope you didn't damage my favourite shoes when you were performing heroics in the hot dust of Spain.'

Katy looked at her sister in exasperation and then laughed. Trust Libby to inject a bit of frivolity into the proceedings. 'Your shoes are back in your dressing room.'

'Phew. I can breathe again.' Libby smiled happily and started to eat peanut butter out of the jar with a spoon. 'I'm going to my room to watch something mindless. Night.'

Katy watched her go, aware that she hadn't even told Libby her news. All day she'd been bursting to tell her and then suddenly the bubble of excitement had burst. Thanks to her father.

Suddenly aware that Jago was watching her with an ominous frown, she stirred. 'I'm glad you arrived when you did,' she said quietly, and he tensed still further.

'Would he have hit you?' he demanded rawly. 'Has he ever hit you?'

Katy hesitated. 'Once,' she said finally. 'When I was a child.'

Jago's fists tightened, his fury unconcealed. 'What happened?'

'Alex hit him with a cricket bat,' Katy muttered, hating to remember those days. 'And Libby called the police.'

Jago threw back his head and laughed. 'You three do stick together, don't you?'

Katy nodded and gave a slight smile. 'He never, ever tried it again but he often came close, particularly when he drank too much. Which he did frequently.' She stared at her hands. 'The truth is that he found other, more clever methods of intimidating us.'

Jago frowned. 'Answer me something else…' He hesitated, running a hand over the back of his neck as he braced himself to ask the question. 'Was he the reason you lost the baby? Libby said that you fell.'

'It was my fault,' Katy said quickly. 'I wasn't looking where I was going and I fell down the stairs.'

Dark eyes locked onto hers with disturbing intensity. 'But why weren't you looking where you were going?'

She hesitated. 'Dad guessed I was pregnant,' she confessed quietly. 'He was shouting at me and...he scared me. I backed away and tripped. It was an accident.'

Jago looked at her in naked disbelief. 'You are so incredibly forgiving, *querida*. How can you bear to see him?'

'He's still my dad,' Katy said simply. 'And I've never given up hoping that one day he'll be proud of me. But I have to confess that these days we usually only get together for family gatherings. I would never choose to see him alone. He caught me by surprise, turning up here tonight. I didn't know he'd managed to get a key.'

'Well, that won't happen again,' Jago growled, stepping forward and pulling her into his arms. 'I'm staying with you tonight, and tomorrow you're moving in with me and I'll brief the security guards. He won't be allowed access.'

Katy stood unresisting in his arms, but the happiness that she'd felt since Spain had totally vanished.

Was Jago really marrying her to avenge himself on her father?

She'd never really understood his reasons for proposing. The only thing she knew for sure was that he didn't love her.

'Jago...' Her voice cracked. 'I—I've changed my mind about marrying you.'

How could she marry him when she knew he didn't love her and when there was so much unpleasant history between them? Her father had treated him appallingly. She could hardly blame him for wanting to extract the ultimate revenge, but that didn't mean that she wanted to be a part of it.

Jago was looking at her blankly. 'Sorry?'

She swallowed. 'I can't marry you, Jago.'

He tensed. 'If this is about Freddie—'

'It's nothing to do with Freddie. It just wouldn't work between us.'

There was a pulsing silence and when he finally spoke his tone was icy. 'This is about your father, isn't it? Did he say something?'

Tears stung her eyes. There was no point in telling him. He was bound to deny it even if it was the truth. She just had to face the fact that it could never work between them.

'It isn't about my father,' she lied. 'It's about us. I can't marry you.'

He stared at her for a long moment, those incredible dark eyes veiled so that she was totally unable to read his response.

Then he turned without another word and walked out of the door.

CHAPTER ELEVEN

KATY arrived at work feeling gritty-eyed from lack of sleep and too much crying.

The department was already in chaos with people standing in the waiting room and the corridors full of trolleys.

She dumped her bag in the staffroom and then found Charlotte. 'What on earth is going on here?'

'Don't ask me,' Charlotte muttered, sorting through a pile of notes and handing her a set. 'Can you start by seeing this guy for me? He's been waiting for four hours so he's bound to be in a good humour. Good luck.'

Relieved that no one had noticed that she'd been crying her heart out for most of the night, Katy made her way to one of the cubicles and used the intercom to call the patient through.

He was remarkably cheerful for someone who'd waited so long and she examined his injured ankle and sent him along for an X-ray.

'You couldn't weight bear after the accident, so we need to check it,' she told him, glancing up as Charlotte popped her head round the curtain, her face white.

'I need you in Resus.'

'On my way.' Katy stood up and gave her patient an apologetic smile. 'I'm so sorry. We're very busy today. Follow the red line to X-ray and then I'll see you when you come back.'

Wondering what was responsible for the tension she'd read in Charlotte's face, she made her way to Resus and stopped dead with shock when she saw her mother standing in the doorway.

'Mum? What are you doing here?'

Jago and Charlotte were already in action, and her eyes swivelled to the patient on the trolley who was being attached to a heart monitor.

'Dad?' Her voice was a croak and she felt a chill run through her body.

Jago's eyes collided with hers briefly and then he turned his attention back to her father as he put a line in and started an infusion. 'You don't have to be here, Katy,' he said roughly. 'Take your mother to the relatives' room.'

Her mother straightened her shoulders. 'I'm not leaving him,' she said stiffly, and Katy walked into the room, letting the door swing closed behind her.

She hurried up to the trolley, her brain working in slow motion. 'What happened?'

Her father was pale and sweaty, gasping for breath as he lay on the trolley.

'We were at home and he suddenly clutched his chest and complained of pains,' her mother said shakily, her eyes on Jago. 'I—I think another doctor should see him!'

'Mum!' Katy was aghast and she looked at Jago with mortification, but Jago didn't react, all his attention concentrated on her father.

'I'm fully aware that Mr Rodriguez hates your father,' her mother said dully, 'and I have to admit he has reason. Why would he want to help him?'

Intercepting Charlotte's startled glance, Katy slipped an arm round her mother. 'Jago's a brilliant doctor, Mum,' she said quietly. 'The best. Who Dad is, or what he's done, doesn't matter at the moment.'

There wasn't anyone else she'd want caring for a member of her family.

Feeling strangely disconnected, Katy watched as Jago examined her father, checking his peripheral pulses to exclude aortic dissection and checking his legs for any evidence of clots in the veins.

'Katy, either help me out here or get me another doctor,' Jago growled suddenly, and Katy leapt into action.

'What do you want me to do?' She wasn't capable of thinking straight but she could follow orders.

'Take blood for U and Es, glucose, CK, FBC, and we may as well check his cholesterol as well.' He glanced up. 'Charlotte, get him attached to a pulse oximeter. I want to monitor his oxygen saturation. And get a radiographer up here. I want a portable chest X-ray.'

'I've done an ECG trace.' Charlotte handed him the strip of paper and Jago ran it through his fingers, studying it carefully.

'He's got ST elevation and inverted T waves,' he said finally, interpreting what looked like a wavy line to the uninitiated.

But Katy knew that what he was describing were changes to the pattern of electrical activity in the heart.

'He's had an MI?'

Her mother glanced between them in confusion. 'What's an MI?'

'Myocardial infarction. It means that Dad's had a heart attack,' Katy explained gently, and Jago looked at her.

'What are his risk factors? Does he smoke? What's his blood pressure like normally?'

Katy opened her mouth but it was her mother who answered, her voice amazingly calm.

'He hasn't smoked for thirty years but his blood pressure has been worryingly high for months now and his GP has been warning him to slow down and take some exercise.'

Katy stared at her mother. It was the first she'd heard of it. 'Mum?'

'You know your father—he never likes to show weakness,'

her mother explained wearily. 'He's also had a very high cholesterol and I've had him on a strict diet. Unfortunately, I don't think he sticks to it when I'm not watching him.'

For the first time Katy realised just how much her mother must love her father. Maybe their marriage wasn't just a business arrangement after all.

She stood still, barely aware of the arrival of the radiographer who bustled around the room preparing to take the X-ray Jago had requested.

'Charlotte, call the coronary care team,' Jago ordered once the X-ray had been taken, adjusting the flow of oxygen through her father's mask. 'I've given him morphine for the pain and aspirin, and we've started thrombolytic therapy. He needs to be transferred to the unit.'

Charles gave a groan and Katy tiptoed to his side.

'It's all right, Dad,' she said quietly, aware that her mother was standing next to her, tears in her eyes.

'Do you hear that, Charles? Despite everything you've done, your daughter is prepared to offer you comfort. I hope you're ashamed of yourself.'

Katy blinked. 'Mum, this isn't the right time.'

'This is exactly the right time,' Caroline said calmly, her eyes fixed on her husband's face. 'If you want to apologise to Katy, then now would be a good time.'

Katy thought she must have misheard. She'd never heard her mother use that tone with her father before, and he was *ill*.

What was going on?

'Charles…' Her mother leaned forward and moved the oxygen mask slightly, her hand trembling. 'I know you can hear me. You know there's something that you want to say to your daughter.'

At that moment the doors to Resus swung open and Libby flew into the room, her blonde ponytail swinging wildly as she hurried across to them.

Aware that a family drama was unfolding, she stopped dead, glancing quizzically at Jago who shrugged his broad shoulders.

Charles opened his eyes and suddenly all the fight seemed to leave him.

'Come here, Katy.' He spoke with considerable difficulty and Jago frowned.

'He needs the oxygen, I don't think he should—'

His patient waved a hand feebly. 'I need to speak,' he said hoarsely, and Katy stepped closer, feeling her heart pounding. What was it that her father wanted to say?

'I haven't been…' He broke off and licked his lips. 'I owe you…'

Her mother's mouth tightened. 'Just say it, Charles!'

'What your mother means is that I'm sorry,' he croaked finally, closing his eyes and sinking against the back of the trolley which had been raised to allow him to be upright and thus improve his breathing. 'I didn't know just how much you loved Jago. I thought it was just a fling.'

Aware of Charlotte's round-eyed curiosity, Katy felt her face colour. The one time her father came near to an apology for his behaviour, it had to be in front of an audience.

And she didn't really want Jago reminded of how much she'd loved him.

Her father cleared his throat and fiddled with the mask. 'I thought you'd get over him, but you never did.'

'Dad, let's forget it now.' Mortified by the disclosure of such personal details, Katy wanted to fall through the floor.

'And he never got over you,' her father continued, turning his head with difficulty so that he could see Jago. 'When you told me that you loved her and wanted to marry her, I was furious. And worried. She was only eighteen and I thought you were wrong for her.'

Katy froze, wondering if her father was rambling. As a doctor she was well aware that a heart attack could cause confusion. Why else would he be saying that Jago loved her? Jago had never loved her. And he'd certainly never wanted to marry her.

'He's trying to apologise,' her mother said, 'but unfortunately he hasn't had much practice. I have to confess that it's probably my fault that he's had a heart attack. He came roaring back from your flat last night, told me what had happened and we had a blazing row.'

Katy stared.

They'd had a row?

To the best of her knowledge her mother had never answered her father back in the entire thirty-six years of their marriage.

Her father struggled to speak. 'I couldn't believe that you and Jago had found each other again and were planning to get married.'

'We're not.' Finally Jago intervened, his tone flat and emotionless. 'You can relax, Mr Westerling. You'll be relieved to hear that your daughter has refused to marry me.'

For some reason this seemed to agitate Charles, and Jago frowned. 'I think that's enough talk now. You need to relax. Everything can be sorted out later.'

Charles ignored him, gulping in air and staring at his daughter. 'I shouldn't have said it. Any of it. None of it was true. He loves you and he always did. And you love him. I suppose that's all that matters.'

Jago's eyes rested on Katy and his firm mouth tightened ominously.

'He said something to you?' His voice was soft. 'I should have guessed. What did he say to you, Katy? What was I supposed to have done?'

She licked dry lips, no longer caring that they had an audience. 'Revenge. He said that you only wanted to marry me because that would be the ultimate revenge.'

There was a long silence. 'And you believed him?'

'I couldn't think of any other reason you'd be marrying me.'

Jago inhaled deeply. 'Could you not?'

He looked at her thoughtfully, but before he could speak the cardiologist arrived with his team and the attention turned back to her father.

Katy stood next to her father, feeling totally numb as Jago talked quietly to his colleague, explaining the history and discussing the ECG trace while the rest of the team listened.

She was only half-aware of what was going on as they examined her father again and made arrangements to transfer him to Coronary Care.

Satisfied that the cardiologists now had the situation well in hand, Jago strode over to the trolley.

'They're going to take you to Coronary Care now, Mr Westerling.' His gaze rested on the older man's face for a moment, his expression totally inscrutable, and Caroline sighed, indicating that she was completely aware of his conflicting emotions.

'Jago, we owe you so much. How can we ever thank you for what you've done? And how can we ever make amends for keeping the two of you apart for so long?'

Galvanised into action by those words, Jago wrenched off his gloves and tossed them into the bin. 'I don't care about that. All I care about at the moment is having a conversation with Katy without an audience.' He lifted his eyes to hers. 'In my office. Now.'

'I'll sort out the transfer,' Charlotte muttered, and Libby smiled weakly.

'Exciting, isn't it? Life with my family. I bet you can't wait for the next episode.' But her eyes were worried as they rested on her father and she stepped closer to the trolley.

Katy stood in Jago's office waiting for him, her legs trembling.

The door clicked shut and she turned on him, her voice shaking with passion. 'Eleven years ago did you really tell my father you wanted to marry me?'

He tensed, obviously surprised by the directness of her approach. 'Yes.'

She gave a groan and sank onto the chair as all the pieces of the jigsaw fell into place.

'So *that's* why my father was so determined to break us up. I could never understand why he was so worried that it was serious. You never seemed serious to me. You kept telling me that you didn't do commitment.'

'I didn't until I met you. When I saw you that day you fell off your horse, it took every ounce of willpower at my disposal not to roll you on your back in the grass and follow my baser instincts,' he confessed rawly, dragging his gaze away from her and pacing across the room to stare out of the window. 'You were so unlike the women I usually dated that I told myself that I had to back off.'

'I was so in love with you,' Katy muttered, 'but I never for one moment thought that you loved me, too. You showed absolutely no signs of it.'

He gave a groan and raked his fingers through his glossy dark hair. 'Of course I did, but you were just too inexperienced to see it. And I was afraid that what you were feeling for me was no more than a childish crush because I was your first lover.'

'My only lover, Jago,' she said quietly, and he stilled, every muscle in his powerful body suddenly tense as he absorbed what she'd just said.

'That can't be true.'

'After what I shared with you, I just couldn't bring myself to sleep with anyone else,' she confessed. 'I had several boyfriends, but when it came to it I just couldn't do it. Part of me always felt that I was yours.'

Jago was across the room in three long strides. 'Freddie?'

She shook her head. 'We were only ever friends. It was very much a marriage of convenience. He didn't even seem to mind when I ended it.'

A smile of pure male satisfaction suddenly transformed his handsome face. 'He never knew the real you. Only I know how hot you can be.'

'Only when I'm with you.' She lifted her flushed face to his. 'I never, ever would have slept with another man, Jago.'

He groaned and dragged her to her feet, wrapping her in his arms. 'And I should never have even thought that of you. Have you any idea how bad I felt that day when you told me what your father had done? I can't believe I didn't see through it, but I was so blindly jealous at seeing you entwined with another man that I ceased to be capable of rational behaviour. And I can't believe that I left you pregnant. I'm so, so sorry about the baby, *querida*. Can you forgive me?'

'There's nothing to forgive,' she said, hugging him back. 'The baby wasn't your fault, and as for the rest of it...' She sighed and gave a slight shrug of her shoulders. 'I should have known that it was my father.'

'And I should have seen what he was doing,' he admitted ruefully, 'but it was only because I was so crazily in love with you and I'd never felt like that about anyone before. It clouded my judgement.'

Katy looked up at him, wobbly with love. 'That's what Libby said when I told her.'

'Well, your sister has more insight than either of us,' Jago groaned, running lean fingers through her silky hair with deep appreciation. 'Why do you think I kept those photographs? Looking at them caused me agony, but they were the only link I had with you. When I realised how badly I'd treated you I just didn't know what to do. I didn't know how to make you love me again.'

'I always loved you,' Katy said simply, lifting a finger to touch his rough jaw. 'Always. I never stopped loving you.'

He froze to the spot, obviously not daring to believe what he was hearing. 'You still love me?'

'So much that it terrifies me,' she confessed shakily, and he gave a disbelieving laugh.

'I can't believe I can be that lucky,' he said hoarsely, 'or that your father nearly ruined it again by making you believe that I was only marrying you out of revenge.'

'I couldn't see any other reason.' She coloured slightly. 'You hadn't thought to mention that you were in love with me.'

He groaned and dragged her against him. 'I thought it was obvious from the way we were together in Spain.'

'Not to me,' she said simply, and he stroked her hair away from her face with his free hand.

'I was working so hard at getting back into your good books that I didn't know what to do. I thought that even if I did tell you that I loved you, you were unlikely to believe me.' He gave a wry smile. 'And I have to admit that I've never been very good with the emotional stuff.'

'That's not true.' She wasn't letting him off the hook that easily. 'I've seen you with relatives, Jago, and I remember how you were with me at eighteen. I *know* you have a sensitive side.'

He gave a reluctant grin that turned her heart upside down. 'Just don't tell anyone. Not that I'll have any credibility left once Charlotte starts talking.' His smile faded and he looked down into her eyes. 'I have never stopped loving you, *querida*. But I thought that you had stopped loving me, and proud Spaniards are not the best at putting their hearts on the line.'

Stunned by his frank confession, she stood on tiptoe and kissed him. 'I think we better have a rule that once a day we tell each other absolutely everything that we're feeling, no matter how uncomfortable.'

He lowered his head with a groan and returned the kiss. 'I think you might be right. So, does this mean that you will marry me after all?'

She gave a shy nod and his grip tightened.

'I'm tempted to call the hospital chaplain and see if he can do it now, before your father comes up with any more of his inventive plans to keep us apart.'

She gave a shaky laugh and bit her lip. 'I can't believe that he said all that. Mum must have given him a real talking to, and she's *never* done that before.'

'Women can be scary when they're crossed,' Jago said, a hint of amusement in his deep drawl. 'I should know. I'll never forget your reaction when I told you about those photographs. I thought you were going to lynch me for being so stupid. And to think I once believed you were shy and gentle.'

She tipped her head on one side. 'I've changed.'

'But, thankfully, not that much, *querida*,' he murmured, kissing her until her head started to swim. 'You still love me.'

Katy clutched at his shirt for support. 'With all my heart.'

And registering the tenderness in his eyes, this time she just *knew* that nothing would ever come between them again. They belonged together for the rest of their lives.

A month later Libby helped put the finishing touches to Katy's wedding dress at the doorway of the church.

'You look spectacular,' she sighed, 'and I just *love* the shoes.'

Katy stared doubtfully at her feet. 'I don't know why I let you talk me into them. I feel as though I'm on stilts. I'm going to trip, going down the aisle.'

'You'll be holding Dad's arm,' Libby pointed out, sitting back on her heels and pulling a face. 'Who would have thought it? Dad suddenly having an entire personality change. It's as if that heart attack made him rethink his whole life.'

'And Mum seems so happy,' Katy agreed.

'Who knows? One day we might be a normal family,' Libby quipped, straightening the hem of Katy's dress. 'OK, you're done. Go wow them.'

Katy looked down at herself. 'Do the shoes make me too tall?'

'You look stunning,' Libby said dryly. 'Fortunately, you're marrying a man who dwarfs you, so you don't need to spend the rest of your life wearing flats.'

Katy felt her stomach tumble at the thought of Jago waiting for her inside the church, with Alex as best man. 'I love him *so* much.'

'I know.' Libby scrambled to her feet and grinned. 'You always did.'

'I almost married Freddie.'

Libby shook her head. 'I hate to break this to you, but that was never going to happen. Alex and I would have kidnapped you rather than let you make a mistake like that.'

'I'm going to miss living with you so much.' Katy leaned

forward and hugged her tightly. 'Alex is lucky to be moving in with you. I know you'll get on well.'

She said it very firmly, as if she was trying to convince herself, and Libby laughed.

'You know we'll probably kill each other,' she said dryly, and Katy sighed.

'Well, hopefully it won't be for long,' she said wistfully. 'I want you to meet someone and settle down.'

'Me?' Libby looked startled. 'You've got to be kidding. I'm a born-again cynic. Now, get down that aisle and stop fantasising.'

At that moment their father appeared, looking remarkably good considering his recent illness.

'The minute we've walked down that aisle you have to sit down,' Katy reminded him firmly, and he looked at her with eyes that were unusually bright.

'I've told everyone that my daughter is a doctor,' he said gruffly, taking her hand in his and tucking it into his arm. 'I know I've never said that I'm proud of you, but I am. Very proud. And I'm proud of you, too, Elizabeth.'

Aware that Libby's mouth had fallen so wide open that she was in danger of swallowing a large insect, Katy couldn't hide her smile.

'Thanks, Dad.' Apparently almost meeting his maker and a confrontation with his wife had been sufficient to make Charles seriously reconsider his ways.

As she heard the music start she moved to the top of the aisle and caught her first glimpse of Jago, standing tall and broad-shouldered next to her brother.

At that moment he turned and saw her and there was no missing the love and pride in his dark eyes. And as Katy took her first steps towards him on her father's arm, she knew that everything about her life was perfect.

* * * * *

Libby

CHAPTER ONE

'LIBBY, you're up for auction. Lot number 16.'

Libby snuggled the tiny baby in the crook of her arm and glanced up at the ward sister in horror. 'Tell me you're joking.'

'Deadly serious.' Beverley squinted down at the baby. 'How's she doing?'

'Better. I'm trying to get her to take more fluids,' Libby said softly, reaching for the bottle of milk that she'd warmed in readiness. 'And, Bev, I'm not taking part in the auction—I already told you that.'

'You have to!' The older woman sat down in the chair next to her and gave her a pleading look. 'You're the best-looking woman in the hospital. We're bound to get a good price for you.'

Libby pulled a face. 'That's so sexist!'

'But true.' Bev beamed at her. 'Come on. Say yes. It's for a good cause.'

'It's utterly degrading and I don't know what made you come up with the idea. You obviously have a sick mind.'

'It was *your* idea,' Bev reminded her placidly. 'But that was before you went off men again. Everyone's really entered into the spirit of things. It's going to be a great evening and we're going to raise a fortune for our playroom. This is going to be the best-equipped paediatric ward in the world.'

'Well, I must have been mad to think of it and I'm certainly not taking part. I'll give you a donation.' Libby gently placed the bottle to the baby's lips. 'Come on, sweetheart, suck for Libby.'

'That's not the same. It's not just about the money, it's about team spirit and you have to be there. You're an important part of the paediatric team. My star performer, in fact.'

'In that case I'll come and watch.' Libby smiled with satisfaction as the baby clamped her mouth round the teat. 'There's a good girl.'

'We need you on that stage,' Bev said firmly, 'and just think of the opportunity to meet a new man! There'll be all sorts there. Short ones, tall ones, thin ones, fat ones...'

A new man?

Libby shuddered. 'It doesn't matter what they look like on the outside. They're all the same on the inside and I'm not interested.'

She'd given up on men totally. There was only so much hurt and disillusionment that a girl could stand.

Bev shifted uncomfortably. 'You have to. It's tomorrow night! They've printed the programmes and you're in it.'

'Oh, for crying out loud!' Libby glared at her colleague, who looked sheepish.

'It'll be fun,' she said lamely. 'A tall, handsome stranger will pay money for you. It's just a blind date really.'

'I don't do dates,' Libby said flatly, 'blind or otherwise.'

The way she felt at the moment, she had no intention of ever dating a man again.

'Well, you could do the choosing,' Bev suggested helpfully. 'It's not as if you're short of money. You could use some of that enormous trust fund that Daddy set up for you to purchase a really hot date.'

Libby shot her a look that spoke volumes. 'Do I look stupid?'

'Libby.' Bev spoke with exaggerated patience. 'You're twenty-nine years old and you're loaded. You shouldn't be single. At the very least, some man should be trying to marry you for your money.'

'Great. So now I'm up for sale to the highest bidder.' Libby looked at her friend in exasperation. 'What's wrong with being single? Women are allowed to be on their own these days. Being single is perfectly acceptable.'

'For some people, maybe,' Bev conceded, 'but not you. You adore children. Children adore you. You're cuddly and loving and fun. You were designed to be married and a mother.'

'The good thing about being a paediatric nurse,' Libby observed, 'is that you can enjoy the benefits of children without the drawbacks of a man.'

Bev sighed. 'Look, I know you haven't exactly had good experiences with men, but—'

'Good experiences?' Libby gave a laugh that was totally lacking in humour and then lowered her voice as the baby shifted restlessly in her arms. 'Bev, do I need to spell out just how utterly ridiculous I feel after what happened with Philip?'

Bev bit her lip. 'No. But you shouldn't feel ridiculous. You didn't do anything wrong.'

'I dated a married man,' Libby said shortly, and Bev frowned.

'But you didn't *know* he was married.'

'Not until I found him in bed with his wife,' Libby agreed. 'That sort of gave the game away really.'

Bev closed her eyes. 'I know you're hurt, but it wasn't your fault—'

'Of course it was. I was too trusting. He didn't mention a wife so I assumed he didn't have one. Silly me.' Libby struggled with a lump in her throat, cross with herself for becoming upset again. She'd promised herself that she wasn't going to waste another tear on Philip and here she was with a wobbly lip again. Pathetic! 'I am obviously totally incapable of spotting a rat so it's safer if I just stay single. So you can forget your auction. There's no way I'm ever voluntarily going on a date again.'

Bev cleared her throat delicately. 'You've got to have a so-

cial life, Libby. What about the summer ball next month? You
need a partner.'

'I'm not going to the summer ball.' Libby concentrated on
the baby. 'I've decided to dedicate my life to work and forget
about romance.'

Bev's eyes widened. 'You're not going to the ball? It's *the*
event of the hospital calendar. If you don't go, Philip will assume that you're pining.'

'And if I do go, and he's there, then there'll be bloodshed,'
Libby predicted darkly, adjusting the angle of the bottle slightly.
'He's a total rat. I've discovered that the better-looking the man,
the higher the rat factor.'

Bev blinked. 'Rat factor?'

'Yes. It's my official measurement of male behaviour.'

Bev giggled. 'We shouldn't be having this conversation in
front of the baby,' she murmured. 'She's only four months old.
We'll shock her.'

'It's never too soon to learn about the rat factor,' Libby murmured. 'She'll have a head start on me. I was grown up before
I discovered the truth.'

Actually, that wasn't strictly true, she reflected, watching as
the baby guzzled the rest of the bottle. She'd had endless clues
during her childhood.

'Men should come with a government health warning.'

'Not all men,' Bev said quietly, looking across the darkened ward at one of the fathers who sat slumped in a chair by
a sleeping child. 'He's going to be with her for the rest of the
night and he's going to have to do a full day's work tomorrow.'

'Yeah…' Libby followed her gaze. 'Dave is a saint. And
Poppy is lucky to have such a devoted dad. But he's the exception. The rest of them are creeps.'

Poppy had cystic fibrosis and she'd developed yet another
lung infection that required her to be back in hospital for treatment. She was well known on the ward and so was her father
who never left her side.

Bev wasn't listening. 'If you wore something short and left your hair loose, you'd make us a fortune. If we hit our target it's going to mean a fantastic playroom for our children. Toys, desks, books by the million, a whiteboard for the teacher. It's just a bit of fun. *Please*, Libby...'

Libby opened her mouth to refuse again and then closed it with a resigned sigh.

It *had* been her idea so people would expect her to be there. But if she attended then she'd have to take part and she really, *really* didn't want to expose herself to an evening with a man.

Or give philandering Philip the opportunity to buy her and force the conversation she'd been avoiding.

Perhaps she could put such a high price on herself that no one would be able to afford her, she mused.

She continued to search for solutions as she eased the teat out of the baby's mouth and lifted her against her shoulder. The baby snuffled contentedly and Libby smiled, breathing in her warm baby smell and cuddling her closer. And suddenly the answer came to her. Her *brother* could buy her. Why hadn't she thought of it sooner?

'All right, I'll do it.' Libby smiled, pleased with her idea. 'Alex can buy me. At least that should ensure that no one else does.'

Especially Philip.

Ever since she'd arrived at Philip's flat unannounced and surprised him in a very compromising position with a stunning blonde who had turned out to be his wife—*a wife he'd never thought to mention*—Philip had been desperately trying to get to see her. He'd called her mobile so often that she'd finally switched it off and told her friends to call her on the ward. At least Bella, the receptionist, could field her calls.

She absolutely did not want a conversation with him about what had happened.

As far as she was concerned, there was nothing to talk about. The man was married. And he'd lied to her.

'Did you manage to get any extra help for tomorrow?' She knew that the staffing situation was dire.

Bev shook her head gloomily. 'The nursing situation is bad, but fortunately the new consultant starts on Monday so at least we should finally have some more medical support.'

Libby nodded. They'd been a consultant short and that had put tremendous pressure on everyone.

'I'll come in early tomorrow,' she offered, and Bev bit her lip.

'I can't ask you to do that, you've worked a double shift today...'

'You didn't ask. I volunteered.'

Bev leaned forward and gave her a hug. 'You're brilliant, and if I were a man I'd definitely buy you.'

'And then you'd go home and sleep with a woman who turns out to be a wife that you conveniently forgot to mention,' Libby said dryly. 'So tell me—is the new consultant a woman or a rat?'

Bev laughed. 'He's a man, if that's what you're asking.'

'Oh well, you can't have everything.'

With a wistful smile Libby stroked the baby's smooth cheek and then laid her carefully back in her cot, tucking the sheet around her.

The baby was so beautiful. It made her terribly broody, caring for her, and she would have loved one of her own.

It was just a shame that having a baby required contact with a man.

Less than twenty-four hours later, Andreas Christakos strolled onto the ward, six feet three of broad-shouldered, drop-dead-handsome Greek male.

The night sister, confronted by this unexpected vision of raw, masculine virility, dropped the pile of sheets she was carrying and lost her powers of speech.

Acknowledging that it probably hadn't been quite fair of him to arrive unannounced, Andreas extended a lean, bronzed hand and introduced himself.

The night sister paled slightly. 'You're the new consultant? We weren't exactly expecting you...' She stooped to pick up the sheets, visibly flustered by his unscheduled appearance. 'Did you want to see—? I mean, it seems a little late—'

'I merely came to familiarise myself with the whereabouts of the ward,' he assured her smoothly, his eyes flickering over the walls which were covered in brightly coloured children's paintings. 'I don't officially start until Monday.'

She clutched the sheets to her chest and looked relieved. 'That's what I thought. Good. Well, please, help yourself to the notes trolley—they're all there and any X-rays are underneath. We're pretty quiet for once, so everyone's slipped off to the auction,' the night sister told him. 'They'll be back when it finishes—or sooner if I call them.'

'*Auction?*' Andreas frowned as he repeated the word. He'd always thought his English was fluent but he found himself very unsure about what she was describing. Surely an auction involved paintings or other valuable artefacts?

'We're selling a date with each member of staff to raise money to buy equipment for our new playroom.'

Andreas, traditional and Greek to the very backbone, struggled with this concept. They were selling *dates*?

Aware that she was waiting for some sort of response, he dealt her a sizzling smile. 'It sounds like a novel way to raise money.'

'It is.' She looked at him for a moment and then smiled cheekily, her nervousness vanishing. 'You're very good-looking. Perhaps you should consider auctioning yourself.'

The smile froze on his face. 'I don't think so.'

He had enough trouble keeping women at a distance as it was, and the one thing he absolutely didn't need was to offer himself to the highest bidder. The thought made him shudder. What sort of woman would that attract? Not the one he was searching for, that was for sure. Recent events had confirmed his growing suspicion that the woman he wanted didn't exist in real life.

'Are you sure I can't persuade you?' The night sister giggled. 'You'd make us a fortune! Well, just in case you change your mind, it's all happening in the doctors' bar in the basement. You could go and meet everyone. Half the hospital will be there. Introduce yourself. Buy yourself a date for the evening!'

Knowing that he had no intention of doing anything of the sort, Andreas merely smiled politely and reached for the first set of notes.

As he flicked to the first page, he reflected on the strange ways of the English. Like most of his countrymen, he was aware of the outlandish behaviour shown by some of the English girls who holidayed in Greece, but in all his time in various English hospitals he'd never come across a scenario where staff sold themselves to raise money.

Was the NHS really in that much trouble?

With a slight lift of his wide shoulders he dismissed the thought and proceeded to read the notes on each child, his sharp brain absorbing the information and filing it away for later.

An hour later he was thoroughly briefed on all the current admissions and he left the ward quietly, walking along the corridors that led to the main entrance, hesitating briefly as he reached the stairs that led down to the doctors' bar in the basement. Loud music drifted up the stairs, along with catcalls and much whooping and laughter.

Intrigued by the concept of anything so alien as an auction involving people, Andreas took the stairs and pushed open the door of the bar just as a leggy blonde sashayed down the improvised catwalk.

He stopped dead, his attention caught.

She was stunning.

Andreas sucked in a breath, his eyes raking over every inch of her slender, perfectly formed body. As he watched, she tossed

her long, wavy blonde hair over her slim shoulders, her slanting blue eyes glinting as if she was daring someone to buy her.

She was wearing an almost indecently short pink dress and
heels that were so high he feared for her safety, but she walked
with a grace and elegance that was achingly feminine.

'Lot number 16.' The auctioneer laughed, raising his voice
over the howls and wolf whistles. 'What am I bid for our Libby?'

There was a chorus of enthusiastic yells and the blonde rolled
her eyes and grinned, striking an exaggerated pose that took
his breath away.

Andreas surveyed her with unashamed lust, oblivious to the
admiring glances he himself was drawing from the other females in the room.

Temporarily forgetting how jaded he was with women, he
studied her closely and came to the conclusion that she was gorgeous. Physically. He didn't fool himself that her beauty went
any deeper than that, but for a short-term relationship did that
really matter? He wasn't inviting her to be the mother of his
children so the intricacies of her personality were irrelevant.

'Ten pounds,' the auctioneer said. 'Let's start the bidding
at £10.'

Andreas glanced at the auctioneer incredulously. Did the
man have no idea of value?

'Yes.' A lanky blond man raised an arm and Andreas watched
with interest as the girl's expression froze. All the warmth and
humour drained out of her pretty face and she stared ahead
stonily. It was clear to everyone watching that she didn't want
to be purchased by the blond man.

She started moving again, and it was obvious from the way
that her eyes slid frantically around the room that she was
searching for someone. She seemed tense, almost desperate,
and then her gaze rested on Andreas.

Startled eyes, as blue as the Aegean sea, widened and stared
into his. Instead of continuing her rhythmic sway down the

stage, she stopped dead, her whole body still, frozen by the connection that sizzled between them.

Taken aback by the strength of the attraction, Andreas felt his body tighten in that most primitive of male responses. His arrogant dark head angled back, he held her gaze, forgetting the recent change to his life that had fired his resolution to avoid women.

Suddenly all he wanted was her.

Naked. In his bed.

No self-respecting Greek male would allow a woman like her to pass by unscathed.

It would be a criminal waste.

Totally sure of himself, he strolled forward, indifferent to the lustful female stares he was attracting from all quarters. He was only interested in one woman and the confidence of his stride made the crowd part to let him through.

'One thousand pounds.' He delivered his bid coolly, his eyes still holding hers as he dropped the words into the expectant hush. He'd never paid for a woman in his life before, but there was no way he was letting the blond man buy her. Or any other man.

He wanted her for himself.

And Andreas Christakos was used to getting exactly what he wanted.

'One thousand pounds!' The auctioneer was almost incoherent with delight. 'Well, none of you tight individuals are going to top that so I'd say Libby's going, going, gone to the tall, dark stranger with the fat wallet!'

Ignoring the laughter, Andreas stretched out a lean, strong hand to Libby, his eyes still holding hers.

Looking slightly stunned, she stepped forward, descended the stage with care and took his hand, chin held high.

It was only when he caught her from falling at the bottom of the steps that he realised that she'd had too much to drink.

The blond man who'd bid £10 stepped forward, clearly desperate to speak to her, but she silenced him with an icy glare and Andreas felt her small hand tremble in his.

He frowned slightly. Why was she shaking?

In an instinctive male reaction, his hand tightened on hers possessively.

'No amount of money would induce me to have a conversation with you, Philip, let alone a date,' she said with exaggerated dignity. Having clarified the situation to her satisfaction, she turned to Andreas with a smile that would have illuminated Athens on a dark night. 'Shall we go?'

Andreas wondered what could have upset her so much that she'd be willing to leave the bar with a total stranger. She hadn't even asked his name and she was clinging to his hand as if it were a lifeline.

A totally inexplicable need to protect her slammed through him and he tightened his grip. 'Yes, let's go.'

He held the door open for her and she walked past him, long-legged and graceful, managing remarkably well on those high heels considering the volume of alcohol she appeared to have consumed. Up close she seemed more fragile than she had on the stage and he was suddenly aware of just how delicate she was compared to him. Her arms and wrists were slender, her waist was impossibly tiny and her long, slim legs seemed to go on for ever.

She climbed the stairs carefully, cheerfully greeting various members of the medical staff who passed. But he sensed that the cheerfulness was for everyone else's benefit and his firm mouth tightened as he contemplated the possible reasons for her distress. Obviously it had something to do with the blond man who thought she was only worth £10.

They reached the top of the stairs and he took her arm as they walked towards the car park.

'Exactly how much alcohol have you consumed?'

'None. I don't drink. Although perhaps I should have done tonight. At least alcohol might have numbed the utter humiliation of being on that stage. I can't believe I ever thought it would be a good idea. Thank goodness you came when you did. That creep almost bought me,' she slurred, bending down to remove her shoes. 'Ouch. Sorry. They're really uncomfortable.'

Did she think he was a fool?

It was perfectly obvious that she'd been drinking.

Andreas frowned. 'If you found it humiliating, why did you agree to do it?' he asked, noticing that without her shoes she had to tilt her head to look at him.

Her shoes dangled from her fingers. 'I did it because I promised that I would and I never break promises.'

'You didn't want to do it?'

'I would rather have dug a hole and buried myself,' she said frankly. 'Standing on that stage and trying to look cheerful was the hardest thing I've ever done in my life. I almost died with relief when you rescued me. For a horrible moment I thought that my rotten brother had abandoned me to my fate. Which reminds me, I need to write you a cheque.'

He looked at her blankly as she rummaged in her bag and produced a cheque book.

'A thousand pounds, wasn't it?' She scribbled on the cheque, tore it out and handed it to him. 'A bit steep, but never mind. It was very decent of you to turn up and buy me.'

She staggered slightly and Andreas closed both hands over her arms to steady her.

'Why are you giving me a cheque?'

She stared up at him vacantly and he found himself noticing the perfect shape of her mouth.

'Because that was the agreement.'

Still studying her mouth, Andreas struggled to concentrate. 'What agreement?'

She hesitated, obviously trying to retrieve something from her memory that the alcohol had wiped out. 'The agreement I made with my brother,' she said finally, a smile of triumph on her face as she remembered. 'He promised that if he couldn't

make it he'd send someone else to save me from Philip, and...'
she smiled at him dizzily '...he obviously sent you.'

Andreas dragged his eyes away from her mouth. 'I don't
know your brother.'

She tilted her head and focused on him. 'You don't?' She
bit her soft lip, confusion evident in her beautiful eyes. 'Alex
promised me that if he was too busy to come he'd send someone to put in an outrageous bid for me so that no one else could
buy me. I assumed it was you...'

He shook his head, totally intrigued. *Her brother had promised to buy her?* 'Not me.'

She swallowed hard. 'Well, if you didn't buy me for my
brother then why did you—?' She broke off and backed away
from him, her eyes suddenly wary. 'Who the hell are you? And
why would you pay that much money for a stranger?'

'I thought that was the idea,' Andreas said mildly. Clearly
she was questioning his motives and he could hardly blame her
for that. 'Surely you wanted to persuade the audience to part
with their money?'

'Well, yes, but not a *thousand pounds*.' She was still staring
at him as if she expected him to attack her at any moment. 'If
you think that paying all that money guarantees you—I mean,
if you think that I'll...' She stumbled over the words, clearly
embarrassed, and then gave up and gave him a threatening
look. 'What I mean is, you're in for a serious disappointment
because *I don't do that*!'

He hid his amusement. 'They were auctioning a *date*, Libby,'
he reminded her calmly, and she glared at him.

'And doubtless you took that to mean sex because that's
what all men expect, and then afterwards I discover the wife
and the child.'

Andreas blinked, trying to keep up with her thought pro-
cesses. 'I don't generally find I have to pay for sex,' he drawled,
and she tipped her head on one side and studied him closely,
her small pink tongue snaking out and moistening her lips.

'No, I'm sure you don't. But, then, I bet you don't usually have to pay for dates either.'

Andreas inclined his head. 'True.'

Normally he had to play all sorts of games to keep women at a distance.

Which made his current behaviour all the more unbelievable.

She obviously agreed with him if the expression on her face was anything to go by. 'So why did you pay such an outrageous amount of money for a date with *me*?'

He was asking himself the same question.

'Because I can afford it and because you're very beautiful,' he replied.

She took a few more steps backwards, clutching her shoes tightly. 'Well, I suggest you take the cheque I'm offering you,' she said coldly. 'I only agreed to do the auction because Alex promised he would buy me. I never, *ever* would have done it if I'd thought I'd actually have to go on a date. I don't date men. Men are rats and creeps.'

Andreas ran an experienced eye down a length of perfect thigh. A less likely candidate for celibacy he had yet to see. But there was no missing the utter misery in her blue eyes.

It didn't take a genius to work out that someone had obviously hurt her badly.

'You've obviously been mixing with the wrong men,' he said softly, and she gave a humourless laugh.

'Funnily enough, I've worked that out for myself. From now on, no more relationships.'

Unable to resist teasing her, Andreas smiled. 'What about sex?'

He watched with fascination as colour bloomed in her cheeks.

'I'm old-fashioned,' she muttered. 'I don't have sex without a relationship and seeing that men are hopeless at relationships, I've given up.'

'So tell me.' He stepped closer to her, his attention caught by the fullness of her lower lip. 'Who was responsible for putting you off relationships?'

'You want the short version or the long version?' She shrugged carelessly but he guessed that she was battling with tears and he frowned, wondering what it was about her that made him feel so protective. Not that she would have thanked him for those feelings, he reflected wryly. These days women wanted to hunt their own dragons and kill them.

'Whichever you want to tell me.'

'Well, I suppose I'd have to start with my parents, who were definitely *not* a shining example of marital harmony. They never touched.' She flashed him a suggestive smile. 'Well, of course, they must have touched *once*, or they wouldn't have had me, but fortunately for them they had triplets so they managed to get all the physical contact out of the way in one go.'

Andreas thought of his own childhood and the love and emotional support he'd been given. It had been something that he'd taken for granted at the time, but his work as a paediatrician had brought him into contact with enough children from less privileged backgrounds than his for him to have been able to appreciate the impact that parental disharmony could have on a child's view of life.

'Their relationship put you off men?'

'That and personal experience in the field,' she said gloomily. 'My most recent disaster turned out to be married.'

Andreas frowned. 'That's what you meant by your comment about discovering the wife and child? You've definitely been dating the wrong men.'

'Don't use that smooth, seductive tone on me,' she advised, swaying slightly as she looked at him. 'It is totally wasted. I don't trust *anyone*. From now on I'm cynical and suspicious. And the more attractive the man, the higher my index of suspicion. I ought to warn you that with you it's soaring through the roof.'

Before he could reply he saw her glance over his shoulder
and her whole body tensed.

Wondering what had caused her reaction, he turned his head
briefly and saw the blond man hurrying towards them, looking agitated.

'Oh, help—here he comes again. What does it take to get
him to leave me alone?' She lifted her chin bravely but he saw
the anguish in her blue eyes.

Andreas knew exactly how to persuade the man to leave
her alone.

Telling himself that he was merely helping a damsel in distress, he pulled her firmly against him and lowered his mouth
to hers.

He felt her stiffen in surprise and then melt against him, her
mouth opening under the subtle pressure of his. She was all
feminine temptation, her floral scent wrapping itself around
him and drawing him in, her lips all sweetness and seduction
as she kissed him back.

Andreas was taken aback by the strength of his reaction to
that kiss. His body throbbed with instant arousal and he cupped
her face with confident hands, feeling her quiver of surprise as
he deepened the kiss. She dropped the shoes she was holding
and clutched at his shirt, whimpering slightly under the skilled
assault of his mouth.

Stunned by her uninhibited response and his own powerful
reaction, he hauled her closer still and stroked a leisurely hand
up her thigh, the warmth of her smooth skin intensifying the
throbbing, pulsing ache of his erection.

Feeling fireworks explode in his head, Andreas continued
to explore her mouth, building the excitement to such dangerous levels that it threatened to engulf them both.

It was the hottest, most erotic kiss he'd ever experienced
and it wouldn't have ended there if it hadn't been for the loud
slam of a car door that jerked them both back to the reality of
their surroundings.

Andreas lifted his head, considerably shaken by his definitely uncharacteristic response to the woman who now stood quivering in his arms.

He glanced around him in utter disbelief, taking in the ordered rows of cars interspersed by the odd streetlamp. He'd always prided himself in his self-control and yet here he was ready to slam this woman against the nearest convenient surface and make love to her hard and fast until she begged for mercy.

What the hell had happened to him?

Not only were they in a public place but he was also aware that, whatever she said to the contrary, she'd had too much to drink and was obviously on the rebound.

Neither factors provided a good basis for any sort of relationship.

Cursing softly in Greek, he released her and then caught her again as she stumbled.

She looked at him, bemused. 'Feel dizzy,' she muttered, her expression dazed and disconnected, her blue eyes cloudy as she lifted a finger to her lips.

He felt pretty dizzy himself.

Remembering just how good it had felt, Andreas fought the temptation to kiss her again. There would be other occasions, he reminded himself, and next time he was going to select the venue more carefully and ban alcohol. She looked as though she was about to collapse in a heap.

'I'd better take you home.'

Before he committed an indecent act in a public place.

And when she was sober he'd arrange a proper date in a place where there'd be absolutely no chance of interruptions.

He stooped to pick up the shoes she'd dropped and then pointed his key towards his car and unlocked it. Suddenly aware that she was swaying again, he swept her off her feet and carried her to his car, trying to ignore her feminine scent and the way her soft hair tickled his cheek.

'Put me down.' Her words were slightly slurred and she wriggled in his arms. 'I hate men. I don't want to go on a date. And I don't want another kiss. It made me feel strange.'

Her head flopped back and he deposited her in the passenger seat, trying valiantly to ignore the fact that her dress had ridden up and was now revealing every perfect inch of her long legs. Her eyes closed and Andreas stared at her in exasperation.

'What exactly did you drink tonight?'

'One glass of really, *really* delicious orange juice,' she murmured sleepily, and he rolled his eyes.

Did she really expect him to believe that?

She was barely coherent!

'I need to take you home,' he drawled, wondering if she knew just how big a risk she was taking by getting so drunk that she didn't know who she was with. She hadn't even asked his name.

'Give me your address.' He slammed the driver's door shut and turned to look at her, groaning with frustration as he saw her curled up in his passenger seat as snug and comfortable as a tiny kitten. She was fast asleep.

His patience severely tested, Andreas sat back in his seat and counted to ten while he contemplated the problem.

So much for taking her home.

He had absolutely no intention of going back to the bar to discover her address, so he really had no option other than to take her back to his house. Which made life extremely complicated because Adrienne was there.

He closed his eyes briefly and swore under his breath.

The evening was definitely not ending the way he'd intended.

CHAPTER TWO

LIBBY awoke with a crushing headache.

With a whimper of self-pity she sat up and found herself looking into a pair of curious brown eyes. A girl sat on the end of her bed. Underneath the unruly brown hair and layers of make-up, Libby guessed her to be about twelve.

'Wow.' The girl studied her closely. 'You look *really* ill.'

Libby bit back a groan and closed her eyes. She had absolutely no idea where she was but she knew she had an almighty hangover.

Which didn't really make sense because she hadn't touched alcohol.

Or, at least, not intentionally.

Suspicion entering her mind she lifted a hand to her aching skull and sat up slowly, wincing slightly as a shaft of sunlight probed through the curtain and stabbed her between the eyes.

Realising that she was lying in an enormous, elegant bedroom, panic swamped her.

Whose bedroom?

Just what had happened last night?

The girl was still studying her closely, as if she couldn't understand how anyone could look so awful and still be alive.

'*Yiayia* made Andreas promise that he'd never bring a woman home while I was in the house, so I suppose that means he's in love with you.'

What?

Who was the girl sitting on the bed?

And who the hell was Andreas?

Searching her aching brain for some recollection of what had happened the night before, Libby had a sudden memory of broad, muscular shoulders, a firm mouth and lots and lots of fireworks.

Yes, there'd definitely been fireworks.

'I…er…who exactly is *Yiayia*?'

'*Yiayia* is Greek for Grandma, and you've said enough, Adrienne.' Cool male tones came from the doorway and the girl scrambled off the bed, suddenly wary.

'There's no need to use that scary tone. I'm old enough to know the facts of life and I know all about sex.' She looked at Libby curiously. 'Did you have sex? *Yiayia* says that loads of women want to go to bed with Andreas because he's seriously rich and very good-looking. Women go mad about him.'

Deprived of her powers of speech, Libby glanced helplessly at the man in the doorway and clashed with the darkest, sexiest eyes she'd ever seen. Despite her somewhat pathetic state, her mouth fell open and she did something she never did when she met a man.

She *stared*.

He was well over six feet, powerfully built, with jet black hair smoothed back from his forehead and bronzed skin that suggested a Mediterranean heritage. He possessed all the arrogant self-assurance of a man who'd been chased by women from the cradle.

She felt herself colour under his sharp gaze. It was evident from the hint of mockery in his dark eyes that he realised that she had an extremely hazy recollection of the events of the night before.

'You talk too much, Adrienne.' Without shifting his gaze from Libby's pale face, he strolled into the bedroom and she noticed for the first time that he was carrying a mug. 'Drink that.' He placed a mug of black coffee on the bedside table. 'It will help.'

Confronted by this final confirmation that he was well aware of her delicate condition, Libby shrank back against the pillow, stricken with guilt at her own behaviour.

She'd obviously been horribly drunk the night before.

What she didn't understand was *how*.

Unlike her, he was fully dressed and she was uncomfortably aware of his wide shoulders and sleek, dark good looks next to her near nakedness. Deciding that so much masculine virility was too much for a woman with a headache, Libby reached for the coffee.

Grandma had a point, she thought weakly. She didn't know about the rich bit, but he was *incredibly* good-looking. Almost enough to make a woman forget that all men were rats.

Which was evidently what she must have done when she'd agreed to go back to his flat with him.

How could she have done such a thing?

She never took risks like that!

She was obviously seriously on the rebound.

Catching sight of her pink dress draped carelessly over the back of a chair, she gave a whimper of mortification.

How had it got there? She had absolutely no recollection of getting undressed. Realising that she was wearing a white silk shirt that she'd never seen before in her life, her stomach flipped.

What exactly *had* happened the night before?

She remembered arriving at the auction and being given a drink of orange juice by Bev.

And she *definitely* remembered fireworks.

'*Yiayia* says that if a man and a woman spend a night together they *have* to get married,' the girl said firmly, and the man said something sharp in a language that Libby assumed was Greek before switching to English.

'Go and get ready for school,' he ordered, 'and wash that muck off your face. They'll refuse to have you back if you look like that.'

'That's why I did it,' the girl said moodily, and he sighed, the long-suffering sigh of a man stretched to the limits of his patience.

'You know you have to go back.' His voice was firm but held a note of sympathy. 'Just until we sort this out. I'm interviewing housekeepers next week.'

Adrienne looked at him. 'If you got married you wouldn't need to employ a housekeeper. It's time you settled down with a decent woman, not someone like—'

'Adrienne!' This time the man's voice was icy cold. 'That's enough. Go and wash your face.'

The girl's slim shoulders sagged. 'But—'

'Now!'

The commanding tone evidently worked because Adrienne subsided and left the room with a last curious look at Libby.

There was a long silence and Libby felt her colour rise.

Feeling that someone ought to say something, she put her coffee down and pushed her tangled blonde curls out of her eyes. 'Er...about last night...'

Not having a clue what had actually taken place the previous night, she left the statement hanging, hoping that he'd be enough of a gentleman to say something reassuring, but he merely looked at her quizzically and waited for her to finish.

Libby sighed. He was obviously one of those enviable people who used silence as a weapon, whereas she, unfortunately, had never mastered the art.

'Look.' Deciding that directness was the best approach, she took a deep breath. 'Did you spike my drink last night?'

He lifted a dark eyebrow. 'You think I need to render a woman senseless in order to persuade her to come home with me?'

No, she didn't think that.

He was the embodiment of most women's fantasies.

She flushed and concluded from his amused expression that he obviously wasn't the one responsible for her pounding headache.

'I'm sorry, it's just that someone must have but I really don't remember that much—except the fireworks. They were great. What did—?' She broke off and cleared her throat nervously. 'Well, obviously you brought me back here, which was very kind of you, but did we—? I mean, I don't remember if we actually— You see, I don't do that sort of thing usually, but I suppose I must have been a bit upset last night and...'

Totally disconcerted by his continued silence, she gave a groan and hid her head under the covers.

Why didn't he say something?

And what exactly had they done?

She was never, *ever* going out again.

It was just too embarrassing.

Finally she felt the bed shift under his weight and the covers were firmly pulled away from her.

'Two things,' he said softly, and she decided that although he didn't say much, it was definitely worth the wait when he did. He spoke with a slight accent, his deep voice caressing her nerve endings and soothing her aching head. The tension oozed out of her and she felt herself relax. His voice was amazing. 'Firstly, you should know that when I make love to a woman, Libby, she *always* remembers it.'

The tension was back with a vengeance. Her breath trapped in her lungs, heart thudding against her rib cage, Libby swallowed hard and stared into his very amused eyes.

He exuded a raw, animal sex appeal that took her breath away and she felt a powerful urge to slide her arms round his strong neck and kiss him.

She could well imagine that a night with him would be an unforgettable experience.

Appalled by the uncharacteristically explicit nature of her own thoughts, she pulled her mind back to the present and tightened her grip on the covers as if they could afford her some protection.

'Right.' Her voice was little more than a squeak. 'And what was the second thing?'

'The second thing is that there *were* no fireworks…' he dealt her a sizzling smile that sent an electric current through her trembling body '…until I kissed you.'

And with that he stood up and left the room, closing the door firmly behind him.

Having dropped Adrienne at her boarding school, Andreas strolled onto the ward an hour later, immediately aware of the consternation his appearance created.

Having recognised him from the night before, the staff were all evidently wondering what had happened to Libby.

'*You're* the new consultant?' The ward sister stared at him and then gave him a weak smile. 'Er, I'm Bev—and you're a day early.'

Andreas lifted a broad shoulder. 'I like to be on top of things.'

Bev bit her lip. 'We noticed you last night. But we didn't know—I mean, we didn't recognise you.'

'Of course you didn't.' He'd been careful not to introduce himself to anyone.

Bev took a deep breath and asked the question that she was obviously dying to ask. 'What did you do with Libby?'

Not what he'd wanted to do.

'I left her to sleep it off,' he drawled, moving to the notes trolley. 'Do the nurses on this ward always party that hard?'

Bev's shoulders stiffened defensively. 'For your information, we're desperately short-staffed and Libby worked sixteen hours on the trot yesterday and the same the day before. She had no breaks and nothing to eat all day. It's not surprising she was tipsy.'

Andreas refrained from pointing out that she'd been more than tipsy. By the time he'd laid her on the bed and undressed her, she'd been unconscious.

But she seemed to be under the impression that she hadn't drunk anything.

'Well, I have to warn you not to expect her in today,' he said smoothly. He remembered how pale and exhausted she'd looked when he'd left her, her amazing blonde hair spread over the pillow in his spare bedroom.

Mindful of Adrienne's presence, he'd resisted the temptation to join her on the bed and apply his considerable skills to bringing some colour to her cheeks.

'She's not due in until later anyway, and Libby's got the stamina of an ox. She'll be here.' Bev grabbed a set of notes and smiled at him hopefully. 'As you're early, I don't suppose you'd see a child for me, would you? The rest of your team all seem to be tied up elsewhere and I think her drain could probably come out.'

Andreas held out his hand for the notes. 'Let's go.'

Libby arrived on the ward later that morning, changed into the bright blue tracksuit bottoms and red T-shirt that all the nurses wore when they were on duty and tied her hair back with a matching ribbon.

The black coffee had helped enormously. Her head was still pounding but it was as much from tiredness as anything else. She'd worked so many double shifts in the last month that she'd forgotten what the inside of her own flat looked like.

And after last night…

She groaned at the memory, stuffed the white shirt and the pink dress into her locker and went in search of Bev.

She found her by the drugs trolley.

'*What* did you put in that orange juice?' Libby glanced over her shoulder to check that no one was listening. 'Someone spiked my drink and I've just worked out that it had to have been you.'

'Vodka,' Bev muttered, not quite meeting her eyes.

Libby stared at her, appalled. '*Vodka?* For crying out loud, Bev! I hadn't had a single thing to eat all day. What were you doing?'

'Giving you courage,' Bev said calmly, her eyes still on the drugs trolley. 'You were nervous.'

'*Nervous?* Thanks to you, I could hardly walk!'

'You looked fine. Better than fine. Really relaxed and sexy. We got £1000 for you. That cheque boosted our funds no end. Do you know how much we made?'

'I don't care how much we made.' Libby groaned and covered her face with her hands. 'Do you realise that I woke up in a strange bed this morning, in the house of a strange man who I don't even remember?' Her hands dropped to her sides and she frowned at Bev. 'What's the matter with you? Why aren't you looking at me?'

Bev looked hideously uncomfortable and Libby felt a sinking feeling in the pit of her stomach.

'There's more, isn't there?'

The ward sister tensed awkwardly. 'Well, there is something I probably ought to tell you—and you're not going to be pleased. It's about the man who bought you last night. Actually, he's—'

Loud screams interrupted her and Libby winced and glanced towards the ward. '*Who* is *that*?'

'Little Marcus Green.' Bev pulled a face. 'He had his hernia repair and his mother's had to leave him to sort out a crisis at home. Not a happy child.'

The screaming intensified and Libby rubbed her aching head. 'Poor little mite. I'll go and see to him,' she muttered. 'We'll finish this conversation later.'

'No!' Bev grabbed her arm. 'Libby, wait, I really need to tell you about the man who bought you. He's—'

'Later.' Libby shrugged her off and walked off down the ward, ponytail swinging as she hurried towards the sound.

One of the staff nurses was trying to distract him and she gave a sigh of relief when she saw Libby. 'I'm glad to see you. He's been like this for hours. His mum had to go and see to the older one at home and he's been hysterical ever since.'

Libby scooped the screaming toddler into her arms, careful not to damage the wound, and carried him over to the pile of colourful cushions that were piled in the corner of the ward.

'There, sweetheart. You'll soon feel better.' She dropped a kiss on top of his head. 'Shall we have a story while we wait for Mummy? I know you love stories.'

Marcus continued to sob and hiccough and Libby cuddled him close as she selected a book and settled down on the cushions with the little boy on her lap. 'You can choose. "Three Little Pigs" or "Little Red Riding Hood"?'

The toddler's sobs lessened. 'Pigs.'

'Three Little Pigs it is, then,' Libby said, reaching for the book and giving a gasp. 'Oh, my goodness, have you seen this?'

At her excited tone the toddler stopped sobbing and stared.

'What a cute piggy,' Libby said happily, and Marcus sneaked his thumb into his mouth and snuggled onto her lap for a closer look.

'Once upon a time...' Libby spoke in a soft voice and several other children slid out of their beds and joined her on the cushions, all listening round-eyed as she told the story.

Having examined the baby and given instructions for the drain to be removed, Andreas walked back through the ward and stopped dead at the sight of Libby, her blonde hair caught back in a bright ribbon, almost buried under a group of contented children.

They were snuggled close to her, listening avidly as she read, one of them holding onto her hand and another settled comfortably on her lap.

She was a little pale, but apart from that she looked none the worse for her excesses of the night before.

In fact, she looked incredibly beautiful and desire slammed through him again.

Bev appeared by his side. 'I told you she'd be here,' she said airily, and relieved him of the notes. 'Don't disturb her now. That toddler has been screaming since he woke up. We were all at our wits' end. We've given him painkillers but they didn't help. He needed comfort and that's Libby's speciality.'

Was it?

Andreas stared, his attention held by Libby who was laughing at something one of the children had said. She was gentle and smiley and thoroughly at home with the children. Frankly, it wasn't what he'd expected. Having seen her on the stage, he'd expected shallow and frivolous and what he was seeing was something completely different.

He watched, feeling something shift inside him. After his recent experiences, he'd given up on meeting a woman who found children anything other than a nuisance.

'She's good with them.' His soft observation drew Bev's glance.

'Yeah, she's better than most drugs. No one cheers the children up like Libby,' she told him. 'She's the best. This ward would have collapsed without her. She does the work of three.'

As they watched, the little boy snuggled closer and Libby curved an arm around him and cuddled him closer.

She was a natural storyteller, her eyes twinkling with enthusiasm and mischief as she emphasised the drama and held their attention.

She'd just got to the part where the wolf fell into the hot water when she looked up and saw him, her eyes widening with recognition. Her gaze slid to Bev in silent question and her cheeks turned pink with mortification as understanding dawned.

Bev gave a weak smile and shrugged helplessly.

'More.' The toddler tugged her arm, frustrated that the story had stopped and oblivious to the drama being played out around him. 'Want more story.'

Libby swallowed, obediently croaked her way to the end and then scrambled to her feet, Marcus still in her arms.

Bev cleared her throat. 'This is Andreas Christakos, the new consultant.' She spoke in a bright, professional voice that did nothing to alleviate the tension in the air. 'Andreas, this is Elizabeth Westerling. We call her Libby. I think you've already met each other...' Her voice trailed off slightly, and Libby closed her eyes briefly, her cheeks still pink with embarrassment.

One of the little girls tugged at her clothes. 'I need the toilet, Libby.'

'I'll take you, sweetheart,' Bev said quickly, catching her by the hand, obviously eager to find an excuse to get away.

Another little boy stepped closer. 'Is that the end of the story?'

Dragging her gaze away from his, Libby glanced down and managed a smile. 'For now. I've got to do some work.'

'Can we have another story later?'

'Maybe. If there's time.' She stroked Marcus's hair and put him back in his cot. She looked pale from lack of sleep and there were dark rings under her eyes but her beauty still took Andreas's breath away.

There were sparks of accusation in her eyes as she turned to face him. 'Well, that was a pretty dirty trick.'

He lifted an eyebrow quizzically and she glared at him coldly. 'Not telling me you were the new consultant.'

'You didn't ask me. In fact, you didn't even ask my name. You just passed out on me,' he pointed out mildly, enjoying the blush that warmed her cheeks. She had incredible skin. Smooth and creamy and untouched by the harshness of the sun.

'But *you* knew who I was,' she said accusingly. 'You knew I worked on the ward.'

'There was a strong chance of it.' He lifted a broad shoulder. 'So?'

She stared at him incredulously. 'Didn't you think that it might be embarrassing? Do you always mix business with pleasure?'

He gave a smile that was totally male. 'That,' he said slowly, 'depends on the extent of the pleasure.'

'Right.' She stared at him for a long moment and then looked away, her chest rising and falling rapidly. 'Well, at least I can save myself postage. Your shirt is in my locker.'

'My shirt?'

'The shirt you dressed me in, *Dr Christakos*.' Her voice was loaded with accusation. 'When I was asleep. Remember?'

Of course he remembered.

He remembered every delectable inch of her. 'I didn't think you'd be very comfortable sleeping in that pink thing. It seemed a little tight.'

'Excuse me?' She arched an eyebrow. 'I'm supposed to be *grateful* that you undressed me?'

'Calm down,' he drawled, his eyes gleaming with amusement. 'I kept my eyes closed the whole time. Well—most of the time.'

Libby's mouth tightened and she grabbed his arm and dragged him into the treatment room.

'I think we'd better get a few things straight.' Her blue eyes flashed at him as she let the doors swing closed behind her. 'I only allowed you to buy me because I thought my brother had sent you. I had no intention of going on a date with anyone.'

'You're angry because I bought you?' He lifted an eyebrow. 'You would have preferred me to have stood aside and let the blond man buy you?'

She stiffened slightly. 'No, of course not.'

'I seem to remember you holding onto me pretty tightly last night.'

His dark eyes glittered with amusement and she coloured. 'Yes, well, at the time I thought you were rescuing me.'

'I was.'

She glanced at him impatiently. 'You know what I mean! I thought my brother had sent you.'

He shrugged carelessly. 'He didn't, but I don't see the problem.'

'There is no problem, providing you take the £1000 back,' she said, and he smiled.

'I don't want the money,' he said smoothly. 'I paid for a date and that's what I want.'

And this time he was going to take the kiss to its natural conclusion.

She lifted her chin. 'And do you always get what you want?'

He smiled. 'Always.'

She sucked in a breath, looking slightly taken aback. 'Well, you won't on this occasion. I don't date men.'

Andreas leaned broad shoulders against the wall and tried to adjust to the fact that he'd just been turned down by a woman. It was a totally new experience.

'So...' He shrugged casually. 'You get to know me a little, and then you say yes.'

Her mouth fell open. 'Confident, aren't you?'

'Remember the fireworks, Libby.'

She stilled and her eyes connected with his. For a long moment she stared at him and then she swallowed and backed away, hoping that distance would cure the fluttering in her stomach. 'Leave me alone. I'm very grateful that you rescued me from Philip last night and I'm grateful that you took me home when I was in a less than coherent state—'

'You were drunk,' he slotted in helpfully, and she winced.

'I hadn't eaten anything all day and I had one vodka—apparently.' She rubbed slim fingers across her temple as if the memory alone was enough to inflict a headache. 'It was hidden in the orange juice.'

Hidden?

'Anyway.' She looked at him warily. 'It's history now.'

His gaze slid down her slim body, noting that she was trembling and that her hands were clenched into fists by her sides.

Despite her protests, it was blindingly obvious that she was as strongly affected by their encounter as he'd been, and it was hardly surprising. The chemistry between them was overwhelmingly powerful.

Gratified and encouraged by her response to him, he folded his arms across his broad chest and reminded himself that she'd been badly hurt. It was just a question of patience. 'It isn't history. You owe me a date.'

'Haven't you learned the meaning of the word "no"? What the hell is the matter with you men?' She glared at him with frustration and then stalked across the treatment room, pausing to look at him as she reached the door. 'In case you've forgotten, you have a little girl at home. I don't think your wife would be too impressed if she could hear you now.'

Andreas tensed, reflecting on how close he'd come to being in exactly the position she'd described.

If it hadn't been for Adrienne he'd have made a colossal mistake.

'I don't have a wife,' he said softly, 'and Adrienne isn't my daughter, she's my niece. But it's true that I do have a responsibility towards her for the time being, which is why you slept in the spare room last night and not in my bed.'

Colour flared in her cheeks and she sucked in a breath. 'I would not have been in your bed, Dr Christakos. I don't do things like that.'

'You didn't know whose bed you were in,' he pointed out, touching her flushed cheek with a strong finger. 'That might be a point worth remembering next time you have a drink.'

'Perhaps you should address your comments to the ward sister,' she muttered, and he frowned.

So it was the ward sister who'd spiked her drink. Which explained why she'd been so worried about Libby when he'd walked onto the ward alone.

Well, next time he took Libby out he was going to make sure that she didn't touch a drop of alcohol. He wanted her stone cold sober.

'What time are you off duty?'

'That is none of your business. What was it your niece said? That women are always chasing you for your looks and your money?' She tilted her head to one side. 'I don't normally tell people this on such a short acquaintance, but it's probably only fair to warn you that my father is one of the richest men in England and I've always been hideously suspicious of really good-looking men. So you have absolutely nothing to offer me.'

'How about fireworks?' He stepped closer to her, amused by the way she snatched in her breath and glared at him. She was trying so hard to pretend that she wasn't interested in him and he found it surprisingly endearing.

'Remember those fireworks, Libby,' he drawled softly, lifting a hand and trailing a finger down the slim line of her throat. 'Next time we're going to set them off in private.'

She stared at him like a rabbit caught in headlights. 'There won't be a next time and I won't be seeing you in private. I'm not interested.'

Her anguished rejection of their attraction made his heart twist. It was like dealing with an injured animal.

'I paid for a date with you, Libby,' he reminded her calmly, 'and I intend to claim it.'

Deciding that the first step in her rehabilitation was to kiss her when she was sober, he slid both hands around her face and tilted it, his eyes dropping to her mouth as her lips parted and she sucked in a breath.

Underneath his fingers he could feel a pulse beating in her throat and he lowered his head slowly, deliberately, closing the gap between them.

Her blue eyes locked with his, their breath mingling, and when their mouths finally touched he gave a groan of satisfac-

tion, his tongue tracing the seam of her lips in a sensual onslaught that left her shivering.

He kissed her slowly and thoroughly and when he finally
lifted his head she just stared at him, visibly shocked, and he
couldn't prevent the smile of all-male satisfaction that tugged
at his mouth.

'Now try telling me you're not interested, Libby.'

Without giving her a chance to recover and deliver a suitable
response, he left the treatment room and went back to work,
deciding that his new job was looking better all the time.

Libby stood frozen to the spot in the treatment room, her
whole body trembling.

Her head had been full of a thousand things that she'd wanted
to say, and they'd all vanished the moment his mouth had met
hers.

She'd never been particularly into kissing if she was honest. Her mind usually wandered and she found herself inventing excuses to end the evening promptly.

But now she realised that she'd never really been kissed before.

Not properly.

Andreas Christakos had kissed her properly. His kiss had
been a full-blown seduction which had affected her ability to
think coherently.

In fact, the way he kissed made her feel *so* hot and he made
her want *more*.

If that was the starter then she definitely wanted the main
course.

Libby gave a horrified groan and covered her face with her
hands.

And the worst thing was that he knew it.

He'd kissed her into a state of quivering, shameless excitement and had then strolled casually out of the room with all the
arrogant self-confidence of a man who didn't know the meaning of rejection.

Libby's hands dropped to her sides and she tried to pull herself together.

No more kissing, she vowed silently. Absolutely no more kissing. It turned her brain to mush and there was no way she was going to be able to keep him at a safe distance if he did it again.

He was *so* good-looking it was hard to concentrate and it would have been very, very easy to give in to all that Greek charm.

But she wasn't going to.

And she definitely wasn't going on a date with him.

He'd be the same as all the others. Worse probably, if his niece was to be believed. What had she said? That women were always chasing after him?

Libby shuddered. Those sorts of men were always the worst. Smug and arrogant. And definitely not to be trusted.

If he expected her to do any chasing then he was in for a shock. She had more sense than to fall for a pair of sexy dark eyes and an incredible body.

She was going to be running as hard as she could in the opposite direction, and now she knew where to find him she'd be delivering him a cheque at the first opportunity.

She lifted her hand to her mouth, touching her lips gently, wondering whether it was obvious to everyone that she'd just been kissed. She felt as though it was branded on her forehead.

Taking a deep breath, she pushed open the door of the treatment room, glancing furtively around her to check that no one was watching.

She could do it, she told herself firmly. She was a professional and she could work with this man.

OK, so he obviously had a Ph.D. in kissing and he was totally different from doctors that she worked with on a daily basis, but she could do it.

Bev sidled up to her, looking sheepish. 'Er, Libby...'

Libby glared at her. This was all her fault! 'Go away. You are *not* my favourite person right now.'

'Libby, the man's gorgeous, you should be thanking me for making it happen.'

'Thanking you?' Libby let out a choked laugh. 'Thanks to you, our new consultant thinks I'm a dizzy, brainless lush with a sad love life.'

'He paid £1000 for one date with you,' Bev pointed out wistfully. 'That's an enormous sum of money. He can't think you're that bad.'

Libby groaned and rubbed slim fingers over her aching forehead. 'I can't believe you got me into this mess. How am I *ever* going to have any credibility with him?'

'You're a great nurse,' Bev said firmly. 'The minute he sees you in action, he'll be bowled over.'

'He undressed me,' Libby hissed in an outraged tone, and Bev's eyes widened.

'Wow. You lucky thing.'

Libby looked at her blankly. 'Lucky?'

'Libby, he's *gorgeous*,' Bev breathed wistfully. 'He is the most stunning-looking man I've ever laid eyes on.'

'Precisely. His rat factor must be off the scale.'

Bev rolled her eyes. 'If someone fancied me enough to pay £1000 for a date, then as far as I'm concerned they could have me for ever. It's incredibly romantic.'

'It's not romantic. It's embarrassing. And, thanks to you, from now on I'm going to have to avoid him. And how am I going to work with a man I have to avoid? *Aargh!'* Libby rolled her eyes in frustration and at that moment one of the more junior nurses hurried up.

'Libby, can you take a look at Rachel Miller for me, please? The GP sent her in an hour ago with a very high temperature and it's showing no sign of coming down. I don't like the look of her. She's still waiting to be seen by one of the doctors but they've been caught up in clinic and I wasn't sure whether to bother the new consultant.'

With a last meaningful look at Bev, Libby followed her colleague down the ward and into one of the side rooms that had cots and beds for parents who wanted to stay.

The baby was in a side ward and Libby could see instantly that she was very poorly. She lay still in the cot, her breathing noisy and her cheeks flushed. Immediately Libby snapped into professional mode, her personal worries forgotten.

The baby's mother was by her side, pale and worried. 'She's really floppy and so, so hot.'

'Can you tell me what happened?' Libby spoke softly, her eyes fixed on the child, assessing her breathing. 'When did she become ill?'

'She was a bit under the weather yesterday morning and then she just got worse and worse. By teatime she was just lying on the sofa.'

And she was just lying now. Totally unresponsive. It wasn't a good sign.

'Could you get her interested in anything—toys, books?'

The mother shook her head. 'Nothing. She just lay there. Finally I panicked and took her to the GP and he sent us in here.'

'And when did she last have paracetamol syrup?'

'Two hours ago.' The mother looked at her anxiously. 'What's going to happen?'

'I'm going to check her temperature now and then ask one of the doctors to see her straight away.' Libby reached for the thermometer. 'Has she had all her immunisations, Mrs Miller?'

'Please, call me Alison and, yes, she's had everything.'

'Good.'

Libby checked the temperature and recorded it on the chart. 'It's very high, as you know. Has she been drinking much?'

'She's just not interested in anything.'

'When did she last have a wet nappy?'

The mother looked startled by the question. 'I don't know...'

'It's a way of judging her fluid output,' Libby explained, and
the woman nodded.

'Oh, I see.' She frowned slightly. 'I suppose I changed it
about three hours ago.'

Libby checked the child's blood pressure and then gave Alison Miller a brief smile.

'OK, well, the next thing to do is to ask one of our doctors
to see her. We need to find out what's causing this temperature.
I'll be back as soon as I can. If you're worried, press the buzzer.'

She gritted her teeth and went to find Andreas. She would
have preferred to have avoided him completely but that wasn't
an option. Bleeping one of the more junior members of his team
would have taken time and she didn't have time.

And, anyway, she didn't really want one of the more junior
members of his team.

She was worried about little Rachel. She needed someone
experienced and he was the consultant after all.

She found him at the nurses' station, checking a set of X-rays,
his shoulders impossibly wide as he stood with his back to her.

Libby swallowed and dragged her mind back to her work.
She already knew he was a fantastic kisser. It was time to find
out what he was like as a children's doctor.

'I need a doctor to see a new admission for me urgently.' Her
tone was cool and ultra-dignified as she struggled to behave
as though she hadn't kissed him senseless and then woken up
half-naked in his spare bedroom. 'I don't like the look of her.
Seeing that the rest of your team are elsewhere, I wondered
whether you'd do it.'

Or was he the type of consultant who preferred to delegate to
his staff? He turned and she backed away a few steps, watching him warily.

In work mode he suddenly seemed very imposing.

'I'll see her.' He flicked off the light-box and moved towards
her. 'What's the history?'

Relaxing her guard slightly, Libby fell into step beside him as they walked back to the side ward. 'She was referred by her GP, but the letter just says that she's worried about the child's temperature. Not much else. The child is floppy, she's refusing fluids and I don't like the look of her.'

She'd been a children's nurse long enough to trust her instincts and her instincts were shrieking about Rachel.

'Great.' He shot her a wry smile. 'It's wonderful to be a GP, isn't it? If in doubt, refer to hospital and let someone else make the decision.'

'Before you insult GPs, you should probably know that my brother is doing a GP rotation—'

He lifted an eyebrow and his mouth twitched in humour. 'This is the same brother who forgot to buy you last night?'

Libby gave a wry smile at the reminder. 'I still have to speak to him about that. But despite his shortcomings as a brother, he's a very dedicated doctor. I expect he was caught up with a patient, which was why he didn't show up. Unluckily for me.'

'But luckily for me,' Andreas breathed softly, his eyes narrowing as he looked at her.

She blushed hotly. 'Stop it!'

'Stop what?' He dealt her a slow smile. 'Libby, I haven't even begun yet.'

Without giving her a chance to speak again, he walked into the side ward and introduced himself to Alison Miller before bending over the cot.

His swift shift from professional to personal and back again flustered her more than she cared to admit, and Libby struggled to concentrate as she followed him into the room.

Andreas didn't seem to be suffering from the same affliction. His eyes were on his tiny patient.

To the uninitiated it might have seemed as though he was just looking at the baby, but Libby knew that he was accumulating vital pieces of information. She saw his eyes rest on the child's chest, assessing her breathing, saw the way that he noted her skin colour and the way she lay limp and unresponsive in the cot.

He lifted his head and looked at Libby, the humour gone from his eyes. 'Temperature?'

'Forty point seven,' Libby said immediately, and his mouth tightened.

'How did you take it?'

'With a tympanic membrane thermometer. I find it the best method in a child of this age.'

It gave an accurate reading of a child's core body temperature and didn't cause undue distress.

Andreas nodded his approval and looked at the chart Libby handed him, his eyes scanning the detail. Then he lifted his head and talked to the mother about the illness, questioning her about immunisations and family history.

As he finished scribbling on the notes, the baby started to cry fretfully.

Alison looked at them. 'Is it OK to pick her up?'

'Of course.' Andreas answered her with a reassuring smile before slipping his pen back into his pocket. 'Cuddle her. Then I will examine her. Libby, can I take a look at the letter from the GP?'

Libby handed it over. 'She did speak to Jonathon, your SHO.'

Alison scooped the baby out of the cot and looked at them anxiously. 'She said that it was probably just a virus but that it was best to be safe as her temperature was so high.'

It didn't sound as though the GP had even examined the child.

Libby glanced briefly at Andreas but his expression didn't flicker.

'Right.' He checked in the notes and frowned. As Libby had commented, there was virtually nothing in the referral letter. 'I'd like to examine her again, please. I'll go and fetch my things while you get her ready.'

Libby nodded and spoke quietly to Alison, explaining what was going on.

'Just hold her on your lap,' she suggested, fetching a chair to make it easier. 'Dr Christakos needs to examine her ears, and it's easier if you hold her like this, and like this...' Libby demonstrated and Alison did as she'd requested.

Andreas examined one of Rachel's eardrums and then waited while Libby helped turn the child round so that he could examine the other ear.

He was very, very skilled with the child. Gentle and swift, with no fumbling.

'Her ears are fine, and so is her throat,' he said finally, unwinding the stethoscope from around his neck. 'I'll just listen to her chest.'

Finally he rocked back on his heels. 'Her chest is clear so we need to start thinking about the less obvious.' He frowned thoughtfully and rubbed long fingers over his darkened jaw. 'Has she ever had a urinary tract infection?'

Alison's eyes widened and she shook her head. 'No. Well, not to my knowledge. Isn't that something that adults get?'

'And some children,' Andreas told her. 'It can be a cause of unexplained fever and I'm wondering if that could be the case with Rachel. There are some tests I want to do. I need to take some bloods and I want a urine sample.'

Libby pulled a face. 'That's never easy in a child of this age, as you well know, but I'll certainly try. She hasn't had a wet nappy for a few hours so we might be lucky.'

'Please.' Andreas gave her a nod. 'UTI is one of the commonest bacterial infections of childhood. It accounts for about five per cent of febrile illness. Rachel is very unwell and her temperature is very high. We need a specimen of urine urgently, and in the meantime we'll give her some ibuprofen to try and bring that temperature down.'

He scribbled on the drug chart and Libby went off to fetch the medicine and the equipment she'd need to take the urine sample.

Andreas caught up with her in the corridor. 'Your instincts are good. That child is very sick,' he said quietly. 'I'll give you an hour to get that sample and if you don't have any luck I'll have to do a supra-pubic aspiration.'

'An SPA?' Libby pulled a face. A supra-pubic aspiration meant inserting a needle into the bladder to draw off the sample of urine. It was sometimes used in very small babies when a sample was needed urgently and other methods had failed. 'Do we have to? That's invasive.'

'I'm aware of that.' Andreas ran a hand over his jaw, his expression serious. 'I'm also aware that the risk of renal scarring in infants and young children with undiagnosed and untreated UTI is high. I want to start antibiotics as soon as possible and I can't do that until I've taken a specimen. Call me if there's any change.'

Despite her best intentions, Libby found her eyes drawn to his mouth.

Being kissed by Andreas had been a totally new experience and for a moment she was lost, remembering.

'Libby?' His voice prompted her gently and she gave a start and her eyes flew to his, registering the gleam of amusement.

Damn.

He'd caught her staring.

She backed away, totally flustered. 'I'll get back to Rachel.'

His smile widened. 'Fine. Call me if you're worried.'

Trying to steady her thundering pulse rate, Libby turned and walked away from him, wondering how on earth she was supposed to get any work done with him smiling at her like that.

Determined to forget about him, she focused her attention on Rachel, trying to obtain the sample they needed so badly.

She didn't succeed and less than an hour later she was forced to find Andreas again.

She came straight to the point, her tone brisk. 'I'm worried about Rachel. Her temperature isn't coming down and I'm nursing her in a nappy and a sheet. I've tried to get a clean sample of urine but it's been a nightmare.'

Andreas frowned. 'Has she drunk anything?'

'Barely.'

'And she hasn't passed urine in the last hour?'

Libby shook her head. 'Her nappies are dry.'

Andreas nodded. 'I'll do a supra-pubic aspiration,' he said immediately. 'I know it's invasive but at least it's definitive and frankly I'm worried about her condition. We'll do an ultrasound to check she has urine in her bladder. I'll need a 21G needle—'

'I know what you need,' Libby slotted in, already on her way to gather the right equipment. She just hoped the new consultant knew what he was doing.

She laid up a trolley and was back by the cot minutes later.

'Someone needs to hold her very firmly in the supine position,' Andreas said calmly, using the ultrasound to check that the baby had a full bladder.

'I'll hold her,' Libby said immediately, 'and I know her mum will want to be with her. She's just nipped to the phone to call home.'

At that moment Alison returned and Andreas quietly explained why they needed to aspirate the bladder.

'Her temperature is going up and we need to obtain a sterile specimen of urine.'

Alison looked pale and tired. 'Libby was trying to get a clean catch.'

'I haven't managed it,' Libby said softly, 'and we really, really need to see if she's got bugs in her urine. In a child of this age this is the only reliable method and we need to send it to the lab before we start antibiotics.'

Alison nodded. 'So do it.' Her mouth tightened. 'Can I stay with her?'

'Do you want to?' Andreas spoke gently and Alison sucked in a breath.

'Yes. It's upsetting but I couldn't bear to think that I wasn't there for her when she needed me.'

Andreas exchanged glances with Libby and then turned away to wash his hands, scrubbing them methodically.

Libby prepared the trolley and then held the child while he cleaned the area with alcohol and allowed it to dry.

She watched as he inserted the needle gently, aspirating as he advanced it into the bladder, speaking softly to the baby as he worked. It was obvious from the skill and speed of his fingers that he'd performed the procedure many times before.

When he had the sample he withdrew the needle and his gaze flickered to Libby.

'Can you apply pressure to that site for about two minutes? Then cover it with a dressing.' He placed the sample on the trolley and turned to Alison. 'It's possible that she will have a bit of blood in her urine for the next couple of days so if you notice that in the nappy don't be alarmed. You can call Libby if you're worried.'

Libby lifted the gauze and checked that the bleeding had stopped and then applied a dressing. Then she swiftly dressed the sobbing baby and handed her to her mother for a cuddle.

'Just hold her for a bit and she should settle,' she advised. 'She's had paracetamol and ibuprofen so hopefully her temperature should come down soon.'

Alison looked at her. 'And the doctor really thinks that she has an infection in her bladder?'

'Yes, he does. The reason he wants to treat it quickly is because it can spread to the kidneys and cause damage.'

'But with treatment she should be OK?'

Libby nodded. 'Dr Christakos will probably want to do more tests to check, but you brought her in straight away so the chances are we've caught it before the infection has had time to spread.'

Satisfied that Alison understood the explanation, Libby followed Andreas to the nurses' station where he was tapping details into the computer.

'What happens now?'

'She's dehydrated so I'm going to put a line in and get some fluid into her. I'm also going to start her on IV antibiotics. When she's picked up a bit we can give her the rest of the course orally.'

'You're not going to wait for the results?'

He shook his head. 'It's important to treat her fast. If necessary we can change the antibiotics when the results come back. If the UTI is confirmed, we'll need to do more tests.' He didn't lift his eyes from the screen. 'All young children have to be investigated for vesicoureteric reflux.'

'So will you do an ultrasound?'

'Amongst other things.' He looked up and smiled briefly. 'Reflux and scarring can be missed by ultrasound in this age group so she will have to have cystography.'

'And you'll send her for a DMSA scan?'

'Yes. And, Libby...' He sat back in his chair. 'We need to try and get her to take oral fluids.'

'I know.' Libby nodded, well aware of that fact. 'Now we've got the urine sample I'll concentrate on that. I've explained the importance of fluids to the mother.'

'Is she breast-feeding?'

Libby shook her head. 'Bottle.'

Andreas finished what he was doing and stood up. 'Let's get that drip up.'

'I'll get a trolley ready.'

Libby spent the rest of the shift looking after Rachel, reassured by the fact that Andreas was within shouting distance if the baby's condition worsened. Apart from one trip down to the A and E department to assess a child, he spent most of the day on the ward, getting to know the children and meeting his team.

Libby tried hard to forget what had happened the night before but it was difficult to concentrate with those sexy dark eyes following her round the ward.

He was a man, she reminded herself firmly. Which meant only one thing as far as she was concerned.

Trouble.

Libby was updating Rachel's charts at the nurses' station when she glanced up and saw a young girl hovering by the entrance of the ward.

Her eyes widened.

'Adrienne?' She recognised Andreas's niece immediately, dropped her pen onto the desk and walked across to her. 'Hi, there. Aren't you supposed to be at school?'

The girl glared at her defiantly but her lip wobbled slightly. 'I've run away. And I'm not going back. *Ever.* I hate it there.'

Oops.

Her dark hair looked more unruly than ever and there were red rings around her eyes where she'd been crying. She looked very vulnerable and very young.

Libby leaned against the wall, her expression sympathetic. 'Do you want to tell me why?'

Adrienne shrugged and stared at her shoes. 'I don't fit in.'

Libby frowned. 'In what way?'

Adrienne didn't look up. 'I'm...different.'

'We don't all have to be the same. Being different can be good,' Libby said softly, but Adrienne shook her head.

'It isn't. It's horrible.' Her voice cracked slightly and she rubbed the toe of her shoe along the floor. 'I'm not trendy. I don't know how to be trendy. I tried to do my hair differently and wear make-up but Andreas made me wash it before I left the house. I hate him.'

Remembering the badly applied make-up, Libby privately thought that Andreas had made totally the right decision.

'How old are you, Adrienne?'

'Twelve. But I'm nearly thirteen,' she added quickly.

Libby nodded. 'It can be really tough being thirteen. I remember it well.'

'You?' Adrienne looked at her in disbelief and Libby nodded wryly.

'I had a terrible time. I was skinny as a rake, had a brace on my teeth and I wore glasses. And, to make it worse, my sister was stunning. Trust me—the other kids had a really big choice of names to call me. I know all about being different.'

Adrienne stared. 'But you're trendy.'

'Now maybe, but not then,' Libby assured her dryly. 'Who goes shopping with you?'

'*Yiayia*—I mean, my grandmother, and she's very, *very* conservative,' Adrienne said gloomily. 'Or Andreas, and he's even worse. He's so strict and traditional he won't let me buy anything remotely daring. Given the chance, he'd dress me in a sack.'

'Hmm, I can see that neither of those would be decent shopping partners,' Libby agreed, examining her nails thoughtfully. 'You know, if you wanted to, I could pick you up from school one day and take you shopping.'

The minute she'd uttered the words, part of her wanted to withdraw the offer. What on earth was she thinking? Offering to help Adrienne would inevitably bring her into contact with Andreas and she'd already decided to avoid him as far as possible.

Adrienne's gasp of delight made it obvious that there was no going back. 'You? Why would you want to do that?'

Because she was a total idiot and a sucker for any unhappy child.

Libby gave a weak smile. 'I adore shopping. Ask my brother or sister. I'm a shopaholic. There's nothing like a bit of retail therapy to cheer a girl up.'

Adrienne's eyes were huge. 'You'd take me shopping? *Really*?'

'Sure.' Touched by the girl's gratitude, Libby decided that she'd done the right thing. 'As long as you promise to smile and not argue with my taste. And then, when we've shopped, I'll do your hair. I'm great with hair. I've been practising for twenty-nine years on my own.'

Before Adrienne could reply, Andreas strode up and Libby stiffened, wondering how he'd react to the fact that his niece had run away from school. She remembered with appalling clarity her father's furious response when she'd done the same thing. *She'd never, ever done it again.*

But Andreas didn't look furious at all. He looked concerned.

'Adrienne?' His tone was incredibly gentle as he stopped in front of the trembling girl. He said something to her in Greek and she took a shuddering breath and looked him in the eye, replying in English.

'I'm so homesick. I want to live with you. *Please*, let me live with you—I won't be any trouble, I promise. I know that it's supposed to be temporary but I can't bear it. Please, don't send me back there.'

Swallowing back an unexpected lump in her throat, Libby glanced at Andreas, noting the tension in his wide, muscular shoulders.

'You're too young to be in the house on your own, *koratsaki mou*, and I haven't found a suitable housekeeper yet,' he said roughly.

Adrienne wrapped her arms around her waist. 'I don't care about being on my own. I'd rather be on my own than with those—those…' Her English failed her and she looked pleadingly at Libby. 'Tell him not to make me go back. *Please.*'

Libby glanced at Andreas helplessly. She really had no idea what to do or say. She knew nothing about the situation but she did know that Adrienne was obviously miserable.

Before she could speak, Bev hurried up, looking worried. 'Dr Christakos, A and E are looking for you. They've got a child with a nasty asthma attack. They want you down there urgently.'

Andreas sucked in a breath and cast a look at Adrienne. 'Of course.' He raked long fingers through his black hair, his frustration evident. 'Adrienne, we can't sort this out now. You'll have to wait in the staffroom until I finish.'

'Why don't I take her home with me?' Libby said quickly, putting a protective hand on the child's arm. 'I'm off duty now anyway and it would be much nicer for her. You can collect her from my flat when you're ready. Bev will give you my address.'

His mouth tightened. 'I'll have to take her straight back to school—'

Adrienne gave a moan of protest. 'No!'

'Adrienne, I have no choice!' He sounded tired and frustrated. 'If I could see another way, believe me, I'd take it. It's just for the short term.'

Libby wondered exactly what was going on.

Why was his niece living with him?

Bev touched his arm. 'Dr Christakos—'

'I'm on my way. Adrienne, we'll discuss this later.' His dark eyes rested on Libby. 'I don't particularly want her waiting around here so if you're sure it's all right, I'll take you up on your offer. Thank you.'

'You're welcome.'

She watched as he strode out of the ward and then turned to Bev who was watching open-mouthed. 'What are you staring at?'

'You.' Bev's eyes twinkled merrily. 'So you're definitely avoiding him, then.'

Libby gritted her teeth. 'This is nothing to do with Andreas.'

Bev nodded solemnly. 'Of course it isn't. I'm sure you'll manage to avoid him when he comes to pick her up *from your flat.*'

Libby glared at her friend. 'Mammoth rat factor, remember?' Turning her back on Bev, she held out a hand to Adrienne and gave her a warm smile. 'Come on. Time to go and raid my fridge I think.'

This had absolutely nothing to do with Andreas, she repeated firmly to herself.

Nothing.

CHAPTER THREE

LIBBY let herself into the flat.

'Let's get something to eat. I'm starving.' She dropped her keys on the hall table and walked through to the kitchen.

A dark-haired man with wicked blue eyes was lounging at the table, nursing a cup of coffee and reading a medical journal.

'You're in *big* trouble, buster,' Libby muttered, glaring at him as she tugged open the fridge door. 'This is Adrienne, by the way. Adrienne, this is my brother, Alex. Don't be taken in by the blue eyes and the charismatic smile, he's a total menace and I'm about to kill him.'

'Hello, Adrienne.' Alex smiled easily and then glanced back at his sister. 'Why are you going to kill me? You should be thanking me.'

'Thanking you?' Libby removed an armful of food from the fridge and slammed the door shut with such force that the contents rattled ominously. 'Where the hell were you last night?'

'Language, Elizabeth, language,' Alex reproved mildly, his eyes flickering to Adrienne. 'And to answer your question, I was in the middle of a tricky delivery. My legendary skills as a doctor were in demand. I was saving lives-snatching the innocent from the jaws of death—'

'Yes, yes, spare me the drama,' Libby interrupted him impatiently, and deposited the food on the kitchen table. 'For your patients' sake, I hope you're a better doctor than you are a brother.' She reached into the cupboard for some plates. 'Here we are, Adrienne. Help yourself. Food always helps in a crisis. Smoked salmon, ham, cheese, salad, chocolate, more chocolate...'

Adrienne sat down at the table and glanced between them, her face slightly pink. 'I'm not very hungry,' she said shyly. 'I'm really sorry if I'm in the way.'

Alex treated her to a smile that was guaranteed to weaken the knees of any female, regardless of age.

'You're not in the way. In fact, I'm very relieved you're here or my future on this planet would be in severe jeopardy.'

Libby noticed the way that Adrienne was staring at her brother and suppressed a groan.

Alex affected all women that way, no matter how young or old they were. He was lethal.

'So come on.' She looked at him pointedly. 'What happened? And don't give me any more of this "I was saving a life" rubbish.'

Alex leaned back in his chair and gave her a slow smile. 'I decided to do you a favour and let someone else buy you. Someone you could actually have a relationship with.'

Libby gaped at him. 'But that isn't what I want. You *know* I don't want a relationship.'

'Of course you do.' Alex suppressed a yawn. 'All women want relationships. It's in the genes. The minute you meet a new man you start scribbling his surname after your name just to see what it looks like.'

Libby was momentarily speechless. 'I don't do that! I don't want a relationship any more than you do!'

Alex regarded her steadily. 'Yes, you do, sweetheart. You're terrified of being hurt but deep down you believe in Mr Right as much as every other woman.'

'You're an insufferable chauvinist.' Libby was simmering and Alex looked amused.

'No, I'm honest. Men have different needs to women. We don't need all that "till death us do part" nonsense to enjoy a relationship. Even when we do end up marrying we only do it because that's what women expect. Not because it's what we want.'

Libby scowled at him, dying to let rip but constrained by Adrienne's presence. 'One day, Alexander Westerling, you are going to meet the woman of your dreams,' she muttered, her teeth gritted as she struggled with her temper, 'and I *truly* hope she refuses to marry you.'

Alex threw back his head and laughed. 'Sweetheart, the woman who refuses to marry me *is* the woman of my dreams.'

Libby glared at her brother with frustration.

He was devilishly good-looking and his ego had been fed a constant diet of adoring, hopeful women since he'd mastered the art of smiling. Consequently he didn't believe that there was a single woman he couldn't seduce into his bed if he put his mind to it.

But that was as far as it went. Libby knew that underneath the light-hearted banter her brother was icily determined never to settle down with one woman. She looked at him sadly, the anger melting away as she acknowledged that he was as much a victim of their upbringing as she was. When things had become heated between her parents, it had frequently been Alex who had intervened. The experience had left him with a serious allergy to long-term relationships.

She'd thought she was the same, but his words had kindled a doubt deep inside her.

Was she secretly hoping that Mr Right was out there?

Was she fooling herself by pretending that she wasn't interested in relationships?

Alex was looking at her steadily and she sensed that he knew what she was thinking. For all their petty arguing, they were extremely close.

'So tell me about the man who bought you,' he said, his voice surprisingly gentle. 'Rumour has it that he was smitten.'

Rumour?

Libby stared at him, wondering just how much he knew. The hospital grapevine had obviously worked overtime. 'Did you know that Philip tried to buy me?'

'No.' Alex's smile faded and his blue eyes suddenly lost their warmth. 'I didn't know he was turning up or I would have been there. He and I need to have a chat.'

Libby watched as her brother's fingers tightened around his mug. For a brief moment both of them had forgotten Adrienne's presence. 'Defending my honour, Alex?'

'Maybe.'

Libby swallowed, touched by her brother's protectiveness. 'Would you have hit him?'

'Into the next county,' Alex drawled lightly, 'so maybe it's just as well I didn't go. I gather someone outbid him?'

Oh, yes. Someone had definitely outbidden him.

Libby stared at her plate, her mind suddenly full of Andreas. His broad shoulders, his powerful musculature and the aura of strength that surrounded him.

All her instincts warned her that he was the sort of man who broke hearts.

He was absolutely the last person that she ought to be day-dreaming about.

So why couldn't she get him out of her mind?

'Lib?' Alex leaned forward, his blue gaze sharp. 'Come on. Tell your big brother.'

Libby felt her colour rise and cursed inwardly as she saw Alex smile knowingly. It was impossible to hide anything from him.

'He's not really my big brother,' Libby told Adrienne, keeping her voice light to disguise the hammering of her heart. 'We're triplets. He was born about three minutes before our sister Katy. I was last.'

Adrienne stared at them in fascination. 'Triplets? You lucky things. How wonderful to be one of three.'

'Not that wonderful,' Libby said, glaring at her brother, but Adrienne sighed wistfully.

'I think it's great. I would have done *anything* to have had a brother or sister and you've got both.'

Alex leaned forward, his voice gentle. 'You're an only child?'

Adrienne nodded. 'And my mum and dad died in a boating accident in Greece when I was tiny. I've lived with my Grandma for the past twelve years but she had to have a hip operation and now she's decided that she's too old to look after me now and that's why I've come to live with Andreas.'

Alex listened carefully to this tumbled speech and his gaze swivelled to Libby.

'And who's Andreas?'

'He's the man who bought me last night, Alex. Remember? I was for sale, and you were supposed to buy me.'

Completely unrepentant, Alex lifted a dark eyebrow. 'How much did he pay?'

'Andreas *bought* you?' Adrienne's eyes were like saucers and Libby suppressed a groan. She'd forgotten that the child didn't know the story.

'He just bought a date with me, that's all,' she said quickly, throwing a warning glance at Alex. 'The money was for a good cause. It was all very harmless.'

Except that the sum hadn't been harmless. He'd paid a small fortune for the privilege of spending an evening with her.

Adrienne's eyes were very round. 'Wow. That doesn't sound like him. Andreas is very picky about women. Especially women he doesn't know. He doesn't trust them. Grandma says it's because he's handsome, Greek and a millionaire,' she said ingenuously. 'They're after him for the wrong reasons. So why you were sleeping in our spare room?'

Aware of her brother's amused gaze, Libby gritted her teeth. 'It's a bit complicated.'

Alex drained his coffee-cup. 'I'll just bet it is,' he muttered under his breath, and Libby rolled her eyes in frustration.

Whoever thought it was great to be a triplet had never had a brother as infuriating as Alex.

'None of this would have happened,' she snarled, 'if you'd fulfilled your brotherly duty and bought me.'

Alex stood up, as cool and relaxed as ever. 'Of course, there's always the possibility that he might have outbid me if he's that rich.'

'You're filthy rich and I'm your sister!' Libby looked at him in exasperation. 'You should have been prepared to pay whatever it took.'

'To keep you out of the clutches of a handsome Greek millionaire?' Alex's eyes brimmed with laughter. 'I don't think so. I think he could be just what my baby sister needs.'

Libby stared at him, a suspicion forming in her mind. 'You did it on purpose, didn't you?' she said slowly, her eyes narrowing as she looked at him. 'You never intended to buy me.'

'I've always been very careful with my money,' Alex said lightly, 'and, anyway, there's nothing like a new love affair to take your mind off your old one. You needed a distraction from Philip.'

He lifted one broad shoulder in a careless shrug and with a conspiratorial wink at Adrienne he strolled out of the room, leaving Libby fuming.

He was *so* infuriating.

'He's *gorgeous*,' Adrienne whispered, her eyes still fixed on the door as if she was hoping that Alex would reappear. 'Really, really handsome. Those blue eyes are amazing.'

'He's dangerous,' Libby muttered, pushing her plate away and reaching for her coffee. 'Wherever he goes, he leaves a trail of broken hearts and sobbing women.'

At that moment her brother was *not* her favourite person.

'Like Andreas,' Adrienne observed wisely, and Libby smiled wryly.

She could imagine that it was true.

Andreas Christakos was staggeringly good-looking and if he was rich as well then that would be enough for most women.

But not her.

She was far too cynical to be taken in by a handsome face and buckets of sex appeal.

And she certainly wasn't interested in his money.

She stood up and smiled at Adrienne. 'Come on. Let's do your hair before he picks you up.'

Andreas rang the doorbell and glanced at his watch in frustration.

He was much, much later than he'd planned. Stabilising the little girl in A and E had taken a long time and in the end he'd admitted her to the ward, leaving instructions with the staff that they were to call him if there was any change in her condition. It had been a nasty attack.

The door opened and, instead of Libby, he found himself staring at a tall, dark-haired man with very blue eyes.

Andreas tensed and the warmth of his greeting froze on his lips.

This was not what he'd expected. It had never occurred to him that Libby could be living with someone.

His reaction to the evidence that she had another man in her life was so intense that he sucked in a breath as he felt a rush of that most basic of emotions—

Jealousy.

The man extended a hand, his expression friendly. 'I'm Alex—Libby's brother. You must be the guy who bought her. I tell you now, you should get yourself a refund. The girl's high maintenance and she costs a fortune in chocolate and shoes.'

Brother?

The tension left his shoulders and Andreas smiled warmly. The knowledge that she lived with her brother and not her boyfriend caused him a significant amount of relief.

'Come on in.' Alex stood to one side to let him pass. 'The girls are in the bedroom. I don't know what's going on but there's lots of giggling.'

'It was kind of her to bring Adrienne home.' Andreas glanced around him, noticing the elegance of the spacious apartment. 'Your sister is good with children.'

Alex gave a short laugh. 'Better with children than she is with adults. Can I get you a drink?'

Andreas smiled and shook his head. 'No, thanks. I need to take Adrienne back to school.' He ran a hand over his darkened jaw. 'That's if I can persuade her to go back.'

At that moment a door opened and Adrienne came flying out, her face happy and smiling.

'Guess what? Libby's promised to pick me up from school and take me shopping one day soon.'

She had? Why would she do a thing like that?

Andreas hid his surprise. A day shopping with a twelve-year-old girl bent on choosing a totally unsuitable wardrobe wasn't his idea of relaxation. Why would Libby have volunteered for the task? She had no reason to want to help Adrienne.

He looked at Libby curiously but she carefully avoided his gaze.

Adrienne slipped an arm through his and looked sheepish. 'I'm sorry I ran away. Did you ring the school? Were they furious?'

'Yes, I rang and, no, they weren't furious. They were worried.' Andreas rubbed a hand over the back of his neck, wondering how he was going to help her to settle in. For all his experience with women, he knew nothing about twelve-year-old girls. 'It's a good school, Adrienne.'

Adrienne pulled a face. 'I suppose the teachers are OK but I haven't got any friends.'

'You've only been there for a week,' Libby said quietly. 'These things take time. Remember what we said.'

'Yeah.' Adrienne nodded and then looked at Andreas. 'Can we go for a pizza before you take me back?'

Relieved to have avoided a long drawn-out debate about whether she should go back at all, Andreas smiled. Whatever Libby had said to the child, it had obviously made an impact. 'Yes, we can go for pizza.'

'And can Libby come?'

Libby stiffened. 'I don't think—'

'Of course she can,' Andreas said smoothly, ignoring the furious look she shot him. 'It's the least I can do after the hospitality she offered you tonight.'

'Fantastic. I just need to say goodbye to Alex.' Adrienne hurried off towards the kitchen and Libby looked at Andreas angrily.

'I've already told you, I don't go on dates.'

'If you think that eating pizza with a twelve-year-old is my idea of a date, you're in for a pleasant surprise when I finally take you out,' Andreas drawled. 'You can relax. This is Adrienne's evening. You're quite safe.'

She sucked in a breath. 'Don't you understand no? Do I need to learn Greek?'

'It's just a pizza, Libby,' he said mildly, noticing with satisfaction that she seemed very tense. She definitely wasn't indifferent to him. 'Trust me, when we go on our date, we won't be eating pizza.'

'I won't go on a date with you.' Her eyes clashed with his and her blue eyes sparked. 'I don't want to go on a date with anyone.'

'But I'm not anyone.'

Her soft lips were parted and he could see a pulse beating in the side of her throat but she was still glaring at him.

'Sure of yourself, aren't you?'

He smiled, intrigued by the complexities of her character. On the outside she was prickly and sassy, but on the inside— his guts clenched as he remembered the way she'd handled the children—on the inside she was soft and all woman.

And he wanted her.

He lifted a hand and brushed her flushed cheek with a lingering touch that made her stiffen. 'Remember the fireworks, Libby.'

He could tell by the expression on her face that she didn't want to remember them. That remembering them disturbed her.

They took Adrienne for a pizza and then drove her back to school.

Libby helped to settle her into her room while Andreas went to talk to the headmistress.

Noting the awed expressions of her roommates as they stared at both Andreas and his incredibly sexy sports car, Libby privately doubted that Adrienne would have any more trouble fitting in, but she chatted away to the other girls, trying to help Adrienne bridge the gap.

When they finally left the school it was dark and Andreas drove back towards her flat.

'I owe you a big thank you.'

She glanced at him briefly, suddenly conscious of the intimacy created by the confines of the car. 'For what?'

'For being so kind to Adrienne.'

'She's a nice girl.'

His strong fingers tightened slightly on the wheel. 'I feel somewhat out of my depth,' he admitted wryly, sounding very Greek and very, very male. 'Dealing with twelve-year-old girls is new to me.'

His broad shoulders were only inches away from hers and she shifted slightly in her seat to try and create some distance.

'How did she come to be living with you?' Maybe if she stuck to neutral subjects she'd be able to forget how good-looking he was. 'She said something about her grandmother deciding that she was too old to look after her.'

Andreas gave a short laugh. 'My mother isn't too old for anything,' he said dryly. 'She was just playing games.'

'What sort of games?'

He hesitated and then cast her a smile. 'It's history now.' There was a brief silence and he returned his attention to the road ahead. 'I was very grateful for your help tonight. She seemed happy by the time we left her and that was because of you.'

Libby frowned slightly, wondering what he'd meant by the statement that his mother had been playing games. 'It's early days,' she said. 'It always takes a while to settle into a new school, particularly when you start halfway through a term.'

She gave a little shudder, remembering all too well the night-mares of school.

'You sound as though you're speaking from experience.'

'I am.' Libby stared out of the window into the darkness. 'We all went to boarding school. Alex was fine—he's as tough as nails—but Katy and I hated it.'

'Katy is your sister?'

Libby nodded. 'She works in A and E. She's married to Jago Rodriguez, the consultant.'

'Really?' Andreas pulled up outside her building and switched off the engine. 'I met him earlier tonight. Bright chap. But at least you and Katy had each other at school. Adrienne has no one. That worries me. And I hate her boarding. As soon as I find a suitable housekeeper she can live at home with me.'

'She's a lovely girl,' Libby said. 'She'll make friends, I know she will. She just needs a little more confidence and her ap-pearance needs a bit of a tweak. I must admit I'm surprised that your mother expects you to keep an eye on her. You're a single guy and teenagers can be a handful at the best of times.'

'My mother is a master manipulator,' Andreas remarked. 'She is desperate for me to mend my wicked ways and settle down. She thought Adrienne might fulfil that purpose.'

Libby saw the amusement in his dark eyes and felt her heart lurch. It would be so easy to fall for him.

Why was she feeling like this? she wondered helplessly.

She had more sense than to fall for a handsome face and a luscious body.

Maybe it was because he wasn't English. All that bronzed virility and exotic sexuality was getting to her.

But she had it under control, she told herself firmly, dragging her mind back to the conversation.

'So how does having Adrienne help?'

'She thinks it will curb my reputedly excessive lifestyle.'

'Oh.' Libby digested this. 'Evidently she thinks you've been dating the wrong sort of women.'

He threw back his head and laughed. 'She does indeed.' His smile faded. 'A bit like you. You've obviously been dating the wrong sort of men.'

Libby stared into those seductive brown eyes and swallowed hard. 'I've already told you, there's no such thing as the right sort of man.'

There was a slight pause. 'And you feel like this because of Philip or because of your parents?'

Libby stared at him. 'How do you know about my parents?'

'You told me.' He threw her an amused glance. 'You *had* drunk an orange juice so it's no wonder you don't remember.'

Libby gave a reluctant laugh and then slunk down in her seat. 'I don't want to talk about my parents.' She never talked about her parents to anyone. Why on earth had she mentioned them to him? 'I don't want to talk about any of it.'

'Not even Philip?'

'Especially not Philip.'

'Were you in love with him?'

He asked the question calmly and Libby looked at him, startled.

'No. I don't think so. But he was very persistent. Going out with him seemed logical.'

'Logical?' Andreas lifted an eyebrow. 'A true love affair should never be logical, surely. It is about emotion and losing control.'

Libby's smile faded under the intensity of his dark gaze.

She'd never had a love affair with anyone.

'Well, it's probably my fault, then,' she muttered. 'I'm not great at losing control. In fact, I'm a control freak. I like to be in charge of everything that happens in my life.'

There was a long silence and then Andreas turned in his seat so that he was facing her.

'Powerful sexual chemistry is not controllable,' he said softly, lifting a hand and pushing a wisp of blonde hair away from her face. 'It's an intense emotional reaction that is beyond human explanation. Evidently you haven't felt that. Yet.'

The gentle brush of his fingers against her skin was unbelievably erotic and she felt excitement swoop inside her and concentrate low in her pelvis.

If sexual chemistry was butterflies in her stomach and difficulty breathing then she was feeling it now.

For him.

Dear God, she wasn't ready for this. After what had happened with Philip she doubted she'd ever be ready for it.

So why was she reacting so strongly?

Totally unnerved by the way he made her feel, Libby reached out and fumbled for her seat belt.

'I'm going. Goodnight.'

Before she could release the catch a strong hand covered hers and her head jerked up, her eyes clashing with his.

'Libby, it's OK. You can trust me—'

'No!' Breathing rapidly, she pulled away from him and opened the car door before turning back to face him. 'Don't turn your lethal charm on me, Dr Christakos. Save it for all those millions of women that must be desperate for your attentions. I'm not interested. Thanks for the pizza.'

And with that she closed the car door behind her, hoping he couldn't see how much her knees were shaking.

CHAPTER FOUR

LIBBY arrived on the ward the next morning, determined to distance herself from Andreas.

She was finding it harder and harder to concentrate on her work with those sexy dark eyes seducing her every time she turned around.

There really was something to be said for having puny, ugly doctors around the place, she reflected. At least they made it easy to keep your mind on work.

If it was at all possible, she was going to bleep Jonathon, the SHO. At least he wasn't a threat to her pulse rate.

Even though it was early, the ward was already bustling with activity and Libby went straight to see little Rachel.

One of the night nurses was checking her temperature and glanced up as she saw Libby.

'Hi, there. I'm glad to see you. It means I can go home to bed.'

Libby smiled and looked at the child. 'How is she? She looks a little better.'

'Her temperature is down a bit so I think the antibiotics must be working. Dr Christakos checked on her in the night and he thought she seemed to be showing a response even though it's

only been twenty-four hours. He thinks it's definitely a urinary tract infection.'

'He saw her in the night?' Given that he'd dropped her off
fairly late, Libby was surprised to hear that he'd paid a visit to
the hospital.

The other nurse smiled dreamily. 'He's *so* impressive. He
was worried about the little girl who had the asthma attack last
night. Apparently it was touch and go for a while in A and E
and when he admitted her to the ward he was concerned that
she could go off again.'

'So he came in to check her?'

'Yes. At about eleven o'clock.'

Just after he'd dropped her home.

Libby cleared her throat, trying to keep her voice casual.
'Has he been in this morning yet?'

Her colleague nodded. 'Oh, yes. He wanted to take some
bloods from Rachel and while he was here he checked Marcus
because he's due for discharge today.'

Libby hid her surprise. He certainly wasn't afraid of hard
work. His team was really stretched and he was obviously more
than happy to roll up his sleeves and help out.

On the other hand, his diligence was going to make it harder
for her to avoid him. She could have done with a consultant
who sat in his office and delegated.

'I'll finish off here. You go home. Where's her mum?'

'Having a wash. Apparently Rachel was awake quite a bit
in the night so she didn't get much sleep.'

'Wet nappies?'

'Plenty, but I have to confess she didn't drink much in the
night.'

Libby nodded. 'OK. I'll make a real effort to get her drinking today and then hopefully we can take that drip down.'

She smiled as Rachel's mother arrived back in the room,
clutching a wash-bag and looking incredibly tired.

'Good morning. She looks a little better.'

Alison looked at her daughter anxiously. 'Do you think so? She certainly seems a little cooler but she was very fretful in the night.'

'It's early days yet,' Libby agreed, 'but hopefully she'll start to pick up today. We need to get her drinking so that we can get that drip out.'

The mother looked at her doubtfully. 'I suppose I could try her with a bottle now…'

'Let's give her another half-hour and see if she wakes up a bit,' Libby suggested, breaking off as Andreas walked into the room.

'Good morning.'

His voice was warm and intensely masculine and Libby felt her whole body hum with sexual awareness.

Colour warmed her cheeks. 'I need to check her temperature, but she's sleeping at the moment,' she explained quickly, as he picked up the chart. 'She seems to be picking up and I thought she'd be better off being left to rest. We'll try her with a bottle in half an hour.'

He scanned the chart briefly, looking at the readings the night shift had recorded. 'Let me know what her obs are when you've checked them and keep her fluids up. If there's a problem, call me. I've got to go down to A and E to see a child.'

Breathing a sigh of relief that he was going to be absent from the ward for at least a short time, Libby got back to work.

She checked on the patients who were her responsibility and then went back to Rachel and found her sitting on Alison's lap, looking much more alert.

'Oh, she's definitely a bit better,' Libby said, pleased by the change in the child in such a short time. 'I'll just check her temperature again and then we'll try and get that bottle down her.'

The temperature reading was down considerably and the baby took the bottle eagerly.

Alison was delighted. 'She wouldn't touch it yesterday so she must be feeling better.'

Libby nodded. 'We'll keep the drip up for now and I'll speak to Dr Christakos about it later. I expect he'll want her to carry on having her antibiotics into the vein for now, but hopefully if she carries on drinking plenty then we can take that drip out later today.'

Making a mental note to discuss it with Andreas next time he appeared on the ward, Libby recorded the results and went to check on her next patient.

Her morning was horrendously busy and she was just starting to hope that she might actually be able to stop for a coffee when a five-year-old child was admitted with vomiting and fever.

Andreas appeared on the ward just as she arrived and Libby grabbed him immediately.

'Her GP sent her in because she's not keeping anything down and she's becoming dehydrated,' she told him as she briefed him about the patient. 'I've put her in a side ward for now, until we know what it is. If it's something infectious then we obviously don't want it spreading over the whole ward.'

He nodded and scanned the letter. 'OK—let's take a look at her.'

Melanie Palmer was lying on the bed, crying and clutching her stomach.

Her mother was sitting next to her, her face drawn with worry. She stood up when Andreas entered the room.

'She's been like this since yesterday morning, and she's getting worse,' she told them, her eyes pleading. 'What do you think it is?'

'I'm going to take a look at her now,' Andreas said immediately, walking over to the sink to wash his hands. 'How did it start, Mrs Palmer?'

The mother closed her eyes briefly, battling with tears. 'Sorry,' she muttered, 'but I've been up all night with her...'

Her face crumpled and Libby slipped an arm around her shoulders. 'Don't apologise. We understand how stressful it is when your child is sick. Take your time.'

'It started yesterday,' Mrs Palmer told them. 'She seemed a bit tired when I left her at Sunday school but nothing that made me anxious.'

'And when you picked her up, how did she seem?'

'She was white as a sheet and complaining of pain in her stomach, but I assumed that was because of the vomiting,' Mrs Palmer said. 'I left it for a few hours, but then her temperature shot up and she seemed so poorly I called the GP. He just said it was a stomach bug and to give it twenty-four hours to settle.'

Andreas walked across to the bed. 'But evidently it didn't settle.'

'She was dreadful in the night. Moaning and crying and clutching her stomach. And her stomach seemed really swollen.' Mrs Palmer bit her lip. 'I didn't know what to do with her so I called the GP again this morning. I think he's probably going to strike me off his list for being such a nuisance.'

'You were right to call him again.' Andreas caught Libby's eye and she knew that he was thinking the same thing as her. That the GP had been too dismissive of Melanie's symptoms.

'Whereabouts was the pain in her stomach?' Andreas asked. 'Did she tell you?'

Mrs Palmer shrugged helplessly. 'Everywhere, I think.'

Andreas nodded and settled himself on the edge of the bed.

'Hello, Melanie.' He spoke softly to the little girl. 'Mummy tells me you've got a tummyache. Can I take a look?'

Libby watched him, full of admiration for the way that he dealt with children. She'd worked with so many doctors who didn't have the first clue how to relate to children. They just waded in with their tests and examinations and then wondered why the child wouldn't co-operate.

But fortunately Melanie was obviously smitten with the handsome Greek doctor.

She looked at Andreas trustingly. 'I've got a poorly tummy.'

Andreas nodded, his dark eyes warm. 'I know you have, sweetheart.'

'Are you going to make it better?'

'I'm certainly going to try, but you'll have to help me.' He lifted his stethoscope out of his pocket. 'First I'm going to listen and then you're going to listen.'

A brief smile touched the little girl's pale face and she lay still as Andreas started to examine her, whimpering occasionally with pain.

Libby watched as he used his fingers to gently palpate the child's abdomen.

'She has oblique muscle rigidity,' he murmured, 'which is a sign of peritoneal irritation.'

Libby looked at him, trying to read his mind. He obviously didn't think that Melanie had gastroenteritis.

Mrs Palmer was biting her nails in agitation. 'What does that mean?'

'I don't think she has a stomach bug, Mrs Palmer,' Andreas said gently. 'I think that she has appendicitis and unfortunately it has burst, which is why her stomach is so very painful and swollen. Libby, can you bleep the surgeons urgently, please, and then come back and help me? I need to get a line in. Mrs Palmer, when did she last have something to eat or drink?'

'She had a few sips of water in the night,' Mrs Palmer told them, 'but nothing to eat since breakfast yesterday morning.'

Leaving Andreas to finish his questioning, Libby hurried out onto the ward and rang the switchboard, asking them to bleep the on-call surgeons.

While she was there she gathered up the distraction box and the rest of the equipment she needed and then returned to the room.

Andreas was talking to Melanie, his deep voice gentle and soothing. 'I need to put a plastic tube in your arm, sweetheart.'

Melanie stared at him. 'Will it hurt?'

'Yes, a bit,' Andreas said honestly. 'But we need to do it to make you better.'

Libby looked at him. 'We could use a local anaesthetic cream.'

'No time.' Andreas reached for a swab and a venflon. 'It takes at least half an hour to work and I need to get this line in now. She needs to go to Theatre.'

Libby looked at the mother. 'If you find this too upsetting you could go and get a cup of coffee while we put the drip up.'

Mrs Palmer shook her head, her eyes glistening with tears. 'No. I can't leave her. Do whatever you have to do.'

'Right, then, Melanie.' Libby sat on the bed and put the distraction box next to the little girl. 'Let's have a look in here and see what we can find.'

'Balloons!' Melanie reached into the box and pulled out a pink balloon. 'Can I have it?'

'Of course. Why doesn't Mummy blow it up while we sort you out?'

Libby handed the balloon to Mrs Palmer who obligingly took it and blew.

Seeing that the child was distracted, Andreas searched for a vein.

'OK—squeeze there for me, Libby, and don't let go.'

Libby knew what he was saying. If they missed the vein on the first attempt, it would be doubly difficult to persuade a child of this age to co-operate, and it was distressing for everyone.

She hoped Andreas was good at finding tiny veins in tiny hands.

He was.

He swabbed the skin, grabbed the child's hand firmly and slid the needle in with the minimum of fuss.

Melanie was so busy watching the balloon grow bigger and bigger that by the time she opened her mouth to protest the cannula was safely taped in place.

Despite all her intentions about keeping her distance, Libby smiled at him. 'You're a genius, Dr Christakos.'

He grinned. 'So are you. I loved your distraction box.'

'It usually helps, but not always.'

Andreas turned to Jonathon, who had just appeared. 'OK, can you take some bloods while we're waiting for the surgeons, please?'

Melanie stared down at her hand. 'What does that do?'

'It means that I can give you medicines straight into your body,' Andreas explained, his voice gentle.

'I haven't listened to *your* chest yet,' she reminded him, and Andreas smiled.

'That's right. You haven't.' He undid a few of the buttons of his shirt and sat still while Melanie lifted the stethoscope to his chest.

Libby suddenly found she couldn't look away, her eyes riveted to the curling dark hairs that covered the hard muscle of his chest. He was incredibly masculine and she felt a kick of sexual reaction deep inside her. Suddenly she felt an overwhelming desire to touch him. To run her fingers over his tanned skin and downwards...

Shocked by her own thoughts, she dragged her eyes away, thoroughly relieved when the surgeons arrived.

Andreas smiled at the little girl and gently retrieved his stethoscope, totally relaxed as he briefly described his findings to Mr Jenner, the surgeon.

'I'll take her down straight away,' Dave Jenner said, after examining the child himself.

Libby collected a consent form and hovered by the bed, her gaze drawn again to the tantalising vision of Andreas with his shirt still undone.

He was powerfully built and strong and just that one glimpse was enough to make her imagine what the rest of him must look like.

She swallowed.

Still in conversation with Dave, Andreas lifted a hand and casually started to button his shirt, pausing suddenly as he intercepted Libby's gaze.

His eyes locked with hers and something passed between them, a mutual acknowledgment of the sizzling attraction that seemed to envelop both of them whenever they were together.

Libby struggled to free herself from the intensity of his gaze and something of her disquiet must have shown on her face because his firm mouth curved into a smile so sexy that her knees shook alarmingly.

Bother the man!

He was totally aware of the effect he had on her.

Turning her attention back to the patient with a huge effort, she concentrated on getting the little girl ready for surgery.

'I don't want to take my pyjamas off.' Melanie wrapped her arms around herself and Libby managed a smile, pleased to have something to look at rather than Andreas.

'You don't have to take your pyjamas off, sweetheart. You can keep them on.' She examined the characters dancing over the fabric. 'I love them.'

'Daddy buyed them for me,' Melanie announced firmly, and her mother tensed.

'We're not together any more,' she muttered in an undertone. 'I suppose I ought to call him.'

'If you need to use a phone, I can arrange it,' Libby said quietly. They had plenty of parents on the ward who were separated or alone so she knew how hard it was when a child became ill.

'We'll see her in Theatre.' With a friendly nod to Mrs Palmer and Melanie, Dave Jenner left the room with his team behind him.

'You and I are going to play hairdressers,' Libby said cheerfully, reaching into her pocket for a band. 'I'm going to tie that lovely blonde hair of yours back. Is that OK?'

Melanie nodded and looked at Libby. 'You've got very long hair. Like a princess.'

Libby smiled as she checked that the child's name and hospital number were on her wrist strap. 'That's me. Princess Libby.' She gathered all the notes and charts together and finally plucked up the courage to look at Andreas. 'Shall we take her straight down?'

He nodded. 'I've done the consent form and everything else is ready.' He looked at Mrs Palmer. 'Try not to worry. Mr Jenner is an exceptionally good surgeon.' He sat down on the bed next to Melanie and took her hand.

'Right, Melanie, this is what we're going to do. There's something in your tummy that's making it bad, so we're going to take it away and then you'll feel better.'

Melanie stared at him, round eyed. 'Will it hurt?'

Andreas shook his head. 'No, because you're going to be asleep for a short time. And if it's sore when you wake up, we'll give you some medicine.' He glanced up as a porter arrived in the doorway, ready to take Melanie to Theatre. 'Ah—this nice man is going to wheel you downstairs now.'

He stood up and watched while Libby flicked the brake on the bed with her foot and manoeuvred it carefully out of the door of the side ward.

Melanie's face crumpled. 'I want Mummy!'

'Well, of course you do,' Libby said quickly, moving out of the way so that the child could see her mother. 'She's right here, sweetheart.'

Libby glanced at Mrs Palmer who was white-faced and tense. 'You can stay with her in the anaesthetic room until she falls asleep if you like.'

Mrs Palmer swallowed. 'Yes—yes, I'd like that.'

She stayed close to her daughter as they wheeled the bed into the lift and pressed the button for Theatre.

In the anaesthetic room a blond man was preparing things for the operation and Libby stiffened.

Philip.

Why did it have to be Philip who was the anaesthetist?

'This is Melanie Palmer,' she said coolly, her tone detached and professional. 'Melanie, this is Dr Graham. He's going to help you go to sleep.'

'Hi, there, Melanie.' Philip smiled at the little girl with the false cheeriness that people so often adopted with children. Libby couldn't help comparing him with Andreas who was a natural with children. He was honest and straightforward with them and had a warmth and strength that they seemed to find reassuring.

How could she ever have found Philip attractive?

Ignoring him as much as she could, she showed Mrs Palmer where to stand so that she could cuddle Melanie without getting in the way.

Philip wafted some gas under the child's nose and gradually her eyes closed.

'You can come back to the ward with me now,' Libby said gently, taking Mrs Palmer by the arm as Philip carried on anaesthetising the child. 'You need a cup of coffee and a sit-down. Mr Jenner will ring when he has some news for us.'

Philip glanced up. 'I'll pop up to the ward and see you soon, Libby.' His gaze was meaningful. 'We need to have a chat.'

Libby shot him a cold look but didn't respond. She didn't want to discuss her private life in front of patients or relatives. It wasn't professional.

And she had no intention of having a chat with him. If he appeared on the ward, she'd make sure that she was unavailable.

Once Melanie was safely under the anaesthetic, they returned to the ward and Libby settled Mrs Palmer comfortably with a cup of coffee before going to check on Rachel.

'Her colour is so much better,' she said, pleased by the way the baby seemed to be responding to the antibiotics. 'She's definitely improving. Has she been taking any fluids?'

Alison nodded. 'She took a whole bottle from me at eleven o'clock. She seemed really thirsty. It's the first time she's fed properly for days.'

'That's great news.' Libby smiled as she checked the baby's temperature. 'That's come right down, too. If she carries on like this we'll be able to take that drip out soon.'

'Will she need to carry on with the antibiotics?'

'Yes, but she can take them as medicine. She doesn't have to have them into a vein,' Libby explained, charting the temperature and noting the baby's respirations. 'Once we've taken that drip out she can have a trip to our playroom and we'll see if we can get her interested in some of our toys.'

It was after lunch when Melanie Palmer returned from Theatre.

'They took out her appendix and irrigated her peritoneal cavity,' Andreas told Libby as they settled the little girl back onto the ward. 'We'll continue the antibiotics and keep her nil by mouth until she's got bowel sounds.'

'Was it the GP's fault?' Libby asked softly. 'Should he have spotted it?'

Andreas pulled a face. 'In my opinion her clinical condition should have alerted him to the fact that it was something serious, but appendicitis in young children is notoriously hard to diagnose. Children tend to present late and a high percentage perforate before they get to see a doctor. In children under the age of three appendicitis is hardly ever diagnosed before perforation, but in her case…' He gave a shrug. 'Hard to say whether her GP could have diagnosed it earlier. I think he should have had a high index of suspicion but it's immaterial now.'

Libby was only too aware that Andreas had made his diagnosis within minutes of examining the child. But, then, she'd already seen enough of him to know that he was a very skilled paediatrician.

What with Rachel and Melanie, it had been a bad couple of days for GPs.

Mrs Palmer hurried into the room, her expression anxious. 'Is she all right?'

'She's fine. She's had painkillers down in Theatre so she's sleeping now,' Libby told her. 'We'll keep an eye on her and if she needs more, she can have them.'

Andreas explained the operation to Mrs Palmer and then

moved towards the door. 'I'm just going to A and E to see a patient but you can bleep me if you need me.'

He walked out of the room and Mrs Palmer looked after him wistfully. 'He's a very good doctor.'

'He is, isn't he?' Libby agreed softly. 'He's a very good doctor indeed.'

Looks and a brain, she thought gloomily. A lethal combination.

She was in the storeroom towards the end of her shift when Andreas strolled up behind her.

'About this date you owe me...' His tone was smooth and enticing and she shivered with a response so powerful that she was forced to snatch in a gasp of air.

He was just *so* good-looking it wasn't fair. It would have been so easy to persuade herself that he'd be different.

Severely shaken by her own thoughts, she made a supreme effort to look bored. 'What date, Dr Christakos?'

Before he could reply, Philip's voice came from behind him. 'I was looking for Libby.'

Libby tensed in horror and backed away further into the storeroom but it was too late. He'd seen her.

Dealing Andreas a frosty glare, Philip walked into the room. 'This obviously isn't the place to say what needs to be said,' he muttered stiffly, 'so I just wanted to check you're still all right for the ball in three weeks' time.'

Libby's mouth fell open.

Did he seriously think that she'd still go to the ball with him after what had happened? The nerve of the man! Did he have no morals?

Wrestling with her temper, she struggled to find her voice. 'No, Dr Graham,' she croaked shakily, 'I'm *not* all right for the ball.'

Philip frowned and looked pointedly at Andreas. 'If you don't mind, I'd like to have a conversation with Libby on my own.'

Andreas didn't budge an inch, his usually warm dark eyes suddenly cold. 'I mind.'

Philip coloured slightly. 'We have personal matters to discuss—'

'We have nothing whatsoever to discuss,' Libby said tartly, relieved that Andreas hadn't abandoned her to her fate. 'And I most certainly won't be going to the ball with you.'

'Oh...' Philip looked slightly taken aback. 'But we agreed—'

'If you're short of a partner, I'm sure *your wife* would be happy to oblige,' Libby said sweetly, aware that Andreas had leaned his broad shoulders against the wall and was watching the encounter with an ominous expression on his handsome face.

Philip coloured unattractively. 'I've already explained to you that we're separated,' he muttered, and Libby lifted an eyebrow.

'Separated?' Sparks of anger lit her blue eyes and she curled her fists into her palms. 'Well, you certainly didn't look *separated* when I saw you the other morning.'

Philip gritted his teeth. 'I can explain, Libby. Listen to me—'

'No, *you* listen to *me*.' Libby took a step towards him, deriving considerable satisfaction from the fact that he backed away from her. 'You are a scumbag, Philip,' she said tightly. 'And if you want to talk to someone, I suggest you talk to your wife.'

Philip flinched. 'I can tell that you're angry and I can understand that you'd rather not go to the ball in the circumstances,' he said stiffly. 'It's going to take you a while to get over this.'

Libby's mouth fell open. 'Believe me, I'm over it,' she said acidly. 'And as for the ball, I never said I wasn't going. I'm definitely going. I'm just not going with *you*.'

Philip looked first taken aback and then horrified, obviously envisaging embarrassing scenes. 'You're never going to find anyone else to go with you at this late stage.'

Making an instantaneous decision, Libby flashed a dazzling smile at Andreas. 'I'm going with Andreas.'

She stepped closer to him and gazed into his eyes with all

the adoration of someone who'd met the love of her life. 'You *did* manage to get the evening off, didn't you, darling?'

Andreas didn't hesitate. 'Of course,' he drawled, lowering his head and kissing her lingeringly on the lips.

Libby's brain ceased to function and she melted against him. She forgot Philip and she forgot the ball. She forgot that she was determined to resist Andreas. She was aware only of sensation. Delicious, tantalising, brain-swamping sensation.

And then Andreas lifted his head.

He brushed her cheek with his knuckles and gave a lopsided smile. 'Libby and I are hoping that there'll be fireworks,' he purred, laughter in his eyes as he looked down at her.

Stunned by the overwhelming chemistry between them, Libby flushed scarlet and Philip glowered at them both.

'Well, if that's the way you want to play it.' He turned on his heel and strode briskly out of the ward without looking back.

'You didn't have to kiss me,' Libby muttered, peering out of the room to make sure that Philip had left.

Andreas narrowed his eyes and surveyed her with all the lazy confidence of a man who knew he had the upper hand.

'I was trying to make it convincing,' he said helpfully, and she managed a scowl, even though her heart rate was still be-having strangely.

'Don't get any funny ideas, Dr Christakos. It's no big deal. I just needed someone to go with and you happened to be stand-ing there.'

A lazy smile settled on his handsome face. 'Of course.'

'If I don't turn up, it will look as though I'm at home, pining for him, and I can't have him thinking that.'

'Of course you can't.'

She glared at him. 'This is *not* a date.'

'Of course it isn't.'

'It's just two colleagues on an evening out. Very platonic.' She bit her lip. 'No kissing or anything.'

His dark eyes gleamed with humour. 'No kissing?'

'Definitely no kissing,' she muttered, dragging her eyes away from his and concentrating on finding the dressing packs she needed. 'So, do you want to come?' She bit her lip, wondering why on earth she'd invited him. Talk about torturing herself. 'It's in three weeks' time. If you're busy it doesn't matter. I can ask someone else.'

Someone who didn't kiss like him.

Someone who didn't turn her brain to porridge.

He stepped closer and touched her flushed cheek with a lean finger. 'I'll take you to the ball, Cinderella, but I'm not promising to keep it platonic.'

Her stomach flipped over. 'Andreas—'

'Every time you see Philip, we seem to kiss,' he pointed out with impeccable logic, 'so we may as well both accept the way it's going to be. If we're spending a whole evening together and you're intending to convince Philip that you're over him, then I predict a significant amount of kissing.'

Libby closed her eyes.

What was she doing?

For a girl who was trying to avoid men, she was doing a pretty lousy job!

She suddenly decided that she needed an urgent talk with her sister.

CHAPTER FIVE

THEY were both on a late shift the following morning and met for a late breakfast in a café next to the river.

'Hi.' Libby dropped her bag onto the padded chair and stooped to kiss her sister. 'You look knackered.'

Katy gave a wry smile. 'Thanks for the compliment.'

Libby looked at her closely. 'Are you ill?'

'No.' Katy dropped her eyes and rummaged in her handbag for her sunglasses. 'Just tired.'

'Hmm.' Libby frowned and looked thoughtfully at her sister but before she could question her further, the waiter arrived to take their order. 'Two regular cappuccinos, please. And a chocolate brownie. I'm starving.'

Katy glanced shyly at the waiter. 'Actually, I don't want a cappuccino. Could I just have a mint tea, please?'

The waiter gave a friendly nod and Libby's eyes narrowed.

'*Mint tea?* All right, now I know there's definitely something going on. You always drink cappuccino. You're addicted to cappuccino.'

A soft flush touched Katy's perfect complexion. 'I'm just a bit off coffee at the moment.'

Libby sat back in her chair and stared at her sister. 'You're pregnant.'

Katy sank her teeth into her lower lip and adjusted her glasses. 'Libby, I don't—'

'I'm your sister,' Libby reminded her softly, leaning forward in her chair. 'Why can't you tell me?'

Katy sighed and removed her glasses, rubbing the bridge of her nose with her fingers. 'Because it's very early days and I'm scared,' she admitted finally. 'I lost the other baby...'

'And you're afraid that you might lose this one too,' Libby finished, suddenly understanding why Katy had been reluctant to confide in her. 'Have you told Jago yet?'

'Last night.'

Libby grinned. 'I bet he was over the moon.'

Katy rolled her eyes and blushed slightly. 'You know Jago—macho Spaniard to the last. You'd think it was his achievement alone. A public declaration of his manhood and virility.'

Libby laughed. 'How many weeks gone are you?'

'Only six.' Katy let out a long breath. 'Ridiculous, isn't it? Getting excited so early. Something will probably go wrong.'

Detecting a hint of tears in her sister's eyes, Libby leaned forward and squeezed her hand. 'Nothing will go wrong, angel. It will be fine.'

'But the last one—'

'You fell, Katy,' Libby reminded her softly. 'You had a really bad fall. And it was more than eleven years ago. That's a long time.'

'Do you think so?' Katy looked at her, desperate for reassurance, and Libby grinned.

'You're the doctor, honey. You should be telling yourself these things. Have you spoken to Alex? He's convinced he's God's gift to pregnant women at the moment.'

Katy shook her head. 'Not yet, but Jago and I are meeting him for supper on Friday. Any chance of you coming?'

Libby shook her head. 'I'm working. And, anyway, Alex isn't my favourite person at the moment. We've had a sort of falling-out. I don't think I could spend an evening in his company without physically abusing him.'

Katy sighed. 'I knew that it was a mistake for him to move into the flat when I moved out. The two of you are always arguing about something. What is it this time?'

'He didn't buy me at the auction,' Libby said darkly, and Katy's eyes widened.

'Was he supposed to?'

'Yes.' Libby scowled at the memory. 'I didn't want to be forced to go on a date.'

'And he forgot?'

'Of course he didn't forget.' Libby's mouth tightened. 'You know Alex. Why miss an excuse to wind me up? Don't worry. I'm going to the ball so we can all get together then and I'll tread on his toes.'

Katy stopped with her cup in mid-air. 'You're going to the ball? But I thought—'

'I know, I know.' Libby pulled a face. 'I sort of trapped myself into it.'

Katy put her cup back down on the table so hard that the tea slopped into the saucer. 'You're not going with *Philip*?'

'No!' Libby gave a shudder. 'I most certainly am not going with Philip. I wasn't going at all but then he implied that I was obviously too broken-hearted to go out so I was forced into a corner. If I stay at home he'll think I'm pining for him and there's no way I want him thinking that. Arrogant rat.'

'So are you going with the gorgeous Greek who bid a fortune for you at the auction?'

Libby stiffened. 'How do you know about that? Who's been talking?'

'The whole hospital,' Katy told her, her eyes amused. 'And can you blame them? He paid one thousand pounds for you, Lib! Everyone else was bidding tiny amounts.'

Libby shrugged carelessly. 'So the guy is rich. It doesn't mean anything.'

'In my experience, rich people don't throw it away,' Katy said mildly. 'It's the reason they're rich.'

'Well, I don't know why he spent a thousand pounds on me,' Libby said testily, picking up a spoon and teasing the froth on top of her coffee. 'Who am I to understand the workings of a man's mind?'

Katy gave a warm smile. 'He must have been pretty keen on you.'

'If he is, it's only because I keep saying no.'

'And why on earth do you keep saying no? Rumour has it that he's gorgeous.'

Libby thought of Andreas, remembering his luxuriant black hair and his incredibly sexy eyes.

'He is gorgeous.'

Katy looked baffled. 'So what's wrong?'

'He's a man,' Libby said flatly, putting her spoon down and staring at the patterns she'd made on the surface of her coffee. 'That's what's wrong.'

'So?' Katy finished her tea. 'You're twenty-nine, Lib. You can't carry on being this defensive. Eventually you've got to trust someone.'

'Why would I want to do a silly thing like that? It's asking for trouble.'

'I can tell you like him,' Katy said softly, and Libby gave a short laugh and picked up her coffee-cup.

'Oh, I like him. I like him a lot.' She felt things for Andreas that she'd never felt for a man before, and that worried her. It made her vulnerable. 'It doesn't change the fact he's a man.'

'Libby, not all men behave badly,' Katy said gently. 'You have to get out there and give it a go.'

'I've given it a go,' Libby said flatly. 'And I found him in bed with his wife.'

Katy frowned. 'But were you in love with Philip?'

Libby sipped her cappuccino. 'No,' she said finally, 'I wasn't. Which just makes me doubly determined not to get involved again. Imagine how much harder it would have been if I'd really cared. I'd be humiliated and broken-hearted, instead of just humiliated.'

Katy looked confused. 'So you're going to go through life picking men you know you can't fall in love with? How is that ever going to work?'

'It isn't,' Libby agreed, 'but, then, I don't actually want it to work. I just can't deal with the pain that goes with relationships.'

'But maybe if you chose someone you really liked, the relationship might stand a chance of working,' Katy suggested logically. 'At the moment you're so afraid of being hurt that you pick people who you can't possibly fall in love with. You'll never meet Mr Right that way.'

'I don't believe in Mr Right,' Libby reminded her. 'He's a myth invented for children by the same person that thought up Father Christmas and the Easter Bunny. Personally I'd rather believe in the Easter Bunny. At least he comes armed with chocolate.'

But, despite her light-hearted words, she found herself thinking about what her sister had said. It was certainly true that she'd never really felt anything for Philip. Did she really pick men that she knew she couldn't fall in love with?

'You're so busy protecting yourself from hurt that you never go out with anyone remotely suitable. You're afraid of falling in love, Libby.'

Libby glared at her. 'I thought you were an A and E doctor, not a psychiatrist.'

'Today I'm your sister,' Katy said softly, 'and I love you. I want to see you settled with babies because I know that's what you want, too. I want to see you in love. And so does Alex, which was why he didn't buy you, I expect. He hoped you might meet someone, and you *have*.'

Libby stared at the river, watching the way the sunlight glittered on the surface. 'I don't want to be vulnerable and being in love just makes you vulnerable.'

Katy gave a humourless laugh. 'I know *that*. I know that better than anyone. I had such a dilemma when I met up with Jago again. He hurt me so badly the first time.'

'That was different. That was because our father meddled.'

'He still hurt me. Believe me, Lib, trusting him again was the hardest thing I've ever done in my life.'

'And Alex and I had to manipulate the two of you back together,' Libby reminded her dryly. 'You were going to marry Lord Frederick Hamilton.'

'I was marrying Freddie because I was scared of what I felt when I was with Jago,' Katy admitted. 'I was doing what you're doing. Running from being hurt. But there comes a point you have to take a risk with your heart, Libby. Otherwise you'll miss out on love. I shiver when I think what might have happened if Jago and I hadn't got back together. I love him so much. Without him, my life would have been so different. Empty.'

Libby sighed, acknowledging that she was envious of her sister's relationship.

'It's different for you,' she said gruffly. 'You and Jago are crazy about each other and you always were.'

She knew how powerfully Jago had affected Katy.

Having loved him, Katy had never been able to feel anything for another man.

But she herself never felt that strongly for a man…
Until Andreas.

Libby arrived on the ward for the late shift to find that Rachel had had her drip removed.

'She's doing so much better,' Bev told her. 'Andreas gave instructions for it to be removed this morning and she's having the antibiotics orally now.'

'Did the results of her urine tests come back?'

'Positive. It was a UTI.'

So Andreas had been right. Libby gave a reluctant smile. He might be good-looking and too pushy by half, but he was clearly a good doctor. Better than good. Hopefully, by treating the child so early he would have managed to prevent any damage to her kidneys.

'And how's Melanie this morning?'

Bev smiled. 'Doing very well. Her wound is a bit sore, obviously, but she's a lovely child. So cheerful.'

'Is her drip out?'

Bev nodded. 'She had bowel sounds so Andreas started her on sips of water last night and took her drip down this morning. I thought maybe you could get her to the playroom today.'

'Good idea.' Like all paediatric nurses, Libby knew how important it was that the children had plenty of opportunities for play. 'I'll get going, then.'

She started with Rachel, checking the baby's observations and noting with pleasure that her colour was good and that she was alert and interested in her surroundings.

'She's like a different baby,' she said to Alison, who nodded.

'I know. Those antibiotics worked like a miracle. Thank goodness the GP sent us in here.' She gave a rueful smile. 'He might not have diagnosed her correctly himself, but at least by admitting her we saw Dr Christakos. He's amazing.'

Right on cue, Andreas strolled into the room looking devastating in a blue shirt and well-cut trousers.

It was really unfair that any man should be so good-looking, Libby thought helplessly as she tried not to look at him. It was like having a job in a chocolate factory and being on a strict diet.

'She owes me a cuddle.' He smiled at Alison and scooped Rachel into his arms. He held her with the easy confidence of someone with plenty of experience with children, talking softly to her and allowing her to pat his cheek with her tiny hand.

'She likes you,' Alison said shyly, and Libby looked at him helplessly.

There seemed to be no age limit to the women he charmed.

Pulling herself together, she quickly changed the sheet on Rachel's cot and got her antibiotics ready.

'We'll give dose IV and then we'll take the venflon out and continue with the drugs orally,' Andreas said, still cuddling the child in his arms.

Libby tried not to look at him, busying herself with the various jobs that needed to be done and then excusing herself and hurrying back to the nurses' station.

Unfortunately he was right behind her.

'By the way...' he looked at her '...this trip you've got planned with Adrienne. She wants to know if you can do it in three weeks' time. She can't do it before that because there are things going on at the school that she wants to go to.'

Libby's face brightened. 'I'm delighted that she wants to stay at school.'

He gave a wry smile. 'Me, too. She seems to have finally made friends. Thanks to you, I think.'

Libby blushed. 'I doubt it. I was only there for five minutes.'

Andreas studied her. 'But some people make an impact in a very short space of time,' he said softly.

Libby's heart hammered against her chest. 'Three weeks, you say?'

'That's the Saturday of the ball so I suppose that may not be convenient. You'll want the time to get ready.'

'Believe it or not, it doesn't take me all day,' Libby said dryly. 'And, anyway, I need to do some shopping for myself, so that's fine. I'm really looking forward to it.'

'So is Adrienne.' Andreas surveyed her under lowered lids, his expression difficult to read. 'It's very kind of you to do it and I appreciate it.'

Did he think that was why she was doing it? To wriggle into his favour?

'I'm doing it for Adrienne, not you.' She looked him in the eye and then wished she hadn't. Head on he was dangerously irresistible.

Andreas smiled. 'Of course,' he said smoothly. 'Can anyone

come or is it girls only? I could treat you both to lunch in the middle of what sounds like an exhausting day.'

Libby hesitated, knowing that Adrienne would like to have him there. It was clear that she was very fond of her uncle.

'You're very welcome as long as you promise not to give your opinion.'

He lifted an eyebrow. 'My opinion isn't valued?'

'Not by a twelve-year-old girl at boarding school,' Libby said dryly. 'I know what she needs.'

'And I don't?'

'You're a man,' Libby drawled, and Andreas gave her a smile so sexy that it melted her bones.

'I am indeed, Libby. And I'm glad you've noticed.'

Libby swallowed. Oh, she'd definitely noticed. It was hard not to.

The next three weeks passed so quickly that Libby barely had time to think. The ward was incredibly busy and Andreas was working so hard that she often went several days without seeing him, which was a relief because it made it easier to keep her mind on the job and not start dreaming about things she couldn't have.

They picked Adrienne up from school on the Saturday of the ball and drove into the centre of London.

'We're going to start by sorting out your hair,' Libby said, turning in her seat so that she could look at the child. 'I'm taking you to the best hairdresser in town.'

Adrienne's eyes widened and she lifted a hand to her unruly mop. 'I've never really had it cut before. I've just been growing it long.'

And it was badly out of condition and desperately needed shaping, Libby reflected, although she kept those thoughts to herself.

'We won't cut it short,' Libby assured her. 'Trust me. It'll look great.'

She directed Andreas through some back streets and then showed him where to park.

'I'm amazed that there's somewhere to park this close to the centre,' Andreas observed, and Libby grinned.

'It's only for very valued customers. And I am a very, *very* valued customer.'

Andreas ran his eyes over her gleaming blonde curls and gave a wry smile. 'I'll bet you are.'

'A girl has to look after her crowning glory,' Libby said airily, pushing open the door of the exclusive salon.

She walked confidently across the marble floor and approached the reception desk.

'Morning, Francesca. Is Mario around?'

The girl glanced up and her face brightened as she recognised Libby. 'Well, hi, there!' A puzzled look crossed her face and she checked her computer screen. 'We weren't expecting you today, were we?'

'Not exactly.' Libby dealt her a winning smile. 'I'm after a favour.'

An extremely slim man wearing a pair of skin-tight, imitation crocodile-skin trousers minced across the salon towards her.

'Elizabeth Westerling, please tell me that this favour isn't happening on a Saturday.'

'Hi, Mario.' Libby followed and kissed him on both cheeks. 'You'll have fun, trust me.'

The man gave a dramatic groan and wiped a hand across his brow. 'It's Saturday, Libby. My busiest day. Everyone is clamouring for my attention—'

'But I'm not everyone,' Libby reminded him with a sunny smile that drew a wistful sigh from the salon owner.

'How can I refuse you?' He spread his hands in a gesture of surrender and then froze as he noticed Andreas for the first time. His hands dropped to his sides and he took a step backwards, his eyes raking appreciatively over the other man's broad shoulders and powerful physique. 'Introduce me to your friend, Libby. *Immediately.*'

Libby laughed. 'Hands off.'

Mario's gaze lingered regretfully on Andreas whose expression was comical.

'Relax,' Libby said, still laughing. 'He's a brilliant hairdresser. The best.'

Mario was pacing the floor of his salon. 'Already I have your sister Katherine booked in and you *know* how fussy she is. Her hair has to look exactly so.'

'You've been doing Katy's hair for years,' Libby pointed out patiently. 'It won't take you any time at all. Now, listen.' She grabbed Adrienne's hand and pulled her forward. 'Mario, do you remember when I was thirteen?'

Mario shuddered at the recollection. 'You were all pouts and teenage rebellion and your hair never behaved itself. Not like your sister's.'

'Absolutely.' Libby smiled happily. 'Well, I've got another ripe case of teenage rebellion for you here. She's having trouble at school, Mario. I want you to transform her. She's going to be cool and a trendsetter by the time she leaves your salon.'

Andreas sucked in a breath and started to protest but Libby placed a hand on his chest.

'You promised not to interfere, remember? What do you say, Mario? Will you do it?'

Mario rolled his eyes dramatically and gave an exaggerated sigh but he stepped forward, loosening Adrienne's hair from the childish band she wore. He pulled a face as he pushed and pulled, feeling the hair and placing it in different positions, his eyes narrowed as he experimented with different effects.

'It is too heavy,' he murmured. 'It's concealing her face. And she has a very beautiful face. It needs layers and texture.'

Libby beamed. 'My point exactly.'

Mario pushed, twisted and lifted for a few minutes and then

sighed and looked at his receptionist. 'Rearrange my morning, Francesca. I'm going to be busy.'

He took Adrienne by the hand and led her through to the basins. 'We'll start with some serious conditioning.'

Libby followed and kissed him on the cheek. 'Thanks, Mario. You're a star. We'll go and grab a coffee and be back in an hour. And remember. She's not quite thirteen. I don't want lamb dressed as mutton.'

Mario looked affronted. 'You are trying to tell me how to do my job?' He clicked his fingers at one of the salon juniors who hurried across to shampoo Adrienne's hair.

'I'm not sure I should be leaving my innocent niece in the hands of that man,' Andreas muttered darkly, following her across the road to a café.

Libby laughed. 'Mario's great. But *you* had a narrow escape.' She shot him a wicked look. 'He really, *really* fancied you.'

Andreas shook his head disapprovingly and sat down at one of the tables on the pavement.

The sun shone down on them and the air smelt of fresh baking and garlic as the many restaurants prepared for their lunchtime trade.

Libby ordered cappuccinos. 'You look really tense. Come on, what's wrong? You're not seriously worrying about Mario, are you? Because you shouldn't. He really is the best hairdresser in London. People wait an average of four months to get an appointment with him.'

'Unless your name is Libby,' Andreas observed dryly. 'No, it isn't that. I'm worried that Adrienne will think that fitting in is all about the way you look,' he confessed, reaching into his pocket for sunglasses.

Libby sucked in a breath. Normally she found it impossible to look away from his sexy eyes, but now they were covered she suddenly found herself focusing on his dark jaw. He was staggeringly handsome and she could hardly help to notice the way that every woman who passed stared at him.

'Appearances matter,' she said, leaning back in her chair as their drinks arrived. She smiled at the waiter. 'Could I have a chocolate brownie, please?'

'Chocolate brownie?' Andreas lifted an eyebrow and she shrugged carelessly.

'A girl's got to have a vice. Mine's chocolate.'

Andreas gave a slow, sexy smile, his expression concealed by the sunglasses. 'And is that your only vice, Miss Westerling?'

'Yes,' Libby replied firmly, wishing that he would remove the sunglasses. It was unsettling not being able to see his eyes. 'But it's a serious one. Now, back to the subject of appearances. You're right that appearances shouldn't matter, but they do, I'm afraid. You know that as well as I do. People form an opinion about you within about thirty seconds of meeting you. And when you're a teenager, the way you look is part of being accepted. Teenagers have a uniform.'

Andreas lifted his cup. 'And you really think a new haircut will help her make friends?'

'I think it will be a start. The rest is up to Adrienne. Mmm. Yummy.' Libby licked her lips as her chocolate brownie arrived and Andreas tensed.

Feeling his gaze on her, Libby felt suddenly hot, every inch of her quivering, female body helplessly aware of the tension that simmered between them.

'D-don't look at me like that,' she muttered, and he lifted an eyebrow.

'Like what?'

His voice was husky and very male and she knew he was teasing her. Suddenly she found she couldn't breathe properly.

Being this close to him affected her *so* badly.

He leaned forward in his chair, his voice soft. 'How do I look at you, Libby?'

His Greek accent seemed very pronounced and she dropped her eyes, concentrating hard on her cappuccino. It didn't really help. Even though she wasn't looking at him, she could *feel* him.

'You look at me as though you—you wish I was the chocolate brownie,' she said finally, and he laughed.

'My vice definitely isn't chocolate brownies,' he drawled. 'And we both know how I look at you. I want you, Libby. I've never pretended otherwise. And you want me.'

Her gaze flew to his. 'I don't.'

He shrugged carelessly. 'Yes, you do. You want me every bit as much as I want you. But you're afraid to admit it.'

Libby bit her lip. It was absolutely true. She *was* afraid.

She was afraid of what he could do to her. Of what he could make her feel.

'You are absolutely the last man in the world I'd have a relationship with,' she said flatly, glaring as yet another nubile female passed and cast a lustful glance at Andreas. 'Do you realise that every single woman who passes this table looks at you?'

Andreas removed his sunglasses and looked at her thoughtfully. 'But I'm not looking at them,' he pointed out quietly, his eyes dropping to her mouth. 'I'm looking at you, Libby.'

Her heart hammered against her ribs and she was consumed by a sexual excitement so powerful that she squirmed in her seat. She looked at him helplessly, thinking that perhaps it had been easier to control her feelings when he'd had the sunglasses on. He had the sexiest eyes she'd ever seen. What was it about him?

He was sitting on the other side of the table, for goodness' sake.

He hadn't even *touched* her and yet she could feel him with every inch of her body.

She swallowed hard and dragged her gaze away from his face. 'Well, I don't want you to look at me,' she said, stabbing her brownie with more force than was necessary. 'Do you want some?'

'What I want is for you to relax with me,' Andreas said, his tone amused. 'You are behaving as though I'm a lethal predator and there is absolutely no need. I want you and I refuse to pretend that I don't, but I have no intention of pouncing on you in the middle of the West End. I'll wait until you're ready.'

Awareness warmed her insides. 'You're awfully sure of yourself, Dr Christakos.' Her hands shook slightly and she placed the cup back down on the saucer. 'What if I'm never ready?'

He gave a slow smile. 'You will be. And in the meantime I'm enjoying the wait. It serves to intensify the satisfaction when we finally get together.'

His words hung between them and she stared at him wordlessly, wanting to say something cutting but totally mesmerised by the look in his dark eyes.

What woman in her right mind would say no to a man like Andreas?

He leaned across and helped himself to a piece of brownie. 'So, after this, are we shopping?'

He was so cool and relaxed, so totally sure of himself that she merely nodded.

'Yes.'

'For you or Adrienne?'

'Both.'

'Are you buying something for tonight?'

Suddenly unable to eat another mouthful, Libby pushed the remains of the brownie to one side. 'Just shoes. I already have enough dresses.'

He lifted a dark eyebrow. 'And you don't have enough shoes?'

'A girl can never have enough shoes,' Libby advised him solemnly, standing up and dropping a note on the table to cover the bill. 'Come on. Mario should be just about finishing by now.'

And she needed a third person to stop her having indecent thoughts about Andreas.

CHAPTER SIX

As LIBBY got ready for the ball that evening, she reflected on what a successful day it had been.

Mario had worked wonders with Adrienne and she chuckled as she remembered the stunned look on Andreas's face when he'd first caught sight of his niece.

Mario had shaped and textured her thick dark hair so that it no longer swamped her delicate features. The new hairstyle cleverly emphasised the shape of her face and made her look exactly what she was. A child on the verge of womanhood.

Thrilled by her own reflection, Adrienne had spent the rest of the trip gazing at her reflection in shop windows.

Libby had dragged her into several of her favourite shops and bought a selection of strap tops and trendy cotton separates that complemented Adrienne's slim figure without making her seem older than she was.

By the time they'd returned her to school, she'd been bubbling with excitement and confidence.

And now it was her turn, Libby thought, reaching into her wardrobe for the dress she wanted.

It was made of pale gold silk and it fell from tiny straps right down to the floor.

And she loved it.

With a smile of satisfaction she slipped into the dress and slid her feet into the gold shoes that she'd found in a tiny shop in one of London's most exclusive shopping areas. They matched the dress perfectly.

She pinned her blonde curls on top of her head, leaving a few tendrils hanging loose around her face, and carefully applied her lipstick.

Satisfied with the result, she reached for her wrap and glanced at her watch as the doorbell went.

Alex had left to collect his date half an hour earlier so she knew it had to be Andreas.

She walked to the door on shaking legs and paused for a moment. Her heart rate accelerated dramatically and excitement curled in the pit of her stomach.

She closed her eyes briefly, wondering why on earth she'd invited the man. She was playing with fire.

Andreas Christakos could hurt her badly.

Taking a steadying breath, she opened the door, trying to control her reaction as she saw him.

Damn.

She should have known that the man would have looked spectacular in formal dress.

She bit back a groan. The truth was Andreas would look spectacular whatever he wore.

He lounged in her doorway, confident, sexy and so masculine that it took her breath away.

He was all temptation and trouble and she'd elected to spend the evening with him.

Great.

'Hi, there.' She sounded breathless and hated herself for it. She hoped he wasn't any good at reading body language but her instincts said that he would be. This man knew everything there was to know about women.

His eyes slid slowly over her and finally he spoke. 'You look sensational.'

Suddenly she wished she'd chosen to wear a different dress. Something that covered her up. Something that would protect her from the way he was looking at her. The dress she'd chosen skimmed her womanly curves and seemed demure enough from the front, but the back was a different matter, and she found herself wishing that she didn't have to turn around.

He was looking at her quizzically. 'Are you ready?'

'I need to fetch my bag.' Which meant turning round.

His gaze didn't shift from hers. 'Fine.'

Swallowing hard, she backed away from him and his eyes narrowed.

'Is something wrong?'

'No.' This was utterly ridiculous! She took a deep breath and turned around, walking quickly to her room to collect her bag.

She returned in seconds. 'I'm ready.'

He didn't answer and slowly she lifted her gaze to his.

'Well, now I know why you were reluctant to turn around,' he said hoarsely, his dark eyes holding hers. 'That dress should carry a health warning. Shall we go?'

He placed a hand on her bare back and it was as if she'd drunk champagne on an empty stomach. Her legs trembled and her head swam. She was acutely conscious of every inch of him as they made their way down in the lift and climbed into the car he had waiting.

It was a warm summer evening but suddenly Libby found herself shivering.

His gaze settled on her face. 'Are you cold?'

Libby shook her head, knowing that she'd never be able to convince him that she was cold.

She wasn't cold. She was just suffering from an acute attack of out-of-control hormones. No man had ever affected her this way before. She'd never experienced this stomach-curling excitement that she felt with him.

'So why are you shivering, *agape mou*?'

She turned to look at him and gave a moan as his mouth descended on hers.

His kiss was slow and erotic and within seconds she was clinging to him, wriggling closer, her whole body throbbing with a heat and desire that was totally unfamiliar.

When he finally lifted his head, her heart was thundering in her chest.

'I've ruined your lipstick,' he said huskily, his eyes resting on her swollen mouth. 'I'm sorry.'

She swallowed hard and reached for her bag. 'J-just don't do it again,' she stammered, ignoring his low chuckle.

Who was she kidding?

Kissing Andreas was like taking a trip to heaven.

Given the choice, she'd happily spend the rest of her life doing nothing else.

They arrived at the hotel and joined the rest of the guests on the terrace where they were drinking champagne.

Libby immediately caught sight of Katy and Alex with their partners. Anxious to be in a group as a method of self-protection, she took Andreas by the arm and walked across to them.

Katy was looking elegant and classy in a long black dress, her blonde hair swept up on top of her head. She had more colour in her cheeks than the last time they'd met and Libby leaned forward to kiss her and then turned to Jago, Katy's husband.

'Congratulations,' she whispered, as she stood on tiptoe to kiss him.

Then she shook hands with Alex's date for the night, a cool-eyed blonde who was a clone of all the women that Alex dated.

Libby smiled politely, noted that the girl's name was Eva and wondered whether she knew that Alex would be seeing someone else within three months. He never dated anyone for longer than that. He was more wary of commitment than she was.

She introduced Andreas and instantly he and Jago started talking about a case they'd had in A and E the previous day.

'No talking shop,' Katy reproved mildly. 'This is supposed to be the one night of the year when we have an evening out without discussing medicine. Anyway, it's time to sit down. We're all on the same table.'

They moved into the ballroom, found their table and Libby seated herself between Alex and Andreas.

She was painfully conscious of how close he was, his lean, brown hand resting on the table only inches from hers, his muscular thigh resting alongside hers and the width of his shoulders under the jacket he wore.

Although they talked and laughed with everyone on the table, she was always aware of him next to her.

From time to time during the meal she caught him watching her and knew that he was playing a waiting game. Andreas was well aware of the effect he had on her and he was biding his time, knowing that the feelings inside her were heating to dangerous levels. It was psychological seduction, mind games designed to drive her slowly but surely to a point of desperation.

Her insides were so churned up by the way he made her feel that Libby lost her appetite. She pushed her food unenthusiastically around her plate and Alex looked at her with a raised eyebrow.

'Following the Hollywood diet, Lib?'

She gave a wan smile. 'I'm just not that hungry.'

'Or, at least, not for food,' Alex murmured softly, his eyes flickering past her to Andreas who was engaged in conversation with Katy, seated to his right. 'I've never seen you like this before. It must be love.'

Love?

Libby's eyes widened and she looked at him in horror. Of course it wasn't love! She'd never be so foolish as to fall in love with a man like Andreas. He was every woman's fantasy and she had no doubt that she was just a temporary interest.

'It's not love,' she said in a strangled voice. 'I've never been in love.'

Alex shrugged. 'Well, something's wrong. That's chocolate mousse sitting in front of you and you're not showing any interest in it.'

Libby looked at her plate and realised that she hadn't even seen the chocolate mousse arrive. Normally she would have devoured it, but tonight she just couldn't face food of any sort.

Not even chocolate.

'If you're off chocolate, it must be serious,' Alex said dryly, glancing from her to the untouched mousse. 'It's either love or gastroenteritis. Trust me, I'm a doctor. I know about these things.'

Thoroughly unsettled, Libby glared at him. 'You're a trouble-maker and can we, please, change the subject?' Her eyes flickered past him to Eva who was talking to a colleague of Alex's from A and E. 'Anyway, you're a fine one to talk. She hasn't stopped drooling over you all night.'

'She'll get over it,' Alex drawled lightly, reaching for his wine.

Libby shook her head slightly, wondering what sort of female it would take to shake her brother out of his customary cool.

'Don't you feel guilty about going through life breaking hearts?' Libby muttered in an undertone. 'It's men like you that have made me the woman I am today.'

Alex lifted a dark eyebrow. 'A crazy, shoe-mad chocoholic?'

'You can joke,' Libby said loftily, 'but you know it's true.'

Alex frowned. 'It's not true. I've never deceived a woman in my life.' His tone was maddeningly cool. 'I'm always totally honest with them. And I'm completely faithful when I'm with a woman.'

'Which is for a maximum of three months,' Libby reminded him tartly.

Alex shrugged his broad shoulders dismissively. 'So? I've never met a woman I wanted to wake up next to every day for the rest of my life.'

Libby rolled her eyes. 'Well, I'm just glad I'm your sister.'

Alex smiled the smile that stopped women in their tracks. 'What you're saying is that I'm so irresistible that if you weren't my sister you'd be in love with me.' His blue eyes gleamed with amusement. 'Go on, admit it.'

Libby's mouth fell open and she was about to deliver a suitable retort when Katy intervened.

'I can't hear what the pair of you are talking about, but I know you're quarrelling, so stop it,' she admonished gently from across the table. 'Alex, stop teasing Libby!'

'Me?' Alex lifted a hand to his broad chest, his expression hurt. 'I would *never* tease my sister. I have the utmost respect for my sister.'

'Alex…' Libby's tone was sugar sweet and she lifted a hand to her plate, her eyes sparkling with mischief as she looked thoughtfully at her brother's pristine white dress shirt. 'I've just thought of a use for this chocolate mousse.'

'Will you two stop it?' Katy stared at them, aghast, and then shot an embarrassed look towards Andreas. 'I'm so sorry. What must you be thinking? They love each other really, it's just that they can't seem to help winding each other up. They're always the same.'

Andreas laughed, totally relaxed. 'Don't apologise. Their conversation is very entertaining.' His eyes rested on Libby thoughtfully. 'And illuminating.'

Libby forgot about the chocolate mousse and Alex's shirt and looked at him in horror. Just how much of the conversation had he overheard? Had he heard Alex suggesting that she was in love? She sincerely hoped not.

The chat started up again but Libby found herself staring at Andreas, trapped by the look in his stunning dark eyes. His gaze was intense and focused and there was no way he was letting her look away.

'So why haven't you eaten anything tonight, Libby?' His firm mouth shifted slightly at the corners. 'Is it the Hollywood diet—or is it something else?'

Libby gritted her teeth and resisted the temptation to slide under the table to hide her embarrassment. He'd obviously heard everything.

She closed her eyes and cursed her brother and his big mouth.

It was becoming harder and harder to keep Andreas at a distance. How was she going to manage it if he thought that she was so affected by him that she was off her food?

'I'm just not that hungry,' she mumbled, pushing her plate away from her and accepting the coffee that the waiter offered. 'I never eat much at these things. Hard to make a serious impact on the dance floor if you're full of food.'

Andreas glanced towards the band, which was playing something with a pounding rhythm. 'If you're aiming to make a serious impact, we'd better get started.' He stood up, broad-shouldered and confident, and extended a hand. 'Dance, Libby?'

Aware that the rest of the people at the table were watching her expectantly, Libby let him pull her to her feet.

It shouldn't be a problem, she reassured herself. The band was playing fast stuff. Nothing that required the slightest bit of physical contact.

But the minute they reached the dance floor she realised that she'd made a major misjudgement.

Andreas was a fantastically good dancer. He closed strong fingers around hers and swung her against him, picking up the rhythm of the music and controlling her moves like a master.

Totally seduced by the pounding beat of the music and his strong lead, Libby let herself go, swaying and spinning, moving away from him and then back again, feeling his hard, muscular strength against her heated body.

A natural dancer, Libby ignored the fact that her hair had escaped from the pin on top of her head and was flying around her face as he spun her around the dance floor.

She was having far too much fun to care.

It was only when the music ended and applause broke out

around them that she realised that they were the only ones that were dancing.

Suddenly self-conscious, she made to retreat to their table but Andreas laughed and hauled her against him.

'Don't you dare. We haven't even begun yet.'

This time several couples joined them on the dance floor, obviously inspired by their exhibition.

They danced continuously until finally the band shifted tempo and played something slow and seductive. On the dance floor the lighting softened and suddenly the atmosphere became more intimate.

'You didn't tell me you could dance,' Libby said breathlessly, pink and laughing from the exertion. 'That was fantastic.'

'I'm Greek,' he reminded her silkily. 'All Greeks can dance.'

Without giving her a chance to argue, he curved a strong arm around her, pulling her firmly against him, and Libby put a hand on his shoulder, feeling the hardness of muscle thinly disguised by the fabric of his shirt. Disconcerted by the way he made her feel, she tried to keep up the conversation.

'I thought you did traditional dancing with lots of plate-smashing.'

'That, too. Now stop talking, Libby.'

He pulled her closer, sliding an arm around her hips so that she was pressed against him.

Aware of every incredible inch of him, Libby dipped her head against his chest and closed her eyes, breathing in his male scent and the subtle hint of aftershave.

The intensity of her body's response shocked her. Butterflies erupted in her stomach and she was sure that he must be able to feel her body quivering. Every part of her felt sensitive. She was incredibly aware of every inch of his body. Unable to help herself, she pressed closer still and he immediately lifted a hand to her face, sliding his lean fingers around her jaw and forcing her to look at him.

The laughter had long since faded and the emotion sizzling

between them was intense sexual excitement. An overwhelming acknowledgement of the astonishing chemistry between them. Skin brushed against skin, breath mingled unsteadily and the heat became almost intolerable.

'P-people are staring at us,' Libby stammered, shivering as she felt his thumb trace the fullness of her lower lip.

'Let them stare,' Andreas murmured softly, supremely indifferent to the curious glances they were receiving. 'On the other hand, I could do with some fresh air. How about you?'

Libby nodded. What she really needed was a cold shower, but fresh air would probably do.

His long fingers closed around her wrist and he strode off the dance floor towards one of the exits, dragging her after him.

Feeling that just about everyone was probably staring at them, Libby didn't look left or right.

'You're behaving like a caveman,' she muttered, mortified by what people must be thinking. 'This isn't very politically correct.'

He shot her a sizzling smile of pure sexual invitation. 'That's because I'm Greek,' he drawled in that dark tone that sent shivers down her spine. 'We're not very good at being politically correct.'

He led her out into the grounds, past the small lights that added a subtle glow to the darkness and illuminated the surroundings just enough to allow them to find their way. After the heat and noise of the ballroom the air was incredibly cool and peaceful.

A few couples were seated at tables outside, but Andreas ignored them and didn't break his stride, taking her across the grass and down towards the ornamental lake.

Finally he slowed down and took a deep breath. 'That's better. It was very hot in there, *agape mou*.'

Libby looked at him shyly. 'What does that mean?'

He didn't answer her and, seeing the lights of the ballroom and hearing the music fading into the background, Libby felt

suddenly vulnerable. All of a sudden it was just a woman alone
with a man in the incredible intimacy created by the semi-
darkness.

She felt breathlessly unsure as he led her down some steps
and through some trees and suddenly they were on the edge
of the lake.

'Oh!' She stopped dead, enchanted by the moonlight flickering on the nearly still water. 'It's magical. How did you know
it was here?'

Andreas maintained his grip on her wrist. 'I saw it from the
terrace when we were drinking champagne earlier.'

After the heat and noise of the ballroom it felt wonderfully
peaceful and she stood for a moment, enjoying the silence,
breathlessly aware of his powerful presence next to her. Even
without turning her head, she sensed that he was looking at
her and she felt her heart thud against her chest in a frenzy of
anticipation. His fingers hadn't moved from her wrist but she
could feel his touch with every part of her body.

'Libby?'

All he did was say her name but his soft tone brushed over
her nerve endings and made her shiver with a sexual excitement that was as intense as it was unfamiliar.

Barely breathing, she turned to face him and collided with
the raw passion in his dark eyes. Suddenly there were butterflies
in her stomach and her head felt woolly. Somewhere in the back
of her mind she registered that she was supposed to be resisting him but for the life of her she couldn't quite remember why.

Why would any woman in her right mind want to resist Andreas?

He was still looking down at her, dark eyes slightly narrowed
in a scrutiny so shockingly sexual that she felt dizzy.

By the time he finally lowered his head to hers she was quivering with expectation, longing for his touch, and the moment
his mouth found hers she moaned and lifted her hands to his

chest, curling her fingers into the front of his shirt, feeling the warmth of his chest through the thin fabric.

He kissed her slowly, teasing her mouth with gentle expertise until she pressed against him, desperate for him to deepen the kiss. Every seductive stroke of his tongue drove her demented with longing and she wrapped her arms round his neck and pulled him closer.

Still kissing her, Andreas shrugged off his jacket, letting it fall onto the grass, and then his arms came round her, hauling her close.

She felt his warm hands slide down her bare back, pressing her against him, making her aware of the intensity of his desire.

And suddenly she wanted more.

He wasn't moving fast enough.

Her arms dropped from his neck to his waist and she wrenched at his shirt, tearing buttons in her need to get closer to him.

She felt his hands slide the straps of her dress down her arms, baring her breasts to the cool night air. He dragged his mouth from hers and trailed kisses down her bare neck and she threw her head back, her eyes closed, all thought suspended as she felt him move lower. Then the coolness was replaced by warmth as he took her in his mouth, teasing her nipple until she cried out, overwhelmed by the exquisite agony of his touch.

His hands were on her thighs, drawing the silken fabric of her dress upwards, and she moved her hips against him, encouraging the contact that he was clearly seeking.

And then his mouth was on hers again and he lowered her to the ground. The damp grass cooled her heated skin and she lay breathless on the bed that nature had provided, aware of nothing except the aching need low in her pelvis and the weight of his body on hers.

His breathing was ragged and he delved deep into her mouth with his tongue, shifting his body so that he lay between her thighs.

Totally abandoned, Libby moaned and kissed him back, arching against him, burning with excitement when he finally touched her where she was aching to be touched.

She gasped his name, wanting more, needing more, totally consumed by the excitement that he'd unleashed.

He lifted his head briefly and she felt his hesitation.

'Andreas...' Her hoarse plea seemed to be the only encouragement he needed because he stared down into her eyes as he adjusted his position and dealt with the thin silk of her panties.

She was dimly aware of his strong fingers biting into her thigh, of the scrape of his rough jaw against her face and then he was there, entering her with a smooth thrust, trapping her gasp of ecstasy with his mouth. She felt his urgency as he drove deep inside her, filling her, increasing her level of arousal with each expert thrust. Dizzy with excitement, her fingers dug into the hard muscles of his back, and she arched up against him, unconsciously drawing him closer still.

The darkness ceased to exist, as did the lake and the press of the cool grass against her back. There was nothing except Andreas and the way he made her feel.

And Libby knew that nothing in her life had ever felt so totally right.

'Open your eyes.' His rough command penetrated the fog of sensation that held her in its grip and she did as he ordered, drowning in the raw sexual hunger that she read in his gaze.

Clashing with the heat of his eyes merely heightened the excitement and she struggled to breathe as he drove them both to such terrifying heights that the only way to go was down. She fell headlong into an explosive climax, aware that she was taking him with her, submitting to the wild, unfamiliar sensations that scorched her body.

Totally wiped out by the intensity of the experience, Libby closed her eyes and lay still, aware of the weight of his body on hers, his solid strength pinning her to the grass.

She could have stayed there for ever, feeling the rhythmic

thud of his heart against hers, the warmth of his breath against her neck as both of them slowly returned to the present.

She was aware of the uneven ground pressing into her back through the soft grass, of the cool night air brushing her bare, heated skin, but most of all she was aware of Andreas.

He was still wearing his shirt but it hung open where she'd all but torn it apart in her haste to undress him and the edges trailed around her, hiding her semi-nakedness. Somewhere nearby lay his jacket, carelessly discarded in their fevered desperation to remove all barriers.

He muttered something in Greek that she didn't understand and shifted his weight, rolling onto his side and taking her with him.

He stroked her tangled hair away from her face with a gentle hand. 'Beautiful Libby. Look at me,' he ordered softly, and she opened her eyes and tumbled headlong into the warmth and heat of his gaze.

I love you.

The words flew into her head and out again before she had time to say them and she caught her breath.

Of course she didn't love him.

How could she possibly love him?

It was just that they'd shared something that she'd never shared with anyone before. Had she imagined the incredible connection between them? Unlike her, Andreas was obviously an experienced male—had he ever felt that with anyone else?

'Don't try and hide from me.' His voice was husky and deep and sent shivers through her body. He pulled her closer and she felt the brush of his chest hair against her sensitised nipples. 'You're shivering. Are you cold?'

Of course she was shivering. She'd just had an explosive experience that had shocked her body.

And she certainly wasn't cold.

She felt hotter than she'd ever felt in her life.

He rolled her under him again and pinned her to the ground

under his powerful body. She felt incredibly vulnerable, aware of every single part of him.

Andreas gave a groan and lowered his head but before he could kiss her they heard voices approaching and Libby froze in horror.

Suddenly the dream shattered and she was horribly aware of where she was.

Lying in the grass by a lake in a public place, about to be discovered.

What was she doing?

Andreas reacted with his customary cool, rolling away from her and sliding her dress back up her arms before attempting to button his shirt.

'Half my buttons are missing,' he murmured, reaching out a lean hand and catching her chin. His eyes danced with humour. 'Do you know anything about that?'

Libby pulled away from him, her face flaming as she recalled how totally uninhibited she'd been. She stooped to retrieve her shoes, wondering what had happened to her.

How could she have done such a thing?

She, who prided herself on her self-control.

But then her self-control had never really been tested before, she reminded herself, her eyes sliding to Andreas and resting on his broad shoulders as he shrugged on his jacket, effectively disguising the fact that half the buttons were missing on his shirt.

He shot her a wicked, sexy smile that made her pulse rate bolt.

'Ready to go back to the party?'

Libby lifted a hand to her tangled blonde hair, still totally confused by her feelings. *She absolutely didn't love him.* 'I can't,' she whispered, painfully self-conscious. 'I look—'

'You look stunning,' he said quietly, stepping towards her and cupping her face in his hands.

He kissed her softly and then threaded his fingers through hers and led her back across the grass, past groups of people who were all enjoying the cool night air after the stifling heat of the ballroom.

Libby kept her face down as they walked and when they reached the terrace just outside the ballroom Andreas stopped and lifted her chin so that she was forced to look at him.

'Your guilt is written all over your face,' he murmured, his tone amused as he stroked her hair away from her flushed face. 'If it really troubles you that much, go to the ladies and redo your make-up.'

Totally shaken by what had happened and glad of an excuse to have five minutes to herself to gather her thoughts, Libby nodded and pulled away from him, hurrying inside to the ladies.

She locked herself in a cubicle and leaned against the door, her eyes tightly closed.

She didn't love him. She couldn't possibly love him.

It was just sex.

But she didn't do just sex.

She wasn't sure which was worse—the fact that she'd done something so reckless in the first place or the fact that she desperately wanted to do it again.

Oh, help!

What had she been thinking? And she knew the answer to that, of course. *She hadn't been thinking at all.* All right, so Andreas was the sexiest man she'd ever laid eyes on but at the same time this was *her*, and she just didn't behave like that. She'd never been interested in sex outside the confines of a serious relationship.

But, then, she'd never experienced good sex before tonight, she acknowledged wryly, opening her eyes and taking a deep breath. Suddenly she was aware of what she'd been missing all her life.

So what happened now?

She wasn't stupid enough to believe that Andreas wanted anything other than a short-term relationship. She was just an interesting diversion to him.

But that just wasn't going to work for her.

She liked him. A lot.

And, given a chance, she knew that it could be more than a lot.

Shaken by the intensity of what had happened between them, she knew that it wasn't an experience that she could risk repeating. Sooner or later she'd end up being seriously hurt. She knew that she couldn't enjoy that sort of physical closeness with a man without it developing into an emotional closeness, and that was something that Andreas wouldn't want.

Neither did she, Libby reminded herself firmly. She didn't want it either.

Which meant that she had to move on and pretend that it had never happened. Yes, that was it. She just needed to pretend that it had never happened. Isn't that what people did after one-night stands? They just went their separate ways and never referred to 'it' again.

She groaned. Unfortunately, 'it' was something that she was never going to forget. And working with Andreas every day just made things doubly difficult.

She ran a hand over her face, wondering whatever could have possessed her to do something quite so stupid.

But she knew what had happened.

She'd been overwhelmed by the chemistry between them, seduced by his warmth and his breathtaking sex appeal. He had an amazing way of making her feel as though she were the only woman in the world.

As if he really cared.

In fact, she'd been so overwhelmed it would have been all too easy to convince herself that he really felt something for her.

Which was utterly ridiculous.

She sucked in a breath and gave herself a sharp talking-to.

She was becoming delusional. Seduced by the romance of the evening. She needed to go home to the familiarity of her flat before she did something stupid.

Having made the decision, she slid out of the ladies' toilets with the minimum of fuss and made her way up the stairs, walking purposefully in the hope that no one would stop her.

They didn't and within minutes she was at the front of the hotel and hailing a taxi.

She stepped into the cab with a feeling of relief, pushing away the feeling of guilt that Andreas would still be waiting for her on the terrace.

He'd probably be a bit annoyed with her at first, but he wouldn't mind that much. To him it had just been a one-night stand.

He was surrounded by women who were desperate to get their claws into him, so losing her wasn't going to matter to him, was it?

She wasn't coming back.

Andreas breathed out heavily as he acknowledged that Libby had fled.

The irony of the situation wasn't lost on him.

For all of his adult life women had pursued him relentlessly, all of them hoping to be the one to finally make him settle down.

But he'd never been even remotely tempted.

Until now.

He still couldn't quite believe what had happened down by the lake. There was something about Libby that seemed to make him lose control in public places.

He'd only known her for a month but he knew without a shadow of a doubt that Libby was the woman he wanted to spend the rest of his life with.

The trouble was, the woman he'd finally fallen in love with had just vanished into the sunset.

CHAPTER SEVEN

LIBBY arrived on the ward the following morning, relieved that she was working. At least she didn't have time to brood. And as it was a Sunday it was extremely unlikely that she'd see Andreas, which gave her another day before she had to face him.

She'd bumped into Alex at breakfast, looking decidedly the worse for wear, and he'd given her a curious look but hadn't questioned her about her mysterious disappearance the night before.

Libby gave a wry smile. Knowing her brother, he'd probably disappeared himself and hadn't even noticed her absence.

She tied her hair up, checked that her sleepless night didn't show on her face and walked onto the ward.

Poppy, the little girl with cystic fibrosis who was back on the ward yet again, greeted her cheerfully from the side ward. 'How was your party?'

Libby lifted her eyebrows. 'And how do you know about the party, young lady?'

Poppy grinned. 'I heard everyone talking about it yesterday and they said that you were going with Dr Christakos. I think you're so lucky. He's so cool.'

Remembering the fiery heat of their encounter by the lake, Libby sucked in a breath.

Not cool.

'The party was fine, thank you, Poppy,' she said, taking the little girl's temperature and nodding with satisfaction as she read the result. 'And if you carry on improving like this, you'll be back home and going to your own parties soon enough.'

Poppy's face brightened. 'Am I better?'

'Definitely better. The physiotherapist will be up soon to sort out those lungs of yours.'

Poppy groaned. 'I hate physio.'

Libby sighed and gave her a hug. 'I know you do, sweetheart, but it helps, you know it does. Where's your dad this morning?'

'Gone for breakfast in the canteen. He was starving.'

Libby pulled a face. 'Well, the food there is enough to cure anyone of hunger so he'll be back soon. Why don't you use the playroom when the physio has been?'

They encouraged the children to get up and use the play-room, rather than sitting on their beds, and Bev had lost no time in spending some of the money that they'd raised at the auction.

Poppy shifted awkwardly on the bed. 'I don't really know anyone…'

'You know me,' Libby said cheerfully, filling in her chart. 'I'll be there.'

Poppy smiled. 'Oh, well, in that case…'

Making a mental note to take Poppy to the playroom later, Libby moved on to her next little patient.

Rachel Miller was back in for some tests. The baby was sit-ting in her cot cooing happily and playing with a stuffed toy.

Alison smiled when she saw Libby. 'She's fine now, but Dr Christakos wanted her to have those tests and they couldn't do them when she was in a few weeks ago.'

Libby nodded. 'They shouldn't take long.' Libby leaned into the cot and pulled faces at Rachel, who chuckled happily and reached to grab her. 'She's gorgeous, Alison. You're very lucky.'

'I know.' Alison smiled proudly at her daughter. 'We wanted a baby so badly and we tried for so long to have her. I still have to pinch myself.'

Libby looked at the little girl wistfully, feeling a sick empty feeling in the pit of her stomach.

She knew all about wanting a baby badly. There were days when she positively ached for a child of her own. But she was rapidly coming to the conclusion that it was never going to happen.

Part of her envied women who happily went ahead and produced babies without the support of a partner and she was aware that it was happening more and more frequently as women made decisions about their lives without the involvement of a man.

But she wasn't like that.

She was old-fashioned enough to believe that a baby was a miracle that should be shared with someone you loved. That a baby was part of the person you loved.

Libby sighed and straightened.

She really must stop being so soppy and romantic. Real life just wasn't like that any more. People got divorced. People had babies without partners. And people had one-night stands. It was a fact of life. It was just that she didn't want it to be a fact of *her* life.

She'd always wanted so much more than that, but it seemed that love and fidelity was an endangered species.

With that thought in her head she went through to the treatment room to fetch something—and came face to face with Andreas.

Libby felt the blood drain out of her cheeks and looked round for a suitable means of escape.

'Well, hello, there. Remember me?' His voice was a lazy drawl and he planted himself firmly in front of the door so that her exit was blocked. 'We were at a ball together and then suddenly you vanished.'

And given the chance, she'd vanish again.

'I went to the ladies.'

He lifted an eyebrow. 'You spent the night there?'

She flushed. 'I don't want to talk about this now.'

'Well, I do,' he said pleasantly, and she glared at him.

'What are you doing here anyway?'

Those dark eyes mocked her. 'I work here.'

'But it's Sunday,' she muttered, screwing her fingers into her palms and trying to stop her knees trembling. She was fast discovering that it was impossible to look at him without remembering what he'd made her feel. 'I wasn't expecting to see you on a Sunday.'

In fact, she'd been banking on it.

He gave a faint smile. 'Avoiding me, Libby?'

'No.' She managed a casual shrug, wondering just how fast a heart could beat before it exploded. 'Why would you think that?'

'Well, it could be something to do with the fact that you vanished in the middle of the evening,' he said, and she looked away from him.

It had been a pretty dreadful thing to do.

Suddenly feeling guilty for the way she'd behaved, she looked at him uncertainly. 'I'm sorry if I damaged your ego.'

He studied her with brooding concentration. 'My ego is totally bombproof, *agape mou*. But I do want to know what made you run.'

Him.

Her feelings.

'I didn't run.'

'You escaped to the ladies and never returned,' he reminded her softly, a hint of a smile playing around his firm mouth. 'I assumed your name must be Cinderella and I searched everywhere for white mice and pumpkins but there was nothing in sight. Not even a stray shoe. All I could see was a cloud of dust as you vanished into the distance.'

'I didn't run. I just thought—I…' Her excuses faltered under

his dark scrutiny. 'Well, I thought that was it so I might as well
go home.'

Before she'd started fantasising about fairy-tale endings.

She absolutely didn't love him.

'You thought that was *it*?' He lifted a dark eyebrow. 'Excuse me?'

She tucked a strand of hair behind her ear and tried to look
casual. 'We had sex, Andreas. No big deal.'

'"No big deal".' Andreas repeated her words slowly. 'So, if
it was no big deal, Libby, why did you run away?'

Oh, why couldn't he just drop it?

'Look…' Libby closed her eyes briefly, wishing he wasn't
quite so astute or persistent. 'It was just a one-night stand.
Plenty of people have them.'

Just not her.

Andreas looked at her thoughtfully. 'You poor thing. You
really are scared, aren't you?'

'Scared?' Libby stiffened defensively. 'What am I supposed
to be scared of?'

Andreas shrugged. 'At a guess—letting go. Trusting someone.' He moved closer to her. 'Obviously what we shared last
night scared you so much that you panicked and couldn't face
me again.'

'That's not true,' she lied, and he gave a wry smile.

'Libby, you know it is true.'

'Stop making it into something it wasn't,' she said frantically. 'It was just a one-night stand. It was just sex.'

'"Just sex".' He repeated her words slowly, and his expression was suddenly serious. 'Libby, are you taking the Pill?'

She stared at him, thrown by his question. Then she shook
her head.

'Right.' His voice was unbelievably gentle. 'So, if what happened between us last night was "just sex", how come neither
of us thought to use contraception?'

She paled and took a step backwards.

Contraception hadn't even entered her head, either before or afterwards.

And obviously it hadn't entered his either.

Oh, help.

Andreas rubbed a hand over his dark jaw. 'The reason neither of us thought about contraception,' he said finally, his Greek accent suddenly very pronounced, 'is because it wasn't "just sex". It was a hell of a lot more than that, as we both know. Neither of us planned it—it just happened—but, looking back on it, it was inevitable. It's been there since the first moment we laid eyes on each other.'

Libby was still staring at him, stunned by the revelation that they hadn't used contraception.

Why hadn't it occurred to her before? She might be relatively inexperienced, but she wasn't naïve. Why hadn't she thought of contraception?

Because she hadn't been thinking about practical things. In fact, she hadn't been thinking at all. All she'd done had been to feel and react.

And now she could be pregnant.

Without thinking, she placed a hand on her abdomen. Andreas, sharp-eyed as ever, caught the movement and his eyes narrowed.

'I am truly sorry for having failed to protect you,' he said softly, sliding his hands around her face and forcing her to look at him. 'There is no excuse and I have to confess that it is the first time in my life that I've ever lost control.'

She could well believe it. Andreas Christakos was the original Mr Cool.

So what was he saying? That she was special? Different?

Did he really expect her to believe that?

Trapped by that dark gaze, Libby was severely tempted.

No, no, no!

She was doing it again.

Losing herself in the fairy-tale when she should know better.

Gentle words were just part of the standard male seduction technique, she reminded herself firmly. Andreas wasn't any different. Except perhaps that he was more skilled at it than the average male.

Any minute now he'd produce the wife or start the 'I don't do commitment' speech.

'It was my fault as much as yours,' she said finally, still unable to understand what had happened. She'd totally lost control and that had never happened to her before. She had never lost control with a man. Never felt remotely like ripping off all her clothes and making love by a lake with a couple of hundred people only metres away.

His voice was gentle. 'We need to talk about what you want to do.'

Do?

Libby looked at him, startled, and noticed that he seemed strangely tense.

'Do you want to take the morning-after pill? I could give you a prescription.'

Trying not to mind that he was so keen for her to sort the matter out, still shell-shocked by the revelation that she could be pregnant, Libby shook her head.

'I—I'll sort something out,' she mumbled evasively, totally confused by her feelings.

She was a single woman with no partner. She ought to be rushing to the chemist to get the morning-after pill.

So why were her legs glued to the spot?

Andreas frowned slightly. 'Libby—'

'I don't want to take the morning-after pill,' she said flatly, unable to be anything but honest. 'It doesn't seem right.'

Suddenly the confusion in her head cleared and her thoughts were clear.

There was absolutely no doubt at all in her mind.

If she was pregnant then she was going to keep the baby.

There was a strange look on his face that she couldn't interpret.

'There's no need to panic,' she muttered, her eyes sliding away from his. 'I don't expect you to take any responsibility.'

Andreas frowned. 'Responsibility? Libby—'

The door opened and one of the staff nurses stuck her head round, interrupting him before he could finish his sentence.

'Dr Christakos, A and E are on the phone. It's urgent.'

Andreas gritted his teeth and strode out of the room, almost sending the nurse flying.

Libby stared after him and she was still staring into space when he returned only moments later.

'That was your brother-in-law,' he said, his mouth set in a grim line. 'There's been a nasty house fire and two children were involved. They're on their way in now but they're already struggling in A and E so he wants some help.'

Libby pulled herself together. 'Of course. I'll just tell Bev.'

She hurried off to find the ward sister and then met Andreas in the corridor and they both made their way to A and E. Andreas didn't make further reference to their conversation but she felt his eyes on her.

The department was frantically busy. The waiting room was bulging with people and the screen was flashing up a waiting time of five hours.

'And it's going to be longer than that,' Katy told them quickly, following their gaze. 'We're having a bad day down here. Thanks for your help. We thought that you could sort the children out—maybe take them straight to the ward if you prefer.'

Andreas gave a brief nod. 'We'll assess them here and then decide. What's been going on?'

'A coach overturned on one of the bridges,' Katy told him, her face drawn and tired. 'We're all struggling. And now Ambulance Control has rung about the fire. Apparently it was a nasty one. The mother jumped from the window with the baby.

She's fractured both femurs and she's in a bad way, although they think the baby is fine. The father went back into the house to try and get to the other child.'

Before they could discuss the case any further they heard sirens as several ambulances pulled into the ambulance bay.

'OK, let's move!' Miraculously, Jago and one of the A and E consultants appeared and took charge. He spoke swiftly to the paramedics, conducted brief triage in the back of the ambulance and then reappeared, his expression grim. 'Katy, I want the mother and the father into Resus straight away, and fast-bleep the orthopaedic surgeons. Andreas, do you want the children on the ward or down here?'

'I'll assess them here.' Andreas stepped forward to talk to the other paramedic. 'What's the story?'

'The baby seems to be unhurt. The mother took the brunt of the fall and she was cradling the child so the little one may be all right, but she herself jumped from the bedroom window, which was quite a drop. Baby's been crying non-stop but no signs of burns. The four-year-old is a different matter. Her pyjamas caught fire and she's got nasty burns to her legs. We've given her oxygen at the scene and covered them.'

'OK—take them both through to Paediatric Resus,' Andreas ordered, and Libby hurried ahead of him to the area of A and E that had been designed specially for children.

The paramedics lifted the howling four-year-old onto the trolley and kept hold of the baby, who was also shrieking.

Charlotte, one of the A and E sisters, hurried forward. 'I'll take her while you examine the older child.'

Andreas was already by her side, talking to her gently, trying to assess the degree of damage. 'Can we weigh her quickly? Once we've done that I want to estimate the surface area of the burns and then get this child some pain relief,' he ordered quietly, and Libby did as he'd instructed. 'We need to get a line in and then we'll give her a bolus of morphine.'

Libby gathered the necessary equipment while Andreas examined the screaming child, calculating the percentage of the body surface that had suffered burns.

'If we take her hand to be the equivalent of one per cent of her body surface area, she's suffered about ten per cent burns, most of them partial thickness,' he murmured, as he examined the little girl's legs. 'Would you agree?'

'Sounds about right.' Libby nodded, running her eyes over the burns on the child's legs.

'These blisters have ruptured and they're weeping. She's obviously feeling pain.'

'Which is a good thing,' Libby said softly, and Andreas nodded.

'Absolutely. As we both know, it's a sign that the nerve endings aren't damaged. I've checked her chest and it seems clear so there's no sign of smoke inhalation. What we have to worry about now is fluid loss.'

Libby nodded. She knew that fluid loss was proportionately greater in children than adults.

'Poor little mite. You'll want to admit her,' she said immediately. 'When you're finished here I'll call Bev and see if she can go in the side room. Melanie Parker is well enough to be on the main ward now.'

Andreas nodded. 'It would probably do her good to be mixing with the other children. OK, let's get on with this. What's her name?'

Libby checked the notes that the paramedic had left. 'Jenny.'

'Right, Jenny...' Andreas positioned himself so that he was close to the girl without actually touching her. She was still screaming hysterically. 'We are going to take that pain away.'

Jenny continued to scream for her mother and Libby exchanged worried looks with Andreas.

'Let's get on with it,' he muttered, and Libby breathed out heavily. It was horrible, seeing the child so distressed.

She was sobbing now and Libby couldn't stand it a moment

longer. She pulled up a chair, wrapped the child in a sterile towel and scooped her onto her lap, cuddling her close.

'There, sweetheart,' she crooned. 'Mummy will be coming in a minute. There's a good girl.'

She continued to talk soothing nonsense while Andreas searched for a vein. Libby prayed that he'd find one quickly, watching his lean, brown hands as he tapped and squeezed until he was satisfied.

He rocked back on his heels and pulled a face. 'Well, I think that looks hopeful.'

The A and E sister stepped forward. 'I'll squeeze.' She wrapped her hands around the tiny wrist and squeezed while Andreas slipped the cannula into the vein with ridiculous ease.

Libby let out a sigh of relief and Charlotte whistled in admiration.

'Nice work,' she said cheerfully, taping the cannula in place and attaching it to the bag of intravenous fluids. 'Here's that morphine you requested.'

She waved the syringe under his nose and Andreas checked it carefully before taking it from her and injecting it slowly into the tube.

'We'll start with this and she can have more in ten minutes if it hasn't done the trick.'

Jenny clung to Libby, shivering and sobbing until gradually the drug took effect and the little girl slumped in Libby's arms.

Andreas straightened and rubbed a hand over the back of his neck. 'OK, let's do a map of those burns and dress them, and then I want to pass a catheter so that we can measure her urine output.'

They worked as quickly as they could and Jenny clung to Libby, obviously seeing her as some sort of substitute mother.

Finally Andreas was satisfied that they'd done all they could. 'We need to check that her fluid replacement is adequate. I want an output of one mil per kilogram per hour.'

Libby nodded and she and Charlotte manoeuvred the child onto the scales, recording the result in the notes.

'Right, let's get her up to the ward and make her comfortable. Keep an eye on her pulses in case her circulation is compromised. Now, how's that baby?'

'She seems fine.' While she'd been helping with Jenny, the A and E sister had put the baby safely in a cot and she was now lying there quietly. 'Do you want to check her here or on the ward?'

'I'll do it here.' Andreas unlooped the stethoscope from around his neck and walked across to the baby.

With Jenny still snuggled on her lap, Libby watched as he examined the baby thoroughly, finally picking her up and making her laugh by blowing raspberries on her stomach.

'She seems none the worse for her dramatic fall,' Andreas observed quietly, holding the child with the easy confidence of someone who was thoroughly at home with children.

Libby watched him, unable to stop herself. He was just so good with children.

It was amazing that he didn't have any himself.

But that would have meant settling down with one woman, and that clearly wasn't his style.

And he obviously wasn't that keen to be a father. After all, he'd been the one to suggest that she take the morning-after pill.

Pushing the thought away, she stood up, intending to place Jenny on the trolley so that she could dress her legs, but the little girl clung to her and whimpered pathetically.

'I'll do the dressings,' Charlotte said immediately. 'She seems to have taken to you so it seems a shame to upset her again. Keep her on your lap and I'll sort it out.'

She bustled around the room, collecting various bits and pieces, and then pushed a dressing trolley close to Libby.

With the deft efficiency of a nurse who was well used to doing dressings, Charlotte covered the burns and made the child comfortable.

'Carry her up to the ward,' Andreas advised softly, placing a large, reassuring hand on the child's head. 'She's had just about all the trauma she can take, poor thing.'

Libby nodded and shifted the child into a more comfortable position, careful not to hurt her injured legs.

'I'll take her up, then,' she said quietly, and Andreas nodded.

'I just want to get an update on the parents and then I'll join you with this little one. It won't hurt to have her in overnight, given the fall she suffered, and we can't exactly discharge her anyway until we know what's happening with the parents.'

Libby nodded and left him to it, carrying little Jenny the short distance to the paediatric ward.

Bev was waiting for them, the room all ready, clucking with sympathy when she saw the child. 'Oh, the poor mite—how are her parents?'

Libby shook her head. 'We don't know yet. Andreas is talking to Jago now.'

Bev sighed and pulled out a chair so that Libby could sit down. 'It looks as though you're going to be occupied for the rest of the shift so I'll reallocate the rest of your patients. Luckily we're not that pushed today so it shouldn't be too difficult.'

'Thanks, Bev.' Libby cuddled Jenny closer. Like the ward sister, she knew that staying with the child was the most important thing she could do at the moment. 'What are we going to do with the baby?'

'We've got a spare cot in with Rachel,' Bev said, hooking Jenny's infusion up to a drip stand. 'I thought we'd put her in there for now.'

'Good idea.'

Libby cuddled Jenny close, talking to her quietly until she fell asleep, her soft hair brushing against Libby's cheek.

'I'm glad she's asleep.' Andreas spoke from the doorway and Libby looked up to find him leaning against the doorframe, watching them, his handsome face inscrutable. 'You look good with a child on your lap, Libby.'

She blushed and changed the subject. 'How are her parents?'

Andreas pulled a face. 'Not good. Her mother is in Theatre now—she fractured both femurs in the fall so she's going to be in hospital for a good while.'

'Poor lady.' Libby considered the implications of his words. The woman had two young children. How was she going to manage? 'Did she suffer burns?'

'Apparently not.' Andreas shook his head. 'She jumped out of the bedroom window with the baby to get away from the smoke. How is the baby, by the way?'

'Seems fine.' Libby spoke softly, careful not to wake Jenny who was still dozing, snuggled against her chest. 'Bev's made up a cot in Rachel's room and put her there for now. I suppose we'll need to find out if there are any other family members to care for her. What about the father? How's he?'

'Suffering smoke inhalation and quite severe burns to his hands where he tried to remove Jenny's pyjamas.' Andreas ran a hand through his dark hair, his expression suddenly weary. 'He certainly isn't going to be in a position to care for a baby on his own for some time.'

Libby sighed. 'Have we managed to contact any other family? Do the neighbours know of anyone?'

'The police are looking into it,' Andreas told her, his eyes resting on Jenny. 'Poor little thing. She looks exhausted.'

'It's all that crying,' Libby murmured, bending her head and dropping a light kiss on the little one's head. 'It's hardly surprising she was upset. The one person you want when you're hurt is your mummy and hers wasn't around.'

Andreas lifted his gaze. 'But she seems to have bonded with you.' His voice was deep and the look in his eyes was extremely unsettling. 'You have a very special gift with children, Libby. They love you.'

Her heart thudded in her chest and breathing was suddenly difficult. 'Better with children than adults,' she said lightly, dragging her gaze away from his. 'Children don't let you down.'

'Neither do most adults,' he responded quietly. 'You've just been unlucky. And we have a conversation to finish, Libby.'

She didn't even pretend that she didn't know what he meant.

He wanted to talk about the possibility that she could be pregnant.

But there was no way she was going to take the morning-after pill and she didn't want him to try and talk her into it.

'It's fine, Andreas,' she said softly, lifting her eyes to his. 'It's not your concern.'

He frowned. 'If you're pregnant then it's my concern.'

She blushed, slightly embarrassed by the intimacy of the discussion and desperately hoping that no one was in the corridor, listening to the conversation. She wondered briefly what had happened to her notion of discretion since she'd met Andreas. First they'd made love in the open air where anyone could have discovered them and now they were discussing the consequences in the middle of a busy hospital ward.

'I'm a modern woman,' Libby said lightly, looking away from him again. 'If it happens, rest assured that I'm not going to chase you for money.'

His gaze darkened ominously. 'Unfortunately, I'm not a modern guy,' he responded icily. 'I'm Greek and Greek men are notoriously old-fashioned about things like that. If you're pregnant, Libby, you'll be getting much more from me than money.'

Without giving her a chance to respond, he strode out of the room, leaving her staring after him.

CHAPTER EIGHT

LIBBY managed to avoid Andreas for the rest of the shift by staying with Jenny.

When the night staff arrived she was still in the little girl's room, cuddling her, talking softly to her, making her feel more secure in her strange surroundings. There seemed no hope that she'd be able to see either of her parents before the morning.

Her mother was still in Theatre and her father was being treated for smoke inhalation.

'The neighbour thinks that there's an aunt living nearby,' Bev told her, 'but no one has any idea how to contact her. We'll just have to wait for one of the parents to tell us. In the meantime, we'll keep the baby overnight. Andreas seems keen to keep an eye on her anyway, given the seriousness of the fall.'

'I can't believe she survived it,' Libby murmured softly, careful not to wake Jenny, who was dozing quietly.

'Well, the mother obviously took the brunt of the impact.' Bev looked at the little girl lying on the bed. 'She seems more peaceful. Has she had more morphine?'

Libby nodded. 'It will be good when she can see one of her parents. She needs the reassurance.'

Bev nodded. 'Well, hopefully we'll manage something tomorrow. We can always carry her up to them if necessary.' Her eyes narrowed as she looked at Libby. 'You look exhausted. You should have requested the day off today. How late did you get to bed?'

Not that late, Libby reflected. But she'd been awake for most of the night thinking about Andreas. *Dreaming about fairytales and happy endings.*

'I'm fine.'

'What you need is some proper time off. You've got a few days' leave due. I want you to take them.'

Libby looked at her. 'Bev, we're far too busy for me to take leave.'

Bev shrugged. 'You're knackered, Lib. You're no use to me like this. You've been working double shifts for as long as I can remember and you need a rest. I'll ring the agency and see if I can get someone for the week after next.'

Libby frowned. 'Holiday leave...'

'Yes, holiday leave,' Bev said firmly. 'You've got five days. For goodness' sake, go away somewhere.'

Libby looked at her blankly. She didn't really want to go anywhere. She didn't have the energy. If she wasn't going to work, all she really wanted to do was go to bed and sleep for ever.

'I'll see how things are,' she said vaguely, thinking that it might actually be nice to have a few days at home, doing nothing. She could lie in bed in the mornings and meet Katy for lunch. 'If you're sure, that is.'

'I'm sure,' Bev said firmly, breaking off as Andreas strolled into the room.

Libby felt her stomach turn over. He was so good-looking he took her breath away and she was starting to have really, really foolish thoughts.

Thoughts about being pregnant and him insisting on marrying her.

Ridiculous!

She closed her eyes briefly, horrified by the way her mind was working.

What was the matter with her? She was thinking like some-one who wasn't thoroughly disillusioned with men.

A holiday was definitely a good idea. It would mean putting space between her and Andreas. And she needed that space.

Her mind seemed to have a will of its own and she was start-ing to believe that Andreas might be different from all the other men she'd ever met.

She definitely needed a holiday.

Libby picked up her bag and left the ward, thinking long-ingly of her bed.

She just hoped that tonight she'd sleep.

Last night she hadn't managed to do anything except think of Andreas. She'd lain in the darkness, reliving every incredible second of their encounter by the lake. The memory had been so vivid that she'd almost been able to smell the damp grass and feel the cool night air on her skin. Her body had tingled with the memory of his touch and she could still hear the rough, masculine timbre of his voice as he'd spoken to her in Greek. She hadn't been able to understand a word that he'd said but it had been an unbelievably erotic experience and she couldn't get it out of her mind.

Damn.

Running a hand over her flushed face, she tried to pull her-self together. It had just been sex, for crying out loud. Just sex, and she'd done it before.

But it had never been like that.

With Andreas it had been a totally different experience and if she was ever going to survive, she had to avoid him. And what better way to avoid him than by taking a holiday?

She could spend the time reminding herself that all men were rats.

Andreas stared at the notes in front of him without seeing them. For the third day running Libby had been in Jenny's room for almost the entire shift, not even coming out for lunch. The little girl was very clingy and she'd obviously bonded with Libby, but all the same it was obvious to him that she was anxious to avoid any further conversation with him and he knew why.

The chemistry between them was so overwhelming that he found it quite unnerving himself. He'd never felt this way about a woman before and he knew that she was experiencing the same emotions.

The challenge was going to be getting her to admit it.

Libby was terrified of being hurt. She found it impossible to trust men and she was incredibly wary and cautious.

He needed to prove to her that he could be trusted but he couldn't do that unless she agreed to spend some time with him. But judging from the way she'd been avoiding him since that night, the chances of her agreeing to that were remote.

He leaned back in his chair and stretched his long legs out in front of him, frowning thoughtfully.

And then he remembered the date.

She still owed him a date.

A slow smile crossed his handsome face as he remembered the conversation he'd overheard between her and the ward sister.

No one had ever stipulated exactly what constituted the date that had been auctioned.

And suddenly he knew exactly what that date was going to be.

A week later Jenny was improving rapidly and spending much of the time in the playroom with Polly, who had taken on a surrogate mother role.

Jenny's parents were still in hospital and her baby sister had been staying with an aunt who lived locally.

The ward had quietened down slightly, Bev had found an agency nurse who'd agreed to work for the rest of the month and Libby was exhausted.

The strain of trying to avoid Andreas was making her jumpy and she wasn't getting any sleep thanks to that one incredible night she'd spent with him. She was totally unable to forget the way he'd made her feel.

She was thoroughly relieved that Bev had insisted she take leave. At least she wouldn't have to peep round corners to check that there was no sign of Andreas. She vowed to get plenty of exercise in the hope that it would make her sleep.

Suddenly she couldn't wait for her shift to end.

She went through the motions of doing her job and at lunch-time Bev bustled up to her.

'You look absolutely wiped out.' The ward sister shook her head disapprovingly. 'Go home.'

'I can't go yet. I haven't finished my shift.'

Bev gave her a gentle push. 'Just go. Now. And if I see you back on this ward before next week, you're fired.'

Libby gave a weak smile. She couldn't actually believe she had a whole week off. 'You can't fire me. I'm your slave labour.'

Bev didn't laugh. 'You've lost your sparkle and bubble,' she said quietly. 'You've been working too hard, Lib. Have a rest.'

Libby didn't say anything. It was true that she was tired, but the truth was her sparkle had gone because she was so disappointed about Andreas. She'd really believed that he was interested in her, but evidently she'd been wrong again.

Apart from that one conversation the morning after, he'd made no attempt to see her since the ball.

All right, so she'd been avoiding him, but he hadn't been that difficult to avoid.

Wondering whether he would even notice that she wasn't around, she went to her locker, retrieved her bag and made her way to the car park, feeling flat and miserable.

A low black sports car pulled up next to her and she sucked in a breath.

Andreas.

He leaned across to open the passenger door, his expression serious. 'Get in, Libby.'

She stared at him blankly. 'Why? Where are we going?'

'Just get in.'

Something about the urgency in his tone prevented her from arguing and she slid into the passenger seat, glancing at him in alarm as he sped away before she'd even finished fastening her seat belt.

'What's happening? Is something wrong?' Suddenly she felt cold fingers of panic touch her spine. 'Is it Katy? Or Alex?'

He covered her hand briefly with his. 'They're both fine. And nothing's wrong.'

'So why are you picking me up? It's not even lunchtime.' She looked at him in confusion. 'And what's the urgency?'

He glanced at the clock and muttered something in Greek. 'We are going to be late.'

'Late for what?'

But he wouldn't answer her. He just stared at the road and drove as quickly as safety allowed, weaving his way through the London traffic until he hit the motorway that led out of town.

'Andreas.' Libby cleared her throat and tried again. 'Where are we going?'

He gave her a sideways glance. 'We're going on that date you owe me.'

Date?

He flicked the indicator and took the exit road that led to the airport and she lifted a hand to her aching head, totally confused.

'What date? Why are we at the airport?'

Andreas pulled up outside the terminal building and shifted in his seat so that he was facing her.

'You still owe me that date, Libby,' he said softly, lifting a hand to cup her face. 'I'm claiming it now. You've got a week off. You're spending it with me.'

She opened her mouth to speak but he was already out of the car, handing his keys to a man in a uniform and removing two bags from the boot.

Libby recognised one of the bags as hers.

She leapt out of the car, waiting while he paid the man and signalled for a porter.

'You packed a bag for me?' She stared at him incredulously and he shrugged.

'Not exactly. I had some help. Katy told me she owed you a suitcase full of clothes.'

Katy.

Libby groaned. 'I switched the contents of her suitcase when she went abroad with Jago. Katy always insisted on dressing really conservatively to hide her looks so Alex and I gave her a completely new wardrobe. She didn't know until she arrived in Spain and unpacked.'

Andreas laughed. 'Well, it seems as though you're not the only sister capable of being devious. And now we need to hurry or we'll miss our flight.'

Libby ran her tongue over dry lips. 'Andreas, I can't just go away with you.'

'Why not?'

Because she didn't trust him.

Because she was trying to put some distance between them and she couldn't possibly do that if they were together all week.

She opened her mouth to voice another protest but he was already striding towards the terminal building and she was forced to run to catch up with him.

'All right, if you want a date, I'll go on a date with you, but this is ridiculous.' She was half running, half walking, but he didn't slow his pace.

'Why is it ridiculous?' He shot her a smile and walked up to the check-in desk. 'I always told you that my idea of a date wasn't pizza. You just never asked what my idea of a date was. Well, this is it. We're going to spend some time together, Libby. No more avoiding me. No more avoiding what we have together.'

She stared at him as he handed over the passports and

checked in, infuriated that he wasn't even giving her a chance to speak.

'We don't have anything together,' she said in a low voice, blushing slightly as the girl behind the desk glanced curiously between the two of them. 'It was just—'

'If you're about to tell me that it was "just sex",' Andreas interrupted, 'then I'd better warn you that the next time you say that I'm going to drag you behind the nearest pillar and prove you wrong. We both know that it wasn't "just sex", Libby, so stop saying things you don't mean.'

He tucked the passports into his jacket and walked towards the international departures area.

Her breathing was rapid and she felt totally out of control.

'At least tell me where we're going,' she asked a little later.

He turned with a smile. 'We're going to Greece, *agape mou*. I'm taking you to my home.'

Greece?

'But where will we stay? What will we—?'

'Stop worrying.' He stepped up to her and covered her lips with his fingers to stop her talking. 'You're not in control any more. I am. This is *my* date, Libby.'

With that Andreas bent his head and kissed her gently, smiling when she gave a start and backed away.

She glared at him. 'This isn't a date. It's kidnap. I could scream.'

His smiled widened. 'If you scream, I'm going to kiss you senseless in front of an audience. Knowing what usually happens when we touch each other, are you willing to risk that, Libby?'

Her heart thudded against her chest. There was no way she wanted him to kiss her again. It was much too disturbing. Strange things happened when he kissed her. Her body burned and her brain ceased to be capable of logical thought.

So instead of screaming she just sighed and pretended to look bored. 'A week is a long time with someone you don't really know, Andreas. What happens when you find that you don't enjoy my company?'

He laughed. 'Libby, we both know that we're crazy about each other. It's just that you're afraid to admit it.'

Crazy about each other…

Libby swallowed hard. 'And you think I'll admit it if I'm with you all week? Are all Greek men as arrogant as you?'

Was he really saying he was crazy about her?

He nodded, giving her a gentle push as they boarded the air-craft. 'We're an arrogant, chauvinistic race who know how to keep a woman in her place,' he teased. 'Now sit down and shut up. And preferably get some sleep. You're exhausted.'

'And whose fault is that?' Libby muttered darkly, fastening her seat belt and wriggling further into her seat.

'You're saying that I'm the reason you're tired?'

His deep voice was right next to her ear and her body heated. He sounded so sexy. Oh, for goodness' sake. So the guy had a sexy voice. So what? She was being utterly pathetic.

She tried to shift further away from him but there was no-where to go. 'I'm tired because I've been working hard,' she said sweetly, and he gave a knowing smile that infuriated her.

'Of course you are. So, sleep, Libby.'

Libby closed her eyes tightly. She had absolutely no hope of sleeping, but at least if she closed her eyes she couldn't see those dark eyes and that sexy mouth. She needed some rest if she was going to resist him.

And she was going to resist him.

No problem.

Andreas shook his head as the stewardess offered him more coffee. They'd been flying for three and a half hours and Libby had been asleep the whole time. At some point her head had flopped onto his shoulder and he'd turned slightly so that he could cuddle her closer and make her comfortable.

He was worried about how tired she looked.

Her cheeks were pale and there were shadows visible beneath her closed lashes. Hc vowed to make sure that she had plenty of rest when they reached their destination.

He still couldn't quite believe that he'd managed to pull it off. He'd hoped that by picking her up straight from work with no warning she wouldn't have time to think up excuses. And it had worked. With a great deal of help from Katy and Bev.

So now he had a week alone with her.

One week to try and persuade her how right they were for each other.

Libby woke feeling warm and safe and then she realised that the person she was cuddling was Andreas and she sat bolt upright, pink with embarrassment.

Bother.

Andreas made no comment. Instead, he shifted his shoulder slightly and reached across to look out of the window.

'Look at that,' he said softly. 'Isn't it fantastic?'

Still foggy-headed from sleep, Libby turned her head to look out of the tiny window and gave a gasp of delight.

Beneath them stretched perfect blue sea, twinkling in the sunlight as though someone had casually tossed a handful of diamonds into the waves. Tiny boats were just visible and she could see several pretty islands with sandy coves

'It's beautiful.'

'It's Greece.' Andreas smiled with satisfaction as he settled back in his seat. 'Still angry that I kidnapped you?'

Libby couldn't take her eyes off the sea. She wanted to dive straight in and feel the cool water on her exhausted body. 'I can think of worse places to be held hostage.'

'The only thing holding you hostage is your inability to trust anyone,' Andreas replied calmly. 'I'm glad you slept. Our journey isn't finished yet.'

Despite her qualms about spending the week with him, she felt suddenly excited.

Why shouldn't she enjoy a holiday?

She could keep Andreas at a distance here as easily as she could on the ward.

'Where exactly are we going?'

'Crete. My home.'

A car was waiting for them when they landed and Libby stared in awe at the scenery that flashed passed.

'It's beautiful. How can you bear to leave it?'

He smiled. 'The lure of British and American healthcare.'

'Well, I think you're mad. If this was my home I'd never leave it.' Libby gave an enormous yawn and settled back in her seat. 'Are we staying in your house?'

Andreas grabbed the bags and shook his head. 'Yes. Although none of the rest of the family will be there. My mother is visiting my cousin who's just had a baby and my uncles spend most of their time in Athens now.'

Libby shot him a wary glance. Would it be just the two of them?

Her heart lurched slightly but before she had a chance to question him further the driver had turned off the road and was driving down what was little more than a dusty track that led towards the beach.

Libby craned her neck curiously, wondering where they were going. Surely there couldn't be a house here? Nothing was visible from the road.

And then the car turned a corner and she gasped.

A beautiful whitewashed villa nestled at one end of a beautiful bay, the sand stretching away from it to form a perfect crescent.

It was the most idyllic spot she'd ever seen and she turned to Andreas in amazement.

'This is your home?'

'I was brought up here,' he told her, nodding to the driver as he retrieved the bags from the boot of the car. 'But we spent

a great deal of time in Athens, too. My father had business interests there. He hated leaving his family behind so we had a
home there as well.'

'You're lucky,' Libby said wistfully, and he looked at her
keenly.

'Did your father travel a lot?'

Libby tensed. 'Yes, but we were all very grateful for that.
Things weren't too great when he was around.'

Wanting to escape from the memories that he'd aroused,
she slipped off her shoes and sprinted down to the sand, sigh-
ing with pleasure as she felt the warm softness ooze between
her toes.

'You're a child, Elizabeth,' Andreas said with a laugh from
behind her, and she shrugged, staring out across the sparkling
sea to the orange sun that was starting to dip behind the mountains.

'I don't know about that,' she said softly, 'but I do know that
if you were brought up here then you were very lucky.'

She'd heard the affection in his voice when he'd spoken of his
parents and suddenly she envied him his childhood. Her own
had been full of rows and totally lacking in parental affection.

Would she have been different if she'd had his family background?

Would she have found it easier to trust people?

'I was lucky,' he agreed. 'I had a secure, loving family around
me when I was a child and I suppose that's why I don't find it
hard to trust people. Unlike you. I know that you've been surrounded by faithless men all your life, but it's time to realise
that they aren't the only sort.'

Her breathing quickened.

It would have been so easy to believe him. So easy…

And so foolish.

She gave a wry smile and kicked at the sand with her bare
feet. 'So…' she lifted her head and gave him a bright smile
'…are you going to show me your house?'

He lifted a hand and touched her face gently. 'You are the mistress of avoidance, do you know that?'

She gave a careless shrug. 'I don't see the point in dwelling on the past.'

'If it's affecting the future, there's a point,' he said quietly, taking her hand and pulling her back towards the villa. 'But we'll talk about that another time. Come on. Let's get settled in.'

She followed him inside, almost drooling with pleasure as she saw the interior. It was decorated in a mixture of white and cool blues so that the overall impression was that it was just a continuation of the ocean.

'I know you're tired so I'll show you straight to your bedroom,' Andreas said roughly, and she looked at him cautiously.

She hadn't given any thought to the sleeping arrangements. 'Andreas—'

'Sleep, Libby,' he said gently, 'and then we'll talk.'

Suddenly realising just how exhausted she was, she followed him into a bedroom, smiling with pleasure when she saw the bathroom. It was the last word in luxury.

'I can't believe you brought me here. I ought to be fighting with you,' she murmured, reaching forward and flicking on the taps, 'but frankly I'm too exhausted.'

'Thank goodness for that.' Andreas gave a wry smile and deposited her suitcase on the floor. 'I'll leave you to it. My bedroom is directly opposite if you need anything.'

She stiffened. 'I won't need anything.'

His smile widened and she sucked in a breath, uncomfortably aware that they seemed to be alone in this villa. Alone for the first time in their relationship.

But he didn't seem inclined to take advantage of that fact. Instead, he flicked her cheek gently with a strong finger and left the room without a backward glance, closing the door behind him.

She stared after him, telling herself firmly that she wasn't disappointed.

He'd left her to have a bath and sleep alone in that gorgeous huge bed with the gauzy cream drapes.

And that was exactly what she wanted.

Wasn't it?

Two days later Libby wondered how she was ever going to bring herself to leave the island.

She'd spent most of her time cooling down in the sea or in the fantastic azure blue pool that overlooked the beach. When she wasn't swimming she slept, and every time she awoke there seemed to be more food waiting for her. Greek salads, dips, plump olives and regional specialities that made her mouth water.

Andreas had explained on the first day that one of the families from the neighbouring village looked after the villa and kept an eye on his mother when she was staying there. They were also responsible for delivering vast quantities of delicious food every day.

'You're trying to fatten me up,' she groaned, leaning back in her chair after a spectacular lunch during which she'd eaten far too much for comfort.

Andreas poured her some more water and she tried not to notice how good he looked in his polo shirt. The fabric hugged the powerful muscles of his shoulders and his arms were tanned and strong.

He was an incredibly good-looking man and she didn't really understand why he was bothering with her.

'It's good to see you eating, rather than picking at your food the way you did the night of the ball.'

As usual, any reference to the ball brought a sudden rush of colour to Libby's cheeks. She couldn't prevent herself from glancing across at him, and instantly regretted it. His dark eyes locked onto hers and she felt heat flare deep in her pelvis.

Terrified of the strength of her reaction, she stood up

abruptly, her chair scraping on the ground. 'It's hot. I'm going to cool off in the pool—'

Strong fingers closed around her wrist and anchored her to the spot. 'You shouldn't exercise when you've just eaten, *agape mou*. And it's time to stop avoiding me. You've rested and the colour has returned to your cheeks. No more running.'

'I'm not running.' She stood, breathing rapidly, trapped by his relentless grip and by the look in his eyes.

'Libby, you've been running since the night I bought you at that auction.' He pulled her closer and she couldn't have resisted even if she'd wanted to. 'It's time you and I communicated.'

She watched, breathless, as his head lowered, transfixed by the inevitability of that kiss. For endless, infuriating seconds his mouth hovered above hers, close enough to set her whole body on fire with anticipation but not close enough to satisfy the raging hunger building inside her.

His eyes were half-closed as he looked down at her, and a hint of a smile hovered on his incredibly sexy mouth. Finally he lowered his head and his mouth brushed against hers, sending shock waves of excitement through her quivering body.

His hands slid up to her face, cradling it firmly, while his tongue traced the seam of her lips and dipped inside. Her lips parted under the pressure of his and she kissed him back, her tongue responding to the demands of his, her body arching against the solid muscle of his powerful body.

He kissed her until her entire body was throbbing with sensation and when he finally lifted his head she stared up at him, dazed.

With considerable effort she found her voice. 'I—I thought you wanted to talk.'

He gave a slow smile and touched her damp, swollen lips with the tips of his fingers. 'I didn't say talk, *agape mou*. I said communicate.'

She gazed at him, heart thumping, hypnotised by the raw passion she saw in his eyes. 'But—'

'We're using body language,' he said huskily, his mouth lowering to hers again.

She gave a tiny sob as he licked her lips suggestively. 'Body language?'

He gave a slow smile that ignited a burning heat deep inside her. 'It's the only way I can be sure that you're telling the truth. When you use words, you say things you don't mean.'

His mouth was still so close to hers she couldn't concentrate. 'Such as?'

'Such as "I'm not interested, Andreas", or "It was just sex, Andreas". Your mouth says one thing and your body says another,' he murmured. 'So for now speaking is banned.'

Libby discovered that she actually didn't want to speak. The gentle, relentless kissing was driving her slowly crazy. She lifted her arms and wrapped them round the strong column of his neck, dragging his head down to hers again.

This time his kiss was hard and demanding, his mouth possessing every inch of hers and his arms hauling her against him. She felt the solid thrust of his erection pressing through her thin shorts and tried to get closer still, frustrated by the barrier created by the clothes they were wearing.

She lifted her hands and slid them under his shirt, groaning as she felt the warmth of his skin and the smooth swell of his muscles under her searching fingers.

His hands followed suit, lifting her tiny strap top, breaking their kiss for only a fraction of a second as he slid it over her head and let it fall onto the sun-baked terrace. Her shorts followed, and then her bra and soon she was standing in only the tiny bikini bottom that she'd worn on the beach earlier.

The slide of his hands over her bare flesh made her shiver in anticipation and she forgot her plans to resist him. Resistance just wasn't an option.

Without lifting his mouth from hers, he lifted her easily in his arms and walked the short distance to the bedroom, kicking the door shut behind him and laying her down on the middle of the bed.

Breathing rapidly, his dark eyes blazing with a sexual need that thrilled her, he yanked off his shirt and came down on top of her, kissing her again until she was writhing and sobbing beneath him.

His hands slid smoothly over her heated flesh, removing the final barrier, and finally she was naked, spread beneath him on the cool, white sheets.

Breathing harshly, he bent his head and teased her nipple, flicking gently with his tongue and then drawing her into the heat of his mouth. Tortured by an almost intolerable excitement, she gasped and stretched her arms above her head, writhing frantically in an attempt to free her body of the sexual need that threatened to consume her.

Refusing to give her the release she craved, he continued to torment her, his strong hand stroking her stomach lightly as he used his mouth on her breasts.

She shifted her hips, aware of his hand resting on her stomach and wanting it lower...

Finally, finally when she thought she was going to explode with frustration he moved his hand and found the moist, warm centre of her longing.

Feeling him touching her so intimately, she lowered her arms and slid them down his smooth, muscled back, pushing impatiently at his shorts, wanting him naked.

With a smooth movement he dispensed with the rest of his clothes and she gasped in anticipation as he moved above her.

'Look at me, Libby.' His hoarse command penetrated her dazed brain and her eyes locked onto his, registering the raw need she saw there.

The eye contact just increased the closeness and intimacy of what they were sharing and when she felt him, hard and strong against the damp heat of her femininity, she wrapped her arms around his neck, feeling him with every centimetre of her quivering body.

He entered her with a smooth, demanding thrust that left her in no doubt of just how much he wanted her and she lifted her hips, encouraging him to thrust deeper still, until there was no knowing where he ended and she began.

He possessed her fully, mind and body, his eyes burning into hers as he thrust in a pagan rhythm that had her gasping and digging her nails into the powerful muscles of his shoulders.

It was the ultimate in sexual excitement, a connection so strong that she felt as though they'd be joined for ever, and she wrapped her legs around him, rocking, giving as much as he took.

Neither of them spoke, but the air was filled with the sensual sounds of their love-making. A soft gasp, a harsh groan and ragged, uneven breathing as his body increased the rhythm, creating an agony of excitement that propelled her towards completion.

She couldn't look away from him. Even when her body exploded in a shattering climax that seemed endless, her eyes were locked on his, drawing him in, feeling him deep inside her both physically and mentally.

And even then he didn't release her. He just slowed the pace, thrusting deeply, building the heat again until she was writhing against him, desperate for the faster, pounding rhythm that would propel her upwards again, towards the mindless ecstasy that she craved.

Finally, when she thought she couldn't stand the sexual torment any longer, he shifted his weight, still staring deep into her eyes as he gave them both the exquisite satisfaction that their bodies demanded.

This time when she peaked she felt his body shudder within hers and felt the pulsing strength of him deep inside her. Her fingers tightened on his arms and she cried out his name, clinging to him in desperation as she tumbled headlong into paradise.

Gradually their breathing slowed and he rolled onto his back, holding her firmly against him, giving her no opportunity to distance herself.

She lay still in his arms, shocked by the explosion of pleasure that had rocked her entire body. Then she turned and gave him a weak smile. 'I thought you said that you shouldn't exercise when you've just eaten?'

He bent his head and kissed her. 'That,' he said slowly, 'depends on the exercise.'

Libby stayed with her head on his chest, feeling the roughness of his body hair against her cheek and the steady thud of his heart. His wonderfully male smell teased her nostrils and she closed her eyes, not wanting the moment to end.

It just felt so perfect.

But it wasn't. Nothing could be that perfect.

'I better get some clothes on—'

'No. This time you're not going anywhere.' He rolled her underneath him and stroked her damp hair away from her face. 'Having communicated honestly through body language, this is the part where you speak and admit that you have feelings for me.'

Achingly aware of the weight of his body touching every part of her, she caught her breath. 'Feelings?'

'That's right.' He gave a lazy smile and shifted slightly.

'What makes you think I have feelings?' She gasped as she felt him against her. 'It was just sex, Andreas.'

He chuckled and bent his head to kiss her again. 'Ah. Back to "just sex" again. Tell me, Lib, how many times have you had sex like that before?'

'Oh, you know—once or twice…' She licked dry lips and tried to look casual but it was pretty hard because he was still lying on top of her and she could feel the hard muscle of his thigh wedged against hers.

He rested his forehead against hers, intensifying the contact between them. 'You're lying, *agape mou*. You've never had sex like that before.'

'You are so arrogant—'

'And the reason I know that,' he said, ignoring her interruption, 'is because I haven't either. Something happens between you and I, Libby, and it's special. Unique to us. Just ours.'

Just ours.

He was doing it again. Making it sound special.

She struggled to catch her breath. 'That's rubbish.'

'Is it?' He shifted slightly so that not one single inch of her body was left untouched by his. 'If it's rubbish, why did you run out on me the night of the ball?'

'The evening was over.' The hair on Andreas's chest teased her sensitised nipples and she struggled to concentrate as her body responded to the lightest of touches.

'You always desert your partner without saying goodbye?' He moved against her and she gasped, realising that he knew exactly what he was doing. 'No, Libby. You ran that night because what we shared was so frighteningly good—so intense—that you were scared witless. You panicked.'

She was writhing under him now, her body arching in an effort to ease the intolerable ache in her pelvis.

'Andreas…'

He gave a low growl and raked a hand through her blonde hair. 'Tell me how you *feel*, Libby. *Tell me*.'

She stared up at him, lost in the expression in his dark eyes, her whole body feverish and quivering. She just felt so *hot*. 'I want you…'

He gave a groan of frustration and bent his head to capture her mouth. 'Admit that it's not just sex.'

Desperate for him, she gasped and arched against him. 'Andreas, please…'

'No.' His voice was a low growl. 'Not until you admit the way you feel.'

Libby whimpered. 'Do you want me to hit you?'

'Admit it.'

'Andreas…'

'I love you, Libby.' He spoke the words softly and her breathing and heart stopped simultaneously.

He loved her?

Afraid she'd misheard him, she lay utterly still and he gave a sigh and shifted slightly so that he could look at her.

'Did you hear me?'

She nodded slowly and he gave a wry smile.

'So this is the point when you tell me that you love me, too.'

Libby felt a rush of panic. *She didn't love him.* She didn't want to love him. It was asking for trouble. He'd hurt her...

'It's just sex, Andreas. Good sex, admittedly, but just sex.'

He gave a frustrated grunt. 'You're lying and if I have to pin you to this bed for the rest of your life I'm going to make you admit the truth.' His dark eyes were unbelievably gentle. 'The sex is good because we love each other, Libby. Why don't you just admit that you've never felt this way about a man before and that you're scared?'

Libby's heart was thumping so hard she could hardly breathe. 'All right. I've never felt like this about a man before and I'm scared,' she parroted, and he sighed.

'Relationships don't have to go wrong, Libby. I know you've seen some bad examples, but that doesn't mean that there aren't good examples out there, too. My parents were happily married for forty years. Why won't you just trust me?'

She bit her lip. 'Because it's been too quick, too good to be true, and because I don't believe that fairy-tales always have happy endings,'

'Then you'd better prepare yourself for a shock,' he said softly, lowering his head to kiss her gently, 'because this particular fairy-tale is going to have the best ending you can possibly imagine.'

CHAPTER NINE

ANDREAS sat on the shaded terrace and sipped his coffee.

It was already midmorning and there was no sign of Libby. But remembering just how little sleep he'd allowed her the night before, he decided that it was hardly surprising.

By contrast, he'd been up since dawn, wading through the mountains of family paperwork that always accumulated in his absence.

He'd just signed the last of the papers when he glanced up and saw her standing in the doorway that led to the terrace, wearing a pair of white shorts and a light blue top.

His eyes dropped to her legs and his body reacted in a surge of sexual hunger that took him by surprise. They'd made love for most of yesterday and all of last night and he still wanted her.

But she still hadn't said that she loved him.

'I'm sorry I slept so late.' She looked extremely self-conscious and Andreas sucked in a breath and ditched the papers he'd been reading, his concentration gone.

There was only one thing he thought of when he looked at Libby, and it certainly wasn't business.

'I'm glad you slept well.' His voice sounded husky and he

wondered if she had any idea of the effect she had on him. Probably not or she wouldn't have worn those shorts. 'Come here.'

She walked towards him and he dragged her onto his lap, stroking her hair away from her face and kissing her urgently.

'I love you.' He groaned the words against her mouth and she pulled away, her blue eyes wary and more than a little frightened.

'Stop saying that.'

'It's the truth. And you love me, too.'

Perhaps if he said the words often enough, eventually she'd find the courage to say them herself.

She slid off his lap and he saw the confusion in her eyes. 'Andreas...'

'Trust me, Libby.'

'Let's go to the beach.'

Andreas suppressed a sigh, wondering what it would take to break through the wall of self-protection that she'd built around herself.

They spent the days swimming and talking and making love, and the time passed too quickly for Libby. She could have stayed there for ever, locked in the tiny world they'd created, safe from outside influences.

There was something magical about the villa and the bay.

Something unreal.

It felt so far away from their real lives.

It was as if anything could happen here, but once they returned home life would just return to normal.

She was lying on a sun lounger with her eyes closed, trying to catch up on some lost sleep, when she felt the familiar tug in her stomach.

Her heart lurched.

Not wanting to believe the messages that her body was sending, she rushed to her room to discover that her period had started.

She'd been so wrapped up in the emotional high of being with Andreas that she'd temporarily forgotten that she might be pregnant.

Swamped by a feeling of desolation that she couldn't comprehend, she went to the bathroom and burst into tears, sobbing against the tiled wall until her head started to ache.

She tried to analyse why she was crying but her head was pounding too hard to allow her access to her thoughts.

Surely she should have been relieved that she wasn't pregnant?

Why did she feel so utterly devastated?

She didn't even know that Andreas had followed her until she felt herself gathered against his hard chest.

For several minutes she just sobbed without speaking and then she took the tissue he handed her and blew her nose hard.

'Why are you crying?'

She shook her head and scrunched the tissue into a ball, too upset to speak.

'Libby.' His tone was urgent and he put her away from him and cupped her face in his hands, forcing her to look at him. 'Tell me.'

'It's nothing,' she hiccoughed. 'It's my problem, not yours.'

His face darkened and his fingers bit into her scalp. 'If this is what I think it is, then it's very much my problem, too. Only actually I don't see it as a problem.'

She closed her eyes and shook her head. He'd misunderstood, and who could blame him? 'Just drop it Andreas—please…'

She needed some time on her own. Time to pull herself together. She was being ridiculous.

'I thought I'd made it clear that I'm very traditional when it comes to certain things,' he said softly, showing no signs of releasing her. 'Tell me why you're crying, because if you're afraid that I won't want you now you're pregnant, you couldn't be more wrong.'

Libby pulled away from him and scrubbed the palm of her hand over her cheeks to get rid of the tears.

'I'm not crying because I'm pregnant,' she gulped finally, her voice jumpy from too much crying. 'I'm crying because I'm *not* pregnant. OK?'

She gave a massive sniff, aware that Andreas was unusually still.

'You're *not* pregnant?'

Just hearing the words upset her again and her face crumpled. 'That's right—I'm *not* pregnant. And now will you leave me alone?'

She turned away from him but he reached out and grabbed her, hauling her round so that she was facing him, his fingers biting into her upper arms.

'If you're not pregnant, Libby, why are you crying?'

She tried to glare at him but instead her face crumpled again and she gave another sob. 'Because I wanted to be pregnant, you dummy! I *wanted* your baby.' She was vaguely aware that she was shouting but she didn't even care. 'Which just goes to show how stupid I can be.'

Andreas stared at her, his dark gaze strangely intent. 'And why did you want my baby, Libby?' His voice was hoarse and she tried to focus on him through watery eyes.

'I don't know,' she muttered, and his fingers tightened on her arms.

'Yes, you do. Why, Libby?'

She hiccoughed slightly. 'Because you're very good-looking and I thought we'd make cute babies?'

He lifted an eyebrow and his firm mouth quirked slightly. 'So you selected me as a prime example of male genetic perfection?'

'Maybe.'

He looked at her. 'Come on, Libby,' he urged softly, 'be honest with me. Be honest with yourself for once.'

Heart racing, she spread her hands and glared at him. 'All right, I love you,' she shouted. 'I love you heaps and tons. And it's terrifying because I know that it won't last because it never does. And finding out that I'm not pregnant is horrible. I didn't even know I wanted to be pregnant until five minutes ago when I found out that I wasn't. How illogical is that?'

'It's the best news I've ever had,' he groaned, dragging her against him. 'I was beginning to think that I'd never get you to admit how you feel.'

Libby stared up at him, her lower lip wobbling. 'I wanted to be pregnant.'

He gave a slow smile. 'I'll make you pregnant,' he promised, lowering his head to kiss her. 'As many times as you like. I adore children, you know that. I'd given up ever finding a woman who felt the same way.'

Libby blinked, still very unsure.

Andreas wanted children?

He wanted to have children with *her*?

'But you wanted me to take the morning-after pill.'

Andreas curved a strong hand round her cheek, staring down into her eyes as he shook his head. 'No. That was the last thing I wanted.'

She stared at him, wide-eyed. 'So why did you suggest it?'

'Because you were panicking enough at the thought of us being a couple, without me admitting how much I wanted to have children with you,' Andreas said quietly. 'If you had wanted to take the pill, I would have supported you, but I was immensely relieved that you decided not to.'

She was still reeling from the shock of finally admitting that she was in love with him. She'd been fighting it for so long she hadn't even admitted it to herself.

She looked at him, her heart thudding. 'So is this the bit where we live happily ever after?'

'I think it probably is,' he agreed, stroking the tears away from her cheek with gentle fingers, 'although the final scene isn't usually played out in a bathroom with the bride-to-be looking traumatised. Wash your face or I'll have to tell our children that I proposed to their mother when she had a red nose.'

She sniffed. 'You're proposing?'

'Not here,' he said dryly. 'I'm going to wait for more romantic surroundings. Wash your face and then join me on the terrace and I'll do it properly.'

Her insides fluttering with excitement, Libby waited for him to go and then tried to concentrate on removing the evidence of hysterical crying.

Did Andreas truly want to marry her?

The thought of spending the rest of her life with him made her feel giddy with happiness.

How could she ever have thought that she didn't love him?

How could she have fooled herself for so long?

She adored him.

And he was about to propose to her. And she knew exactly what her answer was going to be.

Smiling, she wandered back into the bedroom and opened one of the drawers, looking for a tissue.

And then she saw the letter.

She probably wouldn't have looked twice at it if it hadn't been for the fact that the bold handwriting seemed to leap from the page and the first four words penetrated her brain like a sharpened knife.

Andreas, I love you.

Feeling suddenly sick, Libby reached down and picked up the letter, opening it up so that she could read the rest of it.

I really enjoyed this week together and I can't wait to be your wife.

Your loving Eleni.

Libby stared down at the letter for endless minutes, as if hoping that by studying the words hard enough they might alter their shape in front of her horrified eyes.

But they didn't.

They stayed the same, while the sick feeling inside her grew and grew.

Still holding the letter, she walked towards the terrace, hesitating slightly as she saw Andreas standing with his back to her, his broad shoulders blocking the view of the ocean.

He heard her approach and turned, the smile on his face fading as he saw her.

'You're as white as a sheet. What's the matter?'

She swallowed and dropped the letter on the table in front of her. 'This is the matter.'

He frowned slightly and picked up the letter, sucking in a breath as he scanned the contents. 'Libby—'

'Just don't even try and explain,' she advised him shakily, backing away from him so quickly that she stumbled into one of the chairs. She reached out a hand to steady herself and found that it was trembling.

He tensed. 'It isn't—'

'I believed you, Andreas!' She looked at him accusingly. 'When you told me that I was the only woman you'd ever loved, *I believed you*. But you're just like all the others. One woman isn't enough for you!'

Andreas swore softly and stepped towards her. 'Will you listen to me?'

'No.' Libby shook her head firmly, 'When you said that you were intending to propose, I didn't realise that there was a queue. So tell me, Andreas, when exactly did you plan to fit me in?'

'Eleni is not my wife.' His voice was terse and she tried to hide the pain she was feeling.

'Not yet maybe, but she obviously thinks that it's going to happen soon.'

Andreas gave an impatient growl and slammed his fist down on the table.

'Libby, less than half an hour ago I told you that I loved you.

Do you really think I would say those words when I was planning to marry another woman?'

'Of course I do! Men do things like that all the time!' Libby's
chest rose and fell as she struggled to breathe. What usually
happened naturally now seemed to take considerable effort.
'Are you seriously trying to tell me that you had no relationship with her?'

He ran long fingers through his hair in an impatient gesture.
'I'm not saying that, but—'

'But you conveniently forgot to mention her,' Libby interrupted hoarsely. 'When I asked you about other women, you
said that there wasn't anyone special—'

'Because there wasn't,' he said wearily, his hands dropping
to his sides.

'She thinks she's going to marry you, Andreas.' Libby heard
her voice wobble and hated herself for it. 'That sounds pretty
special to me.'

There was a long silence and when he looked up his eyes
were tired. 'For a short time I did think that I would marry
her, but it's history now. On the other hand, perhaps we should
both be grateful that you found that note because it's proved to
both of us that you just aren't capable of trusting anyone.' His
voice seemed to have lost all its warmth. 'I've told you that I
love you more times than I can count, and I've shown you in
as many ways as I know. If you still can't trust my feelings or
your own then there's definitely no future for us. No relationship can work without trust and you just can't give it. You damn
me without even listening to my side of the story.'

Libby looked at him, wondering how anyone could survive
such highs and lows of emotions over such a short time. Less
than an hour ago he'd been promising to make babies with her.
Now their relationship appeared to be in pieces.

And he was blaming her.

In fact, he looked angrier than she'd ever imagined he could

be. She was used to him being good-humoured and relaxed
about everything, but he certainly wasn't relaxed now.

How could he blame her? She shook her head incredulously.
'Look at it from my point of view, Andreas. If you'd found that
letter in my bedroom, what would you have done?'

'What would I have done?' His handsome face was devoid of
emotion. 'I would have asked you about it, Libby, knowing that
you would have had a perfectly innocent explanation. Knowing
that I was the man you loved. You see, I trust you, *agape mou*.'

She looked at him in stunned silence and he shook his head
slowly, his expression sad. 'I love you, Libby, and I know you
love me, but it's never going to work between us unless you
break down that great big wall you've built around yourself and
learn to trust me, too.'

'Andreas—'

'Forget it.' His jaw tightened. 'There's a flight leaving for
Heathrow late this afternoon. I'll book you on it. Our date is
over, Libby.'

CHAPTER TEN

'ALL right, what happened?' Katy dragged Libby into the treatment room, her expression serious. 'It's been a whole week now and you still haven't told me anything. Even Alex is worried about you. He's ready to kill Andreas but he doesn't know what the motive is.'

Libby looked at her. 'It's just the usual.'

Katy frowned. 'What do you mean, *the usual*?'

Libby's eyes filled. 'Andreas had someone else.'

Katy stared at her for a moment and then shook her head. 'No. No way.'

'It's true.'

Katy wrinkled her nose and shook her head again. 'It can't be. Not Andreas. He loves you, Lib, I know he does.'

Libby shrugged and tried to look casual but it was impossibly hard. She felt raw inside. 'So? Since when has that stopped a man from forming other relationships?'

'You've had some rotten experiences,' Katy admitted quietly, 'and I know how badly it's affected you, but I'm sure that this time you're wrong. Andreas is crazy about you. I know he is. Tell me what happened.'

'I found a letter...' Libby found herself telling every detail of that awful afternoon while Katy listened.

'But it doesn't make sense, Lib,' her sister said finally. 'Why would he virtually propose to you if he was planning to marry another woman? There must be a simple explanation.'

'The explanation is that he's the same as every other man,' Libby said stiffly, and Katy shook her head.

'You're not thinking straight,' she said. 'I'm absolutely sure that Andreas isn't the sort of man who would have two women on the go at the same time. He's too traditional. For goodness' sake, Lib, can't you see that?'

Libby stared at her. 'What do you mean?'

Katy sighed. 'For a bright girl, you're very dense when it comes to people. He's Greek, Libby. Family is hugely important to him. You said that he'd virtually proposed to you. Why would he do that if he was in love with someone else?'

'I don't know,' Libby confessed, 'and he didn't offer any sort of explanation.'

'Knowing you, you went in with all guns blazing and didn't give the guy a chance to explain.'

Libby stiffened defensively and then her shoulders sagged. That was exactly what had happened. For the first time she wondered if she'd been too hasty. Maybe there was an innocent explanation for the letter.

'I just find it impossible to trust him,' she said miserably. 'It's me, Katy. It's all my fault. I'm so messed up I don't think I'll ever be able to trust anyone. Perhaps you'd better just shoot me.'

Katy sighed and gave her a hug. 'I'm not going to shoot you. We're busy enough in A and E as it is. And you're not messed up. You're just very wary of being hurt after everything that's happened in your life. It's the same with Alex. You're both commitment-phobes and I suppose our parents can take the blame for that really. We grew up watching a perfect example of a disastrous relationship. But you've got to put that behind you, Lib.'

Libby struggled for control. 'I don't know how.'

'Do you love him?'

Libby gave her a wobbly smile. 'Oh, yes. So much.'

Katy beamed. 'Well, that's good.'

'Is it?' Libby sniffed and rummaged in her pocket for a tissue. It certainly didn't feel good. It felt agonisingly painful and getting through each day was a mammoth exercise in willpower.

'Of course it's good. A month ago you didn't think you could ever fall in love. At least you've moved past that stage.'

'I think I preferred that stage,' Libby said miserably. 'It didn't hurt as much as this stage.'

Katy ignored her. 'All you need to do now is relax and trust him.'

'It's too late,' Libby said. 'He's already decided I'm a lost cause.'

Katy shook her head. 'You really are hopeless sometimes. You can't switch love on and off, Lib. If he loves you then he loves you. And I'm willing to bet he's suffering as much as you are.'

'He said that our relationship didn't have a future.'

'Until you learn to trust him,' Katy finished, and Libby looked at her helplessly.

'You make it sound so simple but I have absolutely no idea how to do that.' She looked at her sister. 'How do I do that?'

Katy smiled. 'You have to believe that what you share is special. That it isn't something he could possibly find with anyone else.' She paused. 'Is it special, Libby?'

Libby stared at her, remembering the way she and Andreas had connected from the first moment they'd met, the laughter they'd shared, how well they worked together—and then she remembered their incredible physical relationship.

'It's special,' she croaked finally, and Katy's smile broadened.

'Good. Admitting that is the first step to learning to trust. Why would he damage anything so special?'

'Because men do that all the time?'

Katy shook her head. 'No. I disagree. There are plenty of mediocre and bad relationships out there and it's hardly surprising that they go wrong because they were always wrong. But when a relationship is special it stays special and it doesn't go wrong, Libby. It just grows stronger. Providing you let it.'

Libby gave a wobbly smile. 'You're back to your psychiatrist mode again. Are you leaving A and E?'

Katy glanced at her watch and pulled a face. 'If I don't get back to work soon, the answer is very probably. But I'm serious, Libby. You have to acknowledge that what you have together is something that neither of you is going to throw away.'

Libby stood still, recognising the truth in her sister's words. What she and Andreas shared *was* special. 'So what do I do?'

Katy grinned. 'You go for it, angel. If you want him—and I know that you do—then don't let him get away.'

'What if he doesn't want me any more? What if it's too late?'

Katy sighed. 'You're doing it again—not trusting your relationship. Not believing in the love you have for each other. Love doesn't die overnight, Libby. Andreas still wants you, but he wants you to believe that what you share is special, too. You need to show him that you do. You need to show him that it's so special you're not going to give up on it.' She gave her sister another hug and then made for the door. 'I want to be your matron-of-honour while I still have something resembling a waistline so you'd better get a move on.'

With that she pushed open the door of the treatment room and left Libby to return to the ward, totally distracted by their conversation.

'There you are.' Bev hurried up, an expression of relief on her face. 'The SHO just called us from A and E. He's taken a call from a GP who's sending in a three-year-old with a high fever and vomiting. Can you get the side room ready?'

Libby hurried off to do as Bev requested and as an afterthought laid up a trolley for a lumbar puncture just in case it was needed.

She'd just finished the room when the little boy arrived on

the ward accompanied by the paramedics who'd been called by the GP.

'This is Max King,' one of the paramedics told her. 'He's been ill since last night but he's gone downhill very fast.'

Jonathon, the SHO, was by his side and looked distinctly flustered. 'I've been calling Andreas, but I'm not getting an answer,' he muttered to Libby. She sensed immediately that he was out of his depth and one glance at the child confirmed the reason.

The little boy was drowsy and irritable and his breathing was rapid. One touch of his dry, scorching skin confirmed that his temperature was sky-high.

'All right, Max,' she soothed gently, 'we'll soon have you sorted out.'

'I'll try bleeping Andreas again,' the SHO muttered, and Libby caught his arm as he went to leave the room.

'Has the child had penicillin yet?' she asked urgently, lowering her voice so that the parents didn't hear her question him.

The SHO shook his head and glanced at the little boy. 'I was waiting for Andreas to look at him. There's no rash or anything, so I didn't think—'

'Get some penicillin inside him now,' Libby ordered softly, knowing that the doctor was still relatively inexperienced and not wanting to take any chances. 'There doesn't have to be a rash for it to be meningitis and that child is very sick. Do it, and then we can do the rest of the investigations knowing that at least we've covered that option. He's showing definite signs of raised intracranial pressure.'

She'd nursed children with meningitis before and she knew that the presentation often varied. But it was still a lethal disease and she wasn't taking any chances while they waited for Andreas.

Jonathon hesitated and then nodded. 'All right. If you think so.'

'I do,' Libby said firmly, reaching for the penicillin that she'd put on the trolley. She turned to the parents, her tone calm and reassuring. 'We're just going to give him some antibiotics. Do you know his weight?'

She calculated the dose based on what the parents told her and then handed it to Jonathon, who checked it and gave it to the restless child.

Max's mother, Heather, was white with anxiety. 'You think it might be meningitis, don't you?'

'It's a possibility,' Libby said gently, 'which is why we've given the penicillin at the earliest time, but our consultant will be here soon and—'

'I'm here.'

Libby felt a rush of relief as she recognised the voice behind her. She'd never been so pleased to see Andreas in her life.

'This is Dr Christakos.' She introduced him to the parents, realising just how much she loved him. Just how much faith she had in him.

Andreas was by the child's side in an instant, taking the handover from Jonathon as he examined the sick little boy.

'You poor little thing,' he murmured gently, his large hands gently palpating the child's abdomen. 'Jonathon, has he had penicillin?'

'Yes.' The SHO shot Libby a look of gratitude. 'Libby thought we should go ahead with that and not wait for you.'

'Good decision.'

Andreas completed his examination and straightened. 'I want to do a lumbar puncture straight away—can you lay up a trolley?'

'It's here.' Libby pushed it forward and a small smile played around his firm mouth.

'Do you ever get anything wrong?'

Her heart beat slightly faster. 'Yes. But when I do, I try to put it right.'

For a brief moment his dark eyes were questioning and then

he strode over to the sink and started scrubbing, talking to the parents as he prepared to perform the lumbar puncture.

He explained what he was planning to do and why, and Heather clung to her husband, the worry visible on her face.

'Perhaps you would rather wait outside while we do this,' Andreas suggested, but Heather shook her head.

'No. I don't want to leave him.'

Andreas looked at Libby. 'We'll do it in the treatment room. I want to get a line in first but then someone needs to hold him for the LP.'

'I'll hold him,' she said immediately, 'and I'll ask Bev to find someone to assist you.'

Moments later they were all gathered in the treatment room and Andreas inserted a line with ease. That done, Libby gently turned Max on his side, talking quietly to him all the time.

She curved the little boy round so that his knees were up by his chin, flexing the spine, and watched while Andreas marked the skin with a pen and then draped and sterilised the area.

Bev settled Heather at the head of the trolley. 'Sit there and talk to him,' she suggested quietly, 'but keep your back to Dr Christakos and then you won't have to watch what's happening.'

Andreas infiltrated the skin with local anaesthetic and then tested the site, his eyes flickering to hers.

'Are you ready?' She nodded and held Max firmly, knowing how crucial it was that the child didn't move during the procedure.

She watched as Andreas inserted the LP needle, talking quietly to the child and occasionally making a comment to Jonathon who was watching.

Bev had three little bottles ready and Andreas let four drops of fluid fall into each bottle.

Once Andreas was satisfied, he withdrew the needle and cleaned the site before covering it with the dressing that Bev had ready.

'All done.' He pushed his chair away from the side of the

trolley and stood up, ripping off his gloves and dropping them in the nearest bin. 'We'll get those samples to the lab urgently and in the meantime we'll get a line in and start getting fluids into the little chap.'

Max had stopped wailing now and was lying on the trolley, moaning quietly.

Andreas turned to his SHO with a list of instructions and tests that he wanted performed. He was leaving absolutely nothing to chance.

'Let's get him back to the room and let him sleep,' he said quietly, his gaze flickering to the parents. 'I'm sorry. This is all very worrying for you, I know, and I'm aware that we haven't had much time for explanations because of the urgency of the situation. If there is anything you'd like to ask me now, please do so.'

Heather's eyes filled. 'He looks so poorly. What will happen?'

'We wait for the results of these tests and we watch him,' Andreas said, his eyes flickering to the child who was shifting restlessly on the trolley. He frowned slightly and pulled back the sheet Libby had used to cover Max. 'He has a rash.'

Libby followed his gaze and saw that the child had indeed developed a rash all over his body.

Andreas looked at her and his eyes were warm. 'You did the right thing, giving that penicillin,' he said softly, and she swallowed.

She really needed to talk to him but she didn't know when an opportunity was going to present itself.

Max started to improve over the next two days and once it was clear that he was no longer on the critical list, his parents started to relax slightly and even take short breaks away from the room.

Andreas had maintained a constant presence on the ward when the child had first been admitted, but once Max was out of danger he'd visited less frequently, kept busy by the other considerable demands of his job.

He made no attempt to seek Libby out and she wondered if it was intentional.

Was he giving her space?

Did he realise that she was desperate to speak to him?

In the end she came up with a plan and waited nervously for him to appear on the ward.

It was almost the end of her shift when he finally arrived, looking grim-faced after dealing with a tough case in A and E.

'I wanted to check on Max before I went home,' he said, walking past her into the room and smiling at the little boy.

'Well, someone's looking better,' he murmured, watching as Max played happily with some toy cars that Libby had found for him in the playroom. 'He is one lucky boy.'

Libby nodded, watching while he checked him over. 'I wonder why the GP didn't give penicillin?'

Andreas straightened. 'Who knows? But the sooner your brother Alex gets out there the better, if you ask me.'

Libby smiled. 'Alex won't be working in London. He's found himself a practice in Cornwall so that he can sail and windsurf and indulge in all the other hobbies he loves.'

Andreas looked at her. 'What will you do about the flat?'

She blushed slightly. 'I don't know yet. His job doesn't start until the end of August.' She took a deep breath. 'Andreas, I wanted to give you something.'

She reached into her pocket and pulled out the envelope she'd been carrying with her all week.

He took it with a frown and was about to open it when Bev stuck her head round the door and announced that he was wanted in A and E urgently.

'Again?' Andreas rolled his eyes and pocketed the envelope. 'I'll see you later. Maybe.' His dark eyes were weary. 'Unless it turns out to be a long one.'

It was a long one and Libby was at home, making herself a

hot chocolate in her oldest jeans and a skimpy pink strap top, when the doorbell rang.

Libby opened the door, her heart pounding when she saw Andreas standing there.

He waved the envelope in her face, his expression wary. 'You gave me a cheque for £1000.'

She nodded and stood to one side so that he could come in, but he didn't move.

Instead, he frowned ominously. 'You don't owe me any money. I paid for a date and that's what we had, Libby.'

'And now it's my turn,' she croaked, wishing that she was wearing heels. She was standing in bare feet and he towered above her. 'I want a date, Andreas, and £1000 seems to be the going rate. A bit steep, but I happen to think you're worth it.'

There was a long silence and then he finally stepped inside her flat and closed the door firmly behind him.

'What are you saying?' His Greek accent was suddenly very pronounced and she fiddled with the hem of her top nervously, wondering whether he was going to walk away once she'd said what she had to say.

'I want a date, Andreas, and as you're obviously not going to ask me again, I thought I'd better ask you.'

'Why do you want a date?' His voice was hoarse and she took a deep breath, wondering why they were having this conversation in the hallway.

'Because I want to be with you,' she said simply. 'And the reason I want to be with you is because I love you. And I know that what we have is too special to throw away.'

He closed his eyes briefly. 'I never thought I'd hear you say that.'

'And I never thought I'd say it,' Libby admitted. 'But then I met you and you changed the way I felt about everything.'

Andreas was very still. 'I thought you didn't trust me.'

'I was wrong. I do trust you. And I'm sorry I overreacted about that letter. It was just that everything between us was so new—so special—I just couldn't believe that it wouldn't go wrong.'

He still didn't make a move towards her. 'Don't you want to know about Eleni?'

Libby shook her head. 'All I need to know is that you love me,' she said softly. 'That's all that matters.'

He gave a groan and hauled her into his arms. 'I love you but I'd given up hoping that you'd ever believe me.'

Libby buried her face in his chest. 'I know. I'm sorry. I'm a hopeless case. The truth is I've never been in love before, and when it finally happened it all seemed too good to be true.'

He slid his hands round her face and forced her to look at him. 'I was at fault, too. I underestimated just how hard it is for you to trust people. You've built this huge wall around yourself.'

'It seemed the only way to survive.'

He stroked her cheek gently. 'Tell me about your parents. I want to understand why you feel the way you do,' he said quietly. 'You hardly ever talk about them.'

Libby pulled a face. 'That's because they're not my favourite topic of conversation.' She took a deep breath and pulled away from him slightly. 'Let's just say that when I was growing up they weren't like everyone else's parents. Alex always says that the only reason the three of us have turned out remotely normal is because they had the sense to send us to boarding school.'

Andreas frowned. 'It was that bad?'

'Worse. For the first twenty-eight years of my life there was absolutely no evidence that my parents loved each other,' Libby said bitterly. 'They argued, Dad drank too much, and when he drank...' She broke off and Andreas looked at her.

'What happened when he drank? Was he violent?'

'Sometimes.' Libby rubbed her fingers across her forehead. 'I suspect it was more than sometimes but we were at school so we didn't really see it. It only happened once when we were at home and Alex went for him with a cricket bat. I called the police and I don't think Dad ever really forgave me for that. But it wasn't just the violence. It was the fact that they showed no affection towards each other and Dad had one affair after another.'

'But they're still together?'

'Amazingly, yes.' Libby gave a wry smile. 'Years ago Dad ruined Katy's relationship with Jago because he didn't approve, and when they met up again years later Mum was so furious about what he'd done that she stood up to him for the first time in her life. I think the prospect of losing her brought him to his senses.'

'Well, in the circumstances it's hardly surprising that you don't think relationships can work.'

'It wasn't just Mum and Dad,' Libby confessed. 'Apart from Jago, all the men I meet seem to be utterly faithless and without morals. Even Alex, who I adore, is a real bastard to women.'

'And Philip?'

Libby laughed. 'I was never serious about Philip, but all the same it was a real blow to my ego. I only ever seem to be everyone's second choice. That's why I couldn't quite believe what was happening between us. It was too good to be true.'

Andreas nodded. 'I understand now why you were so upset about the letter you found. Your confidence was so fragile that you couldn't risk trusting me.'

'That's true.' Libby flushed and bit her lip. 'And it's also true that you're so gorgeous and eligible I just couldn't understand what you were doing with me, apart from amusing yourself.'

'Would you like me to spell it out?' Andreas smiled and then gave a sigh. 'I'm going to tell you about Eleni, Libby, if only to prove to you just how much I love you.'

'There's no need—'

'I want to,' he said firmly. 'I met Eleni when I worked in Boston. She's a lawyer and we knew each other vaguely from functions in Athens that we'd both attended. We started dating, I suppose because we were both Greek as much as anything else.'

'And you were in love with her?'

'No. And that was the problem.' He gave a wry smile. 'She

was desperate to get married. At the time I thought she loved me but I think the truth was probably that she just wanted to achieve the degree of respectability that marriage gives you if you're Greek. She was thirty-two and that's old to still be single in our culture. She saw me as a useful way out of her predicament. That was when she wrote me the letter. I didn't know it was still in the drawer. I hadn't been to the villa for six months.'

'So what happened?'

Andreas pulled a face. 'Adrienne was what happened. My mother was becoming concerned that I might marry Eleni and she knew that she was totally unsuitable for me. So she suddenly decided that Adrienne should live with me.'

'But how did that effect your relationship with Eleni?'

'The minute Eleni knew that I had responsibility for Adrienne she lost interest in me,' he said dryly. 'Eleni is not remotely maternal and the thought of being saddled with a moody teenager quickly destroyed any plans she might have had about marrying me. And also my mother knew I'd never marry a career-woman.'

Libby rolled her eyes. 'I'm in love with a raving chauvinist.'

He grinned. 'I'm Greek, *agape mou*, and Greek men are very traditional. I want a woman who's happy to raise children with me.'

Libby raised an eyebrow. 'Barefoot and pregnant?'

He glanced under the table to her bare feet. 'I actually quite like those ridiculous heels you favour, but I love your bare feet, too. In fact, I love everything about you. The moment I saw you buried under a pile of children I knew you were the woman I wanted to marry.'

'I thought you wanted me because I presented a challenge,' Libby admitted, and he smiled.

'I wanted you because I fell madly in love for the first time in my life. So what do you say, Libby? Are you prepared to marry a very traditional Greek male?'

'Yes. And just to prove it, there's a surprise waiting for you in my kitchen.'

Andreas lifted an eyebrow and glanced towards the closed door. 'A surprise?'

Libby shrugged. 'Why don't you go and find out?'

Andreas pushed open the kitchen door and then smiled with delight. 'Adrienne? What are you doing here?'

His niece flung her arms around his neck and hugged him tightly. 'Libby collected me earlier. She said that I don't have to board any more. She told me that you've finally found a perfect housekeeper.'

Andreas cast a questioning look at Libby and she blushed.

'I thought, between the two of us, we ought to be able to manage our shifts so that one of us can pick her up from school.'

Andreas smiled and held out a hand to her. 'So I take it that your answer is yes? I thought you didn't believe in happy endings.'

She walked up to him and slid her arms around both of them. 'I didn't until I met you, and the answer is definitely yes. As we're going to get married, do you think *Yiayia* will mind if I kiss you in front of Adrienne?'

Without waiting for an answer, she stood on tiptoe and gave him a lingering kiss on the lips.

Adrienne gave a squeal of excitement. 'You're really going to get married? Can I be a bridesmaid?'

There was a brief pause while Libby reluctantly disengaged herself. 'Absolutely! Which means that we girls have got some serious shopping to do.'

Andreas groaned. 'Just don't take me near that hairdresser again.'

Libby's eyes twinkled. 'Afraid you might be tempted?'

Andreas pulled her against him. 'There's only ever going to be one person who tempts me, *agape mou*—remember that.'

Libby lifted her mouth for his kiss. 'I will.'

EPILOGUE

THE reception was in full swing and Libby relaxed back in her chair, smiling as she watched people enjoying the dancing.

'Stop looking so happy.' Alex pulled out the chair next to her and sat down, stretching his long legs out in front of him. 'I suppose it was all the chocolate you put on the menu.'

Libby laughed. 'Did you enjoy it?'

'Apart from the chocolate-coated prawns,' Alex said dryly, helping himself to her glass of champagne. 'They challenged my palate. Where's Andreas?'

'Talking to Katy. She's trying to persuade him to tell her where we're going on our honeymoon.'

'He still hasn't told you?'

'No. It's a surprise.' Libby sighed dreamily. 'Isn't it romantic?'

'Not really.' Alex took a large slug of champagne. 'The guy probably just hasn't made up his mind yet. Don't read anything into it.'

Libby smiled placidly. 'Today I'm too happy to hit anyone. Even you. How's your date?'

Alex's gaze flickered across the room and rested on a curvaceous blonde who was laughing loudly with a group of guests.

'A bit like your chocolate. Better in small quantities.'

'Your problem is that you're dating the wrong women,' Libby said sagely, and he gave a wicked grin.

'I know. It's something that I work *really* hard at.'

Libby reached across and took his hand. 'I want you to be happy, Alex.'

He frowned at her. 'Are you drunk?'

She looked pointedly at the glass of champagne in his hand. 'How can *I* be drunk when *you're* drinking my champagne?'

'Then what's all this sentimental nonsense about me being happy?' He cast her a bored look. 'I'm happy.'

Libby shook her head. 'No, I mean I want you to be settled down with children.'

Alex lifted an eyebrow mockingly. 'I thought you said you wanted me to be happy.'

Libby sighed. 'Don't you ever want children of your own?'

Alex shook his head, his blue eyes suddenly cool. 'No. I do not.'

'You'd be a great father.'

Her brother's broad shoulders tensed and all traces of humour vanished from his handsome face. 'We both know that's not true.'

'Somewhere out there, there's a woman for you,' Libby said firmly, and Alex drained the champagne glass.

'Well, hopefully if I keep my head down she won't see me.' He put the glass down on the table, his blue eyes glittering. 'I don't do commitment, Libby. You know that.'

'I didn't think I did either,' Libby said, 'and look at me now.'

'I'm looking,' Alex drawled, a hint of a smile touching his hard mouth. 'And so are most of the male guests. You're the only bride I've ever met who thinks that "something blue" refers to the length of your dress. Were they short of fabric?'

Libby laughed. 'I didn't want to go down the aisle looking like a blancmange. Not my style. And anyway a long dress would have hidden my shoes. Don't you just *love* my shoes?'

Alex glanced down. 'I think the SAS use something similar for weapons training.'

Still laughing, Libby leaned across and kissed him. 'You're a total pain but surprisingly enough I'm going to miss you. Why do you have to go to Cornwall? Why can't you be a GP in London?'

Alex was suddenly still. 'Actually, I'm not going to be a GP,' he said casually. 'I miss the pace of A and E.'

Her eyes widened. 'You're going back to trauma?'

'I am.'

'Where?'

'In Cornwall. I need a change of scenery.' Alex gave a wicked smile. 'And, anyway, I've been out with all the blonde women in London.'

Libby looked at him thoughtfully. 'Perhaps that's where you're going wrong. Perhaps you should pick a woman who isn't blonde. What you need is a tiny, dark-haired girl with a flat chest.'

Alex threw back his head and laughed, and Libby caught her breath. Her brother was astonishingly handsome. It was hardly surprising that he broke hearts everywhere he went.

He was still smiling as he looked at her. 'Why on earth would I need someone like that?'

'Because all the women you've dated so far have failed to keep your attention for longer than five minutes,' Libby explained with impeccable logic, 'so you need to date someone who is totally opposite to your usual.'

'Thanks for the advice,' Alex said dryly, standing up and nodding briefly as Andreas approached. 'Are you absolutely sure you did the right thing, marrying this woman? I mean, according to Adrienne, women were queuing up to marry you.'

'I did the right thing.' Andreas held out a hand and gave a slow smile that made Libby's heart race. Suddenly she forgot about her brother. All she could think about was her own future, with the man she loved.

She stood up and held out a hand. 'Time to smash some plates, Dr Christakos.'

And Andreas led her onto the dance-floor.

* * * * *

Alex

CHAPTER ONE

'WE'VE arrived, sweetheart.' Jenny switched off the engine. Her mouth was dry and her heart was banging against her ribs so hard that she felt dizzy. 'Get ready to meet your daddy.'

She closed her eyes briefly and then turned to look at the baby, safely strapped in a car seat next to her.

Was she doing the right thing?

She'd ached over the decision for months and now the moment had finally come she was suddenly filled with doubt.

Was Alex Westerling really the right father for an innocent baby?

The answer had to be no.

But what choice did she have?

She brushed the baby's cheek with a gentle finger. 'You do realise that I don't want to do this, don't you? He might be a doctor, but the man has a wicked reputation with women and he's never made a commitment to anyone in his life. The last thing I want to do is introduce him to *you*.' She broke off and nibbled her lip, worry creasing her brow. 'But I just can't see any other way. We need help. We can't manage on our own any more. And you need to know your daddy. It's time Alex Westerling lived up to his responsibilities.'

The baby cooed happily and kicked her legs.

Jenny gave a soft smile. 'Daisy Phillips, you are a beautiful baby. Let's just hope he thinks so too.'

But she wasn't optimistic.

From what she'd heard and read about Alex Westerling, babies, however beautiful, were not on his agenda. The only females who interested him were well over the age of consent.

According to gossip he was a super-cool, rich playboy who moved smoothly through life, leaving a trail of broken hearts littered behind him, and Jenny had absolutely no doubt that the reception awaiting her was going to be decidedly chilly.

Delaying the moment when she would have to leave the car, she turned to look out of the window, her eyes resting on the sea sparkling in the sun. It was a beautiful day. And she'd never felt more stressed in her life.

She absolutely loathed confrontation and you didn't have to be a genius to work out that she was about to get confrontation by the bucketload.

Alex Westerling was *not* going to be pleased to see her.

'Come on. Let's get it over with.' She gritted her teeth and stared down at the row of fishermen's cottages that backed onto the sand dunes. 'At least the man has taste. He lives in a nice place. Right by the beach. You'll like it when you're a bit older.'

Jenny opened her door and walked round the car. Daisy was still blowing bubbles as she undid the straps and lifted the baby carefully out of the seat and onto her shoulder.

Then she took a deep breath, locked the car and paused at the top of the path. 'Brace yourself, Alex Westerling,' she muttered, her hand shaking slightly as she stroked the baby's back. 'Your past is about to catch up with you.'

Three miles away in the accident and emergency department, Alex Westerling finished his examination and straightened up.

'Well? Am I done for, Doctor?' The elderly lady lying on the trolley scowled at him, but he saw the anxiety in her eyes.

'You're not done for, Mavis,' he said gently, replacing the blanket and lifting the sides of the trolley. 'But you won't be dancing for a few weeks. You've broken your ankle.'

'Broken my—' The old lady broke off and frowned. 'Nonsense. It's just sprained.'

'It's broken.'

'You can't know that. You haven't even sent me for an X-ray.'

'I'm going to do that now,' Alex replied, reaching for the appropriate form and scribbling on it. 'But I already know it's broken.'

'How? Are you Superman? Do doctors come equipped with X-ray vision these days?'

Alex handed the form to the staff nurse who was hovering. 'Mavis, you couldn't put any weight on it after you fell and you're tender over the medial malleolus—which is this bone here...' He lifted his trouser leg to show her on himself and she winked at him.

'Nice legs.'

Alex laughed and released his trouser leg. 'Glad you think so.'

'So if you're so clever, why are you bothering with the X-ray?'

'Because I want to have a proper look at the fracture,' he said patiently. 'Check that there isn't anything else I should know about. Do you want me to blind you with science? I can explain exactly what I'm looking for if you like. Talar shift, or—'

'All right, all right, I get the picture. I'll have the X-ray.' Mavis studied him carefully. 'I know you. You're the one that's always in those glossy magazines. Rolling in money. Son of Sir-something-or-other and Lady-something-or-other. They live in a stately home. I saw pictures of it in a magazine. Garden bigger than a park.'

The nurse froze and glanced nervously at Alex. Alex Westerling was notoriously close-mouthed about his personal life and his family connections and certainly no one who worked with him ever dared raise the subject.

There was a moment's tense silence and then Alex shook his head and started to laugh.

'Anything else you know about me, Mavis?'

'Only that you're a bit of a heartbreaker, if the reports are to be believed.'

'They're not,' Alex said dryly, and her eyes twinkled.

'I saw you last winter, didn't I? When I did my hip. I never forget a face. Especially when it's as good-looking as yours.'

'And I never forget a hip. I suppose you were running away from a man at the time,' Alex drawled lightly. 'Perhaps you'd better just stand still and let them catch you. That way you might stop breaking things.'

'Well, if it was you chasing me, I probably would,' the old lady returned. 'You're a handsome devil. It's almost worth breaking something just to bump into you again.'

Alex was visibly amused by his patient and the nurse relaxed. 'Do me a favour, Mavis. Next time you want my company just lift up the phone and we'll meet for a cup of tea or something. It's much simpler than breaking bones.'

'You saucy man! I'm eighty-six! Are you asking me out?'

'Maybe.' His blue eyes twinkled. 'But it's only fair to warn you that I don't do commitment.'

Mavis laughed with delight. 'At my age, who cares? I just want to be a bit wicked and have fun.'

Alex smiled. 'You're my kind of woman, Mavis.' His gaze flickered to the nurse who was still hovering. 'Can you arrange for someone to take her to X-ray, please, and then call me as soon as you have the films. I don't want her hanging around.'

'Oh—aren't you going to leave me waiting for twenty-four hours in a draughty corridor? You hear such dreadful things about accident departments these days,' Mavis said, and Alex slipped his pen back into his pocket.

'Not about my department. I'll see you later. Try not to shock anyone in X-ray or have any more accidents on the way.' He strolled out of the room and bumped into one of the A and E sisters, carrying a stack of X-rays. 'Any of those for me?'

Tina shook her head. 'Don't think so. You've been trapped with that RTA for most of the day so everyone else has been doing your work.'

Alex lifted an eyebrow. 'So if I've had such a slack day, how come I feel exhausted?'

Tina wrinkled her nose. 'Because you were up all night and only had two hours' sleep at your desk this morning?'

Alex rolled his eyes. 'That could have something to do with it. We either need more staff or fewer patients. There's definitely an imbalance somewhere.'

'So are you off home now?'

'As soon as I've checked Mavis Belling's X-rays.'

'Oh, no!' Tina looked dismayed. 'Is the poor thing in again? What is it this time?'

'Ankle.' Alex ran a hand over his jaw and noted that he needed a shave. 'Not as bad as last time, though. But I want to check her myself.'

Tina's eyes were soft. 'Has anyone ever told you you're a nice man, Alex Westerling?'

'Funnily enough, no,' Alex drawled. 'In fact, I'm usually being told the complete opposite.'

'Well, perhaps I should have said that you're a nice man at work. In your personal life you are definitely not so nice.' Tina's eyes twinkled merrily. 'You are very careless with female hearts.'

Alex yawned. 'Don't you start. I've just had Mavis reading my press cuttings.'

'Well, there are rather a lot of them,' Tina pointed out mildly, and he gave a careless shrug.

'Is it my fault if the press have nothing better to do than follow me around? Now, give me a break, Tina. I've been awake for the best part of thirty-six hours with this RTA. I don't need a lecture.'

He strolled to his office to catch up on some paperwork and stayed there, trying not to fall asleep at his desk until one of the nurses called him to tell him that Mavis was back.

He removed the X-rays from the packet and examined them one by one.

'Well, that could be worse. See this?' He tapped on the X-ray with his pen. 'You've got a lateral malleolar fracture but fortunately it's undisplaced.'

'Why fortunately?'

'Because you don't need an operation.' Alex flicked off the light-box. 'You need a below-knee plaster, some painkillers and then you need to keep this leg elevated. I'm going to refer you to the orthopaedic surgeons for follow-up. You'll like them. They're a good-looking bunch. Be gentle with them.'

Mavis beamed. 'And will I see you again?'

'Not unless you break something else,' Alex said, scribbling a referral letter while he talked. 'Now, how are you going to manage at home with that leg in plaster?'

'Are you offering to come and bath me?'

Alex laughed. 'You're wicked, Mavis. What I had in mind was something rather more conventional, like the district nurse or perhaps a care assistant for a short time until you're fully mobile again.'

Mavis pulled a face. 'How boring.'

'But practical. I'll scribble a letter to your GP. He needs to check out your bones, if he hasn't already done so.'

He made the necessary arrangements, picked up his car keys and his jacket from his office and strolled towards his car.

It had been a rough ten days and he was starting to feel the strain. Thank goodness there was only one more day to go before the weekend. He was going to spend the whole time sleeping and surfing.

No responsibilities.

* * *

He wasn't home.

Jenny tried the bell one more time and then stepped back and looked at the house. It wasn't what she'd expected. She knew that Alex Westerling was wealthy beyond her wildest imaginings and she'd assumed that his house would reflect his flashy lifestyle. But it didn't seem to. From the outside it looked like an ordinary fisherman's cottage.

She was trying to work out what that said about him when she heard the growl of a powerful engine approaching.

Every muscle in her body tensed and her heart took off at an indecent pace.

All her instincts warned her that it was *him* and the minute the low black sports car roared into view, she knew she was right.

If the house had been a surprise then the car was everything she'd expected and more. A sleek, blatant declaration of masculine self-indulgence that reflected everything she'd heard about his playboy tastes. Only someone as superficial as him would spend so much money on a lump of metal, she reflected as he turned into the drive and came to a smooth stop.

Jenny dragged some air into her lungs and clutched Daisy against her, taking reassurance from her solid warmth.

Now that the moment had finally come, she felt breathless with panic.

Whatever had possessed her to come here? What madness had made her think that confronting Alex Westerling was a good idea?

Suddenly she felt like running but her legs were wobbling so badly that she couldn't have moved even if there'd been anywhere to run to. And there wasn't. He was blocking the only exit.

Moving at a leisurely pace that served to intensify her anxiety, the driver stepped out of the car and removed his sunglasses. And for the first time in her life, Jenny set eyes on Alex Westerling.

She stared at him stupidly.

She'd seen pictures, of course. He was one of the Westerling triplets and she'd seen his picture everywhere, along with those of his two sisters, and because she'd seen his picture so often she'd assumed that she knew exactly what he looked like. But she realised now that she'd somehow managed to merge the pictures with her own contempt for the man and in the process had managed to distort the truth.

And the truth was that the man standing in front of her was the embodiment of all the most extreme female fantasies.

The sudden increase in her heart rate came as an unpleasant shock.

Handsome didn't begin to describe him. She'd met handsome men before and none of them had had the physical impact of Alex Westerling. Everything about him was exaggerated perfection—his shoulders were unreasonably broad, his eyes a startling blue and his bone structure more striking than any she'd seen before.

He was achingly, spectacularly good-looking—if you liked arrogant, powerful men who thought they owned the world, Jenny told herself quickly, trying to get her reaction under control.

He might be good-looking but he was still the heartless man who'd ruined her sister's life.

And for the first time she was beginning to see how it could have happened. How her sister could have been led to behave in such a wanton and impulsive way. It wasn't just his immense wealth and aristocratic connections that set Alex Westerling apart from other men—it was the raw, almost untamed masculinity that surrounded him like a cloak, an aura of power strong enough to make the most worldly of women act irrationally—and Chloe had certainly not been worldly.

He locked the car with a flick of his wrist and strolled towards her, his jacket slung casually over one broad shoulder.

Brilliant blue eyes focused on Jenny without a flicker of interest, as if he was totally accustomed to having strange females holding babies waiting on his doorstep.

Jenny felt her knees shake. She was hopeless with men like him. She never knew what to say and felt totally out of her depth. Alex Westerling was someone who mixed with models and actresses on a regular basis and she knew he wasn't going to waste a second glance on a plain, flat-chested mouse like her.

He paused in front of her, well over six feet two of raw male power. 'Presumably you're lost,' he drawled, his tone maddeningly indifferent. 'You should have carried straight on at the top of the road. This is a dead end. It doesn't lead anywhere.'

She forced herself to meet his gaze, reminding herself that this was about Daisy, not her.

Her voice was clear and steady as she spoke. 'It leads to you, Dr Westerling.'

The ensuing silence pulsed with tension and his gaze hardened.

'In that case I probably ought to remind you that this is my home and it's the one place in the world that I won't tolerate being pestered by journalists.'

The wobble in her knees intensified and she felt the courage ooze out of her.

She couldn't do this. She just couldn't do this.

He had an air of self-possession and unshakable cool that was thoroughly intimidating and if she had been a journalist she would have run a mile. No story would have been worth the cold, disdainful look that Alex Westerling was casting in her direction.

But she wasn't a journalist and as if to remind her of the reason for her presence, the baby lifted a hand and patted her cheek with a chubby hand.

Daisy.

That was why she was here, facing this man.

That innocent touch gave her the courage she needed and she lifted her chin and forced herself to meet his icy gaze. 'I'm not a reporter.'

His eyes swept over her dismissively. 'I've been awake for the best part of thirty-six hours and I'm not in the best of tempers,' he warned softly. 'Perhaps you could just tell me what it is you want and we can both get on with the rest of the day. Your baby looks tired.'

'She isn't my baby, Dr Westerling,' Jenny croaked, wondering how it was possible to shiver even in the height of summer, 'she's *your* baby. You're her father.'

CHAPTER TWO

THE silence stretched into infinity.

Alex stared at the petite, dark-haired girl in front of him and wished he'd managed to snatch more sleep at the hospital. His usually sharp mind seemed to have ground to a halt.

The girl cleared her throat again and his eyes followed the direction of the sound, noticing a pulse beating in her throat, registering that she was nervous.

In fact, she looked terrified.

Somehow he found that comforting.

If she was nervous then there had to be a reason and the most obvious reason was that she was lying. She had to be lying. For a start she wasn't his type. She was dark-haired and he knew for a fact he'd never had a relationship with someone of her colouring. His sisters delighted in teasing him about the fact that he always had a blonde on his arm. And then there was her manner. All the women he dated were confident and flirtatious whereas this girl was obviously using iron determination to stop herself from running.

His absolute conviction that they'd never had a relationship gave him comfort.

'Perhaps we should go inside to talk about this,' she suggested, and he shook his head.

As far as he was concerned, the only place she was going was back where she came from.

'What is there to talk about?'

She bristled angrily and he saw her dark eyes flash slightly as she clutched the baby more tightly.

He hid his surprise. Maybe she wasn't quite as placid and gentle as she'd first seemed.

She was glaring at him. 'That is exactly the type of comment I'd expect from a man like you.'

'A man like me?' He lifted an eyebrow. 'And you are, of course, intimately acquainted with me.'

He knew definitely that she wasn't and the fact that she blushed deeply merely confirmed it.

She chewed her lip. 'Well, no, but—'

'We're not intimately acquainted?' Alex's tone was mocking. 'And yet you're claiming that we slept together. Maybe your definition of intimate is different to mine.'

She pushed her dark hair away from her face with a shaking hand. 'We didn't sleep together.' She stumbled over the words as if she was uncomfortable saying them. 'And for your information, you're the last man on earth I'd sleep with!'

'And you're the last woman I'd sleep with,' Alex shot back, seething with irritation, 'which makes your claim that I fathered your child utterly ridiculous and totally without foundation. And having clarified that, I think it's time you made your way back to wherever you came from.'

'I n-never said you fathered my child,' she stammered, and he looked at her in growing exasperation. 'Daisy is my sister's child. You slept with my *sister*, Dr Westerling. Slept with her and then left her to deal with the consequences.'

Her *sister*?

There was another prolonged silence, broken only by the distant rush of waves hitting the beach and the occasional shriek of a seagull.

His first impulse was to ask whether her sister was blonde but he suppressed it and looked at her, carefully concealing his emotions.

'And where is your sister now?'

'She's dead.'

Alex saw the anguish in her dark eyes before she quickly veiled it. Suddenly the baby started to cry miserably, almost as if it had understood that something dreadful had happened.

Reluctantly accepting that this wasn't a problem that was going to go away in anything like a hurry, he jerked his head towards the cottage.

'You'd better come inside.'

Vowing that from now on he was going to lead a life of celibacy, Alex gritted his teeth, opened the front door and walked into his house.

There was a gasp of surprise behind him and the girl stopped dead, still clutching the sobbing child.

Alex flung his jacket onto the nearest sofa and glanced at her impatiently. 'What?'

'It's just— I didn't...' She looked around her, unable to disguise her surprise. 'I thought you lived in a cottage.'

'It is a cottage. Well, actually it's four cottages knocked into one.'

She gazed around her. 'It's...not what I expected...'

Alex looked at her with undisguised irritation and then transferred his gaze to the baby, who was still howling. 'Can you do something about the noise? Does it need changing or something?'

She dragged her eyes away from the enormous speakers set in each corner of the spacious living room and glared at him disapprovingly. 'The baby is not an "*it*", Dr Westerling,' she said stiffly, bouncing the baby on her hip in an attempt to soothe her. 'She's a little girl and her name is Daisy. She's your daughter.'

'So you keep telling me.' Alex gritted his teeth as he loos-
ened his tie. He wasn't going to argue with her while there was
so much noise in the background. 'For crying out loud, give her
to me.' Without waiting for her reply, he reached out and took
the child, lifting her onto his shoulder with calm confidence and
placing a large hand on the centre of her back. Without looking at the girl, he walked over towards the huge glass windows
that stretched across his enormous living room and looked out
over the sea. Normally the view soothed him but with the baby
howling in his ear his head was starting to pound.

'She might be hungry...' the girl offered tentatively, and he
shot her an impatient look.

'So feed her. Presumably you've brought some food on your
little trip?'

She nodded. 'I'll need to go back to the car and get my bags.'

Get her bags?

What bags?

He watched her vanish back up the path towards the little
red car that he only now spotted at the top of his drive. How
could he have missed seeing it when he'd driven home? He
closed his eyes briefly and felt an overwhelming urge to sleep.
It was hardly surprising he hadn't seen her car. He was so tired
he would have driven past a herd of elephants without giving
them a second glance.

It suddenly occurred to him that the terrible noise had
stopped and the baby was now staring fixedly at his face.

He stared back, looking for something familiar, some part
of himself that might suggest that this was indeed his child.

She had blue eyes, that was true enough, but, then, so did
plenty of children so that didn't mean anything and she didn't
seem to have much in the way of hair at all so he couldn't use
that as a pointer.

Without warning her mouth spread into a gorgeous smile
and he found himself smiling back.

'So you think you can charm me, do you, blue eyes?' he murmured softly, lifting a finger and rubbing her cheek gently. 'I probably ought to warn you that I grew out of being taken in by a female smile a long time ago. I'm immune.'

She cooed happily and he carried on talking quietly to her until he heard footsteps and turned to find the girl standing in his doorway carrying several large bags.

His smile faded. 'Presumably you'll find the food eventually?'

She flushed and rummaged in one of the bags, pulling out a cool bag, bibs and several small pots. 'Where's your kitchen?'

He lifted an eyebrow. 'You want a tour of my house?'

She bit her lip. 'No, I do not want a tour of your house, but unless you want carrot purée on those pristine white sofas, Dr Westerling, I suggest we feed her in the kitchen.'

The baby gurgled happily and sucked her fists and Alex accepted the inevitable.

'We feed her,' he said through gritted teeth, 'and then we talk. Leave those bags by the door. It will stop you having to carry them so far when you want to take them back to the car.'

'I won't be going back to the car, but I refuse to argue this with you in front of D-Daisy,' she stammered, following him across the gleaming wooden floor towards the kitchen. 'Babies are like barometers. She's picking up the atmosphere.'

'Then she's a bright girl.' Alex stalked into his state-of-the-art kitchen and waved an arm. 'Help yourself. What do you need?'

'Hot water and access to a microwave to heat her food?'

Alex extended a lean brown hand. 'Give me the jar—I'll do the heating.'

'It isn't a jar. I make all her food myself.' The girl handed him a plastic pot and he scraped the mushy contents into a bowl and stuck it in the microwave with an expression of distaste.

'That looks utterly revolting.'

'It's nutritious and she loves it.'

Alex didn't argue. Instead he reached into a cupboard and pulled out a high chair, ignoring her look of amazement.

'I have nieces and nephews,' he said shortly, wondering why he was proffering an explanation, 'but as you seem to think you know everything about me, you probably already know that.'

'How old are they?'

'That's none of your business. I never discuss my family with strangers, and you,' he said icily, 'are most definitely a stranger.'

She flushed slightly and settled the baby on her lap.

He noticed that she was avoiding looking him in the eye and took that as another sign of her guilty conscience.

She had to be lying.

She *had* to be lying, otherwise...

Tensing his jaw, he removed the food from the microwave and put it on the table, but the girl's eyes were fixed on Daisy as she gave her a bottle.

'I have to give her some milk first or she's just too hungry to concentrate on the food,' she murmured, and Alex rolled his eyes.

'Spare me the detail.'

'You're going to need the detail, Dr Westerling. I'm no longer able to take sole responsibility for your child. I need help.'

Still not looking at him, she smiled down at the child who sucked greedily at the bottle of milk.

The smile completely altered her appearance and Alex found his attention caught. She had delicate, almost elfin features, her dark eyes fringed with long, even darker lashes that made her cheeks seem even paler. Her dark hair was pulled back from her face and fastened in a ponytail and she didn't appear to be wearing a scrap of make-up.

He stared at her, fascinated. He wasn't used to women who didn't wear make-up.

All the women he knew wore make-up. Even the ones that favoured the 'natural' look spent at least half an hour in front of the mirror before they emerged from the bathroom.

Not this girl, it seemed.

Despite the fact that it was August and the weather was hot, she was wearing a blouse that buttoned up to her neck and a skirt that buttoned down to her ankles. She looked at him periodically, reproach and a certain wariness evident in her huge eyes. She looked fresh and innocent and very, very young.

Evidently she was expecting him to drag her off to his lair and have his evil way with her, he reflected wryly. She obviously thoroughly disapproved of him and her blatant condemnation made him vaguely irritated and more than a little uncomfortable.

She reminded him of Little Red Riding Hood and she was making him feel like a very, *very* bad wolf.

Assuring himself that she probably wasn't innocent at all, he turned away and cursed softly under his breath.

He had more sense than to be taken in by a pair of wide eyes and an innocent expression. The girl was trouble. It was more than likely that she knew full well that the baby wasn't his but had identified him as an unlimited source of cash.

Thanks to all the press coverage, he was a constant target for women seeking an easy way to supplement their income and this girl was no exception. Despite that innocent expression, she was trying to fleece him.

He paced the kitchen while she finished feeding the baby, his temper held on a very tight leash.

Finally the baby was fed and looked decidedly sleepy.

The girl glanced at her watch. 'It's six o'clock. She usually has her bath and goes straight to bed. Do you have a travel cot?'

'Yes, but be warned that she's only going into it on a temporary basis while we discuss what needs to be discussed,' Alex bit out. 'Once we're finished, you're both going home.'

'She no longer has a mother,' the girl said, her voice decidedly wobbly as she scooped the baby out of the high chair. 'It isn't fair to deny her a father as well. As far as I'm concerned, her home is with you until we work out what to do.'

Alex closed his eyes and cursed all women under his breath and then strode out of the kitchen and up the staircase that led to the bedrooms, aware that she was struggling to keep up with his pace.

He flung open a door that led off the long landing and she gasped in delight.

'What a perfect room!'

Alex gave her a frosty look. 'Well, don't get too used to it. She's only going to be in it for an hour.'

'No, she isn't.' The girl placed the child on the floor and reached for the bag that she'd carried upstairs. 'I need to get her changed. I'll join you downstairs when I've finished.'

Totally unused to being ordered around by anyone, especially in his own home, Alex found himself lost for words and retreated downstairs and poured himself a large whisky.

Jenny took a final look at the sleeping baby, delaying the final moment when she was going to have to face Alex.

She had to admit that she found him monumentally intimidating. He was physically powerful, of course, but it wasn't just that. There was something about him. An air of self-belief that had probably been passed down through generations of Westerlings.

She'd expected him to be shocked by her announcement that Daisy was his baby but he'd barely flickered an eyelid. She wondered what it would take to disturb that legendary cool. Remembering his caustic comments, she shivered slightly.

He was everything she'd expected. Staggeringly good-looking, arrogant and loaded with self-confidence. And he was obviously going to take some persuading that Daisy was his.

She reached the bottom of the stairs and paused. He'd opened the French windows and was standing on the wooden deck outside, staring over the sand dunes towards the sea.

Taking a deep breath, she walked towards him, her nails digging into her palms.

He must have heard her because he turned instantly, a glass in his hand, his startling blue eyes cool and discouraging.

He'd discarded the tie and unbuttoned the first few buttons of his shirt. With his tousled hair and the rough stubble grazing his hard jaw, he looked dangerous and thoroughly disreputable and absolutely nothing like a doctor.

She wondered if he shaved before he saw patients.

'Is she asleep?'

Jenny nodded. 'Yes. I've left the door open so that we can hear her if she wakes.'

'Fine. Let's talk. Fast. I want to get on with my evening.'

Jenny took several deep breaths. He certainly wasn't making things easy for her but then what had she expected? That he'd accept Daisy with open arms? Of course not!

He gave a sigh and ran a hand over his face, as if trying to keep himself awake. She suddenly recalled his comment about having been up for thirty-six hours and her mouth tightened. Obviously he'd been living up to his reputation for partying.

He suppressed a yawn. 'Perhaps you'd better start by telling me who your sister was.'

'Her name was Chloe.' She almost choked as she said her sister's name. 'Chloe Phillips.'

He didn't hesitate. 'I've never met anyone by that name.'

His instant dismissal intensified the lump to her throat. How could he have forgotten Chloe so quickly? Obviously everything she'd heard about him had been correct. That he moved from one woman to another without forming any sort of attachment.

She chewed her lip. 'I wouldn't really expect someone with your reputation to remember one particular night. You've dated so many women it must be impossible to keep track.'

There was a brief pause and then he threw back his head and laughed. 'You really disapprove of me, don't you?'

She hid her surprise. She'd expected him to be angry or embarrassed by her accusations, instead of which he seemed amused. Not by the merest flicker of an eyelid did he indicate that her damning words had had any impact on him whatsoever. Evidently his dreadful reputation didn't worry him in the slightest.

He looked at her keenly. 'How did your sister die?'

His tone was surprisingly gentle and Jenny swallowed hard. 'She had a pulmonary embolus after the birth. It was all very sudden. I—I didn't even know she was having the baby,' she choked, unable to continue, and suddenly she felt his hand on her shoulder, pushing her towards one of the wooden chairs that faced out towards the sea.

'Sit down,' he said roughly. 'I'll get you a drink.'

Jenny struggled to contain the tears, furious with herself. She'd cried so many tears over Chloe she didn't think she had any left inside her. And she really, really didn't want to cry in front of Alex Westerling. He was the last person she'd turn to for sympathy.

He was partly to blame for the whole sorry situation.

He pressed a glass into her hands and she sipped the fiery liquid, choking slightly as it hit the back of her throat.

'Ugh! That's disgusting.'

'It's single malt,' he said dryly, a hint of amusement in his blue eyes. 'Certainly not disgusting.'

She screwed up her face but forced herself to take another tentative sip. 'I'm OK now.' She lifted her chin. 'Sorry. It's just that I still can't quite believe she's…' She broke off and swallowed hard. 'She was younger than me, you see.'

His eyes narrowed. 'Younger?'

'She was twenty when she had Daisy. She died a few days later.'

Alex pulled out the chair next to her. 'Look—I'm sorry about your sister and I can see she's left you with a hell of a problem, but—'

'Daisy isn't a *problem*, Dr Westerling,' Jenny said passionately, her hand shaking so much that some of the contents of the glass sloshed onto her fingers. 'Daisy is wonderful and without her I don't know what I'd—'

'All right, calm down.' Alex reached out and took the glass from her. 'I'll have that before you spill any more.' He put the glass on the table and sighed. 'I'm sorry. That wasn't the most tactful thing to say but I'm decidedly short on sleep and saying the right thing is hard when you're as knackered as I am.'

She looked at him, startled by the apology. She hadn't thought he'd be the sort of man who would apologise easily.

'Perhaps if you spent less time socialising you wouldn't be so tired.'

The moment the words left her mouth she bit her lip, wishing she could retract them. 'I apologise,' she mumbled, her cheeks growing red. 'That was very rude of me.'

Alex laughed. 'You were quite happy to turn up on my doorstep flinging wild accusations—why are you apologising for being rude?'

'They're not w-wild accusations,' Jenny stammered, her cheeks still pink, 'and just because we have a problem it doesn't give me the excuse to forget my manners.'

Alex gave a wry smile. 'I think we've moved slightly beyond manners, don't you? And now you need to listen to me.' His smile faded and voice was firm. 'I don't remember your sister, but I do know that I don't sleep with children and your sister appears to have fallen into that category. I don't know what she told you, but there's no way I can be the father of her baby.'

'She spent the night with you.'

His increased tension was barely perceptible. 'Do you have proof?'

Jenny nodded and reached for her bag, her hands shaking slightly. 'You were at the same party and she was...' She hesitated slightly, and then cleared her throat. 'She was drunk. You took her home.'

She dragged out an envelope and handed it to him.

Blue eyes locked onto hers for a long moment and then he

dropped his gaze to the envelope and reached inside for the contents.

He flicked through them silently, a slight frown touching his brows. 'These pictures—'

'Were taken by one of the magazines. But they clearly show you dancing with her. "Alex Westerling dancing with a friend", the caption says—well, your *friend* was my sister. Chloe. So you see, Dr Westerling, you *did* know her.'

He paused to read the letter and leafed through the remaining photos, his handsome face inscrutable.

She decided that he was a very difficult man to read. He seemed to possess enviable control over his reactions.

'I may have danced with her, but she didn't spend the night in my flat.'

'She said she did.'

He yawned. 'Then she was lying.' He tossed the envelope onto the table and shook his head. 'Is that it?'

It? How could he be so maddeningly cool about the whole situation?

Jenny bit her lip. 'She came home very upset after that night. She didn't want to talk about it, but when the photographs were published the following week she eventually spilled the beans.'

Alex's eyes narrowed. 'And you didn't think that was odd?'

Jenny looked at him, uncomprehending. 'Why was it odd? She didn't want to tell me but when I saw the pictures it was obvious.'

'What was obvious?'

'That you'd had a relationship.'

'We were dancing,' Alex said mildly. 'That hardly constitutes a relationship. I dance with a lot of women.'

'You sleep with a lot of women, too,' she said, totally unthinkingly, and then gasped as she realised what she'd said.

Alex laughed. 'You seem to have studied my lifestyle in minute detail,' he drawled, his deep tones thoroughly masculine and more than a little disturbing. 'Why are you so interested in me, I wonder?'

Her heart suddenly beat faster. 'I'm not interested in you, Dr Westerling. Except when your thoughtless lifestyle affects my family. And you're not going to get away with it. Don't think you can walk away from your responsibilities this time.'

His blue eyes were suddenly cold. 'I have never walked away from my responsibilities, but I did not sleep with your sister,' he said curtly, 'and a simple DNA test should prove that to everyone's satisfaction.'

Jenny looked at him in horror. 'No! I don't want anyone jabbing needles in Daisy unless it's absolutely essential.'

'If you're accusing me of being her father, then it's essential in my book,' Alex bit out, and Jenny shook her head.

'No. I already know you're her father. I don't need proof.'

'Well, I'm afraid I do.' Alex rose to his feet in a fluid movement. 'And I intend to sort this out as quickly as possible.'

'How?'

'If you won't agree to a blood test, I'll contact my lawyers first thing tomorrow.' Alex suppressed another yawn. 'Once they've proved beyond a shadow of a doubt that I didn't spend the night with your sister, you can look elsewhere for the financial support you're obviously seeking.'

Jenny stared at him helplessly.

He'd totally missed the point but, then, someone as rich as Alex Westerling was bound to think that everything in life revolved around money.

'I'm not seeking financial support,' she told him, her voice quiet. 'I'm not interested in your money. I just need help with Daisy and I want Daisy to know her father. She can't grow up not knowing either parent. It wouldn't be fair. She needs to know her daddy.'

Alex closed his eyes briefly. 'I'm not her "*daddy*". What's your name?'

Jenny stared at him. 'Pardon?'

'I asked you your name,' he said wearily. 'If we're going to have an argument it's usually helpful to know how to address each other.'

'Jenny.' Her voice wasn't quite as steady as she would have liked. 'Jenny Phillips.'

His slight smile affected her more than she cared to admit.

'Well, Jenny Phillips, you can take Daisy off to wherever you were planning on staying and as soon as I have a result from my lawyers I'll be in touch.'

Jenny didn't move. 'I'm planning on staying here.'

An ominous silence stretched between them. 'Say that again?'

She swallowed, wondering why she was finding this so hard. It had all seemed wonderfully simple when she'd planned it.

But then she hadn't met the real Alex Westerling and all the imaginings in the world hadn't prepared her for the reality.

'Daisy and I are staying with you, Dr Westerling. It makes sense. You can get to know her and help with her care.'

'Staying with me?' His blue eyes glittered dangerously and his voice was satiny smooth. 'Considering your outspoken views on my wicked reputation I'm surprised you're prepared to risk it, Miss Phillips. Surely there's a strong likelihood that you won't escape unscathed?'

His silky tone doubled her pulse rate but she forced herself not to react to his sarcasm. 'We both know your taste doesn't run to dark-haired women,' she replied, her voice remarkably steady considering the disrupted state of her emotions. 'And as I don't find you remotely attractive I'm fairly confident that I can restrain myself.'

It was a lie, of course. How could any woman not find him attractive? He was impossibly handsome and his total indifference to his startling good looks only intensified his appeal.

But she wasn't interested in a man with no morals, no matter how good-looking he was.

And Alex Westerling had absolutely no morals.

There was a brief silence and then he threw back his head and laughed. 'Ouch. Well, that's put me in my place. All right, stay if you dare. Frankly I'm too tired to argue with you. But what are you going to do when I prove that she isn't my child?'

Seeing the masculine challenge in his eyes Jenny's heart beat slightly faster but she lifted her chin, determined not to show him how uncomfortable he made her feel. 'That isn't going to happen, Dr Westerling.'

'That is exactly what is going to happen, *Miss Phillips*,' Alex returned smoothly, mimicking her formality, 'but if you really want to risk living with me, that's up to you. I'm going to bed and frankly I don't give a damn where you sleep as long as you and that baby don't wake me up.'

And with that he drained his glass, thumped it down on the table and strode away from her.

CHAPTER THREE

ALEX awoke to the smell of freshly baked rolls and strong coffee.

Remembering the events of the night before, he gave a groan of disbelief and covered his eyes with a forearm, trying to block out reality.

People had always warned him that his sins would come back to haunt him and it turned out that they were right.

At this moment there was a bundle of trouble waiting for him downstairs in his kitchen.

A baby who he was fairly sure wasn't his, complete with doting aunt who obviously thought he was a wicked seducer of innocent females.

He glanced at the clock and realised that it was almost seven o'clock. Which meant that he was expected at work in an hour.

Promising himself a really long lie-in at the weekend, he forced himself out of bed and into the shower before making the phone call that needed to be made.

By the time he appeared downstairs he was feeling better. His lawyer had been suitably reassuring and he was confident that the situation would be resolved quickly.

All in all he was feeling back in control and he was totally unprepared for the scene of domesticity in his usually pristine, undisturbed designer kitchen.

In the five years he'd lived in the house, he'd never invited a woman back to his home. This was his territory.

A totally bachelor environment.

But not any more.

Soft rolls, baked to a light brown, lay neatly on a rack, cooling, and a pot of steaming coffee sat in the middle of the table.

The baby was strapped in the high chair, happily gnawing on a piece of roll while Jenny chatted to her and spooned cereal into her mouth. She broke off and blushed when she saw Alex.

It occurred to him that she blushed more than any female he'd ever met.

'Oh— Good morning. We made breakfast— I hope you don't mind.'

If he hadn't been so stunned he would have laughed. She'd invaded his house and here she was checking that he didn't mind that she'd used the facilities? She was like a child at a party, desperate to be on her very best behaviour.

'You're obviously not a very experienced squatter,' he observed dryly. 'You're not supposed to apologise for making yourself at home.'

'I'm not a squatter.' She lifted her small chin and her tone was incredibly dignified. 'But I know I'm not your guest either. I'm aware that I'm here under sufferance.'

'You're here because frankly I was too knackered to throw you out last night,' Alex told her bluntly, eyeing the rolls and wondering why he suddenly felt like eating breakfast. He never ate breakfast. 'You made them this morning?'

Jenny nodded. 'Daisy woke early. She often does. We didn't want to wake you up so we came downstairs. Help yourself.'

'I don't eat breakfast.' The warm, freshly baked smell teased his nostrils and he gritted his teeth.

'Breakfast is the most important meal of the day,' she said, looking at him calmly. 'You ought to eat.'

'When I want your advice on my eating habits, I'll ask for it,' he growled, forcing himself to ignore the delicious smell and focus on the issues in hand. 'I've just spoken to my lawyer.'

She stiffened, the spoon poised in mid-air. 'Do lawyers always start work this early?'

'If you pay them enough,' Alex observed dryly, reaching for a mug and pouring himself some coffee. 'He's confident that he can find out who your sister was with that night.'

Jenny put the spoon to Daisy's lips. 'She was with you.'

'So you keep saying. I disagree.' He took a sip of coffee and almost groaned with pleasure. It was delicious. He hadn't known that he possessed coffee this good. Where the hell had she found it?

'Dr Westerling…' She rested the spoon on the bowl and looked him in the eye. 'I know you slept with my sister so all this denial is pointless. I'm sure your lawyer will confirm the truth soon enough.'

'I'm banking on it,' he said softly. 'I just hope you don't learn something about your sister that you'd rather have not known.'

She tensed. 'What exactly is that supposed to mean?'

'Only that I'm almost totally sure I never slept with your sister—which means that someone else did.'

Her lips tightened and she picked the spoon up again. '"Almost totally sure". Which means you're not sure at all. Has anyone ever told you that your morals are extremely questionable?'

'I'm thirty-four years of age and my morals are nobody's business but my own,' Alex said, wondering why her words irritated him so much. Usually he was totally indifferent to people's opinion of him. 'I'm as sure as I can be that I never had any sort of relationship with your sister, but it was fifteen months ago!'

She regarded him steadily. 'And you have absolutely no idea who you were sleeping with fifteen months ago, have you? You need to employ someone to find out.'

Her quiet tone was loaded with accusation and Alex ran a

hand over the back of his neck, feeling more uncomfortable than he cared to admit. The truth was that she was right. In a way. He *didn't* know exactly who he'd been with fifteen months ago and he didn't need her to remind him that his track record for long-term relationships was appalling.

It wasn't something he cared to dwell on.

'Did your sister actually tell you I was the father?'

'Yes.' She stirred the food slightly to cool it down.

Alex gritted his teeth, wondering whether she always believed everything she was told without question. He was as sure as he could be that the baby wasn't his but only time would prove it.

In the meantime he had a job to do.

'I have to leave for work.' He drained his mug and deposited it on the table. 'You can stay here today.'

And hopefully by the end of the day his lawyer would have resolved the issue and he could boot her out.

She looked at him in that calm, unflustered way that he was beginning to recognise as a prelude to one of her cutting remarks about his disreputable behaviour.

He braced himself.

'If you're hoping to hide us away, Dr Westerling, you're going to be seriously disappointed.' Jenny undid the bib, wiped Daisy's mouth carefully and lifted her out of the high chair. 'We're coming with you. I'm starting work today. I've got a job in your department and Daisy has a place in the crèche.'

Alex stared at her, feeling outmanoeuvred for the first time in his life.

She had a job in his department?

'What the hell are you talking about? What job?'

'I'm a nurse, Dr Westerling,' she told him, cuddling Daisy with one hand while she cleared up with brisk efficiency. 'I've been working in A and E for two years, ever since I qualified, but I had to take a break when Chloe died. But I need to work now. We need the money. I've used up all my savings.'

Alex wasn't interested in her savings. He was struggling with the news that not only was she planning to be under his feet at home but that she was going to be working with him, too.

'How did you find out where I worked?'

'It wasn't hard. Every detail of your life is spread over the gossip columns.' She picked up a cloth and within minutes his kitchen was totally spotless. 'I wanted us to be a family so it was important that we worked in the same hospital if possible. I was delighted when they offered me a job in your department.'

She wanted them to be a family?

Alex opened his mouth and closed it again.

He couldn't even contemplate retribution because neither the nursing staff nor Personnel would have had the slightest clue as to the problem they were introducing into his usually well-ordered bachelor lifestyle by employing Jenny Phillips.

Finally he found his voice. 'Look, I'm sorry about your sister but we need to get a few things straight,' he growled, 'We are not "a family". We will never be "a family". You can stay here for just as long as it takes my lawyer to prove that I'm not the baby's father, and then you're on your own.'

She appeared totally unmoved by his threats. 'And if he proves that you are Daisy's father?'

Alex tensed. He refused to even contemplate that possibility.

'Then we'll deal with it,' he said abruptly. 'But for now you're nothing more to me than a lodger. And a very unwelcome one at that.'

'It's absolute heaven to have more staff,' Tina told Jenny as she showed her around. 'We were so busy yesterday that one of our consultants worked thirty-six hours on the trot with only a quick nap at his desk.'

'I've been up for thirty-six hours.'

Jenny's eyes widened. 'Was that Alex Westerling?'

'You know him?'

Jenny shook her head quickly. 'Well, no, not exactly, but—'

'Don't tell me,' Tina said dryly, 'you've read about him in the newspapers. He's not very good at keeping a low profile is our Alex. Well, I'd better warn you that you don't want to believe everything you read. Whatever he gets up to in his spare time, Alex is a fantastic doctor.'

Jenny hid her surprise. Was he? She had to admit that she hadn't given any thought to his abilities as a doctor. In fact, she couldn't even imagine Alex as a doctor. When she looked at him all she saw was the man. If she'd had to chose a suitable career for him it would have been pirate or highwayman!

She closed her eyes and pushed the thought away, dealing with the sudden awareness that it had been overwork that had contributed to the tiredness she'd seen in his eyes the previous night.

The knowledge made her feel surprisingly uncomfortable.

When he'd mentioned that he'd been awake all night she'd assumed that he was living up to his reputation for wild partying.

She'd just assumed that medicine must be low on his list of priorities.

Tina was still chatting. 'He makes sure the department runs as smoothly as possibly even when we're desperate for staff. And, of course, August is always difficult because we have an influx of new doctors who don't know the ropes.'

Jenny nodded, trying to change the subject. 'So where do you want me this morning?'

'I thought we'd throw you straight in the deep end.' Tina smiled. 'You can work in the main area with me.'

She'd barely finished her sentence when a phone rang.

'That's the ambulance hotline,' Tina told her, hurrying to answer it. 'More trouble on the way, no doubt.'

Jenny listened to the one-sided phone call, trying to pick up clues as to what was coming in to the department. All she could ascertain was that the patient was in considerable pain.

Tina replaced the phone. 'How are you on diving-related emergencies?'

Jenny shook her head apologetically. 'I worked in London. I've never seen one.'

'Then this is your lucky day,' the unit sister muttered, picking up the phone and dialling. 'Alex? You know you said that you wanted to be rescued from that meeting—' She broke off and listened for a second. 'Yeah, they're bringing in a diver—sounds like decompression. OK—see you in a mo.'

She replaced the receiver and hurried towards Resus, taking Jenny with her.

'Obviously, because we're by the coast, we get divers in here periodically. If they're very bad we transfer them to the diving medicine unit. Alex will decide.'

Jenny stiffened slightly. All she could think about was his careless treatment of her sister. 'What about the other doctors? Isn't there anyone else that can deal with it?'

'If they have to, they will, obviously.' Tina grabbed a pack from a shelf and placed it on a trolley in readiness. 'But this is Alex's field really. He's done some diving himself and he spent some time at the diving medicine unit so he knows what he's doing.'

As she finished speaking the doors swung open and the paramedics hurried through, accompanied by Alex.

'What's the story?'

The paramedics moved the patient across onto the trolley. 'This is Pete Warwick. He was on the beach this afternoon and collapsed complaining of numbness in his legs. His friends called us.'

Alex nodded and turned his attention to the patient. 'How are you feeling now, Pete?'

The man groaned slightly. 'Awful. Everything hurts.' He winced slightly. 'Mostly my shoulders and elbows.'

Alex looked at Jenny who was poised at the head of the trolley, nothing in his gaze revealing that she was anything other than another member of the emergency team. 'Give him high-flow oxygen and let's get a line in. I want to take some bloods.'

Jenny placed the mask over the patient's mouth and nose and adjusted the flow of oxygen carefully.

Alex was still examining the patient. 'Does the pain get worse if I move your arms?'

The man gasped and nodded, the pain visible in his face.

'There's no localised tenderness but there is some swelling and you've got a rash.' Alex ran a hand over his skin. 'When did you last dive?'

The man closed his eyes and Jenny moved the mask slightly so that he could answer. 'Yesterday. My legs feel numb now and my back hurts.'

'Did you do multiple dives?'

Pete hesitated and then nodded. 'Yeah. I know you're not supposed to but it was so great down there and I thought I'd be OK.'

Alex continued to talk to the man, questioning him about his method of computing bottom and ascent times, asking about stoppages and the conditions in the water, about the length of time between the dive and onset of symptoms.

It was all totally alien to Jenny. She'd worked in A and E for almost two years but she'd never seen a case like this one. Why did it matter whether the water had been cold or what the currents had been like? Obviously the questions carried some significance or presumably Alex wouldn't be asking them. She was fascinated and dying to know more, but she didn't like to question him while the patient was listening. Besides, they hadn't established any sort of professional relationship yet. She didn't feel comfortable asking questions.

She hadn't managed to separate Alex the doctor from Alex the wicked seducer.

And Alex was using standard resuscitation techniques, she assured herself, handing the venflon to the SHO who was trying to find a vein. There was nothing unfamiliar about the steps he was taking—just the reasons behind them.

'Once you've taken the blood get a unit of saline up,' Alex instructed as he continued his examination. 'Pete, you did too many dives and you came up too fast. You've got something called type one decompression sickness.'

Jenny listened in fascination and resolved to pluck up the courage to ask him about it later.

His gaze lifted and he looked straight at her. 'Get me the diving medical centre on the phone, please. I think we need to transfer him.'

Tina jerked her head towards the phone. 'The number's stuck on the wall.'

Jenny dialled and found herself talking to the duty diving doctor.

Alex strode over and relieved her of the phone. 'Chris? How are you doing? I've got a customer for you...' He quickly outlined the patient's condition and gave details of the dive and the history before listening to his colleague.

Finally he replaced the phone and strode back to his patient. 'We're transferring you to the diving medical centre,' he told him. 'Tina, can we give him some aspirin, please, and arrange for an ambulance?'

Considering the amount of pain the man seemed to be suffering, Jenny was surprised that Alex was giving Pete aspirin.

His gaze flickered to hers. 'Severe decompression can cause capillary sludging,' he told her, obviously reading her mind, 'and it's the only analgesia I'm prepared to risk. Strong analgesia can mask recompression responses.'

Jenny nodded, grateful for his explanation, wishing that she'd been more knowledgeable for their first working encounter.

They prepared the man for the short transfer and in no time at all the ambulance crew arrived, ready to collect him.

Alex did a quick handover to the SHO who was going to accompany the patient and then went with the team to load him into the ambulance.

Jenny set about restocking Resus with Tina. 'I've never looked after anyone with decompression sickness before. I felt decidedly out of my depth,' she confessed, and then smiled as she realised what she'd said. 'Pardon the pun.'

Tina laughed. 'You did fine.'

'How come he only started getting symptoms today if it was yesterday that he was diving?'

Tina frowned. 'I don't know, actually. You'll have to ask Alex. He knows everything.'

As if on cue, Alex strolled back into the room. 'What do I know?'

'Jenny was asking why it took so long for the diver to show symptoms.'

Jenny coloured slightly. She would rather have not drawn attention to herself and she was still having trouble regarding him in a professional capacity.

Doctor, she reminded herself firmly, concentrating on the stethoscope looped casually round his neck. Today he was a doctor. Doctor. Doctor.

'Symptoms can occur from several minutes up to forty-eight hours after diving,' Alex explained, not by a flicker of an eyelid betraying the fact that they were at loggerheads. 'Decompression sickness is the result of gas bubbles travelling to various parts of the body.'

'And that's why he had pains in his joints?'

Alex nodded. 'It's known as "the bends".' He didn't follow his dive tables closely enough. He spent too long on the bottom and came up too fast. It could have been worse. He'll be OK once they've sorted him out at the dive centre.'

Tina smiled. 'In all the rush and panic, I didn't even have the chance to introduce you to our new staff nurse. This is Jenny. Jenny Phillips.'

Alex's blue gaze was decidedly cool as it flickered in her direction. 'We've met,' he said shortly, and turned on his heel and left the room without further conversation.

Tina stared after him, visibly shocked. 'What's got into him?'

Jenny ripped open a giving set and unravelled it ready so it

could be attached to a bag of saline quickly if the next patient
required it. She had absolutely no intention of confessing, but
she knew exactly what had got to Alex Westerling.

Her.

Jenny enjoyed her first day more than she'd anticipated. It had
helped that she'd been incredibly busy and that had prevented
her from dwelling on her problems with Alex.

But she found working so closely with him distinctly unsettling as she tried to reconcile the doctor she saw in action with
her preconceived views on the man.

Her head buzzed with conflicting signals.

She'd dismissed him as careless and shallow but as a doctor
he was obviously extremely talented and well regarded.

The entire staff seemed to worship him.

How would they react if they knew what he was really like?
she wondered as she collected a very contented but tired Daisy
from the hospital crèche and drove out of town towards Alex's
home. What would they say if they knew how badly he'd treated
Chloe? They only saw the capable, self-assured doctor and obviously he behaved in a suitably responsible fashion when he
was at work. They didn't know that he was a man with so few
morals that he was capable of leaving a young girl pregnant.

Her mouth tightened as she parked the car outside the cottages and lifted the baby out of the car seat.

From his comments, it seemed as though he was going to do
everything possible to dodge his responsibilities towards Daisy.

In a way she was glad that he'd contacted his lawyer. She
had every confidence that he would produce concrete evidence
to show that Alex Westerling was Daisy's father.

And then surely he wouldn't refuse to be part of her future?

Alex let himself into the house, dropped his bag on the polished
floor and threw his jacket over the nearest chair.

He was hot, tired and seething with irritation following another fruitless discussion with hospital management over staffing levels in the A and E department.

It was high summer, the place was flooded with tourists and everyone was worked to the bone.

In theory he had the weekend off—the first one for a month—but he was well aware that there was every likelihood that he'd be called in to help if things became too stressful for the staff.

And if that happened he had every intention of calling the chief executive of the hospital. If he had to forfeit his precious weekend off then so could the hospital management.

Perhaps if the guy experienced the reality at first hand he might be more sympathetic to requests for more staff.

Alex flexed his aching shoulders and looked out of the huge windows across the sand. Normally the tension leached out of him as soon as he reached his home, but not any more.

His home had suddenly become a source of tension too.

He'd passed Jenny's car on the way in so he knew she was here.

With the baby.

The baby that wasn't his.

Any hope he'd had that his lawyer would have been able to clear the matter up quickly had been dispelled by a quick conversation before he'd left the hospital. It seemed that it was going to take some time and the help of a private investigator to produce the evidence that Alex required.

Which meant that for the time being he was stuck with them. Unless he threw them out.

His head was suddenly filled with the disturbing memory of the baby smiling up at him and Jenny's eyes filling as she'd told him about Chloe.

He gritted his teeth and knew that he couldn't throw them out. Not until he'd been given some answers.

Cursing himself for being a soft touch, he decided that what he needed was exercise. Something to take his mind off the frustrations of the day.

He could run or he could swim.

The sea sparkled temptingly and he opted for the swim. Although it was early evening it was still surprisingly warm and hopefully the cool water would clear his head.

He took the stairs two at a time and then paused when he heard laughter coming from one of his bathrooms.

He'd given her a key so that she could let herself in, only too aware that if he hadn't she would have been more than capable of forcing a confrontation in A and E in front of his colleagues, and that was something he was keen to avoid.

For the time being he didn't want anyone knowing she was staying with him.

Hearing more laughter, he pushed open the bathroom door and stood still, his attention caught by the antics of the little girl.

She was chuckling with delight as she splashed herself, totally confident and happy in the water.

Jenny was completely soaked and Alex's eyes flickered downwards, his gaze drawn to the swell of her small breasts under the damp, clinging material.

Unaware of his presence, Jenny leaned forward to kiss the baby.

'Ow!' She winced as Daisy locked a fist in her hair and tugged at her ponytail. 'Now look what you've done, you minx.'

Her dark hair tumbled loose around her shoulders but she ignored it and scooped the baby out of the bath and laid her carefully on the towel that she had ready.

Alex watched, curiously. Whatever the circumstances of the baby's conception there was absolutely no doubt that Jenny adored her niece.

'There—was that nice, angel?' She dried the baby carefully and then reached for a nappy and noticed Alex. Her smile vanished and she looked at him warily, self-consciously adjusting her T-shirt. 'Oh. Hello. We didn't hear you.'

'Evidently.'

With her soft dark hair around her shoulders and no bra she looked completely different from the disapproving young woman he'd met at breakfast or the professional nurse he'd worked with all day.

She looked…

She looked…

Damn! What the hell was the matter with him? This woman had come into his life for the express purpose of causing trouble and here he was lounging in the doorway noticing all sorts of things he shouldn't be noticing.

He definitely needed to plunge himself into cold water.

'I'm going for a swim,' he said shortly, and she looked surprised.

'Oh. But you've only just come in.'

He ground his teeth. This was why he'd never lived with a woman. They expected an explanation for everything.

'And I'm immediately going out.'

'Right.' She brushed her hair out of her eyes. 'It's just that I thought you might want to spend some time with Daisy before she goes to sleep.'

'Well, you thought wrong.'

Daisy chose that particular moment to chuckle and smile at him and the muscles in his shoulders tensed even more.

He didn't need this.

'Look…' His tone was harsh. 'I don't do family stuff, OK? I never have and the sooner you realise that the better for both of us. I live on my own and that's the way I like it. If I want to swim in the sea, I swim. I don't answer to anyone and I have absolutely no wish to cuddle a child who isn't mine.'

Her gaze was steady. 'But she *is* yours, Dr Westerling. You may not be able to remember the names of your girlfriends but my sister was different. She wouldn't have—well, she didn't have lots of partners.' She blushed slightly. 'If she said you were the father then that's good enough for me.'

'It isn't good enough for *me*. This is England. I'm innocent until proven guilty and, for goodness' sake, stop calling me Dr Westerling. If you're intent on living in my house and ruining my life, you might as well use my first name,' he said irritably, casting an impatient look in her direction before striding off towards his bedroom to collect what he needed for his swim.

Jenny dressed Daisy and sat her on the floor.

'Your daddy behaves like a little boy,' she said wearily. 'Everything seems to revolve around him with no thought for others. He comes from a very rich family, you know. He was probably brought up by a series of nannies and doesn't really know what family life is. We're going to have to show him.'

Daisy cooed and sucked her fists and Jenny stuffed some supplies into a bag and lifted the baby onto her shoulder.

'We're going to start by hiding that whisky bottle and making him eat breakfast. How do you fancy having your supper on the beach? We can watch him swim.'

She was absolutely determined that Alex wasn't going to avoid them.

Daisy was his child and the sooner he started accepting her as part of his life, the better.

She carried Daisy to the kitchen, prepared her bottle and then walked out onto the sand, carefully locking the doors behind her.

There were a few other people on the beach and she narrowed her eyes and squinted into the distance, trying to identify Alex.

She made out a lone swimmer moving smoothly through the waves and decided that it must be him.

Finding a towel and some shoes abandoned at a safe distance from the water's edge, she decided that they must belong to Alex.

'We'll just settle ourselves here and wait for him,' she said to Daisy, dropping the rug that she'd found in one of the cupboards and settling herself comfortably. She just wished that she could relax herself but the tension was really starting to get to her. Her heart was thumping and she felt incredibly nervous.

You didn't need to be a genius to know that he was going to be annoyed to see her there.

But what else was she supposed to do?

If he was going to continue to ignore Daisy, then it was up to her to try and bring the two of them together.

'You deserve to know your father, angel,' she muttered, settling Daisy on her lap and offering her the bottle.

The baby sucked greedily and while she fed Jenny stared out to sea at the swimmer, watching the steady lift and fall of his arms as he cut through the water. Whoever it was, he was a powerful swimmer and she just knew it had to be Alex.

She sat on the blanket and fed the baby, totally unable to relax, knowing that the moment he saw her there'd be trouble.

When he finally emerged from the sea she tensed, preparing herself for the inevitable confrontation.

But as he moved closer all thoughts of confrontation vanished from her mind.

He was wearing the briefest pair of trunks she'd ever seen. They seemed to accentuate the muscular perfection of his powerful body and suddenly Jenny found she couldn't breathe.

She averted her eyes quickly, looking at the sea, the beach, anywhere as long as it wasn't at him.

But it was too late.

Just one glimpse had been enough. With the accuracy of a camera, her eyes had recorded the vision of Alex and stored it with appalling clarity in her befuddled brain.

'Are you stalking me?' He reached down and picked up his towel, his dark lashes clumped together, drips of water glistening on his hard cheekbones.

'No.' She sat stiffly, desperately trying not to look at him. 'But I won't let you avoid Daisy. She's part of your life, whether you like it or not.'

'Not,' he said grimly, rubbing the towel over his face and

hair and draping it around his broad shoulders, 'as my lawyer will shortly prove. I thought I already made clear to you that I value my independence. I don't like being followed.'

He was drying his shoulders now and against her will her eyes followed the contour of his muscles, tracing the perfect curvature which indicated the degree of physical demands that he placed upon himself.

Unlike so many of the doctors she met, Alex Westerling had the body of an athlete, a physique that undoubtedly would have been the envy of most men.

Jenny looked away quickly, horrified by the direction of her thoughts.

Why did she care what sort of body he had?

She didn't want to notice his physique. She didn't care about his physique. She wasn't that shallow.

Looks didn't matter.

There were other things far more important, such as behaving in an honourable way, something which Alex evidently knew very little about.

Her slim shoulders sagged slightly.

Maybe this whole idea had been a mistake.

It was all very well to want Daisy to know her father, but what if her father wasn't worth knowing? What if he was the sort of man who never faced up to his responsibilities?

She was about to speak when she heard a shrill scream from further down the beach.

Alex stopped drying himself and stared in the direction of the sound. 'What…?'

A woman was running in their direction, carrying a little girl who was screaming loudly. 'Help me!'

Alex dropped the towel and sprinted towards her while Jenny stooped to pick up the rug and Daisy before hurrying to catch him up.

'What happened?'

'She trod on a jellyfish—there's a bit still stuck to her foot.'

The mother started to sob hysterically and Alex's gaze flickered to Jenny, his message clear.

The mother was making the situation a thousand times worse.

Jenny immediately took the woman's arm. 'Try not to panic. Most of the jellyfish in these waters are relatively harmless.' She flung her rug on the ground and sat Daisy down, thankful that she was still too young to move about. 'Let me hold your daughter so that Dr Westerling can take a proper look at her.'

The woman relinquished her grip on the child without protest. 'You're a doctor?' She was looking at Alex as though he were an oasis in a desert. 'Oh, thank goodness. I was so worried—we're such a long way from civilisation and you read such dreadful things.'

They were on a Cornish beach— Hardly that far from civilisation!

Thinking that the woman was overreacting, Jenny glanced at Alex, expecting him to make a caustic comment, but he didn't. Instead, he bent down to examine the child's foot.

'It's swollen and it's obviously going to be causing her pain,' he said finally, glancing around him with a frown. 'We need some sea water.'

'We've left buckets and spades over there.' the woman gestured vaguely across the beach. 'But I don't want to leave her.'

Alex smiled, his blue eyes reassuring. 'She'll be fine with us and I need that sea water. Would you mind?'

Staring into his handsome face, the woman suddenly stopped crying and gave a self-conscious smile. 'I— If that's what you want, I'll go and fetch the bucket.'

'That's great,' Alex said smoothly, and Jenny resisted the temptation to roll her eyes.

What was it about her sex that made them behave like such idiots in the presence of a good-looking man?

She watched while the woman hurried away across the sand

and then realised that Alex had turned his attention back to the little girl who was still crying quietly.

'What's your name, sweetheart?'

The little girl gulped. 'Amy. Are you really a doctor?'

Alex grinned. 'I'm really a doctor, Amy. Don't I look like a doctor?'

The girl stopped crying and her eyes were suddenly huge. 'You don't wear clothes and most doctors wear clothes. My doctor at home wears a tie.'

Alex laughed. 'I wear clothes when I'm at work, but at the moment I'm not working. I'm wearing my beach clothes. Just like you. And ties look silly with swimming trunks, don't you agree?'

Amy giggled but Jenny felt her face heat at yet another re-minder of his decidedly disturbing state of undress.

Alex seemed supremely indifferent to the fact that he was wearing virtually nothing.

'Well, Amy…' he treated the little girl to another one of those smiles that seemed to knock women sideways '…as soon as your mummy comes back, we're going to rinse this foot of yours.' He glanced at Jenny. 'We need some vinegar.'

'I'll go and get some from the house,' she said immediately, and then hesitated and looked at Daisy.

Alex intercepted her glance. 'I'll keep an eye on her. But don't read anything into it.'

She ran back to the house, flinging open cupboards in the kitchen until she found the vinegar.

On impulse she sprinted up the stairs, pushed open the door to Alex's bedroom and grabbed a shirt that she saw lying on the bed.

She returned to find Alex bathing the foot in sea water while the mother stared at him in ill-concealed admiration.

Gritting her teeth, Jenny thrust the shirt in his direction. 'I thought you might like to put this on.'

'Thank you.' He took the shirt without further comment but something gleamed in his blue eyes and she coloured slightly.

Bother.

She hoped he didn't realised that seeing him naked was making her uncomfortable.

Satisfied that there were no more tentacles stuck to the little foot, Alex reached for the vinegar. 'This should help,' he said. 'Do you have paracetamol syrup at home?'

'We're on holiday,' the woman said, looking at him meaningfully. 'We're staying at the Cliffside Hotel.'

Alex calmly ignored the blatant invitation. 'That's near a chemist so you should be able to pick some up. They stay open late at this time of year.'

Finally he was satisfied and he dressed the foot and lifted the little girl into his arms.

'Better now?'

She nodded. 'It still hurts a bit.'

He nodded sympathetically. 'It should feel better soon.' He handed her back to her mother with a smile. 'Any worries, take her up to A and E, but I don't think you'll have any problems. And next time you need to watch where you're stepping, young lady.'

The child nodded and stuck her thumb in her mouth. The mother cast a last longing look at Alex before picking up the bucket and struggling back along the beach towards the rest of their things.

Alex watched them go and Jenny wondered whether he even realised that he was still half-naked. It seemed not. Didn't he know the effect he had on people? All right, so he'd dragged the shirt on, but he hadn't bothered doing it up and she kept catching thoroughly disturbing glimpses of a muscular chest covered in curling dark hair. Against her will her eyes traced the line of dark hair down to where it disappeared into his swimming trunks and she felt her mouth dry.

'Well, that added a bit of excitement to my evening swim,'

he said casually, stifling a yawn and reaching for the towel that he'd tossed on the rug.

'I'm surprised you didn't take up her invitation,' Jenny muttered, and he gave a cool smile.

'Maybe I will,' he drawled carelessly, but she suspected that he was just baiting her and watched silently as he draped the towel round his neck and ran his fingers through his damp hair to straighten it.

Suddenly aware that from her position on the rug her eyes were level with his powerful thighs, Jenny scrambled to her feet, her face flushed. All of a sudden all she could think about was the significant bulge she'd seen in his swimming trunks.

What was the matter with her?

She *never* thought about things like that.

'You're not very romantic, are you?'

Alex gave a soft laugh. 'I can be very romantic when the need arises.'

'You mean when you want to persuade someone to s-sleep with you,' she stammered, unable to hide her distaste. 'I can't believe women fall for your patter.'

His eyes glittered and he moved towards her with all the graceful stealth of a jungle cat. 'Is that a challenge, Miss Phillips?'

She backed away so fast she almost stumbled, hideously aware of every muscular inch of him. 'No. It certainly isn't. Unlike most of the women you mix with, I know exactly what sort of man you are, Alex Westerling.'

Dangerous.

'So you keep telling me,' he said silkily, 'but you're obviously finding me incredibly hard to resist.'

She gaped at him. 'No wonder you need four cottages to live in! Your ego would never fit into just one. For your information, I don't have any trouble resisting you.'

'No.' He was maddeningly cool and relaxed and there was a hint of laughter in his wicked blue eyes. 'Then why did you bring me the shirt, sweetheart? Go on, admit it. The sight of my body was really disturbing you.'

Her heart was banging against her ribs and she stared at him, dry-mouthed. 'You are the most arrogant, hateful—'

She broke off and he laughed.

'Jenny, you brought me the shirt,' he said mildly. 'You wanted me to cover up.'

Cheeks hot with anger and another emotion that she couldn't identify, Jenny scooped up Daisy and then proceeded to struggle with the rug.

'Here—give me that.' His tone still amused, he took it from her and thrust it under his arm before strolling back across the sand to fetch his shoes.

She fought the impulse to throw something at him and followed him back to the house, glaring at his broad back. She was still simmering when he dropped the rug inside the door, poured himself a drink and disappeared up the stairs to his room without a backward glance.

Frowning after him in total frustration, Jenny made her own way upstairs and prepared Daisy for bed.

Her heart was thumping and she felt hot all over.

'Your father is a total nightmare,' she muttered as she finally tucked the little girl into her cot. 'And I have no idea how we're going to persuade him to take notice of you. Maybe once his lawyer has confirmed the truth he'll start acting in a more responsible manner.'

She lifted a hand and stroked the baby's back gently, smiling as she saw Daisy's eyes close. Just being with the little girl soothed her and she sighed, wishing that she hadn't reacted so strongly to Alex's teasing. And she was sure now that he had been teasing her.

'I suppose he thinks that if he's horrid enough then I'll leave,' she whispered quietly, knowing that the baby wouldn't care what she was saying as long as the voice was suitably restful.

'But we're not going to leave, are we? He's your daddy and he's going to get to know you.'

But she wasn't going to let Alex bait her again.

Satisfied that Daisy was asleep, she made her way downstairs, tensing as she reached the living room. There was no sign of Alex and she assumed that he must be up in his bedroom, changing after his swim.

Jenny walked into the kitchen and gathered together the ingredients that she'd bought earlier.

However tired or angry he was, surely he had to eat some time?

And if they ate together maybe they could establish at least some sort of relationship—that was going to be essential if he was to be part of Daisy's life.

It would have been a great deal easier if they weren't so different, she reflected helplessly, digging around in his kitchen for the equipment she needed.

She heated some oil in a huge wok that she found in one of his cupboards, tossed in some fresh garlic and ginger and then added spring onions. Hopefully the smell would tempt him downstairs.

By the time he appeared in the doorway she'd added strips of chicken and vegetables and everything was sizzling temptingly.

'What the hell do you think you're doing?'

His soft tone made her catch her breath but she stayed outwardly calm, concentrating on draining the noodles instead and adding them to the wok.

'I'm cooking dinner.'

'Very domestic,' he said sardonically. 'I didn't realise that this little agreement of ours included catering. What else is on offer, I wonder?'

She wondered whether he was trying to shock her on purpose.

Determined not to react, Jenny ignored his insinuation and took a deep breath. 'Dr Westerling—Alex—you didn't eat breakfast and to the best of my knowledge you worked through lunch. As you don't seem to have planned anything for dinner either, I thought I'd better prepare something.'

'What makes you think I haven't already planned something for dinner?'

'The contents of your fridge.' She shook the wok and risked a glance in his direction. 'It's full of beer.'

He lifted an eyebrow in blatant mockery. 'What's wrong with that?'

She kept her tone light. 'You can tell a lot about someone from what's in their fridge.'

'Is that right?' He lounged against the doorframe, his blue eyes glittering dangerously. 'And what does my fridge tell you about me?'

'That you don't take care of yourself,' she said bluntly, tossing the contents of the wok with skilful turns of the long-handled metal spatula she'd found. 'You drink too much and you don't eat properly.'

There was an ominous silence.

'Anything else?'

She ignored his sarcastic tone and emptied the contents of the wok onto two plates.

Yes. He had a wicked reputation with women.

But she wasn't bringing that up now, she reminded herself firmly. The atmosphere was already tense enough. If she wanted him to be a father to Daisy then she had to build some sort of relationship with the man, and she wasn't going to do that if she was constantly reminding him that she disapproved of his morals.

Instead, she handed him a plate with a calm smile. 'I hope you like Chinese—I didn't ask you.'

His eyes clashed with hers and then drifted down to the plate.

For a moment she thought he might refuse to eat it but instead his eyes narrowed and his firm mouth lifted at the corners. 'So you want to eat dinner with me—very cosy.'

His voice was silky smooth and he reminded her of a lethal predator tempting his prey into his lair.

Her breath stuck in her throat. 'I have no particular desire to eat dinner with you, Dr Westerling,' she said, struggling to keep her voice steady, 'but seeing as we both have to eat I thought I might as well cook for both of us.'

'We'll eat outside.'

Having delivered that statement, he turned and strode through the living room, clearly expecting her to follow him.

She did so at a slower pace, wondering whether she was actually going to be able to eat anything. Her insides were so churned up that she had a feeling the food might stick in her throat.

She settled herself near the door and his eyes flickered to the intercom that she placed next to her.

'What's that for?'

'It's so that I can hear Daisy.' She lifted her fork and stabbed a piece of broccoli and made an attempt at civilised conversation. 'It's very beautiful here. Do you swim every evening?'

'Yes.' His answer was terse and she gave up on conversation, choosing instead to sit quietly and concentrate on her meal.

It was all very well wanting Alex to get to know Daisy but she was only too aware that it meant that he had to get to know her, too. And he'd made it perfectly clear that she was the last person he'd choose to spend time with. If she hadn't been here she had no doubt that he would be doing something much more exciting than sitting on his deck eating noodles.

They ate in a tense silence for a few minutes more and then she tried again.

'This is a fantastic spot.'

'I chose it for its privacy.' His meaning was crystal clear and she sighed, wondering how she was ever going to build any sort or relationship with him.

The truth was, she just wasn't used to dealing with men like him. He was way out of her league and just being within a metre of the man made her nervous. If it hadn't been for Daisy she would have legged it the moment he'd stepped out of his flashy sports car.

'What's the sauce?'

She jumped, startled that he'd actually spoken to her. 'Pardon?'

'I like the sauce.' He took another mouthful and nodded approvingly. 'It's delicious.'

He liked her cooking?

She hid her surprise. 'I—I made it. It's a mixture of things.'

'Well, it's good.' He lounged back in his chair, his glass in his hand. 'You're very domesticated, aren't you? Home-made bread for breakfast, baby food from scratch, dinner in the evening...'

Jenny flushed, sensing that he was mocking her again. 'I love cooking.'

'Very wifely.'

She winced at his acid comment.

'I'm not trying to be wifely, Dr Westerling,' she replied steadily. 'But both of us have to eat so it seemed sensible for me to cook. You may find this hard to believe but I don't have any designs on you at all.'

Alex cleared his plate and lounged back in his chair. 'I do find it hard to believe,' he said shortly. 'Women have used all sorts of tactics in the past to try and persuade me into marriage, but you're the first one to actually go to the lengths of producing a baby. You'll have to forgive me if I'm a little sceptical about your motives.'

Marriage?

She gaped at him. 'Is that what you think? That I want you to *marry* me?'

He shrugged carelessly. 'Why else would you move in here and start cooking me dinner?'

Marry Alex Westerling? It would mean sentencing herself to a lifetime of torture. She would never, ever be comfortable with him. He was just too...too...*male*.

'I moved in because I want you to get to know Daisy,' she said, utterly appalled by his arrogance, 'and I cooked us dinner because we both have to eat. Believe me, given the choice, the last place I'd want to live is with you and I wouldn't marry you if you paid me.'

Alex yawned. 'Is that right?'

He didn't believe her.

She looked at him in genuine amazement. 'Frankly, I can't understand why so many women are desperate to marry you.' She stabbed a piece of chicken. 'They must be mad.'

Her last comment was muttered under her breath but he heard her and he shot her a look that she couldn't interpret.

'You really wouldn't want to marry me?' There was a strange light in his eyes and she looked at him and shook her head, her shyness temporarily forgotten.

'Absolutely not. You lead a totally selfish lifestyle, you're insufferably arrogant and you've obviously been getting your own way since the day you were born. As a husband you'd be a nightmare.'

There was a silence and then Alex threw his head back and laughed in genuine amusement.

'Oh Jenny, Jenny.' He was still chuckling as he reached forward for his drink. 'Aren't you worried about my poor ego?'

She shot him a look of contempt. 'Your ego is so inflated that I could chip away at it for weeks and not make any impression.'

His eyes were still brimming with humour. 'I'm beginning to think you might be my type after all. Where have you been all my life?'

Jenny felt more and more unsettled. Why didn't his reactions ever match her expectations?

Surely he should have been offended that she didn't want to marry him, not amused.

'I've been avoiding men like you.'

He ran a hand over his rough jaw and she found herself noticing the way the sides of his firm mouth creased when he smiled.

'What I want to know,' he said in that lazy upper-class drawl that was doubtless the product of a vastly expensive education, 'is why, if you find my lifestyle so distasteful, you want me to be Daisy's father. Aren't you worried about my pernicious influence?'

'I don't *want* you to be Daisy's father,' she delivered coolly, giving up on her dinner and placing her fork carefully on the plate. 'I didn't choose you, but apparently my sister did and we have to live with that fact.'

His eyes narrowed. 'You really do believe I'm her father, don't you?'

She stared at him, thinking that it was an odd question.

'Absolutely. Why else would I be here?' She held his gaze. 'Why would my sister lie?'

'I have absolutely no idea,' he replied thoughtfully, 'but I have every intention of finding out.'

With that he stood up and walked away from her, indicating that the conversation was over.

He was like a tiger, she reflected helplessly, watching as he prowled back into his enormous living room and fiddled with the stereo. A solitary male, moving through life on his own, careful never to form a relationship with anyone. Even from her short acquaintance with the man she could see that he never allowed anyone close to him.

Who or what had made him that way?

As far as she was aware, his family was stable enough. His father was one of the richest men in the country and she knew that he'd inherited enormous wealth himself. He certainly didn't have money worries.

In fact, judging from the careless way he lounged on the sofa, eyes closed as he listened to the music, one arm flung across his forehead, he didn't seem to have any worries at all.

Jenny stared at him in helpless frustration.

He was obviously determined to ignore the fact that Daisy was his child.

How on earth was she ever going to encourage him to build a relationship with her?

CHAPTER FOUR

IT WAS the cry that woke him.

Dragged from a deep sleep by the terrified wails, Alex jerked upright in bed and waited for the cries to stop.

They didn't.

He muttered a curse and sprang out of bed, padding barefoot along the landing towards the room he'd had decorated as a nursery.

The baby was sobbing in her cot and Alex frowned, glancing behind him, expecting to see Jenny hurrying to take over.

But there was no sign of Jenny.

Cursing softly under his breath, he stepped into the room and scooped the baby out of the cot, feeling the dampness soaking through her cotton sleepsuit.

He rolled his eyes. 'No wonder you're yelling,' he muttered softly, tucking the baby against his shoulder. 'You need changing. You need your mummy.' He broke off as he said the words, remembering that she no longer had a mother.

But she had Jenny.

Where the hell was Jenny?

He glanced impatiently towards the door again but the landing was still in darkness and there was no sign of movement from the other bedroom.

The baby had stopped crying and was snuffling softly against his neck but he knew that the moment he put her down she'd start crying again, and no wonder. She was soaking wet.

Muttering under his breath, he glanced around the room. Nappies were neatly stacked next to a changing mat, along with wipes and everything else he was likely to need.

There was no reason why he couldn't change her himself.

Except that it just wasn't the sort of thing he did.

Even with his sisters' children, he avoided the nappies.

He glanced impatiently towards the door again but there was still no sign of Jenny.

For a moment he was tempted to wake her, and then the baby smiled up at him again and for the first time in his life Alex Westerling found himself utterly captivated by a female.

Her soft, baby smile warmed something deep inside him, reaching a part of himself that he hadn't known existed.

Staring down into her gorgeous blue eyes, Alex decided that maybe they didn't need Jenny's help after all.

He dealt with life-threatening situations on a daily basis.

He could deal with one wet nappy.

'OK, young lady, I suppose we'll have to do this ourselves, but you're going to have to be patient. This whole nappy business is new to me. Whenever my sisters visit with their offspring, I always avoid this bit.' He laid her gently on the mat on the floor and undid her sleepsuit. 'Ugh. This is totally disgusting. No wonder you were screaming.'

He tossed the damp sleepsuit on the floor with an exclamation of distaste and glanced towards the bathroom.

'I'm going to be right back—don't move.' He straightened up and walked into the bathroom, wetting a flannel and picking up a towel. By the time he returned the baby had rolled off the mat and was kicking happily on the carpet.

Alex laughed softly. 'Think you're clever, do you? Drying

yourself off on my carpet.' He knelt down, lifted her back onto the changing mat and gently washed her while she gurgled and tried to grab his face with her tiny hands. 'Keep still. You're dealing with a total amateur.'

Finally he was satisfied that she was dry and reached for a nappy, opening it up and looking at it doubtfully.

'Which way up does this thing go? Have you any idea?' He pulled a face at the baby who chuckled and clapped her hands. 'Stop laughing. Tapes at the front or tapes at the back?'

He experimented, decided which was correct and then tried to slip it under Daisy's bottom, but she'd decided that this was a great game and proceeded to twist and wriggle until he grunted with frustration.

'For crying out loud, baby,' he growled, wincing as the tapes stuck themselves to the hair on his arms for the third time. 'Ouch! This is worse than sticky plasters. Thank goodness my sisters Katy and Libby can't see me now. I'd never hear the last of it. Just lie still, will you? Don't you know a beginner when you see one?'

Finally he managed to secure the nappy and dress her in a clean sleepsuit.

'There. You're dry now.' He picked her up and she snuggled against him, her eyes drifting shut immediately.

Alex looked down at her and sucked in a breath. She looked utterly defenceless.

'You poor scrap. You've lost your mother and no one seems to know who your father is,' he murmured, stroking her head softly as he supported her. 'I honestly don't think it's me but we're trying to find out for sure and if it is-well, I suppose we'll come to some agreement. Try not to worry. At least you've got your Aunty Jenny and she seems pretty good at homely things. She makes your food from scratch and I'm sure it's very healthy—even though it does look disgusting.'

He wondered why Jenny hadn't woken up. Maybe she was exhausted. It occurred to him that she must have had a very tough six months, what with losing her sister and being landed with a baby that wasn't hers.

No wonder she was looking for help.

He settled the baby in the cot and watched her sleep, his expression suddenly thoughtful.

He'd always thought that having a baby would be just about the worst thing in the world but suddenly he wasn't so sure.

There was certainly nothing horrifying about Daisy.

She was incredibly sweet.

Shocked by his own thoughts, he swore softly and raked long fingers through his dark hair.

What the hell was happening to him?

Babies were not sweet. Babies marked a very definite end to a bachelor existence and a start to a lifetime of self-sacrifice.

It wasn't a route he intended to take.

Jenny stood in the corridor, hardly daring to breathe.

She'd been woken by the first cry but then it had occurred to her that this was a golden opportunity to force Alex closer to Daisy. Surely he wouldn't be able to ignore the baby's cries?

And he hadn't.

She'd stayed in her room, suppressing the natural urge to rush to the baby, biting her nails until she'd heard his heavy tread on the landing and his rough male voice talking to Daisy.

She had no idea what he'd done but Daisy had stopped crying so whatever it was had obviously worked.

And he was still in her room.

Not sure whether that was a good thing or not, Jenny crept back to her room and slid into bed.

Hopefully, exposing Alex to the baby would improve their relationship, but on the other hand it was a strategy that could totally backfire. Alex was a hardened bachelor who valued his independence above everything. Spending too much time with Daisy could just reinforce his prejudices about the effects of babies on his lifestyle.

He could decide that he wanted nothing to do with Daisy. And then what would she do?

Jenny was downstairs giving Daisy breakfast the next morning when Alex strode into the kitchen full of purpose.

'Get Daisy's things together. We're going shopping.'

Jenny paused with the spoon halfway to Daisy's mouth. 'Sorry?'

'Shopping.' He glanced round the kitchen expectantly. 'Is there any of that delicious coffee?'

Jenny blinked, registering the fact that he thought her coffee was delicious. 'It's on the side,' she said warily, wondering what was going on. 'What are we going shopping for?'

'Toys.' He helped himself to coffee and stared at the freshly baked batch of rolls cooling on a rack in the centre of the table. 'Are those spare?'

His tone was casual and she hid a smile. 'Help yourself.'

She felt a thrill of satisfaction that she'd finally persuaded him to eat breakfast. 'Why are we shopping for toys?'

'Because Daisy doesn't have any.'

Jenny stared at him, unable to hide her amazement. 'You want to buy Daisy some *toys*?'

He didn't look at her, instead reaching for a roll and covering it in butter and honey. 'Every child needs toys. I know a great toy shop. I take my nieces and nephews there. We'll go there and find something for Daisy.'

Still flabbergasted by his sudden interest, Jenny hesitated. Should she remind him that at six months a baby didn't need much in the way of toys? No. Any interest from him was surely to be encouraged.

'But why?' She nibbled her lip, unable to comprehend his sudden interest in the baby. 'You don't think Daisy's your child.'

'I'm sure she isn't.' He poured himself some coffee. 'But that doesn't mean I can't buy her toys. The kid's had a rough time.'

Had a rough time?

Jenny looked at him curiously, considerably heartened by the fact that he at least seemed sympathetic to Daisy's situation.

That had to be a good thing. It would make him more likely to help when his lawyers confirmed her parentage.

'If that's what you want,' she said, and he nodded, biting into the roll with a grunt of approval.

'You're a good cook.'

Not used to receiving praise, Jenny coloured and concentrated on Daisy. 'Thank you.'

'OK, here's what we're going to do.' He finished the roll and reached for his coffee. 'I can see that life must have been tough for you over the past six months and I'm willing to help you until we can find out who Daisy's father is.'

Jenny opened her mouth to point out that she knew that it was *him* and then closed it again. She had no wish to antagonise him and he obviously had it all worked out.

There'd be time enough for him to take full responsibility when his lawyers found out the truth.

'You can stay here until you find her father. Once we trace the guy I'll get my lawyers to sort it all out so that you have decent financial support for Daisy.'

He obviously felt he was being extraordinarily generous and Jenny sighed.

'It isn't just about financial support, Dr Westerling.'

'Alex,' he prompted immediately, and she gave a brief smile.

'Alex. It isn't about money. Most of all I want Daisy to have a father. It's really important for a little girl to know her daddy. I had such a great relationship with my dad when I was growing up. He was such an important part of my life. I don't want Daisy to be denied that.'

Alex gave a humourless laugh. 'Better find out what sort of person the father is before you commit Daisy to a relationship,' he advised, his tone suddenly harsh. 'If he's anything like my father, she'd be better off on her own.'

Jenny looked at him, sensing his sudden tension. 'Why? What was your father like?'

His expression was suddenly blank, all evidence of emotion gone. 'I have no intention of discussing him with you. Just because I'm prepared to help you, it doesn't mean I intend to start spilling my guts. Not my style.'

'You prefer to drink and work and lose yourself in blonde women whose names you can't remember,' Jenny shot back, and then bit her lip. 'Sorry.'

To her surprise Alex laughed, some of the tension leaving his broad shoulders. 'Ouch. There you go again, forgetting your manners—but as it happens you're absolutely right. Do you have a problem with that?'

Heart thumping, Jenny tried to look away but her eyes were trapped by the wicked gleam in his.

'I—I just think there are b-better ways of relaxing,' she stammered quickly, and he flashed her a smile that made her realise immediately why women fell into his bed so easily.

'If you think that,' he drawled softly, 'then you've obviously never had really good sex.'

Her face turned a fiery red and she couldn't think of a single suitable retort.

Alex Westerling was used to dealing with sophisticated women and she was anything but sophisticated.

She could just imagine his amusement if he discovered that she'd never even had a proper boyfriend.

She concentrated on feeding Daisy and hoped he'd drop the subject.

He didn't.

'I can't make you out, Jenny Phillips.' He spoke in that lazy, masculine drawl that seemed to connect with her nerve endings. 'Are you really as innocent as you appear? Every time I mention sex you turn the colour of a fire engine.'

Oh, help.

'My sex life is none of your business, Dr Westerling,'

His eyes gleamed. 'Perhaps I'm levelling the playing field. You seem to take a keen interest in my sex life so I don't see why you should escape unscathed.'

'I'm only interested in your relationship with my sister,' Jenny said in a strangled voice, wondering how this conversation had started. She really, *really* didn't want to be talking about sex with Alex Westerling.

It was conjuring up images that she found incredibly disturbing.

Alex smiled. 'All right, Little Red Riding Hood. We'll leave it at that for now, but just remember—if you expect privacy yourself, it pays to afford others the same courtesy.'

Vowing never to ask him anything personal again, Jenny changed the subject hastily. 'Why do you call me Little Red Riding Hood?'

He leaned forward, his blue eyes faintly mocking. 'Because you arrive at Grandma's cottage, knock trustingly on the door, clutching your freshly baked rolls, and don't notice the wolf,' he said softly, and Jenny caught her breath at the look in his eyes.

She'd never met a man with such wicked, laughing eyes. They seemed to tease and seduce at the same time.

'I—I noticed the wolf,' she stammered, her fingers shaking slightly as she held the spoon. 'But I know he would never be interested in me. Or I in him.'

His eyes held hers for a long moment and then slid down, surveying every inch of her before returning to her shocked face. 'Is that right?'

For an endless, breathless moment of aching intensity their eyes held and then Daisy bashed her spoon on the table and Jenny was jerked back to the present.

What was she doing?

And what was *he* doing?

She knew she wasn't his type, and he certainly wasn't hers.

Was he just trying to make her uneasy? If so then he'd definitely succeeded.

Thoroughly flustered by feelings that she couldn't identify, Jenny wiped Daisy's mouth and scooped her out of the high chair.

'About this shopping...'

Alex rose to his feet in a fluid movement and reached for his car keys. 'We'll go as soon as you're ready. I'll put her car seat in my car.'

Refraining from asking how he was going to fit a baby seat in his flashy sports car, Jenny concentrated on Daisy, gathering together a selection of things that they might need for the trip.

Still thoroughly unsettled by the conversation over breakfast, she would have done anything to avoid more close contact with him, but as this was the first real interest he'd shown in Daisy she didn't want to reject his offer.

It would be fine, she told herself firmly as she carried Daisy out to the car.

He hadn't meant anything by his comments.

He'd just been teasing her.

She knew for a fact that she wasn't his type. And he certainly wasn't hers.

She had absolutely nothing to worry about.

Three hours later Alex handed over his credit card with a satisfied smile.

At least now it couldn't be said that Daisy didn't have toys.

'Thank you, Dr Westerling,' the assistant said smoothly, eyeing the enormous bill with the smug satisfaction of someone who received a bonus on sales. 'Will there be anything else?'

Anything else?

Alex flashed him a look of intense irritation and refrained from pointing out that he'd already bought half the shop. He pocketed his credit card and glanced benignly at the object of his largesse.

Daisy was sleeping soundly in her pushchair, oblivious to the fact that she was now the proud owner of several dolls complete with changes of clothes, stuffed toys, rattles, chunky bricks and a baby gym guaranteed to turn every child into a genius.

Alex gathered up the bags, noticing that Jenny was looking at the toys, the floor, the ceiling—in fact, anywhere but at him.

And that was totally his fault, of course.

Ever since that conversation at breakfast when he'd mentioned their sex lives, she'd avoided eye contact.

He gritted his teeth.

He hadn't intended to embarrass her but frankly he didn't know any girls of her age who were embarrassed about sex. They seemed to talk about it quite freely.

But not Jenny, obviously.

Little Red Riding Hood.

He let out a sigh as they strolled back to the car, wondering what he had to do to make her relax with him again. She obviously had him pegged as a real seducer of women. After the way he'd teased her at breakfast she was probably worrying about her virtue.

And she really didn't need to.

As she'd rightly pointed out, she wasn't his type.

He always went for blondes.

Reminding himself of that fact, he took Daisy from her but found himself looking at Jenny, noticing the thickness of her dark lashes and the smoothness of her cheeks.

It didn't matter what her colouring was, he told himself firmly, strapping Daisy into her seat. The main reason that he wasn't interested in her was because she was so obviously different from the sort of women that he usually spent time with.

Jenny didn't do casual sex.

You only had to witness her appalled reaction to his lifestyle to know that.

He shocked her, and Alex didn't tangle with women who were easily shocked.

Keeping his eyes on the road, Alex waited for her to strap herself in and then hit the accelerator.

This whole business was stressing him out and the sooner his lawyers identified Daisy's real father, then the better for all of them.

Jenny was relieved when Monday came.

She was finding it harder and harder to relax around Alex.

Everything about him was aggressively masculine, from the way he always took command of every situation to the way he lay sprawled on one of his sofas, watching cricket on his wide-screen TV or listening to music through headphones.

She'd thought that she wanted Alex to spend more time with Daisy but what she hadn't considered was that spending time with Daisy inevitably meant spending time with him. And being forced into close contact with Alex Westerling for the best part of two whole days had left her feeling decidedly unsettled. Even though she knew he couldn't possibly be interested in her, she couldn't forget his comment about her walking into the wolf's lair.

But at least he'd started to show an interest in Daisy.

The day before, he'd insisted that they all go to the beach and he'd carried the little girl into the sea, dangling her feet in the water until she'd chortled with laughter. Jenny had watched quietly from her position on the sand, a lump in her throat as she'd seen Alex smile indulgently as the little girl had kicked her legs and splashed him.

When she'd nervously cooked dinner he'd reined in the sarcastic comments and merely complimented her on her cooking.

In fact, he'd proved to be such entertaining company over dinner that she'd had to forcibly remind herself that he was the same man who had seduced Chloe and then left her.

All in all the whole weekend had left her feeling increasingly confused and unsettled. Before she'd turned up on his doorstep she'd thought she'd known exactly the sort of man Alex Westerling was. Now she wasn't so sure.

Fortunately she was prevented from dwelling on the situation by the arrival of an ambulance.

'Little boy tried to run in front of a car,' the paramedic told her as he pushed the trolley into the main area of the A and E department. 'Mother managed to grab hold of him but he fell and hit his face on the pavement. He's going to have a nasty black eye.'

Jenny glanced up as a young woman rushed into the department, dragging a toddler behind her and carrying a baby. She looked unbelievably upset and harassed.

'I just can't believe he did that.' She pressed a hand to her chest, her breath coming in gasps. 'One minute I was in the bank cashing a cheque, and the next minute he just grinned at me and dashed out of the door as if it was all a big game. I only just stopped him from going into the road and there was this lorry...'

She closed her eyes tightly and Jenny winced, experiencing the same mental images as the mother.

If she hadn't caught up with the child—

'Try not to think about what might have happened,' Jenny said hastily, taking the woman's arm and guiding her into Resus. 'I'm sure he's going to be fine. I'll just take some details from you and then we'll ask a doctor to see him.'

The woman was battling with tears. 'It's just too much.' She broke off and rubbed a hand over her face. 'He's such a monkey. He's always in trouble and I've been up all night with the baby and you only have to turn your back for a minute and he gets himself into trouble.'

'Some children are like that,' Jenny agreed, her tone sympathetic. She settled the little boy on the trolley and listened while the paramedic gave her the rest of the details.

The mother hurried over to the trolley and hugged the child with her free arm, tears spilling out of her eyes. 'How many times have I told you that you don't run away from Mummy?'

The little boy's face crumpled and he started to sob miserably.

Jenny said a hasty thank you to the paramedic and hurried over to the trolley to try and help.

'OK.' Her voice was calm and steady and she smiled at the toddler. 'What have you been up to, mischief? You've frightened the life out of your mum.'

She filled his details on a card and then checked his obs.

'He hasn't been unwell at all, Mrs Newton? No temperature or anything?'

'Please, call me Helen, and, no, he hasn't been ill.' She frowned slightly. 'Why do you ask?'

'Because when children fall we need to be sure that there isn't something else going on,' Jenny told her. 'Sometimes an ear infection might cause him to lose his balance.'

'He just tripped because he was running away from me,' Helen said tightly, and Jenny nodded.

'And are you're sure he wasn't knocked out?'

Helen shook her head. 'No. He howled immediately so I know he was conscious.'

'OK, well, I need to ask a doctor to check him over,' Jenny told her, scribbling on the notes. She glanced up and noticed that Helen had her eyes closed and was breathing slowly. 'Are you all right?'

Helen gave a wan smile. 'Not really, but I don't suppose anyone is with three children under five and the amount of sleep I get. I'm fine really. Just tired and unfit. I was so breathless after I chased after Jack and it was only a few feet.'

Jenny smiled. 'You can't be that unfit if you're chasing round after these three all day.'

'Well, I am.' Helen hurried over to her little girl who was tugging at one of the cupboards in Resus. 'Stop that, Bella! Come and sit down.' She sighed and cast Jenny an apologetic look. 'Sorry. Controlling them is a nightmare. It's no wonder I get chest pains.'

'Chest pains?' Jenny frowned, but before she could question her further, Alex strolled in, broad-shouldered and a vision of unshakable confidence.

Awareness slammed through her and she looked away quickly, shocked by the intensity of her own reaction.

What had happened to her over the last few days?

Had she lost every bit of common sense?

Despite everything she knew about Alex Westerling, he still made her heart beat faster and her breathing stop.

Which just proved that she was as vulnerable to his lethal charm as every other member of her sex.

Horrified by the realisation that he could affect her so strongly, she stared at him stupidly and he lifted an eyebrow in her direction.

'Tina mentioned that you needed a doctor in here.'

'Yes.' Jenny croaked the word out and waved a hand towards the trolley. 'This is Jack. He fell and hit his head on the kerb. He wasn't knocked out and his GCS is 15.'

Alex strolled over to the trolley and smiled at the little boy. 'Hello, there, Jack. That's a pretty impressive eye you've got there.'

Helen groaned. 'Don't tell him that, he'll do it again.'

Alex grinned. 'He's a boy. He's bound to do it again, only next time it'll probably be someone's fist rather than the pavement.' He turned back to the little boy. 'I just need to have a little feel of your head, is that OK?'

Jenny watched him with grudging admiration. She didn't want him to be a good doctor. She really didn't. But he was.

And he had a nice way with children.

She watched while he examined Jack, chatting easily to him about subjects that she wouldn't have expected him to know about, like Thomas the Tank Engine and Bob the Builder.

Bob the Builder?

What did Alex Westerling know about Bob the Builder?

He reached for an ophthalmoscope and examined Jack's eyes, one large hand steadying the child's head as he altered the angle.

'Well, that looks OK.' He ran his fingers around the bony orbit of the eye, checking that it was intact. Then he turned to Helen. 'I don't think he's done himself serious damage. The bruising should improve gradually. Obviously he had a bang on his head so you'll need to keep an eye on him for twenty-four hours. Any sickness or headache—anything at all you're worried about—bring him back in or call your GP. Jenny will give you a form that explains everything.'

He chatted for a moment longer and then left the room. Jenny reached for a head injury form, watching as Helen walked over to extract her little girl from the cupboard for the second time.

She was wearing shorts and Jenny noticed that her left leg seemed swollen.

Was it her imagination?

She looked closer and decided that it wasn't. Helen's leg was definitely swollen.

'Helen...' She hesitated, unsure how to voice her concerns. 'Your leg seems a little swollen. Is that usual for you?'

Helen dragged the little girl out of the cupboard, her expression harassed. 'No, but the weather's been hot and I'm on my feet all day.'

Jenny chewed her lip. It was possible that the heat was the reason, but still...

'The chest pain you mentioned having when you chased after Jack—have you ever had that before?'

'For the last few days.' Helen scooped the little girl into her arms and walked back towards the trolley, holding the squirming toddler. 'I've had a cough so I presumed it was related to that.'

'What sort of cough?' Alarm bells were ringing in Jenny's head.

'Just a cough.' Helen gave a rueful smile. 'I'm a smoker so that's probably got something to do with it.'

'How many do you smoke?'

'About thirty a day, but don't tell my husband.' Helen gave a tired smile. 'You'd smoke too if you were looking after these three.'

'I'm not judging you, Helen,' Jenny assured her quickly, 'I'm just worried about you. Would you mind if I just take a look at your leg?'

Helen looked startled. 'You want to take a look at me? But it's Jack who's had the accident.'

'I know that, but I'm slightly concerned about the symptoms you're describing.'

Helen looked at her. 'You don't think I'm just run down?'

'Possibly, but I'd like to be sure.' Jenny pulled up a chair. 'Sit down there for a moment.'

Helen sat with the toddler on her lap while Jenny examined the leg.

'Does it hurt if I press here?'

Helen winced. 'Yes.'

'Are you taking the Pill, Helen?'

The woman nodded. 'Yes. Why? What's that got to do with my legs and my cough?'

'Maybe nothing,' Jenny admitted, 'but I'm going to ask a doctor to look at you anyway. I've got one more question. Have you ever coughed up any blood?'

'A bit.' Helen was starting to look alarmed. 'I just assumed it was because I coughed too hard.'

'That was probably it,' Jenny agreed, rising to her feet and making for the door. 'Stay there, Helen. I'll be back in a minute.'

She walked briskly into the department and searched for Alex.

He was checking a set of X-rays for one of the more junior doctors.

'You can see a fracture if you look.' He pushed another film into the light-box. 'You were looking at the wrong view.'

'Alex.' Jenny's tone was urgent and he tilted his dark head in her direction, his eyes still fixed on the X-ray.

'What's the matter?'

'It's Helen. The mother of that little boy you just saw.'

'What about her?'

'I'm worried about her. I think she might have a pulmonary embolus.' The moment the words left her mouth she felt stupid. She wasn't a doctor, for goodness' sake. She shouldn't be going around making diagnoses. She waited for him to laugh or say something cutting, but he didn't.

Instead, he abandoned the X-ray and turned towards her, giving her his full attention. 'What are her symptoms?'

Grateful to him for taking her seriously, she swallowed and brushed a strand of hair out of her eyes. 'She's breathless, she has chest pain and she's coughed up blood. She's got some pitting oedema of her right leg and ankle and some tenderness in her right calf.'

Alex stared at her. 'How the hell did you find all that out? She wasn't even the patient.'

Jenny blushed. 'She happened to mention that she became breathless when she ran after Jack to try and stop him going on the road and I noticed that one leg was swollen. If she hadn't been wearing shorts I don't suppose I'd have noticed. It may be nothing…'

'Doesn't sound like nothing to me. Let me just finish off here and I'll be with you.' Alex yanked the X-ray out of the lightbox and handed it to the other doctor, who was still hovering. 'Send this guy to fracture clinic for a below-knee plaster and refer him to the orthopaedic lot for follow-up.' He turned to Jenny. 'Let's take a look at your patient.'

She hurried to keep up with him as he strode towards Resus. 'She's a smoker—thirty a day—and she's on the Pill.'

He turned to her with a wry smile, pausing with one hand on the door of Resus. 'Is there anything you didn't find out about her?'

Jenny returned the smile tentatively, thinking that he shouldn't be allowed to smile. It made him dangerously attractive. 'I only asked a few questions...'

'But all the right ones,' he observed softly, his blue eyes suddenly intent. 'Come on, let's see if you're suspicions are right.'

He pushed open the door of Resus and walked over to Helen. 'I gather you've not been feeling too great yourself, Mrs Newton.'

Helen was trying to control the wriggling toddler while reading a book to the other child. 'Well, that's true, but I must admit I just thought it was because of these three. They're hardly relaxing.'

'I can imagine.' Alex scooped the little girl into his arms and looked at Jenny. 'Could you nip and get some toys from the paeds area? These little ones have been here long enough and they're bored stiff. Let's give them something to play with other than surgical instruments, shall we?'

Jenny smiled and hurried off to do as he'd suggested, thinking that for a man who didn't want children he was remarkably sensitive to their needs.

She returned with the toys to find Alex examining Helen's leg. 'Does this hurt?'

Helen pulled a face. 'A bit. Nothing dramatic.'

Alex nodded and his eyes flickered to Jenny. 'I want to get a line in.'

Judging from the urgency of his tone, he obviously agreed with her diagnosis and she reacted immediately, reaching for a venflon and a swab.

Alex squatted down next to Helen who was still sitting on the chair, occupying the toddler.

'Helen, I think it's very likely that you've developed a clot in one of the veins in your leg,' he said gently. 'We call it a DVT. Deep-vein thrombosis. I also think that the clot may have moved up to your lungs, which is why you're coughing. I want to run some tests.'

Helen stared at him. 'You mean stay in hospital?'

'For now, yes.' Alex took the tourniquet that Jenny handed him and slid it over Helen's arm. 'I'm going to put a cannula into your vein so that we can take blood and give you drugs if the need arises.'

He swabbed the back of her hand and then selected a vein and slid the venflon in with practised ease.

'OK.' He straightened and tossed the debris onto the trolley. 'I want a chest X-ray, an ECG and an ultrasound of that leg.'

Jenny hurried off to make the necessary arrangements and Alex called the medical team.

'I can't stay in hospital,' Helen fretted, reaching down to pick up a toy that the little girl had dropped. 'I've got three children under the age of five, one of them with a banged head.'

Jenny glanced at Jack who was lying on the trolley, playing quietly with a toy car.

'Is there anyone we can phone?'

Helen sighed and tipped her head back. 'My husband, I suppose, but he won't thank me.'

Alex walked back over to her, his phone call finished. 'Why won't he thank you?'

'He's got a very busy job,' Helen muttered, concentrating on the children. 'He hates being called when he's working.'

Jenny caught Alex's eye and hid her surprise at his obvious disapproval. Somehow she would have expected him to empathise with a businessman who didn't have time for his children, but again it seemed that she'd misjudged him.

'Jenny will call him,' Alex said smoothly. 'She's good at reminding people of their responsibilities.'

Jenny caught the gleam of amusement in his blue eyes and glared at him.

'I'll be happy to call him,' she said, delivering a sweet smile in Alex's direction. 'I'm sure he'll be only too happy to come at once when he knows that you need him.'

Helen didn't look convinced but at that moment a radiographer hurried into the room, along with two ECG technicians.

Alex gave a brisk nod. 'Great. Let's move you up onto a trolley, Helen, next to Jack. Jenny will take the other two for a little walk while we do the X-rays.'

Noticing that little Bella was showing more than a passing interest in the metal drip stand, Jenny nodded her agreement and gently took the baby from Helen.

'I'm not sure if she'll go with you,' Helen fretted, releasing the baby reluctantly. 'She's terrible with people she doesn't know.'

'She'll be fine with Jenny. Jenny's great with babies,' Alex said immediately, signing the form that the radiographer handed him. 'Babies love her.'

Jenny blinked at the unexpected praise and lifted the baby gently against her shoulder.

Fortunately the baby did seem to love her. Or at least it didn't protest at being cuddled by a total stranger.

Assuring Helen that she'd bring the baby back at the first signs of distress, Jenny left Resus and walked down to the paediatric area to find a phone and look for more distractions.

Still holding the baby, she showed Bella a box of toys and watched with satisfaction as she involved herself with a train set.

Then she called Helen's husband, choosing her words carefully so that he understood the seriousness of the situation.

'Who's this?' Tina strolled up to her as she replaced the phone. 'Shall I call you a doctor to take a look at her?'

Jenny shook her head. 'Nothing wrong with the baby,' she said, and quickly explained what had happened.

Tina's eyes widened. 'You spotted that?'

Jenny blushed. 'Well, I was just—'

'Quick off the mark,' a very male voice interjected from behind them, and Jenny turned to find Alex lounging in the doorway.

Her pulse rate doubled. 'How is she?'

'She has a pulmonary embolus and the medical team is looking at her now.'

'Oh, so it was something—' She broke off and he gave a wry smile.

'It was rather more than *something*, Nurse Phillips. If you hadn't noticed her symptoms, she might well have died.'

Unaccountably warmed by his praise, Jenny cuddled the baby closer. 'Well, I'm glad she's all right.'

Alex pulled a face. 'She's worrying herself silly about the children. Did you get hold of the husband?'

Jenny nodded. 'He's coming straight away. He was very worried.'

'Was he, indeed?' Alex laughed. 'Then you obviously did a good job.' He looked at the baby who was snuggled contentedly against her shoulder. 'Perhaps you'd better take the kids back into her. The medical reg is just seeing her now. He's going to admit her for anticoagulation and observation.'

'Right, well, her husband said he'd be here in the next fifteen minutes so at least he'll be able to take the children.'

Jenny walked with Alex back to Resus and found the medical reg making arrangements to transfer Helen to the ward.

Fortunately her husband arrived quickly and was able to help with the children.

Alex let out a long breath as the doors of Resus swung closed behind them. 'Maybe now we can snatch a quick cup of coffee.'

Jenny glanced at her watch and realised that they'd missed both coffee and lunch but before she could comment the doors swung open again and Tina hurried in, followed by a team of paramedics pushing a trolley.

Alex's gaze flickered to Jenny. 'Obviously no coffee,' he drawled, and she gave a smile of mutual understanding as she hurried to help with the man on the trolley.

It was obviously going to be one of those days.

CHAPTER FIVE

JENNY was just returning the casserole to the oven when she heard Alex's key in the door.

Her heart rate increased and she took a deep breath, bracing herself for more confrontation.

She'd hesitated before making dinner but in the end she'd decided to go ahead.

Doubtless he'd make some caustic comment about the fact that she was behaving like a wife, but she hadn't eaten all day and she knew that he hadn't either. It seemed ridiculous not to eat dinner together.

She looked up to see him standing in the doorway to the kitchen.

'Hi.' She knew she sounded nervous and hated herself for it. 'I cooked dinner because I thought you might be hungry but I'm not trying to be wifely and if you'd rather not then—'

'I'm starving.'

'Oh.' She relaxed slightly and gave him a hesitant smile. 'Well, that's good. It will be about half an hour. I've already bathed Daisy and put her to bed.'

'No hurry.' He lifted a lean hand and yanked at his tie. 'I'll be on the deck.'

Drinking, no doubt.

Jenny watched with a frown as he strolled out of the kitchen. She knew for a fact that he'd had a long and stressful day, but still…

On impulse she followed him through to the living room and hesitated, watching as he poured himself a whisky.

His tie had been discarded and his shirt was now unbuttoned at the neck, revealing a hint of tanned skin covered in curling dark hairs.

He was disturbingly attractive and suddenly she felt strange inside.

'You know, there are other ways of relaxing apart from drinking.'

The moment she'd said the words she wished she could retract them but it was too late.

He was still for a moment and then turned slowly to face her. 'Sorry?'

'I—I just think you drink too much,' she stammered, taking a step backwards as she suddenly became the focus of his attention. 'It isn't good for you.'

The atmosphere was suddenly chilly. 'And since when did my drinking habits become any of your business?'

'You're Daisy's father,' she said simply. 'That makes it my business.'

He gritted his teeth. 'I don't need this, Jenny. I've had a long day. If I want to drink, I'll drink.'

'There are better ways of relaxing.'

He lifted an eyebrow mockingly. 'Just what exactly are you suggesting, Red Riding Hood?' he drawled softly, stepping closer to her. 'I just meant that you could take a bath.' She swallowed. 'Or something like that.'

He studied her in amazed silence. 'A *bath*? You think a bath would relax me?'

His eyes glittered dangerously and she wished immediately

that she hadn't suggested the bath. Suddenly her mind was filled with all sorts of disturbing visions of Alex naked.

Ever since she'd seen him in swimming trunks, the image of his body had been imprinted on her mind and the image disturbed her in ways that she couldn't comprehend. She didn't usually notice men in that way. And she didn't want to notice Alex.

'It's what I always do when I've had a bad day,' she said quickly, taking a step backwards. 'I light candles and have a bath...'

His gaze never wavered from hers. 'Do you, now? Come to think of it, I think it sounds like a great idea.' He moved towards her. 'Let's go.'

Her breathing stopped. 'L-let's go?'

'Certainly.' His smile was almost devilish and she felt goosebumps break out on her skin. He was wickedly handsome and it was absolutely impossible to look away from those blue eyes. They seemed to strip away all her defences and leave her emotionally naked before him.

'Dr Westerling—Alex...' Her voice was little more than a croak and his eyes slid down her body with a thoroughness that left her struggling for air.

'I'm more than willing to try your alternative form of relaxation.'

'Y-you're being ridiculous,' she stammered. 'You know I didn't mean that.'

'You propositioned me.'

'I—I didn't.'

'You were the one who suggested the bath,' he said silkily, and she rubbed damp palms down the seams of her jeans, knowing that he was teasing her. He had to be teasing her.

'You know I didn't mean it *that* way.'

He lifted an eyebrow and moved closer still. 'How do I know that?'

Her heart was thumping so fast she felt as though it was

going to burst out of her chest. 'Well, for a start because I'm not your type.'

He shrugged carelessly. 'It's true that generally I prefer blondes, but you'll do fine. You've got a great body.'

She flushed and looked away from him. 'It isn't fair of you to tease me.'

There was a long silence. 'Tease you?' There was a sharp edge to his tone, all traces of mockery gone. 'What makes you think I was teasing you?'

Because she knew she didn't have a good body.

'Look—can we, please, change the subject?' She was squirming with embarrassment and, as usual, he looked totally relaxed.

'No, we can't.' He was frowning now. 'I want to know why you think I'm teasing you.'

She gave a sigh of exasperation. 'Because I'm small and flat-chested and even a push-up bra can't give me a cleavage. I don't have a great body by anyone's standards but that doesn't mean I enjoy being teased about it.'

For a moment he stood still and then she felt his hands slide round her face and he tilted her head until she was forced to look at him.

'I wasn't teasing you. You have a great body,' he said quietly. 'Incredibly delicate and feminine. The only problem is in your head. Someone has obviously made you feel unattractive. Are you going to tell me who?'

She pulled away from him, totally flustered. He thought she had a great body? *Alex Westerling thought she had a great body?* No one had ever paid her a compliment before and she didn't know how to react. Especially when it came from a man she was supposed to despise.

'Please—let's just forget it.'

There was another silence and then he smiled, the mockery back.

'I thought you wanted me to scrub your back in the bath.'

'That wasn't what I was suggesting, and you know it,' she

muttered, wishing that she was immune to him. She wanted to be. Oh, she really, really wanted to be, but it seemed that she was as susceptible to that killer smile as the rest of the female population.

He folded his arms across his broad chest and smiled. 'You could teach me how to relax.'

She was thoroughly flustered and he knew it. 'I didn't mean—'

He gave a soft laugh. 'Then take some advice. Don't play with fire, Jenny. And don't try and reform me.'

With that he drained his drink, his eyes never leaving hers, challenging her to comment.

She didn't.

She was too busy trying to work out why Alex had such a powerful effect on her. He was everything she avoided in a man.

But just being in the same room as him had an alarming effect on her pulse rate and she was achingly aware of his powerful physique and his overwhelming masculinity.

'I'd better check on Daisy,' she croaked finally, desperate to get away from him.

'Coward.' His soft laugh followed her as she hurried up the stairs and sought refuge in Daisy's bedroom.

She curled her fingers round the cot rail and closed her eyes briefly. She didn't know how to cope with his banter. She wasn't any good at clever retorts and she was hopeless at flirting. That had been Chloe's forte. Aware that she couldn't lurk in Daisy's room for ever, she slid into the bathroom, tidied her hair and then went back down to the kitchen to finish off the dinner.

'I shouldn't tease you. I'm sorry.' Alex's voice came from behind her and she turned, startled.

'That's all right.'

'No, it isn't all right.' He gave a wry smile. 'The truth is, I'm not used to women like you, Jenny Phillips. You don't flirt—in fact, you don't play any of the games that women usually play.

I know that I shock you and some wicked part of me seems to need to see how far I can go before you slap my face.'

'You're pretty safe.' She gave a hesitant smile. 'I hate violence.'

He laughed. 'I bet you do. You're the most placid person I've ever met. Do you ever lose your temper?'

'It isn't one of my vices.'

'You have vices?' He shot her a disbelieving look and she smiled.

'Of course I do.'

'All right, name one.' He sounded thoroughly sceptical and she lifted the casserole out of the oven and placed it on the table.

'Chocolate.'

Alex groaned. 'Not another one. What is it with women and chocolate? My sister Libby can't live without chocolate. Chocolate and shoes.'

'She sounds nice.' Jenny put the plates on the table. 'Is she the one with the children?' She blushed and bit her lip. 'Sorry, I know you said you don't want to talk about your family...'

Alex shrugged. 'That was when we were strangers.' He sat down at the table and reached for some bread. 'We're not exactly strangers any more, are we?'

Jenny served the casserole, wondering what was happening to her emotions.

She'd arrived here full of anger and hatred for the man and somehow here they were, eating dinner in a relatively amicable fashion.

But if she was ever going to persuade him to take an interest in Daisy then they had to be amicable, she reasoned, handing him a plate and pushing a bowl of freshly cooked vegetables towards him.

'Libby has two little girls of four and two, and my other sister Katy has five-year-old twins—a boy and a girl. Multiple births run in the family, it seems.' Alex spooned some vegetables onto his plate. 'We're triplets but I expect you already know that if you read the papers. My sisters used to feature regularly until they married. Then the press seemed to lose interest.'

'And now it's all concentrated on you?'

'Something like that.' He forked up a piece of meat and gave a wry smile. 'Apparently I'm an object of fascination until I get married.'

'An eligible bachelor,' Jenny observed, pouring herself a glass of water.

'Water?' Alex mocked her gently, a smile playing around his firm mouth as he reached for the wine he'd uncorked. 'Don't you ever drink anything stronger than water?'

She smiled. 'Of course. But, to be honest, since Daisy was born I'm too exhausted to risk drinking. She wakes up quite often in the night and I need all the sleep I can get.'

He frowned slightly. 'It must have been very hard for you.' His voice was gruff. 'Tell me about Chloe.'

She stiffened slightly. 'Why do you want to know about Chloe?'

'Well, for a start because I'm being accused of corrupting her,' Alex said dryly. 'I think I at least deserve to know something about her.'

'I don't really think that you corrupted her. I do realise that it takes two…' Jenny pushed the food around her plate and then put her fork down. 'Chloe was very beautiful.'

'Describe her.'

Jenny hesitated. 'She was the sort of girl that made men do stupid things.' She gave an embarrassed smile. 'Long blonde hair like a mermaid, a figure with more curves than a country road.'

'Was she the reason you don't think you're attractive?'

Jenny looked at him warily. She'd never had this conversation with anyone before. And here she was having it with a man that she was supposed to loathe.

But the truth was she didn't loathe him, and he was an amazingly good listener.

'She was so beautiful that it was hardly surprising that men didn't pay me much attention when she was around,' she said lightly, picking up her water and taking a sip. 'It really didn't bother me. I loved her.'

'What was she like? Gentle, like you?'

Alex asked the question in the most direct fashion and she bit her lip.

'Chloe had a very difficult life. When Mum died she was only twelve, and Dad did everything he could to make it up to her. I think perhaps he overcompensated slightly.'

'You mean she was spoiled.'

'No!' Jenny denied it quickly and then bit her lip. 'Well, maybe, just a little, but it wasn't her fault. She was so young when Mum died.'

Alex frowned. 'You were young too, but he obviously didn't spoil you.'

'It was different for me.'

'Why?'

Jenny hesitated. 'Chloe was already quite…troubled.'

'Troubled?'

'A bit wild. Mixing with the wrong set. It started after Mum died. Dad tried his best but he couldn't really control her and his heart wasn't in it. He missed Mum too much. He died two years after she did.'

Alex pulled a face. 'You poor thing.'

'I was eighteen and already training to be a nurse but Chloe was living at home and she was hit really badly by it.' Jenny bit her lip. 'I switched hospitals so that I could live at home with her but I just couldn't get through to her. She stopped studying, fell in with a crowd who did nothing but party and after that—'

She broke off and he waited, his eyes on her face. 'After that, what?'

'She just seemed to go off the rails,' Jenny mumbled. 'I never knew where she was or who she was with. Sometimes she'd stay out all night without phoning. I'd wait up, worried sick. There were some nights when I didn't go to bed at all.'

'But you weren't her mother.'

Jenny gave a sad smile. 'That's exactly what Chloe said. After our parents died I did my best to keep everything to-gether but I was pretty useless.' Her voice cracked slightly and she cleared her throat. 'Anyway, you don't want to hear all this.'

'I do want to hear it,' he said softly. 'It involves me, too, re-member?'

It was the nearest he'd come to admitting that he'd had a re-lationship with her sister.

Jenny put her fork down. 'Eventually Chloe got fed up with me.' She gave him a brave smile. 'She said I was always breath-ing down her neck and I suppose I was. So she moved out of the house and lived with a group of friends. I hardly ever saw her after that. Every time I went round there she always seemed to be out and she never rang. It was purely by chance that I found out that she was pregnant.'

He gave a wry smile. 'And knowing you, I'm sure you were horrified.'

'Of course!' Jenny shot him an appalled look. 'She was only nineteen and really young for her age. And I know she was frightened, although she'd never admit it.'

'Did she tell you anything about the father?'

Jenny hesitated. 'All she'd say at first was that it was some-one famous. She boasted that she was going to—' She broke off and closed her eyes briefly. She felt uncomfortable repeat-ing her sister's words. 'Well, she said that she was going to—'

'Fleece him for money,' Alex finished, reaching for his glass. 'Don't be embarrassed to say it. When you have money there's always someone chasing after it. It's a fact of life.'

Jenny looked him in the eye. 'But that isn't why I'm here. Whatever Chloe had in mind, I'm not interested in your money.'

Suddenly it seemed really important that she convince him.

He looked at her thoughtfully. 'Strangely enough, I believe you. Anyway, carry on with the story.'

'Well, that's it really.' Jenny let out a breath. 'I tried to stay in touch but she avoided me as much as possible. I didn't even know she'd had the baby until the hospital rang to say she was very ill. Obviously she'd given me as next of kin. I dashed there as fast as I could. It was a nightmare.'

'And that's when she named me.' Alex leaned back in his chair, his face expressionless.

'Yes.'

'So why didn't you come and find me straight away?'

Jenny licked her lips. 'I was totally shattered by her death. I blamed myself for months. You know what it's like when someone dies—there's always guilt. And for me the guilt was that I'd allowed her to go through her pregnancy without me.'

Alex frowned. 'But she cut you out.'

'I know, but grief isn't rational,' Jenny muttered, taking a sip of her water. 'I felt I should have been there anyway, and as for coming to find you...' She broke off and he lifted an eyebrow.

'What?'

'I was angry with you,' she said simply. 'I thought you'd seduced her and abandoned her. Every paper I opened seemed to have a picture of you with a different girl in it.'

'Lots of those pictures are perfectly innocent,' Alex pointed out mildly, 'but the general public seem to be inordinately interested in my love life so the press print anything they can lay their hands on. It sells papers.'

Jenny nodded slowly. Now that the anger had died slightly she was beginning to see just how badly the man was hounded by the press. 'How come they don't come to your house?'

He gave a wicked grin. 'Because I actually have a different address that I use from time to time just to distract them.'

'Oh. That's clever.' She smiled. 'Well, anyway, I struggled by myself for a while but our quality of life was non-existent because the rent was so high in London.'

Alex pulled a face. 'And you were just on a nurse's salary?'

Jenny smiled. 'It wasn't that bad, but I decided that I was short-changing Daisy. She only had me and she deserved more than that. So I decided to find you.'

Alex looked at her in silence and then shifted in his chair. 'I'm almost sure she isn't mine,' he said gruffly, 'but either way I'll help you.'

Jenny looked at him warily. 'Why would you do that if she isn't yours?'

'Because I'm a sucker for a woman in trouble,' he said lightly, draining his wineglass and placing it carefully back on the table. 'And you, Jenny Phillips, are most definitely a woman in trouble.'

Her eyes meshed with his and something in the way he looked at her made her stomach turn over. She tried to look away but she found herself trapped by the look in his blue eyes.

She might have gazed at him for ever if Daisy's cry hadn't broken the connection.

Startled out of a forbidden daydream that shocked her, she was on her feet in an instant, knocking over the chair in her haste to get away from him. 'I'd better check if she's OK,' she mumbled unsteadily, and he gave a soft laugh.

'Saved by the baby,' he drawled, and although she was careful not to look at him, she knew that he was still looking at *her*. She *felt* it. 'Better run, Little Red Riding Hood, before the wolf gets you.'

She knew he was teasing her and her eyes flew to his, expecting to see laughter there, but for once his expression was deadly serious and she swallowed hard before she backed out of the room.

Oh, help.

What exactly had happened back there?

What had she been thinking?

Appalled by the strength of her reaction to a man she supposedly disapproved of, she lifted Daisy with shaking hands and wondered whether perhaps it was time she looked for a small flat for herself and Daisy.

Living with Alex was proving to be more unsettling than she could possibly have imagined.

Work continued to be horribly busy and things weren't helped by a flu bug that seemed to hit half the staff in the hospital.

'This can't be happening. It's the middle of summer,' Tina grumbled as she tried to allocate the staff for the morning shift. 'We shouldn't have flu. I've got two nurses off and the agency is so stretched it can't provide any cover.'

Jenny wasn't in a position to offer to work extra shifts because she had to be at home with Daisy, but she knew that some of the nurses were putting in a vast amount of overtime. And so were the doctors.

Alex was working punishing hours and for the next four days he was hardly at home.

She was forced to concede that her first opinion of him had been horribly skewed by the reports she'd read in the press.

It might be true that he avoided commitment like a life-threatening disease, but it was also true that he was an amazingly skilled and dedicated doctor, something the newspapers always failed to comment on.

Even when one of the consultants was on duty, it was still Alex who was called upon to deal with the really difficult cases. And there was no shortage of difficult cases.

As if to confirm that observation, the ambulance hotline rang, disturbing her thoughts, and Tina rushed to pick it up.

As she replaced the phone, Jenny looked at her expectantly. 'Well?'

'Thirty-four-year-old woman, thirty-one weeks pregnant coming in.' Tina was already hurrying towards Resus. 'She was found at the bottom of the stairs. Give Alex a yell, will you? I'll bleep the obstetric team.'

By the time Jenny had located Alex, the ambulance had arrived.

'Her pulse has been very rapid and I can't find a blood pressure at all,' the paramedic muttered as they quickly transferred her to the trolley. He gave a quick handover to Alex, outlining the patient's physical state.

'Give her high-flow oxygen and I want her tilted to the side. Use a pillow or a wedge, but I don't want her lying flat because the weight of the baby will press on her major blood vessels.' Alex talked as he worked, checking the airway and feeling for a pulse again. 'Get her attached to a monitor and I want two lines in—one in either arm. Everyone remember we're dealing with two patients here. Move!'

The whole team was aware of the seriousness of the situation and they worked fast to stabilise the woman but her condition deteriorated.

Alex talked clearly and calmly to the patient, even though there was no evidence that she was even aware of them. 'You're going to be fine, Jilly. You're in hospital now and we're going to sort out this problem and make sure that your baby is OK.' He glanced at one of the other doctors. 'Take blood for group and cross-match, urea and electrolytes, and then give her some Haemaccel. She's bleeding from somewhere and we need to start replacing fluid. Get the rest of her clothes off so that we can assess her properly and call the radiographers so that we can do some X-rays.'

Jenny glanced at him. 'What about the baby?'

His eyes lifted to hers and she read the tension there. 'We'll keep the abdominal and pelvic X-rays to a minimum and she can wear lead abdominal shields for the rest. Not ideal, I know, but I have to find out what's going on. 'Where the hell is the obs team? Did you call them, Tina?'

'They were in Theatre but they're coming as fast as they can.'

'Well, it's not fast enough,' Alex growled. 'Phone the ward and get a midwife down here with a CTG machine. I want the baby monitored. And someone get a Caesarean section pack ready. Just in case.'

Jenny exchanged stunned glances with Tina. Was he really contemplating doing a Caesarean section in A and E?

Despite the tension, everyone worked quickly and calmly and Alex was examining the first set of X-rays when the special registrar sucked in a breath.

'She's arrested,' he said, and Alex was back by her side in an instant.

'I need to intubate her.'

Jenny calmly handed him the laryngoscope and adjusted the light above his head.

'ET tube,' he snapped, but it was in his hand before he'd finished his brief order and Jenny found herself holding her breath as he attempted to intubate the patient.

She knew that inserting a tube into a patient's lungs was even harder when she was pregnant but fortunately Alex completed the procedure with no apparent difficulty and proceeded to ventilate the patient while the SR performed cardiac massage.

'Tom…' He turned to the SHO who'd inserted both the lines. 'I need you to take over here.'

The more junior doctor did as he was instructed and Alex strode over to the sink and started scrubbing. 'Open that Caesarean section pack and someone bleep the obstetricians again.'

Tina gaped at him. 'You're doing a Caesarean in here?'

'The baby is now in a hypoxic environment,' Alex reminded her roughly, lifting his forearms so that the soapy water ran down into the sink. 'We need to get it out of there if there's to be any hope that it'll survive. And getting the baby out will take the pressure off her inferior vena cava and improve the mother's blood supply so it might help her as well. Is anyone with her?'

Tina nodded. 'Her partner's in the relatives' room. He's really worried.'

'With good reason.' Alex's mouth was set in a grim line and he glanced up as one of the A and E consultants walked in. 'Mark! I need to do an emergency section—can you go and talk to the husband?'

They had a brief conversation, during which Alex slipped his arms into the gown that Jenny had carefully opened and snapped on a pair of sterile gloves.

In the meantime, one of the midwives from the obstetric unit had appeared and scrubbed up, ready to assist.

'Whatever you do, don't stop CPR,' Alex ordered, nodding with relief as the anaesthetist hurried into the room. 'Great. You can take over at the head end. Hurry up. I want to start. What's the foetal heart rate?'

The midwife checked. '105.'

'We need to get that baby out fast.' Alex cleaned the skin while the scrub nurse laid drapes over the woman. 'I'm starting.'

The anaesthetist nodded to indicate that he was ready and Alex picked up the scalpel and made an incision, his movements sure and confident.

Jenny watched in stunned amazement as he cut through layers of skin and muscle with such speed that she could barely keep up with what was happening.

In no time at all he was lifting the baby out, holding it head down and below the level of the mother's abdomen.

Somewhere in the course of the drama the paediatric and obstetric teams had arrived but seeing Alex confidently performing the emergency operation no one had interfered.

But now the baby had been delivered, they moved into action, taking the infant so that Alex could clamp and cut the cord.

The paediatricians took the baby away for assessment and Alex turned his attention back to the mother.

The atmosphere was tense and Jenny held her breath as she watched Alex work.

Would he be able to save the woman or would this be another little baby that ended up losing its mother?

Visions of Chloe, blonde-haired and laughing, flashed into her head and she swallowed down a lump in her throat.

Chloe shouldn't have died. She'd been so young.

Life was so unfair.

Oblivious to her distress, Alex was still concentrating on the mother. 'Here's the problem,' he said finally, gently removing the placenta from the uterus. 'Her placenta has started to come away. We need to give her some blood.'

'The lab just called with her results,' Jenny told him quickly, pushing aside the painful memories, 'so we've ordered some blood from the blood bank. It should be here any minute.'

'Right.' Alex glanced towards Hugo, the obstetric consultant. 'Over to you to close, if you don't mind. I want to try and sort the rest of her out.'

Hugo gave a wry smile. 'That was a pretty impressive section. I used to think I was fast until I saw that. Remind me never to travel in a car with you, if that's the speed you do everything.'

Alex smiled but he was already ripping off his gloves and turning his attention back to the patient, his eyes flickering to the monitors that gave him vital clues as to her condition.

There was a sudden wail from the corner of the room and Jenny gave a silent prayer of thanks.

The baby was crying.

Alex glanced up sharply. 'Is he OK?'

The paediatrician nodded. 'Seems to be. Bit on the small side, of course. Probably going to need a bit of help with his breathing but he's pretty good on the whole.'

Hugo glanced up from closing the uterus. 'Good job, Westerling. A few more minutes and that baby would have been dead. For a wealthy playboy you don't do half badly.'

But underneath the humour there was respect in his tone and Jenny bit her lip, realising that Alex had saved the baby's life.

But Alex wasn't listening to the praise being heaped on his head, he was concentrating on the mother, refusing to give up. Having saved the baby, he was obviously equally determined to save the mother.

'She's in sinus rhythm.' The anaesthetist glanced at Alex in amazement. He grinned like a little boy.

'Good work.'

Only when he was totally satisfied that the woman was stable did Alex sanction Jilly's transfer to the intensive care unit.

Mark strolled back into the room just as everyone was preparing for the transfer.

'She's doing all right?' There was no hiding the surprise in his voice and Alex gave a brief nod.

'For now. But we'll have to see how she goes.'

Mark looked stunned. 'And the baby?'

'The baby is on special care,' Tina told him, reaching up to hug Alex. 'And you are a clever man.'

'God's gift to women, that's me,' Alex drawled lightly, gently disengaging himself, 'especially pregnant ones.'

'Will you talk to her husband?'

Alex gave a nod. 'I'll do it now. We have no idea how she'll do in the long term, of course, but I'll discuss it with him.'

Jenny looked at him. 'Do you want me to come?'

'Yes.' He gave a nod and led the way out of the room. 'You're better at the emotional stuff than me. Are you OK? You look a bit pale.' His blue gaze was disturbingly acute. 'Were you thinking about Chloe?'

For a man who didn't think he was good at emotional stuff, he was amazingly intuitive. 'Yes.' She gave him a brave smile. 'Life's hard, isn't it?'

Alex nodded and lifted a hand to squeeze her shoulder. 'I'm sorry about your sister.'

Jenny swallowed, feeling his strength through the thin fabric of her uniform. 'Thanks. Oh, and by the way, I think you're fine with the emotional stuff,' she said softly, remembering just how hard he'd worked to save the mother and the baby. There hadn't been a man who didn't care. 'Except when it's about you.'

He paused outside the door, a wry smile playing around his firm mouth. 'More psychology? Don't push your luck, Red

Riding Hood.' His masculine voice was silky smooth and she caught her breath.

'You always keep yourself at a distance.'

His smile widened and he flipped her cheek casually with one lean finger. 'I can assure you that I don't.'

She coloured. 'I meant emotionally. And you're teasing me again.'

'I know.' His blue eyes glittered. 'But teasing you is such fun. It's fast becoming my favourite pastime.'

Without giving her a chance to answer, he pushed open the door and held it open so that she could walk through.

Later that evening they relaxed on the deck, eating a light supper while they enjoyed a spectacular sunset.

'Had you done one before?' Jenny couldn't forget the dramatic events of the day.

'Had I done what before?' Alex yawned and twisted some pasta around his fork.

'A Caesarean section.' Jenny wasn't really eating. She was still too wound up. 'You had that baby out in minutes.'

Alex shrugged. 'It was an emergency and, yes, to answer your question, I had done one before. Several, in fact.'

She looked at him curiously. 'You did obstetrics?'

'For a year. Why?'

'Because you just don't seem like the type of guy who'd enjoy it. All that emotion and children and you don't even like—' She broke off and he let out a long breath.

'I like children, Jenny,' he said quietly. 'I just don't want any of my own because I know I'd make a lousy father. And in a way you're right. Obstetrics didn't suit me. I did it because for a while I considered doing a GP rotation, but then I discovered that I missed A and E so I went back to that. But obviously I learned some skills along the way.'

'Like how to do the fastest section on record.'

Alex shrugged. 'Well, speed isn't always the most important

factor, of course. For a routine section it's better to take more time, but in Jilly's case it was literally a matter of life or death so you take your chances and go with speed.'

'A sort of Ferrari version of a Caesarean section.' Jenny laughed and he smiled back, his eyes glittering dangerously.

'And just what do you know about Ferraris, Little Red Riding Hood?'

'Only that they're fast.' Her smile faded. 'Do you think they'll both be all right?'

Alex shrugged and pushed his plate away. 'Who knows? We did our best. Now we have to wait and see. The baby's still small but he should be OK.'

Jenny stared at him, blushing slightly. 'You were amazing.'

He lifted an eyebrow mockingly. 'I thought I was a rich playboy with wicked habits?'

Her blush deepened. 'You do have wicked habits but you were still amazing. You're a good doctor. And I don't think you'd make a lousy father at all. I think you'd be a very good father.'

He leaned back in his chair, his face inscrutable. 'That's not true.'

'Who has made you think otherwise?' It was almost an exact replica of the conversation they'd had about her appearance and his wry smile told her that he was aware of it.

'Trying to get smart, Red Riding Hood?'

'I just think the problem is in your head,' she said daringly, reminding him of his words to her, and he leaned forward, his gaze locked on hers.

'The problem,' he said slowly, 'is that I like my selfish, bachelor existence.'

'But you'd still make a good father.'

And with that she stood up quickly and picked up the plates, hurrying out of the room before he could reply.

CHAPTER SIX

TWENTY-FOUR hours after giving birth Jilly was well enough to be transferred to the maternity ward and everyone was hailing her recovery as a miracle.

'Which is a load of nonsense,' Tina said briskly as they prepared for another busy day. 'The only miracle around here was Alex Westerling.'

Jenny had to agree. 'I'll never forget how quickly he delivered that baby. I didn't even know he knew about babies.'

'Alex knows about everything,' Tina said dryly. 'He's a fantastic doctor but the press usually ignore that side of him. And he keeps it very quiet.'

And indeed Alex seemed almost embarrassed by all the fuss. When his skills weren't needed in Resus he spent most of the day in his office, wrestling with a report on staffing.

It was towards the end of the day that Jenny noticed that he didn't seem his usual self.

He looked flushed and there were lines of tiredness around his blue eyes.

She handed him some X-rays to check, her expression concerned. 'Are you all right?'

He stared at the X-ray. 'I'm fine.'

He didn't look fine.

He looked terrible and Jenny wondered whether he'd caught the flu bug that was going round.

Hopefully not, because without Alex she had a distinct feeling that the department would fall apart. He gave a great deal of himself to the hospital.

One look at him when they arrived home told her that she was right.

'I think you'd better go straight to bed,' she said gently, and he shot her a mocking glance that showed he'd lost none of his faculties.

'Propositioning me again, Miss Phillips?'

She gave him a placid smile. 'You're too ill to be a threat to my virtue, Dr Westerling.'

'Don't count on it, Red Riding Hood,' he said, but his voice rasped and his cheeks were flushed.

'Do you want supper?'

He shook his head and frowned slightly, lifting a hand to his head as if he were suddenly dizzy.

'No.' His jaw hardened and she sensed that for a man as strong and in control as Alex, being ill must be incredibly hard to cope with. 'I'm fine.'

She wished he'd stop saying that when he was clearly anything but fine!

She watched him drag himself up the stairs towards his room and let out a sigh. He most certainly was not fine but it was obvious that he wasn't going to reveal anything remotely like weakness to her.

Resolving to check on him later, she walked into the kitchen, made herself a salad and then curled up on one of his sofas with a book.

It was wonderfully peaceful after the hectic pace of the day and she was soon absorbed by the story, pausing only to sip the coffee she'd made herself.

She read until her eyelids started to ache and then closed the book and made her way to bed, checking on Daisy on the way. The baby was fast asleep, curled up in a ball on her tummy.

Jenny used the bathroom, changed into the T-shirt she wore to bed and went to check on Alex.

He was probably fast asleep, but still…

She padded along the landing and gently pushed open his bedroom door, frowning as she saw him sprawled over the bed, still fully clothed.

He was flushed and restless and she could see immediately that he had a high temperature.

Suddenly anxious, she hurried across to him and touched his forehead.

He was burning hot and he definitely shouldn't be wearing all those clothes.

'Alex…' She spoke gently but there was no response and she bit her lip.

She needed to get him undressed and into bed where at least he'd be more comfortable.

Deciding to start from the bottom and work upwards, she removed his shoes and then moved upwards to the button on his trousers. Her fingers shook slightly as she undid the button and slid his zip down.

Now all she had to do was remove his trousers.

Hoping desperately that he wouldn't wake up while she was doing it, she pulled the trousers gently over his hips, tugging harder as the fabric became stuck.

He gave a groan and his eyes flew open, his feverish gaze burning into hers.

'What are you doing?' His words slurred together and he moaned in protest as she finally removed his trousers and tried to shift him into the bed.

She hoped he didn't realise what she was doing. She could just imagine his comments if he woke up properly and realised that she was removing his trousers.

'You've fallen asleep with your clothes on. You need to get into bed, Alex.'

She tried to move him again but he was over six feet of powerfully built male and she didn't stand a chance of shifting him without some help.

'Alex—' she tried again '—can you move a bit—?'

He grunted and his eyes drifted shut again but he moved further onto the bed and she was able to yank the duvet out from under him and settle him against the pillows.

Having undressed him down to his pair of black silk boxer shorts, she decided that enough was enough and went back onto the landing to find a fresh sheet. The last thing he needed was a duvet.

She tucked the sheet around him, checked his temperature again and then went back to her own room, carefully leaving the door open so that she could hear him if he needed her.

Alex was ill for three days, his temperature so high that Jenny called the doctor twice because she was so worried.

The doctor told her impatiently that it was just flu and that all she could do was make him as comfortable as possible. So she did that, even though he hardly seemed to know that she was there.

He was so hot that twice she changed the sheets, struggling to shift his powerful body enough to enable her to remake the bed.

It was fortunate that she had four days off and that Daisy was relatively content just to play in the upstairs rooms. In the end Jenny gave up on her own room and camped out in Alex's bedroom, nursing him night and day, wishing desperately that he'd get better.

The doctor had assured her that his temperature would come down but there was no sign of it and she sponged him regularly, trying to make him more comfortable even though he didn't even seem to know she was there.

The nights were the worst, sitting there, trying to calm him down as he shivered and muttered incomprehensibly under his breath, totally unaware of her presence.

On the evening of the third day she was so worried about him that she curled up at the bottom of his bed so that she could doze but still be aware of any change in him. She'd already resolved to call the doctor again in the morning if there was no change. She didn't care how irritated he was with her. She wanted him to check Alex again. She was due back at work but there was no way she could go. Alex needed her.

'Jenny—Jen…' His hoarse voice woke her and she propped herself up on her elbows, muzzy-headed from sleep.

It was the first time he'd said her name since he'd become ill and she let out a sigh of relief.

He was better. He must be better.

She'd left a small light turned on so that she could see him in the night, and without thinking she crawled up the bed and touched her face to his cheek, noting that it was cooler.

'Oh, thank goodness.' She sank back on her heels, her slim shoulders sagging with relief. 'You had me worried for a while there.'

Very worried.

'I feel terrible.' His jaw was darkened with three days' worth of stubble and his hair was tousled but somehow he still managed to look dangerously handsome.

It occurred to her that for the past three days she hadn't thought of him as a man but as someone who needed nursing.

Now that the worst had passed she realised with appalling clarity that he was very much a man and she was kneeling on his bed in front of him, wearing nothing more than a skimpy T-shirt that only just covered her bottom.

Hopefully he wouldn't be able to see much in the dimly lit bedroom.

'Of course you feel terrible. You've been really, really ill.' She tried to slide away from him, scarlet with mortification, but long fingers curled around her wrist, preventing her escape.

'Don't go.' His voice was scratchy and she glanced at him, feeling hideously self-conscious.

She was half-naked, for goodness' sake!

'I'll just get some clothes on and I'll be back.' She tugged at her wrist again but his grip merely tightened.

'You didn't seem to care about what you were wearing when you thought I was asleep,' he pointed out, and she flushed.

'Well, of course I didn't. I was worried about you. You've been very ill.'

His gaze was curiously intent. 'And you looked after me.' His dark brows came together as he obviously searched his mind for some memory of the past few days. 'What the hell happened?'

He sounded so much like the old Alex that she smiled with relief, forgetting for a moment that she was still kneeling on the bed with his long fingers clamped round her wrist.

'You caught flu, that's what happened. And you caught it badly. I've had the doctor out twice. Your doctor hates me, by the way,'

He looked at her blankly. 'The doctor?'

'That's right,' she said lightly. 'One of those creatures who think they know everything.'

His eyes narrowed as he studied her closely. 'You don't look too great yourself.'

'Thank you.'

'I mean you look exhausted. You've got dark circles under your eyes. Did I keep you awake?'

For three whole days and nights.

'Just a bit,' she hedged, wishing that he'd stop looking at her. Being the focus of his attention was decidedly unsettling, 'But now you're better I'll go back to my room.'

'Not yet.' He showed no signs of releasing her and she chewed her lip, horribly conscious of the short T-shirt. It only just reached the tops of her thighs. 'Was I a terrible patient?'

She shook her head. 'Surprisingly not.' She gave a wry smile. 'You're easier to handle asleep than awake.'

Despite the fact that he was obviously still feeling rough, his eyes gleamed. 'Is that so?'

She was suddenly achingly aware of the breadth of his shoulders, of the nest of dark hair on his chest and the fact that he was wearing virtually nothing. She knew that for sure. After all, she'd been the one who'd undressed him.

She was desperate to escape from the room and dress in something more appropriate. 'Would you like a drink or something to eat?'

He shook his head. 'What I do need is a visit to the bathroom.' He grimaced and shifted in the bed, 'How have I been managing that?'

She flushed scarlet and tugged her wrist away from his grip. 'I've been helping you.'

'Have you now?' He gave a humourless laugh. 'It's a good job you're not romantically attached to me, isn't it? I'm sure helping me to the bathroom would have killed any relationship stone dead.'

'That's because you associate relationships with sex and not caring,' she said quietly, and he cast her an odd look.

'Do I?'

'Yes. You only do the physical stuff, not the emotional stuff. But we're not going to talk about your deficiencies in that area now. Do you want to use the bathroom or not?'

For a moment he appeared to be speechless and then he coughed and winced slightly. 'I'll give it a try on my own.'

She couldn't resist teasing him. 'You don't need to be shy. I'm fairly well acquainted with your body, having sponged it with tepid water for the past three days.'

'So why are you dying to escape?' he drawled, and her smile faded. Even in his weakened state he was devastatingly attractive.

'Because the wolf has woken up,' she muttered, backing towards the door, wishing that she hadn't teased him. Teasing

Alex was playing with fire. Even when he was ill he was lethally attractive and mentally alert.

He stood up and immediately staggered. She was back by his side in an instant, concern for him overwhelming any shyness that she felt. She took his arm so that he could lean on her.

'You're not well enough to be out of bed without help,' she scolded, helping him towards the bathroom, trying not to notice as he slid an arm round her shoulders.

He was just using her for support, she reminded herself firmly, escorting him as far as the bathroom.

'There we are—you can manage this bit by yourself. I'll go and get you a drink. I'll be back in a minute.'

When she'd had time to dress in something more appropriate and remind herself that Alex Westerling was absolutely not her type.

Alex lay in bed watching as Jenny straightened the sheets and replenished his drink. She was a born nurturer, he reflected. A woman who was never happier than when she was taking care of people. You only had to look at the way that she cared for Daisy to see that. And the child wasn't even hers.

And now he was on the receiving end of that warmth and it felt good. Better than he ever would have imagined.

He couldn't remember ever being cared for like this before, not even as a child.

Her hands were unbelievably gentle, her voice warm and soothing, and just having her there made him feel a hundred times better.

She was peaceful and soothing and calmed the atmosphere more effectively than the scented candles she'd insisted on placing in his room.

She'd dragged on a dressing-gown that covered her from neck to ankle but she may as well not have bothered. He had a very vivid memory of a pair of sensational long legs that had been the first thing he'd seen when he'd opened his eyes.

He'd pretended not to notice because she'd clearly been embarrassed by her lack of attire, but he was incredibly touched by the fact that she'd been sleeping at the bottom of his bed. She must have been seriously worried about him.

And she obviously hadn't had much sleep herself. She looked done in.

'How the hell did you cope, looking after Daisy as well as me?'

She smiled. 'You were much more demanding than Daisy. She's a very easy baby. I put her on the mat on the floor and she played happily. At night she slept.'

But Jenny had been awake all night looking after him. And then all day looking after Daisy. No wonder she looked so exhausted.

The fact that she'd made such a sacrifice for someone she disapproved of as thoroughly as him made him feel vaguely uncomfortable.

He shifted slightly in the bed but the feeling remained and he realised that it wasn't physical.

She placed a hand on his forehead and frowned anxiously. 'How are you feeling now?'

'Pretty weak.'

It was true, but he also knew that in normal circumstances he would have died rather than admit weakness to a woman. But he'd discovered that there was no nicer feeling than being cared for by Jenny. And he liked the fact that she no longer seemed so wary of him.

Not that he could have done anything remotely shock-inducing if he'd wanted to, he reflected wryly. He was too weak to pounce on anyone, even someone as slightly built as Jenny.

Alex's eyes followed her as she tidied up the room, noticing the long, sooty lashes and the fullness of her lower lip. Even the bulk of the dressing-gown couldn't disguise her slender, feminine body. She was incredibly beautiful, he decided, especially now when she didn't know that he was watching her. He struggled with an impulse to drag the dressing-gown off and discover if the rest of her was as good as her legs.

She finished tidying and glanced at him. 'You should get some sleep,' she said softly. 'I'll leave the door open so that you can call if you need me.'

He felt a pang of disappointment that she was no longer going to sleep on the end of his bed. And then he realised that what he really wanted was for her to sleep *in* the bed.

With him.

He closed his eyes and clenched his jaw. What the hell was the matter with him?

Jenny wasn't his type.

Not because she wasn't blonde but because she wasn't the sort of woman that played by his rules. Jenny didn't even know how to flirt. In fact, he wouldn't be surprised if she was still a virgin. Something had to explain why she always looked so shocked and uncomfortable whenever the subject of his sex life was raised.

She disapproved heartily of his wicked ways and the sooner he booted her out of his house, the safer for her.

And him.

Alex returned to work three days later despite Jenny's strenuous attempts to persuade him to stay at home.

'You've been really ill,' she protested as they ate breakfast together, and he shot her that impatient look that she was getting to know so well.

'You're being wifely again.'

She bit her lip. 'I just don't think you're ready to go back to work.'

'If I collapse you can resuscitate me,' he promised, flashing her a wicked smile that made her catch her breath. She couldn't stop her eyes drifting down to his mouth.

What would it be like to be kissed by Alex?

Exciting...

'Stop looking at me like that, Red Riding Hood,' he said hoarsely, the expression in his sharp blue eyes telling her that he knew exactly what she'd been thinking. He drained his coffee and put the mug down on the table with a thump. 'Let's get out of here before we both do something we'll regret.'

This time she didn't argue.

She'd never been so confused in her life. This was the man who treated women with a carelessness that appalled her. He went through life avoiding any sort of commitment. He was totally wrong for her.

So why was she suddenly noticing every small thing about him? Like the way he teased old ladies and showed the utmost patience with people who were frightened and in pain? And the way he waded in confidently, determined to do his utmost to save a mother and her unborn child? And the way his cheeks creased when he smiled and the way he always seemed to have the beginnings of stubble on his hard jaw? Why did she suddenly want to run her fingers through that glossy black hair, just to see how it felt?

But he wasn't hers to touch, she reminded herself, feeling suddenly helpless under the pull of emotions she'd never experienced before.

In fact, he wasn't anybody's.

Alex was a loner. A man who kept himself at a safe emotional distance from everyone around him.

And he wasn't going to make an exception for a small dark-haired girl with a flat chest, who worried about his drinking habits and had never even had a proper boyfriend.

Pulling herself together, Jenny fastened Daisy into her car seat and drove to work, trying to think about anything other than Alexander Westerling.

Fortunately work was so busy that she had absolutely no chance to dwell on her confusing response to him.

From the minute she arrived on the unit she was working

flat out, and as the day progressed she wondered how Alex was coping. She knew that he must still be feeling rough.

'I need you in Resus, Jenny,' Tina said briskly, her face drawn and tired. She'd been coping with a staffing crisis for more than a week and it was beginning to show. 'They're bringing in a 64-year-old man who collapsed in a shopping centre.'

The ambulance arrived before she finished her sentence and the man was hurried into Resus.

Jenny glanced up with relief as Alex strode into the room. He looked grim-faced and pale but he applied himself with the same ruthless efficiency as ever.

'What have we got?'

'This is Geoffrey Palmer...' The paramedics handed over quickly and Jenny carefully placed an oxygen mask over the man's face lifting it slightly as he gestured to talk.

He looked at her with frightened eyes. 'What's happening?'

'We're going to find that out now,' Jenny said firmly, her voice steady and her eyes sympathetic as she checked his pulse and blood pressure.

Alex was already examining the man, his gaze flickering briefly to Tom who'd accompanied him into Resus. 'Two lines in, please. Large-bore cannulae.'

Tom nodded and reached for the equipment while Alex continued his examination.

'I want him on a monitor, Jenny. Mr Palmer, can you describe the pain for me?'

The man groaned. 'Round my stomach and my back...'

'We'll give you something for the pain right now.' Alex quickly undid the buttons of the man's shirt to give him access to the abdomen.

Tom moved away from the trolley. 'Two lines are in.'

'Give him some morphine for the pain and cyclizine and then take blood for FBC, U and Es, glucose, base-line coagulation screen, LFTs and emergency cross-matching.' Alex listed the investigations he wanted and then paused briefly, his eyes on the more junior doctor. 'And I want ten units of red cells and two units of platelets.'

Tom stared at him and then gave a brief nod as he reached for the necessary blood bottles.

Jenny bit her lip and concentrated on the patient. It was obvious from the volume of blood that Alex had ordered that he thought that the patient was at risk of a major bleed.

'Jenny, can you fast-bleep the vascular surgeon, the on-call anaesthetist and warn Emergency Theatre?' Alex finished examining the patient's abdomen and Jenny noticed that the patient's skin was mottled over his lower body.

Alex was staring at the monitor. 'He's tachycardic and hypotensive. Tom, give him a unit of Haemaccel.' He turned his attention back to the patient and put a reassuring hand on the man's shoulder. 'Mr Palmer, we need to pass a tube into your bladder and then you're going to need an operation I'm afraid.'

The man groaned. 'What's happening to me?'

'You have what we call an aortic aneurysm,' Alex said briefly, looking up as a man hurried into the room dressed in theatre scrubs. 'Paul—thanks for coming.'

He briefly outlined the condition of the patient and the vascular surgeon examined him and pronounced that he'd operate immediately.

'I'll clear the corridors and get them to hold the lifts,' Jenny said, knowing that the transfer to Theatre was crucial and that any delay could be life-threatening.

She made the necessary calls, checked the oxygen and suction and made sure that all the right equipment was ready for the short trip to Theatre.

If anything happened on the way, they needed to be prepared.

'Mr Palmer, is there anyone you'd like me to call?' she asked, and the man nodded, his face pale and sweaty.

'My daughter. Can you phone my daughter? She works on Anderson Ward.'

Jenny made a note of the name and handed it to one of the other staff nurses who promised to call straight away.

Fortunately the transfer passed without incident and the patient was wheeled into Theatre within minutes.

Jenny hurried back to A and E and made her way to Resus to clear and restock the room.

Tom and Alex were still there, deep in conversation.

Tom raked his fingers through his hair, visibly stressed. 'But how did you know it was an aortic aneurysm? You knew straight away.'

'He had classic symptoms.'

Tom pulled a face. 'Well, you gave me a fright when you ordered all those units of blood.'

'My guess is he's going to need every one of them. If that aneurysm bursts, he's going to have a massive bleed,' Alex said grimly, his handsome face pale and drawn. 'We were lucky to get him to Theatre.'

Jenny looked at him, hiding her concern.

She knew he wouldn't thank her for it, but she was worried about him.

There was absolutely no doubt in her mind that he should have been at home, resting, not working a punishing schedule in the A and E department.

She was desperate to persuade him to go home but she knew there was no point. Alex would do exactly what he wanted to do.

All she could do was finish her shift, go home and hope that he wasn't in too bad a state when he finally appeared.

CHAPTER SEVEN

HE FELT terrible.

It was almost nine when Alex eventually arrived home and the first thing that hit him as he walked into the house was a delicious smell coming from the kitchen.

He closed his eyes briefly and gave a wry smile.

He was rapidly adjusting to having a woman in the house. There was something amazingly restful about coming home to Jenny's cooking.

She walked out of the kitchen, her green eyes anxious, and he realised with profound shock that it wasn't coming home to her cooking that was restful, it was coming home to Jenny.

It was the patient syndrome, he told himself firmly. He was fixated on his nurse.

Goodness only knew what a psychiatrist would make of that.

'You look awful.' She frowned at him in concern. 'You never should have stayed so long.' She touched his arm gently in a gesture of sympathy and he felt his body harden in response to her touch.

Suddenly all he wanted was to drag her off to bed and re-discover those incredibly long legs.

Damn.

This was getting really bad.

The sooner his lawyer called the better for both of them.

'Where's Daisy?'

'Fast asleep.'

So even the baby wasn't going to provide a distraction. Gritting his teeth, he disengaged himself from her and paced across the room to pour himself a drink.

He paused with his hand on the bottle and then glanced over his shoulder towards her with a sigh.

'Go on. Say it. I shouldn't be drinking.'

'You've had a lousy day, Alex,' she said quietly, her green eyes warm with sympathy. 'You're entitled to a drink if you want it.'

Suddenly he found that he didn't want it.

He could think of a much better way to relax.

But what he really wanted was totally off limits.

Jenny was staring at him in consternation and it occurred to him that if she could read his mind she'd run a mile.

In fact, she ought to be running a mile. He wasn't sure that he was safe around her any more.

He sucked in a breath and ran a hand over the back of his neck to relieve the tension. It was taking all his willpower not to drag her into his arms and it was getting to the stage where he didn't trust himself around her. Normally if he met a woman that he liked and she played by his rules then he was perfectly happy to pursue the relationship to its natural conclusion. Which was nearly always bed.

But Jenny was different.

Jenny didn't do bed.

Not in the casual sense, anyway.

She was looking at him with concern. 'Can I do anything? Would you like me to run you a bath or something?'

Despite the building tension, his eyes gleamed. 'Ah—we're back to the bath again.' Maybe if he teased her it would help. 'Jenny's answer to all of life's problems.'

He waited for her to blush, the way she always did when he teased her, but this time she smiled, her cheeks dimpling slightly.

'You should try it,' she suggested mildly. 'It works.'

'Only if you show me how.'

He was trying to shock her into backing off. Trying to warn her to run for cover while she still had the chance.

But she didn't run. Instead, she gave him that lovely smile that almost made him groan with longing.

'Don't be ridiculous, Alex,' she said mildly. 'I know you're joking.'

He wondered what she'd say if she knew he was deadly serious. At the present moment there was nothing he'd like more than to share a bath with Jenny.

She was totally unlike any woman he'd ever been involved with before, but maybe that was part of the attraction, he mused silently.

One thing was sure, she'd be hideously shocked if she could read his thoughts.

Hell, he was shocking himself.

'I'm going for a swim.' Hopefully the freezing water would dampen down some of those hormones of his that were raging out of control. 'I'm stiff after standing in one position for too long.'

She stared at him, appalled. 'Alex, you can't swim now! It's already dark.'

He shrugged carelessly. 'It's fine. I often do it.'

'Please, don't.' She bit her lip. 'I've had about as much trauma as I can stand for one week. You've only just got over a horrid bout of flu. You've been at work all day. If you get into trouble in the water…'

His tension increased and he moved his shoulders and grimaced. 'My shoulders are aching from standing in one place for so long.'

'Then lie down on the sofa and I'll give you a massage,' she suggested, and then rolled her eyes. 'I suppose you'll take that the wrong way, too.'

He gave a wry smile. 'You're becoming harder and harder to shock, Jenny Phillips. That's what comes of living with such a disreputable rake as me.'

Her eyes slid away from his. 'You're not so bad, but as you've brought the subject up…' She hesitated and cleared her throat. 'I have rung a couple of agents looking for a flat.'

He felt as though he'd been kicked in the stomach and then frowned. Hell, wasn't that exactly what he wanted? For Jenny to move out?

No.

It was the last thing he wanted. 'Why would you do that?'

She avoided his gaze. 'Because the issue of Daisy's paternity is taking longer to sort out than I thought it would. I—I truly hadn't intended to land myself on you indefinitely. Sooner or later Daisy and I are going to need somewhere of our own,' she said quietly, 'and obviously I want to stay near to you so that you can see Daisy.'

Was he bothering her as much as she was bothering him?

He narrowed his eyes and looked at her closely, searching for clues, but he couldn't tell much if she refused to look at him.

Unless that was a sign in itself.

'Why would you want to move out? You're struggling with money as it is and if you start paying rent…' He shook his head. 'No. Forget it. You and Daisy stay here until my lawyers come up with an answer on her paternity. Then we'll work out the best course of action.'

He didn't want her moving out.

He wanted her where he could keep an eye on her.

But before he could argue the point further, the pressures of the day finally caught up with him and he felt the room shift.

She noticed immediately. 'Go upstairs. Lie down on the bed and I'll bring you some supper.'

He didn't argue.

Instead, he dragged himself upstairs and sprawled on the bed, eyes closed, and moments later he heard her soft tread as she walked into the room.

He was still wondering whether he could be bothered to get undressed when he felt the bed dip as she sat down beside him.

'Take your shirt off and roll over.'

He opened one eye and gave her a wry look. 'Is that your best pick-up line?'

'It's my massage line.' She reached out and undid the buttons on his shirt herself. For a moment he thought he saw her fingers tremble slightly but when he looked at her face she was perfectly calm and he decided that he must have imagined it. 'You take it off while I light the candles.'

'Candles?' He shrugged out of his shirt, noticing for the first time that she'd placed several candles next to the bed, along with some tiny bottles. 'Why do we need candles?'

'I'm trying to create the right atmosphere to help you relax.'

She lit the candles, flicked off the main lights and the bedroom was immediately plunged into semi-darkness, lit only by an intimate glow.

Relax?

Alex shot her an incredulous look and then realised that she truly had no idea what she was doing. He swore softly under his breath. She was unbelievably naïve about sex. Here she was with a half-naked man on the bed and she was lighting candles.

She obviously believed that she was creating an atmosphere of relaxation whereas, in fact, what she'd created was an atmosphere of seduction.

The dimly lit room, the scented oils and a half-naked man on the bed...

And he didn't feel relaxed at all.

In fact, his whole body was throbbing with suppressed sexual tension.

He propped himself up on his elbows and watched as she walked back into his bathroom and picked up some towels.

She spread one out on the bed next to him and then gave him a shy smile.

'You might want to take your trousers off. If you fall asleep you're going to be uncomfortable in them.'

Fall asleep? There was absolutely no way he'd fall asleep the way he felt at the moment, and as for the trousers—well, at least they were covering up his reaction to her.

Nevertheless he found himself undoing his trousers and sliding them down his thighs.

She was warming some oil between her hands. 'Now, lie on your front and I'll cover your lower half so you don't get cold.'

He gritted his teeth and did as he was told, although lying on his stomach wasn't easy given his current physical condition. At least it would make it easier to disguise how she made him feel.

He had a feeling that she didn't have a clue and he didn't want to embarrass her. He liked the fact that she seemed to have lost some of her wariness around him.

He closed his eyes and tried to think of something suitably neutral and boring, something that didn't involve being semi-naked while Jenny rubbed oil into his body.

Even so, the first touch of her hands on his skin made him groan and he knew that if her intention was to make him relax, she'd chosen the wrong activity. There was no way he would ever be able to relax while Jenny was sliding her palms over his shoulders in such a seductive fashion.

He never would have guessed that she had such good hands.

She hadn't seemed a particularly tactile person—at least, not with him.

But her hands slid over him in a smooth, seamless motion that ignited the most wicked of fantasies in his active mind. She had the most incredible touch.

The touch of a lover.

He lay still, his eyes closed as she worked on his shoulders and then moved slowly down his back.

She didn't speak and the silence merely intensified the erotic thoughts throbbing in his brain.

Her hands slid smoothly over his body, gliding lower, and he groaned again.

She paused. 'Am I hurting you?'

She really had no idea.

He decided enough was enough and rolled onto his back, his jaw tense and his eyes closed.

'I think you'd better stop.'

She frowned, puzzled. 'But—'

His eyes opened and what she read in them must have made an impact because she sucked in a breath.

'Run, Red Riding Hood,' he said softly, his gaze fixed on her face. 'Run while you still can.'

She froze then, her green eyes locked on his. But she didn't seem able to move. She reminded him of a delicate, gentle animal who has just realised that she's been playing with the ultimate predator.

Torn between fascination and terror.

He gritted his teeth and fought the very male impulse to grab her and roll her under him.

'Go, Jenny,' he said hoarsely. 'For heaven's sake, just go.'

She spoke then, her voice breathy and very feminine. 'I'm sorry if I did something wrong…'

Damn. She should be running to her room and locking the door behind her.

'You didn't do anything wrong.'

'But—'

She obviously had no idea of the danger she was in.

Swearing softly under his breath, he reached for her and pulled her down, rolling her under him as he'd been dying to do from the moment she'd lit the candles.

Or maybe from before that. He didn't know. All he knew was that he wanted Jenny and that she wasn't running fast enough.

'You should have run, Red Riding Hood, while you had the chance.'

She stared up at him, her breath coming in little pants, her pupils dilated. 'I can't run...'

'Well, you should,' he growled, lifting a hand and pulling her hair out of the clip that she always wore. He combed his fingers through the silky strands of dark hair, deciding that he'd never felt anything so soft and smooth. 'Push me away, Jenny.'

His mouth hovered above hers and he could feel the warmth of her breath mingling with his.

'Stop me, Jenny.'

She stared up at him helplessly, enthralled and hypnotised by his burning gaze. 'I can't.'

His mouth brushed lightly against hers and he groaned as delicious sensation arced through his tense body. 'I'll hurt you.'

'You wouldn't.'

Her tongue flickered against his lips and Alex gave up all attempts at restraint.

He touched his mouth gently to hers, dipping his tongue inside, persuading her to open for him. And she did. His hand still locked in her hair, he kissed her deeply, tasting her sweetness, feeling her shuddering response against him.

Her tongue tangled with his and she kissed him back without restraint, kissed him until the blood throbbed in his veins and he felt as though his body might explode.

He knew he ought to lift his head to let them both breathe, but kissing Jenny was shockingly addictive and he couldn't bring himself to end it even for a moment.

His free hand slid downwards and heat flared inside him as he gently drew a thumb over one pebbled nipple. She gasped against his mouth and he repeated the movement and then slid his hand under her T-shirt, his whole body throbbing with the need to have her naked under him. He unclipped her bra without the slightest difficulty and then finally dragged his mouth away from hers.

She lay looking up at him, flushed and fevered from his kiss, her eyes totally trusting.

He knew he should stop.

He was going to stop.

And then she breathed in deeply and he heard the jerk in her breath and felt the brush of her nipple against his searching fingers.

Unable to help himself, Alex slid her T-shirt up, exposing her breasts to his hungry gaze.

She was small and delicate and utterly female, and the male in him struggled to control the powerful surge of desire that swamped his body.

Aware that he was torturing himself, he lowered his head and flicked at one dusky pink nipple with his tongue, groaning as it hardened under his skilled touch.

She gasped his name and clung to the muscles of his shoulders as if she was falling and he was the only one who could keep her safe.

But he wasn't going to keep her safe.

He was going to hurt her.

He always hurt women.

He lifted his head and gave a soft curse, fully intending to end the kiss while they both still could, but his eyes locked onto her nipple, glistening damply from his touch.

Her breathing was shallow and her hips writhed subtly against the sheets as she sought to relieve the incredible tension that was building inside both of them.

She was all softness and warmth and feminine temptation, her eyes and her body begging him for more, and Alex, who had never lost control of his reactions in his life before, suddenly lost control

He moved upwards again and brought his mouth down on hers, his free hand sliding lower until he found the hem of her skirt. He drew it upwards, feeling the warmth of her skin against the ends of his fingers, feeling the press of her sweet body as she arched against him. He shifted slightly to allow himself better access, his hand gliding smoothly up her inner thigh and brushing the damp silk of her panties.

His desire fuelled still further by this explicit evidence of her need for him, his fingers slid inside the elastic and gently touched the very heart of her.

Sensitive as he was to her every tremor, he felt her sudden tension and his hand stilled.

'Alex…' She croaked his name against his mouth and he lifted his head slightly, his breathing decidedly unsteady, his fingers still resting gently on the most private part of her.

'Do you want me to stop?'

'No—yes…' She closed her eyes and gave a whimper. 'I don't know. It's just that I've never—I haven't…'

She was a virgin.

And suddenly Alex found the willpower he'd been looking for.

He moved his hand and rolled away from her, closing his eyes as he struggled to calm his throbbing body.

There was a moment's silence while he fought to regain control—while he wrestled with his conscience.

'Alex?' She said his name, her voice barely a whisper, and he gave a sigh and opened his eyes.

'I told you to run.'

'But I didn't want to run.'

'Well, you should have done,' he said roughly, sitting up and sliding off the bed in a lithe movement. He needed to get away from him. Fast. 'I'm no good for you, Jenny. You know that. We should never have started this.'

'But—'

'Jenny, I'm everything you accused me of being the day you first turned up here with your accusing gaze and your innocent expression.' His voice was harsh. 'Nothing's changed.'

'That's not true. I didn't know you when I arrived. I said

things—' She broke off and bit her lip. 'I said awful things about you, I know, but that was before I knew you.'

He gritted his teeth. 'Jenny, I'm everything you thought I was, sweetheart.'

She shook her head. 'You're a brilliant doctor. You give so much of yourself to others but you like to hide it. And you're wonderful with Daisy. You're going to be a great father.'

He raked long fingers through his tousled dark hair. 'Jenny, I will make a lousy father. I don't do relationships. You know that. I don't get close to people.'

She looked at him. 'Why?'

He recognised the look in her eyes and swore under his breath. She thought she could change him. She thought she'd be different from the others, but what she didn't realise was that the problem didn't lie with the other women he'd been with— the problem lay with *him*.

He just couldn't commit to anyone.

He didn't want to. And Jenny was no exception.

All he wanted was a brief, uncomplicated relationship.

'Because that's the way it is.' He saw the hurt in her eyes and cursed himself. Why the hell had he ever let it get this far?

Hating himself for what he had to do, he ran a hand over his face and looked at her.

'I don't sleep with women like you.'

'Because I'm not blonde?'

Her feeble attempt at a joke did nothing to relieve his tension. However had he got himself in this position? 'Because you don't do just sex, do you, Jenny? And that's all I'm offering.'

His blunt words made her flinch and she looked at him like a kitten that knew it was being sent away from its mother. 'I'm not a threat to you, Alex,' she said softly, and he gave a wry smile.

With her gentle warmth and her calm nature she was the biggest threat that he'd ever encountered.

And tomorrow he was putting serious pressure on his lawyer to find an answer to Daisy's paternity.

He wanted the issue settled so that he could get Jenny out of his life.

Before he did something that was going to hurt both of them.

Ending the conversation abruptly, he strode into the bathroom and locked the door, turned the shower full on and switched the setting to cold.

Jenny stared at the locked bathroom door, feeling totally numb.

He'd rejected her.

But that wasn't surprising, was it? How could she possibly compete with the women he usually mixed with?

And she'd totally blown it by reacting like a gauche schoolgirl. But his touch had been so overwhelmingly intimate and she'd been terrified by the power of her own response.

She slid off his bed, filled with embarrassment, wondering how on earth she was going to face the man in the morning.

It was all her fault. What on earth had possessed her to give him a massage? The minute he'd removed his shirt and exposed his smooth, well-muscled chest she'd realised the depth of her mistake but it had been too late to correct it without drawing attention to the sudden awareness that had engulfed her.

And to be fair to the man, he'd given her every opportunity to pull away.

But she hadn't been able to do so.

She'd been trapped by the chemistry that had pulsed between them, in the thrall of something far stronger than common sense.

All the warnings in the world wouldn't have stopped her from experiencing Alex's kiss.

Groaning at the memory, she slid back into her room and closed her eyes briefly.

What had she been thinking of?

Guilt stabbed her. This was the man that Chloe had loved. They'd made a child together.

How could she have forgotten that this was the man that broke Chloe's heart?

Because he wasn't the man she'd thought he was.

If he hadn't detected her lack of experience, where would they be now?

Making love…

Only it wasn't love, she reminded herself. It was sex and, as Alex had said, she didn't do sex.

Or did she?

She certainly never had before but she was painfully aware that if Alex hadn't exerted his awesome willpower to break off the physical contact she would have gone wherever he'd chosen to take her.

Jenny sat at the table in the kitchen, feeding Daisy, dreading Alex's arrival.

She'd thrown herself at her sister's lover and he'd had to tactfully reject her.

She ought to be grateful to him for saving them both from a huge mistake but at the moment she couldn't see past the humiliation of having thrown herself at a man who didn't want her.

Where on earth did they go from here?

But when Alex strode into the kitchen five minutes later he didn't show even a flicker of embarrassment.

But, then, he must be used to women flinging themselves at him, she reflected miserably, concentrating her attention on Daisy as he poured himself coffee and pulled out a chair.

He sat down, stretched his long legs out in front of him and reached for a freshly baked roll.

She was making a determined effort not to look at him but she knew he was looking at her.

'Good morning.' His voice was soft and very male and connected with every female part of her.

How did he do that? she wondered helplessly, trying to stop her hand shaking as she lifted the spoon to Daisy's mouth. He was sitting on the other side of the table but already her heart was thumping and her pulse was racing. The moment Alex entered a room it seemed to throb with sexual tension.

'Good morning.' She answered without looking at him and there was a brief silence.

'You're going to have to look at me some time, Red Riding Hood,' he murmured finally, a touch of amusement in his velvety tones. 'It was just a kiss, sweetheart. There's no need to be shy.'

Just?

The man obviously had no idea just how well he kissed.

But the fact that he could dismiss it so easily just confirmed her belief that it had meant absolutely nothing to him. She already knew that, of course. He'd been the one who'd ended it. And she'd virtually begged him not to…

Embarrassment swamped her again and she wished he'd go to work and leave her alone.

But he obviously wasn't going anywhere.

Instead, he poured himself some more coffee and her eyes slid to his hands, fixing on the dark hairs just visible below the cuffs of his shirt. Everything about Alex was sexy. Even his hands. *The same hands that had touched her so skilfully the night before.*

She dragged her attention back to Daisy. This was ridiculous. Since when had she started noticing a man's hands?

He gave an impatient sigh. 'Listen, Jenny, I don't—'

'Please, don't say anything else.' She stood up so quickly she almost knocked the chair flying, but she just couldn't bear to hear him list the reasons why he didn't want to be with her. 'I'd rather not talk about it.'

She'd rather not think about it either, but unfortunately that wasn't so easy.

She unstrapped Daisy and lifted her out of the high chair, cuddling her close. The feel of her soft, sturdy little body gave her courage.

'It was all my fault and I'm sorry.' She plucked up courage to look at him, trying to look relaxed about the whole thing. 'I was the one who gave you that stupid massage and I didn't think—I mean, it didn't occur to me that you'd—' She broke off and bit her lip, cursing her shyness. Everyone else seemed to be able to talk about sex. Why couldn't she? 'What I mean is, the kiss was all my fault and, please, don't think you've offended me by stopping when you did. You were Chloe's lover and I never should have—'

'I was never Chloe's lover,' he said impatiently, a frown touching his dark brows. 'And Chloe has absolutely nothing to do with what happened between you and I last night.'

'I still believe Daisy is your child,' she said hoarsely. 'The only thing that's changed is that you're not the man I first thought you were and I'm sorry I misjudged you.'

His longer fingers tapped a rhythm on the table. 'You didn't misjudge me.' His handsome face was inscrutable. 'I drink too much, I party too hard and I'm very careless about women's feelings. I've never had a relationship that's lasted longer than three months. I'm everything you believe me to be. You didn't misjudge me.'

She gave him what she hoped was a light-hearted smile. 'Well, at least I've taught you to eat breakfast.'

There was no answering smile in return. 'You've taught me more than that,' he drawled softly, his eyes never leaving her face. 'Like the fact that I do have a conscience. And that conscience, my dear Jenny, is the reason that you're still a virgin this morning.'

She was mortified that he'd guessed but after her reaction to him the night before it was hardly surprising.

'We wouldn't have—'

'Oh, yes, we would.' He drained his coffee. 'And I'm warning you to keep your distance, Red Riding Hood. The wolf let you escape last night. I can't guarantee it will happen a second time.'

Her heart banged hard against her ribs and her mouth was suddenly dry.

So he did find her attractive.

It wasn't just her that felt the special connection between them.

'I agree that you should move out,' Alex replied bluntly. 'There's no way I'll be able to keep my hands off you if you're continually wandering around my house.'

She stared at him. 'But I don't try to—'

'You really don't know much about men, do you?' he observed dryly. 'It's the fact that you're not trying that makes you so appealing. That and the fact that you have absolutely no idea how attractive you are. Even clothed, I'm struggling to keep my hands off you.'

Her stomach tumbled and she suddenly found breathing difficult. 'But I'm not doing anything.'

'You don't have to do anything,' Alex drawled. 'You can bath Daisy in an old T-shirt and I still want you. You can wear that ridiculous outfit that buttons from neck to hem and all I want to do is rip it off. The truth is that I have absolutely no interest in what you're wearing because all I want to do is rip it off, spread you on my bed and introduce you to the pleasures of sex. And now I've told you the truth, you'd better run.'

She stared at him, her breathing rapid, two spots of colour on her cheekbones.

He wanted to introduce her to the pleasures of sex?

No one had ever spoken to her in such a—such an explicit way before, and it did strange things to her insides.

'Alex—'

'Am I shocking you, Red Riding Hood?' His voice was silky smooth. 'Because I should be.'

Finally she found her voice. 'You're not shocking me. But you won't convince me that you're so wicked either. I know you now, Alex. I know you have a caring side.'

'Not in my relationships,' he said bluntly, and suddenly she realised her problem.

She'd come after him for Daisy, but now she'd got to know him she wanted him for *her*.

She was in love with Alex Westerling.

Appalled by the sudden revelation, she froze.

'You're right, of course,' she said finally, her lips stiff as she formed the words. 'You're not the right sort of man for me.'

And in a way she was telling the truth. For Alex a relationship was something purely physical. He didn't do the emotional stuff. How many times had he told her that?

There was a brief pause and his eyes burned into hers. 'Jenny—'

The soft chime of the doorbell interrupted whatever it was he'd intended to say and his darkened jaw tensed.

'Who the hell is that at this time of the morning?'

'Do you want me to go?' She looked at him anxiously. 'If it's a journalist I could tell them that you are out.'

He laughed out loud and flipped her cheek with a gentle finger. 'You are so damned innocent. What do you think a journalist would make of a pretty girl opening my door, holding a baby?'

Her eyes widened and she stared at him. 'I hadn't thought of that.'

'But fortunately I had.' He rose to his feet and walked towards the kitchen door. 'Better stay in here. Just in case.'

With that he closed the door firmly behind him, leaving her alone.

Jenny stared at Daisy helplessly. 'Oh, Daisy. What have I done? What on earth possessed me to fall in love with a man like him? I thought I had more sense than that.'

But the truth was that her emotions were outside her control for the first time in her life.

She hadn't chosen to fall in love with Alex Westerling but it had happened.

And who could blame her?

Alex was the ultimate catch. He had a mind like a rapier, he was sinfully good-looking and he could kiss a woman until she forgot her own name. He was good company and a surprisingly good listener. He was kind to his patients and a dedicated doctor. And he'd be a great father once he woke up to the fact that Daisy was his.

Not realising that she hadn't once thought about his money, Jenny tidied the kitchen with her free arm and then froze as she heard female laughter.

She felt as though she'd been showered with cold water.

Here she was, happily playing house and make believe, and she hadn't given any thought to Alex's current girlfriend. And there was bound to be one, of course. He just wasn't the sort of man to deny himself.

She dropped the cloth and held Daisy tighter, bracing herself as the door opened and Alex strolled in, his arm looped casually around the shoulders of a stunning blonde woman who was wearing the shortest skirt Jenny had ever seen.

Jenny tried to smile and she hoped that it looked more convincing than it felt.

'Hi, there—I'm Jenny.'

'And I'm Libby.' The girl looked at her curiously, switched her gaze to Daisy and then glanced at Alex.

'There's obviously quite a lot that you haven't been telling me, you naughty boy.' Her voice was a seductive purr and her amazing blue eyes teased wickedly. 'I should drop in on you unannounced more often.'

'Not if you want to survive to old age,' Alex drawled, suppressing a yawn. 'Jenny, this is my sister Libby. Don't answer any of her questions. She's worse than any journalist.'

Sister?

Jenny wasn't sure which was worse. The pain of thinking that he was involved with this beautiful creature, or the intense feeling of joy that swamped her when she realised that he wasn't. If she'd needed conformation about the strength of her feelings for him, she had it now.

Alex poured a coffee and handed it to his sister. 'So, to what do I owe the honour? Have they run out of shoes in London?'

Libby laughed and sipped the coffee. 'No. I just happened to be passing.'

Alex lifted an eyebrow. 'Passing where? This is a dead end, Lib.'

Libby shrugged. 'All right. Actually, Andreas is away in Greece with Adrienne for a few days and I thought I'd take the opportunity to visit you.' She turned to smile at Jenny. 'Adrienne is Andreas's niece. She's seventeen.'

Alex looked at his sister suspiciously. 'And that's it?'

Her eyes twinkled naughtily. 'Well, Katy and I haven't heard a squeak from you lately and that's always a sign that you're otherwise occupied.'

Alex raised his eyes to heaven. 'And knowing that, you didn't think that I might want to be left in peace?'

'Absolutely not.' Libby smiled at Daisy. 'We're only staying for one night. I promise we won't be in the way. We'll just lounge on the beach.'

Jenny glanced between them, puzzled. 'We?'

'Libby has evidently brought my two nieces to visit me,' Alex said wearily, raking a hand through his dark hair and gazing at his sister in frustration. 'You really must learn to ring first.'

'Why?' His sister's gaze was disturbingly intent and Jenny suspected that there was something going on. 'Am I interrupting something?'

Alex hesitated for only the briefest second. 'No,' he said finally. 'But the nursery is already in use.'

Libby stared at him, momentarily struck dumb. 'But no one ever stays here.'

'Well, Jenny is staying here, with Daisy,' Alex said irritably, 'and you'd better get the girls out of the car, Lib.'

'They're asleep,' Libby said absent-mindedly, her eyes still on her brother. 'So are you saying there isn't room?'

Jenny cleared her throat. 'Of course there's room,' she said quickly. 'We can all share the nursery. This is Daisy. I'm sure she'll enjoy the company.'

'Pleased to meet you, Daisy.' Libby tickled the baby's cheek and made noises that drew a chuckle from the baby.

'I'll get the girls.'

Alex strode out of the room, leaving the two women together.

'I really, *really* didn't mean to intrude,' Libby said softly, her tone contrite. 'I had no idea. Alex never invites women back here. If he invited you then you must be very special.'

Jenny closed her eyes briefly. What was she supposed to say?

She could hardly confess that Alex hadn't invited her. That she'd landed herself on him together with a paternity suit and that life had never seemed more complicated than it was at the moment.

Fortunately Alex was back in the kitchen within minutes, carrying two little girls in his arms.

They cuddled against him sleepily and he dropped a kiss on each of their dark curls before handing them to Libby.

'We really need to go to work. You know where everything is.' He gave a wry smile. 'I don't need to tell you to make yourself at home because you always do. We'll see you later.'

'We?' Libby was clearly consumed by curiosity and Alex let out a breath.

'Jenny works in the same department as me. Now let it go, Lib.'

'So you met at work?'

Jenny threw a helpless glance at Alex who rolled his eyes.

'How we met is none of your damned business.'

Libby gasped and covered the older child's ears. 'Alexander Westerling, you shouldn't use language like that in front of my four-year-old!!'

'Then you shouldn't bring her to stay with her wicked uncle

unannounced,' Alex drawled, but he stooped to kiss the girls. 'See you later. We'll go and play in the sand.'

The youngest one gazed up at him. 'Thand castles?'

'Definitely thand castles,' Alex mimicked gently, reaching out to pick up his car keys from the table. 'Have a good day and don't get up to any mischief.'

The moment she'd dropped Daisy at the crèche Jenny went in search of Alex.

She found him in the treatment room, examining a wound that had come in to be redressed.

'It's infected,' he was saying in that definite voice he always used. 'I'll give you antibiotics and you need to come back and get it checked.' He broke off briefly when he saw Jenny hovering anxiously in the doorway and then turned his attention back to the patient, finishing his instructions.

Then he strolled over to Jenny, his handsome face blank of expression. 'My office. Now.'

She blinked and wondered whether she'd ever get used to the way Alex always had to be in control.

But she had little choice other than to follow him through to his office, and she had to admit that they needed privacy for the conversation that they were about to have.

She closed the door quietly behind her and hovered in front of it.

'You'd better sit down.' Alex collapsed into the chair behind his desk and closed his eyes. He looked worn out and it struck her that he was still obviously recovering from his bout of flu. 'I suppose you want to talk about my damned sister.'

Jenny bit her lip. 'I just don't know what we're going to say to her.'

Alex yawned. 'Why do we need to say anything to her?'

How could he be so relaxed?

'She'll want an explanation.'

'I never explain myself to anyone,' he said in a cool tone, and then sighed. 'Don't look so worried, Red Riding Hood. You're still safe in the wolf's lair, remember? I'll sort it out.'

'But what will you tell her?'

Alex shrugged, totally indifferent to what she saw as a massive problem. 'I don't know. I'm not in the habit of discussing my relationships with my sister.'

Jenny coloured. 'But we're not having a relationship.'

He shot her a strange look. 'No, we're not, are we? Yet.'

His smooth tones heated her blood and she felt warmth spread through her body.

'I—I'll try and find a flat today,' she croaked, and he gave a short laugh.

'You'll be lucky. This is a tourist resort in the middle of the tourist season. You'll be lucky even to find a metre of sand that someone hasn't already bagged.'

'But you said—'

'Yeah, I know what I said.' He gave a wry smile. 'It's certainly safer if you move out but seeing that isn't going to be possible we'll have to go with the more dangerous option.'

'What do you mean?'

'You continuing to live with the wolf,' he said slowly, leaning forward and looking at her with an intensity that made her pulse accelerate alarmingly. 'Until we find out about Daisy.'

Jenny stared at him, heart pounding. 'She's yours, Alex.'

'So you keep saying.' A muscle worked in his lean jaw. 'I think for both our sakes it's time we found out the truth so that we can get on with our lives.'

CHAPTER EIGHT

JENNY arrived home from work first and found Libby feeding both children in the kitchen.

Alex's usually pristine bachelor environment had been transformed into a girly paradise. Shoes seemed to be scattered everywhere, items of clothing had been dropped haphazardly on the floor and the kitchen looked as though someone had used a blender without the lid.

'I'm afraid that's Athena's fault,' Libby explained cheerfully, following the direction of Jenny's gaze. 'She's a terribly messy eater. Don't worry. Alex is used to her. There's no point in clearing it up halfway through. I always wait until she's finished. Then we get the hose out.'

Jenny giggled. 'I bet Alex has a shock when you come to stay.'

'He just reaches for the whisky bottle,' Libby said dryly, smiling tolerantly as Athena grabbed a handful of pasta and rubbed it into the table. 'My husband, Andreas, is the same. He adores the girls but he's a typical macho Greek. He doesn't know one end of a nappy from the other. Which is utterly ridiculous because the guy is a paediatrician and an incredibly good one at that. He just isn't great at the practical stuff. A bit like Alex.'

Not like Alex.

Jenny slipped Daisy into the high chair, thinking that Libby would be surprised if she knew just how involved Alex had been with Daisy.

After that first night, when she'd forced the issue, he often helped out with her and seemed to relish spending time with the baby.

'She's beautiful,' Libby said, her eyes resting on Daisy thoughtfully. 'How old?'

'Six months. How old is Athena?'

'Just two.' Libby pulled a face. 'And Zoe is four. Jolly hard work, I can tell you. I used to work on a paediatric ward. I can't imagine how I used to look after twenty-four little patients. I can't manage two when they're mine. Fortunately my husband is addicted to his daughters so I get some help once he's home. That's why I run to Alex when Andreas is away. I can't cope on my own. Pathetic.'

'They're gorgeous,' Jenny said wistfully, thinking how lucky the children were to have two parents who adored each other. Daisy would never have that.

'They're both horribly spoilt,' Libby admitted, smiling indulgently, 'Andreas is Greek and he adores his little girls. Of which I'm one, fortunately.'

Jenny smiled. She could well imagine it. Libby was the girliest 'girl' she'd ever met and so bubbly that you wanted to put the lid on her in case she fizzed over the carpet.

'So come on—' Libby's eyes gleamed mischievously '—tell me everything about Alex.'

Jenny tensed. 'There's nothing to tell.'

'Oh, come on…' Libby slipped her shoes off and curled her legs under her on the chair, obviously totally at home. 'Jenny, my brother has never invited a woman into his home before. I want to know why you're the exception.'

Jenny chewed her lip. 'I'm not exactly the exception. You see, it's—it's—'

'None of her business,' came a deep, dark drawl from the doorway. 'Back off, Elizabeth.'

His tone contained a definite warning and Libby pouted.

'You're a horrible grouch and I can't think why I ever come and visit you.'

'You come and visit me because your husband is away and you don't want Athena to make that sort of mess in your own kitchen.' Alex strolled into the kitchen and stopped in front of his niece, frowning deeply. 'I wish you'd stop using my walls for target practice, madam.'

Athena chuckled happily and reached up to him with gooey hands. 'Lexth, lexth—cuggle—'

Alex leaned down and dropped a kiss on her curly head, keeping a safe distance from her chubby hands. 'I never cuddle my women while they're covered in tomato sauce,' he said dryly. 'When your mother has hosed you down we'll have a cuddle.'

He sat down next to Zoe.

'Hi, there, Zoe. How are you doing?'

'Good, Uncle Alex.' The little girl smiled up at him. 'Can we go to the beach?'

'Sure.' Alex glanced at Libby and lifted an eyebrow. 'Is that OK with you?'

She beamed. 'Definitely. We'll all go. Or is that a problem for Daisy?'

'Daisy loves the beach,' Jenny said quickly. 'She eats the sand.'

'They all do at that age,' Libby said sagely, and Alex rolled his eyes.

'Athena still eats it. In fact, that girl eats everything.'

Jenny stood up. 'I'll make up a bottle for Daisy and heat up her food here.' She bustled around the kitchen, preparing what she needed, clearing up as she went.

Libby stood up and lifted Athena off the chair. 'Oh, yuck

I wonder if you actually ate anything. Most of it seems to be stuck to your bottom.'

'Her aim is hopeless,' Alex said mildly, observing the food stuck to the floor and the walls. 'She has absolutely no idea where her mouth is.'

Libby laughed and reached for a cloth to wipe Athena's face and hands. 'She does when it's chocolate. She never misses.'

'Now, why doesn't that surprise me?' Alex rolled his eyes and reached into the fridge for some beer. Then he glanced at Jenny, his gaze gently mocking.

Jenny blushed and gave a shy smile. She knew that he was challenging her to scold him for drinking but she had no intention of doing any such thing. Instead, she reached out a hand to take the bottles of lager.

'You can put those in Daisy's bag,' she said calmly, and he gave a reluctant smile.

'Put one in for me,' Libby said, turning Athena round to check she hadn't missed any splodges of tomato. 'There we are, you're clean.'

'Clean?' Alex surveyed his niece and raised an eyebrow. 'You seriously call that clean?'

'It's clean for Athena, Uncle Alex,' Zoe said solemnly, and he laughed and swung her into his arms.

'I suppose it is, sweetheart. Now, then, what are we going to do on the beach?'

'Can we go over by the cliffs and play caves?'

Alex nodded. 'Sounds good to me.'

He held onto her and Jenny watched them, a lump building in her throat.

How could he possibly think he wouldn't make a good father? He was so lovely with his nieces. He would have made an absolutely wonderful father for Daisy. Except that he was determined to deny that she was his. She remembered his comments about contacting his lawyer and wondered whether he'd had any news during the day.

Presumably not or he would have mentioned it.

On the other hand, he would hardly have mentioned it at work and he wasn't in a position to bring it up now because Libby was staying there.

She shifted Daisy slightly, wondering how he'd react when his lawyer confirmed that there was every possibility that he was the baby's father.

She'd have to move out, of course.

There was no way they could continue to live together.

They'd have to come to some arrangement whereby he could continue to see Daisy regularly.

And as for her—well, she'd only see him on an occasional basis.

She felt as though a heavy lump of lead was sitting in her stomach. The thought of leaving Alex dismayed her more than she could ever have imagined.

She'd dismissed him as a superficial playboy but the truth was that there was nothing superficial about Alex. Nothing at all.

He was incredibly complex.

On the surface he was sophisticated and independent, the ultimate Mr Cool, a man who possessed a wild streak that had earned him a wicked reputation. But underneath there was so much more to him. He had a brilliant brain, a sharp sense of humour and was capable of great warmth towards those in trouble. He was impatient with freeloaders and the press but who could blame him for that?

She'd even started to understand his womanising. He was a stunningly good-looking man who'd been born to one of the richest families in Britain. It was hardly any wonder he'd had a string of girlfriends.

But he hadn't made a commitment to any of them, she reminded herself gloomily.

That was one aspect of his personality that she couldn't understand.

Despite his caustic comments about children, he was actually very good with them.

So why had he never settled down?

Despite the fact that it was late afternoon, the beach was still crowded and they found themselves a spot near to the caves that Zoe was keen to explore.

Libby settled herself on the sand with Athena and let the toddler play with a bucket and spade while Jenny snuggled Daisy on her lap and gave her a bottle.

Alex took Zoe's hand and they wandered off inside the cave.

'You know, Katy and I always said that Alex would end up with someone small and dark. No, don't eat the sand, darling.' Libby leaned forward to brush the sand away from Athena's mouth. 'Yuck. Amazing, isn't it? Her dinner doesn't make it anywhere near her mouth but with the sand she's spot on. Dig, Athena. Dig. Not eat. He's always dated blondes.'

Jenny tried not to mind about that. 'Libby, we're not exactly dating, we're—'

'Well, there's something going on,' Libby said calmly. 'I've known Alex for thirty-four years and I've never known him protect a woman the way he protects you. The slightest whiff of an uncomfortable situation and he dives in and rescues you.'

Jenny frowned. Did he? She'd never even thought about it.

'Truly, we're not—'

'Jenny—' Libby's tone was patient '—I can see you're in love with him. Every time you look at him it shines out of your eyes.'

Jenny stared at her, appalled. Her first instinct was to deny it and then she realised helplessly that there was probably no point and anyway her main concern wasn't Libby.

'Do you think your brother knows?' she croaked, glancing towards the cave to check that Alex wasn't within earshot.

Libby looked taken aback. 'I don't know. Probably. Women are always in love with him, so he sort of expects it. But what's the problem? He's clearly crazy about you too.'

Crazy about *her*?'

Jenny shook her head. 'No. He isn't. It isn't like that.'

It was true that he seemed to be attracted to her for some reason, but she didn't fool herself that it was anything other than novelty value.

Libby brushed some more sand away from Athena's face but her eyes were on Jenny. 'Why don't you tell me what's going on?'

It was severely tempting to confide in someone who knew Alex well but Jenny shook her head.

The issue of Daisy was between her and Alex and she didn't feel comfortable sharing it with anyone else until Alex chose to acknowledge his responsibility for Daisy. And as for the other issue—her relationship with Alex—there was absolutely nothing going on.

Unfortunately.

Libby was looking at her with sympathy. 'Well, if it's any consolation, he seems to treat you differently to all the other women he's ever been with.'

Jenny concentrated on Daisy, not wanting to think about the other women that Alex had been with. It just hurt too much.

Daisy finished the bottle and Jenny and Libby chatted casually until Alex arrived back with an excited Zoe.

'We went right into the cave and it was so *dark*,' she said, her voice an awed whisper. 'Uncle Alex was scared so I had to hold his hand.'

Libby laughed and then gave a startled gasp and lifted her hand to her neck, knocking off an enormous bee that had landed on her skin.

Her face blanched and she jumped to her feet, her expression one of pure panic as she looked at her brother. 'Alex, I've been stung.'

Alex was by her side immediately, his expression grim. 'Jenny, call the air ambulance *now*! Tell them we've got a case of anaphylactic shock.' He took his sister by the shoulders and looked down at her, his tone urgent. 'Where? Where did it sting you?'

For a moment Jenny stood frozen to the spot, uncomprehending, and then she fumbled in her bag for her mobile phone and dialled the emergency number without question. She had no idea what was going on but she knew better than to doubt Alex about anything medical. If he felt that he needed the air ambulance then he needed it.

As she slipped the phone back in her bag, Zoe caught her hand, her eyes terrified.

'Mummy's allergic to bees,' she said, her little voice trembling.

Allergic to bees?

Jenny glanced at Alex in horror but all his attention was on his sister.

'Where did it sting you, Lib?'

'Neck.' Libby was white and Alex tipped her head over and examined the skin.

'I see it. The sting is still in there.'

'Get it out! Alex, get it out!' Libby was gasping now and Alex scraped at the sting with his finger until he finally managed to remove it.

'It's out. Tell me you're carrying adrenaline,' he said through gritted teeth, and Libby nodded, lifting a hand to her throat, her eyes wide with panic.

'It's starting. I can feel it. I can't breathe, Alex. Oh, no, *I can't breathe.*'

She started to gasp and sob, clutching at him with her free hand, and he scooped her up in his arms and laid her gently on the blanket.

'It's all right, baby, I'm here.' His voice was rock solid and reassuring but Jenny noticed his hand shaking slightly as he reached out to grasp Libby's bag. Jaw clenched tight, he lifted it and emptied the contents unceremoniously onto the rug. 'You're going to be fine, sweetheart. Try not to panic.'

'My throat…' Libby's voice was a rasp as she clutched at her brother's shoulders.

'It's OK, Lib— I'm here, sweetheart. Jenny, find the adrenaline,' he growled. *'Quickly!'*

The gravity of the scenario swamping her with horror, Jenny dropped to her knees and rummaged through the contents of Libby's handbag, her hands shaking so badly that she couldn't grasp anything. There seemed to be thousands of different lipsticks, notebooks, numerous screwed-up chocolate wrappers, but finally her fingers closed around a pre-loaded syringe of adrenaline.

By now Libby was gasping and her face was swelling rapidly. She clutched her brother, her eyes terrified as she stared up at him desperately. 'Don't let me die! Don't let me die, Alex.'

'You're not going to die, baby,' Alex soothed, snapping his fingers at Jenny in an attempt to hurry her.

Sick with reaction, Jenny pushed the syringe into his hand and he sucked in a breath as he jabbed the syringe into Libby's thigh without a second's hesitation. 'You're not going to die, Libby. I promise you won't die.'

Jenny watched in appalled silence, frozen to the spot in shock. Only moments earlier they'd been chatting happily and now Libby was fighting for every breath.

In all her years working in A and E Libby had never seen anyone deteriorate so quickly. It was a nightmare of the worst proportions and she didn't need to see Alex's white face to know just how gravely ill his sister was.

'Uncle Alex…?' Zoe's voice quivered. 'What's happening to Mummy?'

Jenny gave a gasp of horror and scooped the child into her arms. In the urgency of the situation, they'd both forgotten the children.

'Mummy will be fine, angel,' Alex said firmly, giving the little girl a quick smile before transferring his gaze to Jenny.

'Get the children away.' His voice was remarkably calm.

'Ask that family over there to look after them for a minute and then get yourself back over here. I'm going to need your help.'

Jenny did as he ordered, her palms clammy as she ushered the children to the family sitting near them on the beach.

Zoe was trying to ask more questions but fortunately the other family immediately saw the problem and took over, comforting and distracting the little girl.

By the time she'd sprinted back to Alex, Libby was barely conscious. Her lips were tinged blue and she was wheezing badly.

Alex was trying to reassure her but Jenny could see the tension in his broad shoulders.

'The adrenaline hasn't touched her and I don't have any with me. I left it in the house. Everything is swelling up,' he muttered, raking long fingers through her hair in a gesture of frustration. 'Go through her handbag again and see if you can find hydrocortisone. I told her to carry both.'

Frantically hoping that Libby had followed her brother's advice, Jenny pushed aside lipsticks, mirrors, nail varnish, ribbons and closed her fingers around an ampoule of hydrocortisone and a syringe.

'I've got it!'

'Draw it up,' Alex ordered, struggling to keep Libby's airway patent.

Jenny did as he asked and handed him the syringe.

'I can't stop what I'm doing—you're going to have to do it,' he said immediately. 'She carries a tourniquet. Put it on her arm and find a vein. I want you to give it IV. *Where the hell is that helicopter?*'

Jenny didn't argue but she was suddenly terrified that she wouldn't be able to do what he asked.

Working in a well-equipped accident and emergency department was very different to delivering lifesaving first aid on a beach. Especially when the victim was someone you knew.

Her hands were shaking and she felt physically sick.

She tightened the tourniquet, aware of the sound of a helicopter in the distance.

By now a small crowd had gathered and Alex was giving instructions.

'Make an "X" in the sand so that they can land, and clear everyone away! Hurry!'

Jenny concentrated on Libby's arm. 'That looks like a good vein.'

Please, let it be a good vein.

'Go for it. And don't miss.' Alex lifted his eyes and his gaze burned into hers, giving her courage. 'Good girl. You can do it.'

She swallowed hard and then swabbed the skin and picked up the syringe. She pushed the needle, felt the skin give and then she was in the vein.

'Well done.' Alex was still watching. 'Now inject it—that's right. A bit faster.'

As Libby removed the syringe, the paramedics sprinted up to them with oxygen.

Alex grabbed it and covered Libby's mouth and nose with the mask. 'Get me some more adrenaline,' he ordered swiftly. 'I've given her one lot and it's done nothing. I want to try some more.' He turned his attention back to his sister, stroking her hair and talking gently to her while maintaining her compromised airway. 'If this doesn't work I'll need to intubate her.'

He swore softly, the strain clearly visible on his handsome face, and Jenny stood watching, totally powerless to help as the paramedics handed Alex a syringe.

He gave Libby another injection of adrenaline. 'Come on, sweetheart,' he said calmly, discarding the empty syringe and smoothing Libby's blonde hair away from her forehead with a hand that wasn't quite steady.

As if in response to his voice, Libby's eyes flickered open and she started to retch.

Alex let out a breath and immediately turned her on her

side. 'Good girl. You're going to be fine. I'm here, sweetheart. I'm here.'

Hearing the shake in his usually confident voice, Jenny felt her eyes fill. If she'd ever doubted that Alex was capable of love, those doubts had now gone. His love for his sister was obvious to all watching.

He looked at the paramedics, his face white. 'I'm coming with you and we need to be prepared to intubate her. Can you call ahead and warn the unit that we're bringing in a severe case of anaphylactic shock caused by a bee sting?'

Alex turned his attention back to Libby who seemed to be improving by the minute.

The swelling around her mouth and tongue had reduced slightly and at last she appeared to be aware of what was going on.

'Alex—'

'You're going to be OK, sweetheart,' he said hoarsely, running a hand over his rough jaw. 'You're going to be fine. Which is more than can be said for the rest of us. You gave us the fright of our lives. Do that to me again and I'll bloody well kill you myself.'

But he held onto his sister's hand tightly and there was no missing the depth of love in his eyes as he watched her closely, checking that her condition continued to improve.

He looked totally wrung out and it was hardly surprising. Handling a medical emergency on a public beach was stressful enough, without the patient being an adored sister.

Libby didn't respond for a moment and then she tried to speak again. 'The girls—'

'I'll take them,' Jenny said quickly, placing a hand on Alex's shoulder in a gesture of sympathy. 'I'll stay with them for as long as you need me to.'

At the very least she could do that. She wished she could do more. Anything to ease the tension in Alex's shoulders.

The paramedics were back with a stretcher and Jenny stood to one side while they prepared to lift Libby.

'I'm going to need to stay with her,' Alex said, his eyes still on his sister, and Jenny nodded.

'Of course. Stay as long as you need to.'

'I'll call Andreas from the hospital.' He turned to her with a harassed smile. 'I'm landing you with three children, Red Riding Hood.'

She gave a calm smile. 'I can cope with three children.'

'Athena is a monkey.'

'I can cope. You just worry about Libby.'

'I am.' He let out a breath and then shook his head slowly. 'Thanks, Jenny.'

'No thanks needed,' she whispered, but he was back beside Libby, checking her airway, talking to her, reassuring her while they carried her across the sand to the waiting helicopter.

Once it took off the crowd dispersed and Jenny thanked the family that had taken the three children.

'Will Mummy die?' Zoe looked at her with huge eyes, her lower lip trembling ominously.

'No, darling.' Jenny stooped to hug her, feeling her own tears start. It had been a horrifying, frightening experience for all of them, especially the children. 'Uncle Alex has already made her better. They're just taking her to hospital to give her some more medicine.'

And to be ready if she relapsed. Oh, God…

Zoe nodded solemnly. 'Uncle Alex is very clever. Mummy and Daddy told me that. He'd never let Mummy die.'

Jenny brushed the tears away from her cheeks. She didn't even want to think about Libby dying, but she knew just how close it had been.

Aware of her responsibility to Libby's children, she made a huge effort and managed what she hoped was a relatively normal smile. 'He is clever. Very clever. Now, then, how do you fancy going home and playing an amazing game in the bath?'

CHAPTER NINE

IT WAS two next morning when Alex finally arrived home.

The children were fast asleep together in the nursery and Jenny was lying on her bed, reading.

The moment she heard his footsteps on the stairs she put the book down and held her breath. She'd been longing for news but she hadn't wanted to call the hospital and disturb Alex so she'd forced herself to be patient.

He paused in the entrance to her bedroom, his broad shoulders filling the doorway.

'I thought you'd be asleep.'

'I was too worried about Libby,' she confessed shakily, 'and I wanted to listen out for the children. Particularly Zoe. She's old enough to understand that her mummy is really ill. We talked about it and I think she was all right, but I've been worried she might wake up and go looking for Libby.'

His eyes glittered strangely in the semi-darkness. 'You're a good, kind person, Red Riding Hood.'

Jenny shook her head. 'I felt totally useless out there on the beach.'

'You weren't useless,' he said gruffly. 'You did a good job.'

Jenny's eyes filled. 'It was so awful.'

He held out his arms and she went into them, feeling the reassuring warmth and hardness of his chest against her cheek.

'How is she?'

'Off the critical list, I hope.'

She lifted her head and even in the limited light she could see the evidence of stress in his handsome features. Given that he'd been ill with flu only days earlier, it was amazing that he was still standing. 'We're keeping her in hospital for twenty-four hours at least because people can have prolonged reactions and I'm not taking any chances. Andreas is flying back now. He should be here in the morning.'

Libby bit her lip. 'You saved her life.'

Alex gave a laugh that was totally lacking in humour. 'Unfortunately it isn't the first time. It happened once before, at one of my parents' wretched garden parties. None of us knew she was even allergic to bee stings before then. She collapsed and, of course, we had nothing. No adrenaline. Nothing. It was touch and go.'

'So now she always carries adrenaline?'

Alex nodded. 'Thank goodness. Although I'm going to tell her that she needs to carry more than one syringe of the stuff.'

Jenny lifted hand and touched his cheek gently. 'You must feel worn out after that. I can't imagine what it must have felt like, seeing your sister collapse like that.'

'It was traumatic,' he muttered wearily, and she shrugged helplessly.

'Can I get you anything? A whisky?'

Despite the obvious tension, he gave a soft laugh. 'You're actually offering to pour me a whisky?'

She gave a hesitant smile. 'I think you need to relax. If it didn't taste so revolting I'd have one myself.'

His blue eyes burned into hers. 'And what if I prefer to use one of your other methods?'

Her breath caught at the look in his eyes and she felt her legs wobble. 'Which method did you have in mind?'

He hesitated for a long moment and then he gave a groan and slid his hands into her hair, pulling her hard against him.

She held her breath, aching with anticipation as she waited for his kiss, but he just stared down at her, his expression inscrutable.

'You are such a gentle, kind person, Jenny,' he muttered hoarsely, 'and I am totally wrong for you.'

The blood was pounding in her ears and her insides melted. 'You're not wrong for me.'

He stroked her hair away from her face, his eyes devouring hers. 'I can't give you a relationship.'

'I know that.'

His breathing was unsteady. 'So why aren't you running?'

'Because I love you,' she said simply, and he closed his eyes and gave a groan.

Jenny...'

'It's OK,' she whispered. 'I'm not asking anything of you. I just wanted to be honest with you. I know you don't love me back. I don't expect you to.'

Suddenly she didn't care about his relationship with her sister. Being with Alex felt totally right.

For this one night, they were meant to be together.

He opened his eyes and his hands tightened on her face. 'You don't know what you're saying.'

'Oh, yes, I do.' She gave a shy smile. 'I know exactly what I'm saying.'

Breathing heavily, he lowered his forehead to hers. She could feel the hard bite of his fingers through the thin fabric of her T-shirt and the warmth of his powerful body pressing against hers. The excitement was so intense that it threatened to swamp her.

'The children...'

'Athena and Zoe never wake up,' he muttered, inhaling her scent as he kissed his way down her neck.

'Alex...' She gasped his name and lifted her hands, terrified that her legs wouldn't hold her any longer. But fortunately they didn't have to. He scooped her up easily into his arms and carried her into his bedroom, laying her gently on his bed before coming down on top of her.

He was all powerful muscle and hard male strength and she felt her heart pound uncontrollably as she placed her hands on his arms in a gesture of pure female surrender.

She stared up at him, her fingers digging into the curves of his biceps, waiting, wanting, and finally he lowered his head and kissed her.

His mouth played gently with hers and his tongue flickered out and traced the seam of her lips until she opened to him with a gasp of longing. He delved deeper, exploring her mouth with a thoroughness that left her trembling and clutching his shoulders. He pulled away for just long enough to strip off his clothes and then she felt the smooth slide of his hand on her T-shirt. He removed it in a swift movement and then he was touching her breast, teasing her nipple until moist heat pooled between her thighs.

Alex dragged his mouth away from hers and she briefly caught the glitter of his eyes before he shifted himself slightly so that he could gaze at her breasts.

'I'm really flat-chested,' she joked feebly, and he lifted his head and his eyes burned into hers.

'You're absolutely beautiful,' he said hoarsely. 'Don't ever believe anything different. And you have gorgeous breasts.'

She lay still, transfixed by the expression in his eyes, knowing that he meant it. And the knowledge made her feel more like a woman than she ever had before.

And then he lowered his head to her breast and heat exploded in her belly. With a skilled flick of his clever tongue he teased one pink nipple while his fingers played gently with the other. Her response was instantaneous, her hips shifting restlessly against the cool sheets in an effort to relieve the building pressure in her pelvis. The excitement was so intense that she thought she'd explode and perhaps he knew that because he ceased the flicking motion and instead drew her nipple into the damp heat of his mouth.

Jenny's whole body burned with longing.

She writhed and sobbed underneath him, clutching at his dark hair in a fevered desperation.

'Alex…'

He lifted his head, his blue eyes suddenly fierce. 'Don't ever tell me you're not attractive,' he said thickly, his thumb slowly tracing the contour of her damp, pouting nipple. 'You're incredible. And intensely sexual.'

Her breath was coming in pants. 'Alex, please…'

'Please, what?'

'I need you to—' She broke off, unable to believe that she was being so brazen. 'Please, touch me—please…'

Alex shifted slightly so that he was looking directly down at her and then his hand slid down her heated flesh, impatiently removed the barrier of her panties and then returned to rest lightly on the dark curls that protected the heart of her femininity.

'Is this what you want?'

This time, instead of stopping him she arched against him, her whole body begging for his touch, encouraging him.

His eyes locked on hers, increasing the intimacy as he parted her legs with long, clever fingers, caressing her with a sure touch.

She gasped, her hands biting into the powerful muscles of his shoulders, unable to look away from the raw sexual need that glittered in those blue eyes.

His gaze stripped her naked, both physically and emotionally, and the knowledge that there were no barriers between them left her heady with excitement.

Amazingly she felt no shyness, only a sinful desire to know this man in every possible sense.

She stroked her fingers over the dark hair that covered his chest, tracing its course down his sleek, heated flesh until finally they brushed gently over the throbbing heat of his arousal.

He gave a harsh groan and she touched him as she'd never touched a man before, intrigued by the silken heat that pulsed in her seeking hand. Gently she explored him, her eyes still locked with his, the blood pulsing in her veins as she learned his power and masculinity.

'Jenny, I can't...' He eased away from her, his breathing rapid. 'You have to give me a minute.'

'No!' She coiled her legs around him in explicit invitation but the muscles of his shoulders bunched and he held himself away from her.

'Not yet—you're not ready.'

Not ready?

How much more ready could she get?

She gave a sob of frustration, lifting her hips towards his in desperation, but he ignored her seductive movement and slid downwards, intent on tormenting her still further.

She'd thought that excitement had pushed her beyond shyness but when she felt the cool flick of his tongue against the damp core of her womanhood she tensed and tried to wriggle away from him, but he held her firm, ignoring her shocked protests. His hands holding her still, he took what he wanted, exploring her in the most intimate way possible until she forgot about shyness, consumed by an excitement more powerful and delicious than she could possibly have imagined.

And then finally, when she felt the pulses start deep inside her, he slid back up the bed and took her mouth, his kiss both erotic and explicit as he moved over her, his weight on his elbows.

'Curl your legs around me,' he ordered roughly, and she did as he instructed, in the grip of sensations totally beyond her control.

It was going to happen...

Finally, now, it was going to happen...

Alex hesitated briefly, staring down into her face, and suddenly she was terrified that he was going to change his mind again. Terrified that she wouldn't please him.

Her fingers slid down the sleek skin of his back, urging him forward, bringing him closer to her feminine heat, and with a sharply indrawn breath he slid an arm under her hips and lifted her, positioning her to take him.

She tensed as she felt the hard probe of his shaft against her and then he thrust gently, pausing to allow her to accommodate him before deepening his possession. She felt herself open to him, relishing each movement, feeling his pulsing strength as she drew him in.

He paused, his breathing unsteady, a sheen of sweat on his brow as he stared down at her, his eyes fierce with restrained passion.

'Am I hurting you?'

She shook her head and urged him closer, refusing to acknowledge the flash of pain that tried to intrude on the rising heat of her excitement.

But he must have felt her body's faint resistance to the alien male intrusion because he swore softly and smoothed her dampened hair away from her face with a hand that was far from steady.

'Relax, sweetheart,' he urged hoarsely, and she did as he instructed, hypnotised by the look in his blue eyes. 'Better?'

She nodded, everything she felt reflected in her eyes as she gazed up at him, and he closed his eyes and moved deeply within her.

'You're mine now, Jenny,' he groaned hoarsely, each movement of his hips taking him deeper, building the tension. 'All mine.'

Her eyes closed.

All his.

She wanted so much for it to be true and for this one, wild, suspended moment in time she surrendered to the fantasy and clung to him, feeling the tiny shivers build within her as he drove them both to a peak of pulsing ecstasy that seemed to last for ever.

Sated and limp, she clung to the sleek muscle of his shoulders, relishing each moment of their intimacy, knowing that it couldn't last.

How could it?

He wouldn't want the children to find them like this, locked together, when they padded into his bedroom in the morning, and neither would she.

And despite the fiercely possessive words he'd spoken at the height of passion, she knew that, for him, the night had just been a lush oasis of pleasure in an otherwise barren day of stress and anxiety.

He rolled onto his back, taking her with him, holding her tight against his hair roughened chest.

'You are amazing.' He slipped his fingers under her chin and forced her to look at him, his expression stunned. 'Jenny...'

'Shh...' She placed a finger over his lips, wanting to stop him before he said something that would pierce the bubble of happiness that still bloomed inside her. 'Let's not talk about it.'

Alex gave a totally male smile. 'Trust you to be different,' he said gruffly, snuggling her back into the crook of his arm. 'A woman who doesn't want to talk after sex.'

Jenny felt a tiny stab of disappointment.

Sex.

Of course, that's all it would have been to Alex. What else had she expected? That after enjoying one night of passion with her he'd suddenly discover that all his years of avoiding women had been for the express purpose of keeping himself free for *her*?

She slid an arm around him, desperate to hold onto him for as long as possible. For tonight, at least, he was hers. And if that was all she could ever have of Alex then she was going to relish every minute.

* * *

Jenny awoke feeling warm and comfortable and realised that she was still snuggled against Alex, her limbs tangled with his. She moved her head and glanced at the clock. Five o'clock. Still early for grown-ups but not small children and she had three of them to look after.

Conscious that she didn't want them to find her in Alex's bed, she slid away from him, trying not to wake him, quickly retrieved her discarded T-shirt from the floor and hurried back to her own room.

She was only just in time.

Within minutes she heard Athena cry out and tiptoed into the nursery to see if she could settle her down again.

But the little girl was wide awake and ready to play, and her cries had woken Daisy who was suddenly equally alert.

Resigning herself to an early start, Jenny lifted Daisy out of her cot and took the two youngest children down to the living room to play.

She didn't want them to wake Alex.

Remembering just how little sleep he'd had the night before, her face heated and she gave a wistful sigh.

She'd thought that one night with Alex was better than none but now she wasn't so sure. He'd taught her more about her body in one night than she'd learned by herself in twenty-three years. He'd released a part of herself that she hadn't known existed and now it was loose she didn't know how to handle it.

She felt like a different person—her whole being focused on the feminine part of herself that he'd awakened with his clever touch.

For the first time in her life she felt like a real woman. An attractive, flesh-and-blood woman.

Restless and tense after everything that had happened, she took the children into the kitchen, strapped Daisy into the high chair and let Athena help her make bread.

She nipped upstairs once to check on Zoe and found her curled up in bed with Alex, both of them fast asleep.

Jenny looked at the two of them and felt her heart turn over.

If Alex truly thought he'd be a bad father then he was fooling himself.

He'd be a fantastic father.

She walked quietly back downstairs, leaving the two of them sleeping and they eventually emerged at eight o'clock, yawning and tousled. Zoe was still in her pyjamas and Alex had pulled on a pair of jeans.

Unshaven and with his chest bare, he looked breathtakingly attractive and Jenny blushed as she caught his eye.

She had absolutely no experience of morning-after conversation. Fortunately the presence of the children made everything easier.

'Athena and I have made rolls,' she said cheerfully, and Alex glanced round his kitchen with a wry smile.

'So I see. Did any of the dough make it into the oven?'

'Just a bit.' Jenny smiled. 'She woke very early and I wanted to keep her busy so that she didn't...well...'

Alex nodded to indicate that he'd understood that she hadn't wanted the little girl to miss her mother's presence.

He stooped to put Zoe in one of the kitchen chairs and then stretched, and Jenny's eyes were drawn to the ripple of muscle in his shoulders. He had a fantastic body and just remembering what he'd made her feel in bed made her shiver with longing.

Suddenly she was aware of every unfamiliar ache of her body.

He looked at her keenly. 'Are you OK?'

She knew exactly what he was asking and met his gaze boldly. 'Very OK.'

Not for a moment did she want him thinking that she regretted what had happened between them.

How could she possibly regret anything so utterly perfect?

There was an expression in his eyes that she couldn't interpret. 'Good.' His eyes searched hers for a moment longer and then he reached across the table for a roll and put one on a plate for Zoe. 'I've spoken to Andreas. He arrived during the night and went straight to the hospital.'

Jenny poured some milk for Zoe. 'He was lucky he was able to get a flight so quickly.'

'His family has a private jet,' Alex said in such a matter-of-fact voice that Jenny felt herself deflate like an overfilled balloon.

He'd mentioned the private jet with a total lack of interest. If ever she'd needed a reminder of the difference in their social circumstances then he'd just provided one.

What was she doing with this man?

He moved in circles that were so far removed from her own that it was ridiculous. Their paths never would have crossed if it hadn't been for Chloe.

But even knowing that, she couldn't regret what had happened the night before.

Oblivious to her distress, Alex drank a mug of coffee and then stood up. 'I'm going back to the hospital. Are you OK here with the children?'

Jenny nodded. 'Of course.'

'I'll see you later, then.' His eyes meshed with hers and she read the promise there. Despite all the efforts of her brain to maintain common sense, her heart lurched with excitement. He was definitely telling her that last night hadn't been a one-off for him.

Joy bubbled up inside her and she watched while he left the room and then tried to concentrate on giving the children their breakfast.

'Why are you smiling, Jenny?' Zoe's innocent question made her bite her lip with guilt.

Their mother was lying ill in hospital and here she was smiling like an idiot because of Alex.

'It's always good to try and smile, Zoe,' she said quietly, remembering all the times she'd almost forgotten how to smile after Daisy's birth. 'Do you want some more milk?'

Zoe held out her cup. 'Will I be able to see Mummy today?'

'I hope so.' Jenny poured milk into the cup. 'Your daddy arrived last night so he'll come and see you soon, too.'

'Daddy?' Zoe's face lit up with excitement and she drank her milk while Athena flung a half-eaten bread roll across the kitchen floor.

They spent a quiet morning at home, playing with toys and painting pictures, and halfway through the morning the phone rang in Alex's study.

Jenny hesitated. Should she answer it?

What if it was Andreas, calling from the hospital?

Deciding that she couldn't risk ignoring a phone when Libby was so ill, she checked that the children were occupied and hurried into Alex's study.

The phone stopped ringing as she reached it and she realised that there was a fax coming through.

Relieved that it obviously hadn't been anything to do with Libby, she turned to leave the room but then she recognised her name on the top of the paper.

Feeling vaguely uncomfortable, she reached for the first sheet and saw the bold letterhead of a major London law firm followed by a heading that contained her name.

Hands shaking, she clutched at the paper, reading the report that followed. Her face paled and she sank down onto one of Alex's chairs as she read the detail of the lawyer's investigations.

She was still staring at the paper in mute horror when Zoe pushed her way into the room.

'Daisy's finished her milk and Athena has dripped paint on Uncle Alex's floor,' she said, tilting her head to one side as she looked at Jenny. 'You look sick? Are you sick?'

Jenny struggled to find her voice. 'I'm not sick,' she

croaked, standing up with an effort and putting the papers down on Alex's desk. 'I'm fine.'

Considering the fact that she'd just discovered that Alex couldn't possibly be Daisy's father. According to the report, he'd done no more than dance one dance with her sister that night and Chloe had left with someone entirely different. Someone who she'd then spent the night with. A high-profile public figure who was married and already had three children by his very beautiful wife. A man whose marriage was held up as a perfect example of family life.

No wonder Chloe had been reluctant to tell her who the father was.

Jenny covered her eyes with her hands, utterly consumed by the enormity of Chloe's lies.

It was clear now why she'd refused to name the baby's father right through her pregnancy. To have exposed this man would have led to a massive public scandal that would have harmed everyone, including Chloe and her unborn child.

Jenny sucked in a breath.

Had this man ever known about the baby? Had her sister even tried to contact him? Or had he regretted his affair and turned his back on her?

Perhaps she'd never know the answer, but one thing she did know for sure—Alex Westerling was not Daisy's father.

She thought about all the accusations she'd flung at him and gave a groan of horror. How could she have said all those terrible things? And she'd forced herself and Daisy on him, moved into his house, interrupted his life...

She raised a hand to her mouth, totally appalled at her own behaviour.

How could she have done that?

But she knew the answer, of course. She'd believed Chloe. And Chloe, knowing that she was dangerously ill, had obviously wanted to secure protection for Daisy. A mother's instinct to do the best for her child.

But whatever Chloe's motivations had been, the truth was that Alex had absolutely no responsibility towards Daisy at all and she didn't fool herself that he felt anything for *her* other than lust.

There was no doubt at all that he'd be delighted to receive the lawyer's letter.

'Jenny?'

Realising that Zoe was still looking at her with a worried look on her little face, she forced herself to stand up and walk through to the kitchen, dealing with the children on automatic.

She'd already decided what she must do.

She had to leave.

And she just couldn't face Alex. She'd moved into his house with a baby who wasn't his, had said such dreadful things to him, had believed him capable of—

She closed her eyes briefly and sucked in a breath. As soon as Andreas arrived from the hospital, she'd leave.

And Alex could return to the bachelor existence that he treasured so much.

CHAPTER TEN

ANDREAS arrived towards lunchtime and the girls flung themselves on him with undisguised delight.

Jenny had already packed her little car and had left a short note to Alex. She'd torn up six versions, her brain totally refusing to produce the right words as she'd tried to apologise for the dreadful things she'd said. How did one even begin to apologise for being so completely and utterly wrong?

In the end she'd given up trying to say what was in her heart and had just left a short, succinct letter of apology that stated the facts but left out the emotion.

And now that Andreas had arrived, she could leave.

The prospect left her feeling utterly depressed.

'How is Libby?'

'Much better.' Andreas smiled and Jenny could see immediately why Libby had fallen for him. He was a very charismatic man. 'We hope to bring her home in the morning. In the meantime I'm going to take the girls to see her. She's missing them terribly.'

'And they've missed her.' Jenny gave him a wan smile and Andreas looked at her keenly.

'Is everything all right?' His Greek accent was suddenly

very pronounced. 'You look very troubled about something. Have my girls been hard work?'

She shook her head immediately. 'They've been wonderful. I love them.'

It was true. The little girls were completely adorable and they'd been enchanted by Daisy, caring for her as if she were a tiny doll.

Andreas looked at her closely. 'But you are upset about something—I can see that.' His tone was unbelievably gentle. 'Can I help?'

She shook her head, not trusting herself to speak. His kindness was the final straw. She really had to get away.

'I made some chocolate-chip muffins for Libby,' she muttered, hurrying into the kitchen so that he couldn't see the tears in her eyes. 'She's probably not up to eating yet but I wanted to do something.'

'If it's chocolate, Libby will eat it,' Andreas said dryly, 'and it was very kind of you. But, Jenny—'

'I have to go and see to Daisy,' she said quickly, and without giving him a chance to say more Jenny handed him the tin of cakes and left the room.

Alex checked the monitors and glanced at his sister. 'Everything looks OK.'

'I know that. They've been in here a hundred times to check on me.' Libby looked at him with affection and gratitude. 'I don't know what to say, Alex...'

'Say that from now on you'll carry two adrenaline injections,' Alex drawled, back to his cool self now that his sister was out of danger. 'One wasn't enough.'

Libby closed her eyes at the memory. 'I was *so* scared—I keep remembering—'

'Don't—it was the worse moment of my life.' Alex's voice was suddenly gruff and he leaned forward to hug his sister just as Andreas walked into the room with the children.

There was an emotional reunion and the children totally ignored hospital protocol and crawled all over the bed to get to their mother.

Andreas took his brother-in-law to one side. 'I met Jenny.'

Alex smiled. 'Great, isn't she? Doubtless she was cooking.'

Andreas didn't return the smile. 'Have you spoken to her today?'

Alex frowned slightly, his eyes on his sister. 'Yes—briefly this morning. Why?'

'She looked very upset about something when I arrived,' Andreas said quietly. 'She wouldn't tell me what.'

Alex turned, suddenly giving him his full attention. 'Upset?'

'It was probably nothing.' Andreas shrugged dismissively. 'The children had made a terrible mess—it was probably that.'

'Jenny doesn't care about mess,' Alex said tersely. 'And small children don't faze her in the least. In fact, I haven't really seen anything much faze her.'

Suddenly he felt an intense feeling of foreboding.

'You're sure something was wrong?'

'Well, I don't know her, of course, but, yes…' Andreas lifted a broad shoulder '…I'd say something was very wrong. She looked… stricken.'

Stricken?

After what they'd shared the night before he hadn't expected Jenny to look anything but happy.

But what did you really give her last night? a tiny voice nagged him as he struggled to make sense of his feelings. He wasn't the type of man who said 'I love you', even in the middle of the hottest sex, and he was well aware that he hadn't said it to Jenny. But she hadn't minded that. Had she?

In fact, she'd even told him that she didn't expect commitment.

Which just about made her his perfect woman.

So why was he panicking about losing her?

He'd never worried about losing a woman before. Ever.

Shaken out of his customary cool by emotions he didn't understand, Alex looked at his sister. 'I need to go home. I need to check on Jenny. I'll see you later.'

Libby shifted Athena out of the way so she could concentrate on her brother. 'She loves you, Alex. Really, really loves you.'

Alex tensed, his conscience pricking him for the first time in his life.

Damn. He never ever should have made love to her.

But it had been so perfect…

Suddenly he felt as though he was being suffocated and he left the hospital at a run.

He just had a bad feeling.

He drove at a pace that would have horrified Jenny and the minute he pulled up outside his house he knew that Andreas was right. Something was very wrong.

Her car had gone.

Not even bothering to slam the driver's door, he sprinted into the house, hoping to find some evidence that her absence was just temporary. But he knew that it wasn't and a quick glance into the rooms upstairs confirmed that she'd taken all her things.

It wasn't just her car that had gone.

She'd gone, too.

He checked in the kitchen and saw the note left on the table.

His hands shaking, he ripped open the envelope and read the short letter and then strode through to his study to pick up the fax that she'd mentioned.

He skimmed it quickly, taking in the fact that he wasn't Daisy's father, and then dropped the fax back on his desk and turned the air blue with words that would have horrified his sister.

He should have been relieved to have his innocence confirmed but instead he felt an unfamiliar panic surge inside him.

Jenny had gone.

She'd gone because his lawyer had confirmed that he couldn't be Daisy's father.

And suddenly he realised just how much he'd wanted to be exactly that.

He glanced around him, acknowledging for the first time just how much Jenny had changed his life in the short time since she'd entered it. She'd filled all the empty spaces with her warmth and gentleness and she'd turned his house into a home. Not by her cooking or the way she'd nurtured both him and Daisy, but just by her presence.

And he didn't give a damn whether Daisy was his or not. He wanted them back in his life.

For the first time in his life he'd found a woman that he didn't want to lose.

Alex let out a long breath and realised that if he lost Jenny and Daisy he would have lost everything that was important to him.

Without dwelling on his feelings a moment longer, he strode back to his car and drove at a breakneck speed down the road that led away from the coast. He didn't know where she was heading but he guessed that she would have started on this road and his car was a lot faster than hers.

His shoulders rigid with tension, he shifted gears like a racing driver, peering impatiently along every new stretch of road in the hope of seeing her little red car.

But there was nothing and he started to wonder whether he could have been wrong about the direction she'd taken.

Maybe she'd stayed in the village after all, or maybe she'd taken back roads.

Growling with frustration, he was about to hit the accelerator once more when he saw a flash of red up ahead.

He slowed his pace and then felt a lurch of horror.

The flash of red wasn't on the road.

There was a car lying in the ditch, and it was Jenny's.

He hit the brakes and the car came to a halt with a shriek of tyres.

'Jenny!' His voice was hoarse as he slid down the bank to the driver's side. 'Jenny, sweetheart!'

She was slumped against the steering-wheel, eyes closed, blood pouring from a cut on her head.

Glancing into the back seat, Alex saw that Daisy was still safely strapped in her car seat and was crying noisily.

She seemed to be OK, which was more than could be said for Jenny.

Panic pulsing through his veins for the second time in twenty-four hours, he fumbled for his mobile phone and rang for an ambulance, his voice shaking as he gave their position, all the while tugging at the door which had obviously become jammed in the accident.

Ordering them to bring a fire crew as well, he tried the other side of the car and managed to get the door open.

With a rush of relief he slid into the passenger seat. 'Jenny. Jenny, it's Alex. Talk to me.'

He lifted a hand to her neck, checking for a pulse, and then heard the sound of a siren.

He checked her airway, satisfied himself that it was clear and that she was breathing, and did a quick assessment of the rest of her injuries. She didn't appear to be bleeding anywhere apart from the cut on her head and he could see her feet and legs.

Then he leaned into the back seat and swiftly checked Daisy.

'Well, at least you're crying, angel, which means you're conscious,' he said softly, checking her as best he could while she was still in her car seat.

'Alex?' The face of one of the paramedics appeared at the window and he turned with relief.

'Mike, get the baby out of here—and be careful with her. I think she's all right but I can't be sure. Then get back here with a backboard. Jenny might have hurt her neck.'

There was no way he was going to risk moving Jenny without some sort of support to her cervical spine.

As the fire engine arrived, Jenny opened her eyes.

'Jenny!' Alex's voice was hoarse and he stroked a gentle hand over her head. 'Sweetheart, can you hear me?'

Her eyes drifted closed again and he fought against the panic that rose inside him.

'Jenny!'

She opened her eyes again and looked at him. 'Daisy?'

He let out a groan of relief at her croaked question. At least she could remember something about what had happened.

It was typical of Jenny that her first thought was for Daisy.

'Daisy's fine and we're going to get you out of this car really soon. We're just fetching a backboard.'

'My head hurts.'

'Anything else? Does it hurt anywhere else?'

His tone was urgent and there was a brief pause while she thought about his question. 'No. I don't think so.'

The next half-hour was a blur of frantic activity while everyone worked to free Jenny from the car.

Finally she was in the ambulance and Alex scrambled in beside her. 'OK. *Move!*'

Jenny looked at him, her face bruised and battered. 'You can't leave your precious car by the side of the road—someone might drive into it.'

'I don't care about my car.' He took her hand in his. 'Jenny, do you remember what happened?'

She didn't appear to be suffering from memory loss but she'd been knocked out and he wanted to check.

'I remember.' She closed her eyes and then they fluttered open again. 'How did you know where to find me?'

He gave a wan smile. 'Lucky guess. What happened? Why did you crash?'

Her eyes slid away from his. 'I don't know. I suppose I wasn't concentrating.'

His grip tightened on her hand. 'All right. Don't worry about that now. The only thing that matters is that you're both OK.'

And, thank God, they seemed to be.

He just wanted to get her to the unit so that he could check that she hadn't done any damage to her cervical spine.

'Alex—' her voice was a croak '—did you get my letter?'

His jaw clenched. 'Yes.'

'She isn't yours.' Her eyes filled. 'I really believed she was. I'm so sorry for everything I said.'

His body tensed and he fought the impulse to drag her roughly into his arms and kiss her senseless. He didn't want to risk making her injuries worse and anyway they had a paramedic sitting in the back with them.

'We can't talk about this now,' he said gruffly, squeezing her hand to reassure her. 'Wait till we've sorted you out then we've got all the time in the world to talk.'

'But—'

'Later,' he said, glancing impatiently out of the window. 'Where the hell are we?'

'Nearly there,' the paramedic said quietly, and sure enough Alex recognised the entrance to the hospital.

He just wanted to arrive so that he could give Jenny and Daisy a thorough check-up.

And then they had some serious talking to do.

Jenny lay in the bed with Daisy in a cot next to her.

'Do I really have to stay in overnight?' she asked the nurse, who was checking her blood pressure yet again.

'You had a nasty bump on the head,' the nurse reminded her, recording the results with a satisfied nod. 'Fortunately everything seems to be all right but Alex will hang us out to dry if we let you move a muscle before he says so.'

Jenny gave a weak smile. 'He's a bully.'

'That's me.' His dark drawl came from the doorway and he took the chart from the nurse and glanced at the monitors. 'How are you feeling?'

Jenny pulled a face. 'Headache, but apart from that—fine.'

'Have you been sick?'

She shook her head. 'I'm all right. Really.'

'Well, we're keeping you in to be on the safe side.' He rolled his eyes. 'What with you and Libby, we can virtually fill a ward with our family.'

Our family.

The words caused a pain so intense that she closed her eyes. They reminded her of just how desperately she'd wanted to be just that.

A family.

With Alex.

Somehow she'd got used to living with him. Even though she'd always known that there could never be anything permanent between them, she'd played the role so convincingly for Daisy's sake that now she was finding it hard to let go of the dream.

Alex looked at her stricken face and turned to the nurse. 'Can you leave us, please?'

She vanished immediately, closing the door behind her.

'Right.' Alex sat on the bed, his handsome face inscrutable as ever. 'Time for you and I to have a chat.'

'Yes.' She pinned a smile on her face, knowing what was coming. He wanted an apology. 'I just don't know how to apologise for what I said to you—all the things I accused you of. There's nothing I can say, except that I was so wrong about you.'

'Only about Daisy's paternity,' Alex said flatly, all traces of humour totally absent. 'You were pretty much right about everything else. I am a selfish, thoughtless bastard.'

Jenny stared at him, startled.

She'd expected him to be condemning *her*, not himself.

'That's not true and you know it,' she said softly. 'You're incredibly generous.'

He gave a wry smile. 'I think you've painted a rather glossy picture of me, sweetheart.'

Looking at the slightly tousled dark hair, the rough jaw and the devilish blue eyes, Jenny failed to see how any picture of

Alex Westerling could ever come near to doing him justice, let alone be too glossy.

'Did you read the fax?'

She was still reeling with shock at the discovery of Daisy's true paternity and Alex's mouth tightened.

'Yes.' He gave a short laugh. 'What are you going to do?'

Jenny shook her head and turned to look at Daisy who was sleeping contentedly. 'I've decided not to do anything.'

Alex's mouth tightened. 'He owes you some sort of support.'

She turned back to him, her smile sad. 'He's married with three children, Alex. The only support he'd be able to give us is financial and I don't need that. What I really want for Daisy is a loving father. A good man in her life. Every little girl should have that.'

Alex sucked in a breath. 'So you're going to let him off?'

'It isn't an easy decision, but I'm thinking of his family rather than him,' Jenny said softly. 'How can I approach him, knowing that it could ruin his marriage and have dreadful consequences for his children? I'm pretty sure that what he and Chloe shared was just a one-night thing—a mistake for both of them.'

Alex took her hands in his. 'You're so damned forgiving.' He stroked a thumb over the palm of her hand, seeming strangely hesitant for once in his life.

'Well, after last night I'm not quite so naïve about sex,' Jenny confessed, a rueful smile touching her soft mouth. 'I can see how people might be swept away by the excitement. Common sense can go out of the window, even for a one-night stand.'

How could she condemn Chloe when she herself had followed the intensity of her emotions the night before?

'A one-night stand?' Alex's tone was hoarse. 'Is that what you think last night was for us?'

She blushed slightly and tried to tug her hand away from his, but he held it firmly. 'Alex, I know what sort of man you are. I know about your three-month rule.'

'I've always believed that rules are there to be broken.'

Alex's voice was rough and his hands tightened on hers. 'Jenny, I need to tell you a few things about myself. Things I've never shared with anyone apart from my sisters.'

She lay still, hardly daring to breathe, wondering what was coming. It was so unlike Alex to talk about himself. And it was obviously a struggle for him.

'My parents had the worst marriage you can imagine,' he said flatly. 'They fought, argued and my father had a string of very public affairs which my mother chose to ignore.'

Jenny held onto his hand. 'And you witnessed it all?'

'Fortunately the girls and I were sent to boarding school from a very young age.'

Fortunately?

Her heart contracted as she imagined what it must have been like for a small boy to be sent away from home. Away from all family contact. 'That must have been awful for you.'

'Awful?' He gave a bitter laugh. 'Actually, it was an escape from hell. It was the holidays that were awful but I usually managed to wangle myself an invite to a friend's house.'

Jenny looked at him helplessly. No wonder he was so fiercely independent. He'd been managing on his own from an age when most children were still utterly dependent on their parents.

'Is that the reason you've never wanted to commit to one woman?' she asked softly. 'Because you think that all marriages are like your parents'?'

He shook his head. 'No. I know that all marriages aren't like that. Libby and Katy are prime examples. They're both crazily in love with their respective partners. I just never thought that marriage was for me. Before today I never saw the point, to be honest. I always believed that marriage just forces people to stay together, who shouldn't be together, and sometimes children are caught in the crossfire.'

Before today?

What did he mean, before today?

Squashing down the tiny bud of hope which started to bloom

inside her, Jenny hardly dared to breathe. 'What's different today?'

Alex released her hands and cupped her face, looking deep into her eyes. 'Today,' he said softly, 'was the day you tried to drive out of my life. Today was the day that I finally understood why people get married. Today I finally discovered what people mean by the word "love". It's what I feel for you, Red Riding Hood.'

Jenny stared at him, mute. He couldn't be saying what she thought he was saying. She must have misunderstood.

'Alex?'

Her voice was a wistful croak and he lowered his head and kissed her gently on her parted lips. 'Jenny, I want to be that man in Daisy's life. And I want to be the man in your life. One night isn't enough, and three months won't be either.'

She stared at him. He wanted Daisy? He wanted her?

'Are you going to say something?' His blue gaze was suddenly intense. 'Last night you said you loved me, Jenny. Did you mean it? Do you mean it enough to marry me?'

She ran a tongue over her dry lips. 'You want to marry me?'

He gave a wry smile. 'I never thought I'd have to say the words twice. There's arrogance for you. Yes, I want to marry you. I want to marry you because there is no damn way I'm letting another man lay a finger on you. Last night I made you mine and I intend to keep you as mine. You let the wolf into your life and now there's no escape.'

Swamped by a cloud of euphoria, Jenny smiled. It seemed too much like a fantasy to be real and she couldn't quite let herself believe it.

Did real life really have endings like this?

'You really want to marry me?' She bit her lip and looked up at him. 'I disrupted your bachelor lifestyle.'

'Totally.'

'I make you eat breakfast '

His eyes dropped to her mouth. 'I love your breakfast.'

'I hide your whisky.'

His blue eyes gleamed. 'I never thought I'd say this, but I've discovered that there's something I prefer to single malt.'

She blushed. 'Alex…'

'I wonder if eventually you'll stop blushing,' he mused, stroking her cheek with a gentle finger. 'Maybe after fifty years with me you'll have got used to my wolfish ways.'

Her eyes twinkled. 'I haven't said yes yet.'

He grinned, his mouth hovering a breath away from hers. 'But you will.'

'You're very sure of yourself, Dr Westerling,' she whispered, feeling her heart rate increase dramatically. 'What if I say no?'

'I don't understand the word no,' he groaned, leaning forward to claim her mouth in a gentle kiss. 'I had a very limited education.'

'I can't believe you truly want the two of us.'

'Well, I do. And I'll do my best to be the very best father to Daisy. I know I've been pretty wild in the past, but you calm me down, Jen. I can learn the father stuff.'

She lifted a hand and touched his cheek. 'I never had any doubts that you'd be a brilliant father. It was only ever you who believed that.'

'Because I didn't think I could commit to anyone,' he said, 'and I wasn't willing to risk bringing children into a doomed relationship.'

'And now?' She gazed up at him. 'Do you believe you'll be a good father now?'

'With you as the mother, definitely,' he groaned, kissing her until the room started to spin. 'If I step out of line, you'll soon tell me. And now do you think you could put a chap out of his misery and give me an answer? Will you marry me or are you going to load up your basket of bread rolls and go back into the forest to search for Grandma?'

'She lived in the cottage,' Jenny reminded him, and his broad shoulders lifted in a shrug.

'See? I'm really going to need your help to do the daddy stuff properly. So what do you say?'

'Yes.' What other answer could there possibly be but yes? 'Very yes.'

He grinned. 'Very yes?'

'Very, very yes.'

'In that case you might want to wear this, just in case any of those doctors who keep slinking into your room to check up on you get any funny ideas.' He slid a hand into the pocket of his trousers and withdrew a tiny box which he flipped open.

Jenny gasped as she saw the beautiful diamond ring. 'That's for me?'

'Unless you want Daisy to have it.'

'B-but when did you get a chance to buy it?' Suddenly she couldn't bear the fact that he might have chosen this ring for someone else.

'I bullied the jeweller's into opening early for me,' Alex said, slipping the ring onto her finger. 'I know what you're thinking, but I've never bought a ring for anyone else in my life, angel— trust me on that one. This is just for you.'

Just for her?

Jenny stared down at her finger and her eyes filled. 'This is like a fairy-tale.'

'Not exactly,' Alex mocked gently. 'In the fairy-tale it wasn't the wolf who ended up with Red Riding Hood.'

She gave him a watery smile. 'I always thought the wolf was terribly misunderstood.'

Alex gave her a smile that was totally male. 'I wouldn't be so sure about that.'

And he bent his head and kissed her.

EPILOGUE

THE garden party was in full swing. An army of waiters circulated with champagne and the guests mingled in groups on the lawn.

'I cannot believe that Dad agreed to a bouncy castle,' Alex drawled, watching with amusement as the children slithered and jumped, shrieking with delight.

'He didn't.' Libby smiled smugly at her brother. 'I ordered it. My two absolutely adore bouncy castles and I didn't see why they shouldn't enjoy the party. It's more than we ever did as children. I arranged for it to arrive a few hours ago so Dad didn't have time to protest.'

Alex laughed and then glanced down to find Daisy tugging at his trouser leg. 'Hello, my angel.' He scooped her up in his arms and planted a kiss on her cheek. 'Having fun?'

'She's gorgeous, Alex.' Libby smiled as she looked at the little girl. 'I can't believe she's two and a half. Just think, it's been two whole years since I first met her. Remember my bee sting? It was so awful.'

Alex lifted an eyebrow. 'Bee sting? What bee sting?' But despite his mocking tone, his gaze was soft as it rested on his sister. 'I assume you carry adrenaline?'

Libby nodded and patted her handbag. 'Of course. Andreas is utterly paranoid about it. He has stocks of it everywhere.'

'Good.' Alex glanced across the lawn and grimaced. 'Have you seen Athena? What *has* she been eating this time?'

Libby smiled happily. 'Ketchup. Andreas banned it but she smiled at one of the waiters and he found her a giant bottle. I just stopped her wiping her fingers on the Prime Minister's jacket.'

'A Prime Minister with "red" streaks,' Alex said, his blue eyes amused. 'An interesting political statement.'

Libby looked from him to Daisy. 'It's been two years, Alex. Are you ever going to tell us who her real father is?'

Alex tensed and his blue eyes hardened. 'I'm her father,' he said softly, holding the little girl more tightly. 'She's my baby girl, aren't you, sweetheart?'

He nuzzled her neck and Daisy chuckled happily just as Jenny arrived looking cool and pretty in a blue linen dress.

'You look great in that colour,' Libby said warmly, 'and those shoes look fantastic with that dress.'

Jenny glanced down at herself and smiled shyly. 'It was kind of you to lend them to me. I'm being really careful how I walk. I'm not used to heels this high. I'm afraid I'll fracture something. On the other hand, it is nice not to feel so small compared to Alex.' She turned to him with an awed expression on her face. 'Did you know that Libby has *sixty-three* pairs of shoes?'

Alex yawned. 'Is that all? She's obviously sold some of them then.'

Libby laughed and thumped him on the shoulder. 'Vile man. It's just as well you have Jenny to reform you.'

Alex's eyes gleamed as they rested on his wife. 'Reform me?' He stepped closer to Jenny, enjoying her soft blush. 'I don't think so.'

'Alex!' Jenny backed away and glanced round self-consciously. 'I don't want to shock your father.'

'Oh, but I do,' Libby said happily. 'It's my favourite pastime. Go ahead. Shock away.'

'Don't start, Lib.' Katy joined them, holding the hands of her two seven-year-old boys. 'Dad is so much better. He's trying really hard to relax.' She turned to Jenny. 'Where are your twins?'

'With Andreas and Jago,' Jenny said, pointing across the lawn. 'They're using them as a climbing frame.'

Katy laughed. 'Isn't it amazing? Two sets of twin boys in the family.'

Alex reached out a hand and pulled Jenny towards him in a totally male gesture of possession. 'Actually, I would have rather had them separately.' He dropped a gentle kiss on Jenny's head. 'I worried about you right the way through your pregnancy. You seem too delicate to carry one baby safely, let alone two.'

Jenny gazed up at him lovingly and Libby and Katy melted into the background with knowing smiles.

Jenny and Alex found themselves on their own with Daisy.

'So...' His voice was husky and so sexy that it made her nerve endings tingle. 'Do you fancy slipping away somewhere more private?'

Jenny's eyes widened. 'Alex, we can't.'

He gave a slow smile. 'You've been married to me for almost two years, Jen. I've given you two babies. How can you still blush?'

'It's you!' She bit her lip and looked away, flustered, 'You always make me feel—feel...'

'Yes?' He stepped closer again, this time not giving her the chance to back away. 'How do I make you feel?'

Staring into his wicked blue eyes, Jenny felt her stomach drop away. 'Oh, Alex, I love you so much.'

He sucked in a breath and stooped to put Daisy on the ground. 'Sweetheart, go and play with your cousin Zoe for five minutes.'

Daisy ran off happily and Alex followed her with his eyes for a few seconds, checking that she was safe. Then he turned his attention back to his wife.

'Come with me.'

He took her hand and walked along a path that wound its way away from the guests towards an ornamental lake.

'Where are we going?'

'Somewhere more private.' Alex flashed her a smile. 'Since I'm aware that you don't like public displays of affection.'

They reached the lake and he hauled her into the shade of a weeping willow.

'Now, then, Jenny Westerling.' His voice was loaded with promise and he pushed her against the tree trunk, blocking her escape. 'What were you saying about loving me?'

She gave a moan and lifted her mouth for his kiss.

Heat flared between them and Jenny wrapped her slim arms around his neck, trembling as he deepened the kiss.

When he finally lifted his head, neither of them was smiling. 'Damn.' His voice was husky. 'Let's go home.'

Still in the grip of sizzling sexual attraction, Jenny stared at him stupidly. 'Alex we can't.'

'Jenny, I want you. Now.' He stroked her hair away from her face with a hand that was far from steady. 'We either leave, or we make love here and risk an audience. Your choice.'

Her knees were shaking. 'Alex, the children—'

'Will be more than happy to leave, too,' he said gently. 'Believe me, Dad isn't going to notice whether we're here or not. He's too busy networking. Frankly I'd rather get home to the cottage where I can rip that dress off you and do what I've been longing to do since we left Cornwall this morning.'

Jenny blushed. 'Alex, it's only been about eight hours since we—' She broke off, thoroughly embarrassed, and his blue eyes gleamed with amusement.

'Yes, angel? Since we…?'

Jenny looked at him helplessly. It didn't matter how often they made love, she still wanted him with a desperation that shocked her.

'I love you, Alex,' she breathed, and he gave a groan and lowered his head to hers.

'And I love you, sweetheart. More than anything in the world. Let's go home.'

And they did…

* * * * *

Dear Summer Reader,

One of the best things about being a writer is that you can travel without ever leaving home. After one dull, grey, cold winter, I found myself dreaming of a Mediterranean summer with its kaleidoscope of bold colour—pink bougainvillea tumbling over whitewashed walls, pretty fishing boats rocking against a picturesque waterfront, blue skies, soft sand and the sparkle of sun on the ocean.

So I wrote these three interconnected stories about triplets, two sisters and a brother with aristocratic connections, all of them different in personality but sharing a close bond forged during a difficult childhood.

Katy's story takes her from London to Seville, with its winding medieval streets, rich history and hidden tapas bars. Wild Libby finds herself chasing love all the way to romantic Greece and soon she's dining at beach-side tavernas filled with the scents of summer cooking. What could be better than eating fat ripe tomatoes drizzled in local olive oil, plump glossy olives and fish bought straight from the boats? And, closer to home on the wild coast of Cornwall, is heartbreaker Alex's story.

This summer why not travel through the pages of a book? Whatever the weather, pour yourself an iced drink and dive into another world. Switch off your phone and bask in the sunshine, the scents and the flavours of a #SummerRead.

So here, from me to you—*Summer with Love.*

Sarah

xx

To see where Sarah writes her books visit:
www.millsandboon.co.uk/sarahmorgan

0813/MB431

Who was the inspiration behind Jago Rodriguez?

How do you create such strong heroines like Libby?

Introducing…

Sarah Morgan

So you've just finished reading **Summer with Love**…

Before you head straight back to page one and start reading it again, maybe you have a question for the author?

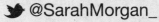 @SarahMorgan_

#AskSarahMorgan

Tweet your questions to Sarah now… and don't forget the hashtag!

Do you have a writing routine?

When is your next book out?

Soak up the sun this summer with more Sarah!

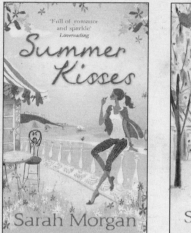

If you loved *Summer with Love*,
you'll love Sarah's other
#SummerReads!

To read the first chapters now visit:

www.millsandboon.co.uk/sarahmorgan

Where will *you* read
this summer?

#TeamShade

Join your team this summer.

www.millsandboon.co.uk/sunvshade

SUNSHADEb

More summer! More Sarah!

← *Scan me!*

Scan this code (or the one on the back of this book) for our *Summer with Love* video, Sarah's music playlists and photos of locations in this book!

The Mills & Boon® Guide to QR Codes

What are they?

They are links. Links through to more goodies!

Where do I see them?

On products, on adverts, in shops, on the back of romance books…anywhere!

What do I need to do?

Download a 'QR code scanner' to your phone and then use it to scan the code on the back cover of this book!

www.millsandboon.co.uk/sarahmorgan